TO STEAL A BRIDE

PART 1 OF TEO AND ESTELA'S DUET

ENTANGLED WITH THE ENDUAR

DANIELA A. MERA

This is a work of fiction. Names, characters, places, and incidents either are the product of the author's imagination or are used fictitiously. Any resemblance to actual persons, living or dead, events, or locales is entirely coincidental.

Copyright © 2023 by Daniela A. Mera and Golden Glow Press

All rights reserved. No part of this book may be reproduced or used in any manner without written permission of the copyright owner except for the use of quotations in a book review. For more information, address: authordanielaamera@gmail.com

First ebook edition November 2023

Book Cover Design by Artscandre

Book couple art by Amira

Map by Daniela A. Mera

Book Artwork by Daniela A. Mera

ASIN (ebook): B0CF83KRNN

ISBN (paperback): 978-1-960343-19-2

ISBN (hardback): 978-1-960343-18-5

PRONUNCIATION GUIDE

Characters

Estela (es-tell-ah)
Teo/Ma'Teo (tay-oh/mah tay-oh)
Keksej (Keck-se-sh)
Rholker (Roll-ker)
Mikal (Meek-ahl)
Arlet (Are-let)
Vann (Van)
Liana (Lee-ahn-ah)
Erdaraj (Er-dah-rash)
Aitana (Eye-tan-ah)
Lijasa (Lee-jaw-sah)

Ceremonies

Grutaliah Bondyr (grew-tah-lee-ah bon-deer)—Mating Ceremony
Dual'moraan (do-al-more-ahn)—First Cut

PRONUNCIATION GUIDE

Hlumrynna (hu-loom-ree-nah)—parting ceremony

Enduar Words:

Enduar (en-doo-are)—knowledgeable ones
Ruh'duar (ruh-doo-are)—cave-born enduares

Creatures:

Cave rat - **Ruc'rad** (ruck-rad)
    Cave bear - **Ruh'Glumdlor** (ruh glum-dl-ore)
    Cave bat - **Ruc'ciel** (ruck-cee-el)
    Crystal wraith - **Glacialmara** (glass-ee-al-mar-ah)
    Glow spiders - **Aradhlum** (ah-rahd-loom)
    Glow wyrms - **Wyrmhlum** (worm-loom)
    Crystal Dragon - **Drathorinna** (dra-thor-ee-nah)

Enduvida

Tunnels

Mining
Section

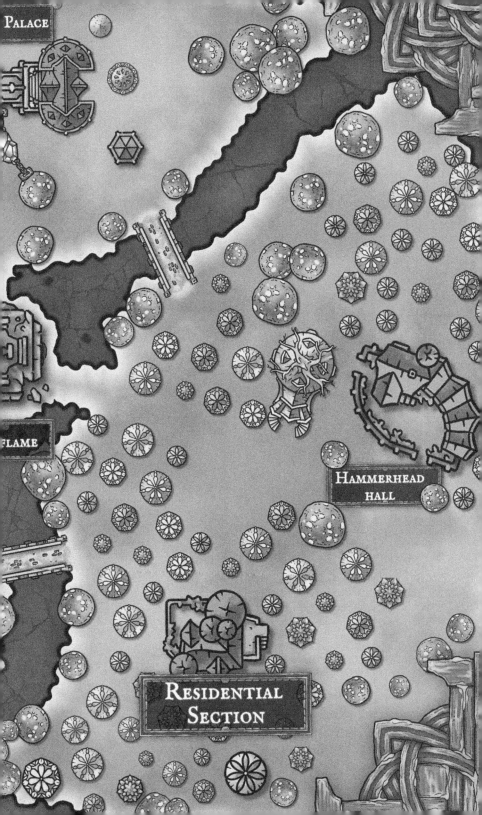

WELCOME TO ENDUVIDA!

Dear reader,

First off, thank you for picking up my book!

If you have ever read one of my solo books, you know that there is a pretty hefty dose of Spanish. I have included a bit of that in this book, but I have continued to flex my creative wings to find something that is easily accessible.

I hope you like it!

Finally, reading is wonderful—it's what brings us together today. However, no book is worth your personal peace.

I want to remind you all that this book is new adult, and includes some pretty heavy themes. So, please note there are mentions of sexual assault, crude language, violence/gore, misogyny, slavery, and death. Take care of yourself, dear reader.

Con mucho amor,
Daniela

For everyone who has ever made Skyrim a foundational part of their personality.

I don't have any ruby claws for you, but there's a puzzle inside this book nonetheless.

THE SONG OF THE ENDUARES
TRANSLATED BY ANTONIO CASTILLAS

In ancient times of lore and might,
elves danced under starry night.
Giants roared with forests tall,
But trolls emerged from shadows' thrall.

Great war brewed in realms untold,
More battles raged than the eye beholds.

Trolls, with jagged teeth and hunger wild,
scoured lands like demons riled.

Elven songs echoed, magic weaved,
Through valleys deep, their foes deceived.

Giants' footsteps shook the earth,
Mighty forces enslaving the mortals, a realm's rebirth.

As kings clashed, tales were sown,
Amidst the chaos, destinies unknown.

THE SONG OF THE ENDUARES

Trolls of cunning, dark intent,
Brewed chaos with a plan unbent.

From deep within the earth's own core,
They birthed a mountain's fiery roar.

With ancient crystals and twisted spells,
They carved a path to magma's fiery hell.

A volcano rose, fierce and tall,
Spewing fire.
Consuming all.

From war's ashes, elves and giants grew,
The trolls—now called Enduares—fell silent, hidden from view.
To the Enduar Mountains, souls incline,
Where death and treasures are disguised by a diamond's shine.

PROLOGUE

Trolls. We are known to the world as vicious, bloodthirsty monsters.
    We build, only to destroy.
Our victims weep.
And then we do it all again.
    My father raised me to butcher giants with all the hopes of a new father that I would follow in his footsteps as a supreme ruler. He would writhe in his grave if he knew that I had cast off both his weapons and ambition—that I took a new name for me and my people after he died. There was no more Ma'Teo the Butcher. No more trolls. Merely *King Teo* and the *Enduares*.
    Fifty years later, I wonder what purpose there was in trying to reinvent my court. My people still mourn their families, the same as the elves and giants. A name does not erase more than ten thousand dead. We could not eat our identity before it ate us. Just like the ocean eats everything—including our old home.
    Today I stand outside, on one of the rare occasions when my people leave the under mountain, and hold a newborn in my arms. We all stare at the ocean, the icy waves lapping against the

shore and the singers cast their voices to the murky white quartz, filling the air with joyful harmonies.

"I think you should do it, King Teo," Iryth says as she smiles at her son. Her braid hangs over her shoulder, and her silver-blue eyes shine with such joy. "I am sure Mother Liana will not be angry."

As the wise woman, Liana usually holds up the child, but she is late by more than an hour. I nod, "It would be my pleasure as king to perform the ceremony," I say and step in the middle of my people.

"Your mothers have given you the name Sama, and today, you join your people, the Enduares," I say loudly.

The little thing flicks its tail back and forth, squirming in the cold wind. Svanna and Iryth are one of few mated pairs, and they adopted Sama after his birth parents died in a mining cave-in last week. We do not mourn Mele and Irsh today—they would've wanted us to celebrate their son.

The singers hold up their crystals higher as their volume increases. The open-air sings, igniting the joy inside of us and making the atmosphere more boisterous.

"I bless you with the names of our gods, Grutabela and Endu. Be strong, little one. Grow with the stone," I call up to the heavens where Grutabela sits on her starry throne. "May your eyes one day see Vidalena."

As if on cue, the little one opens his mouth and lets out a cry loud enough to make my ears ring. Everyone laughs and shouts blessed words to the new babe.

"My son is strong," Iryth says proudly. Her mating mark is displayed proudly on her neck, and I conceal my lingering look.

Despite how deeply I long for a child, I am alone and cannot take on Sama. A king without a queen is laughable.

"He will be a strong miner!" Svanna shouts.

The rest of us shower the babe with blessings of goodwill,

and I try to hold the happiness close before a cloud settles over my people once more. I hold Sama up for a little longer, waiting as the singers finish their songs, and then turn to pass the wailing creature off to Svanna.

It is a shadow of what we once were, but for now, it is enough. While turning, I catch Ulla's eyes in the crowd. She turns away. I watch her smiles while I grieve the distance between us. We weren't meant to be, but I dislike causing her pain.

"*Stop!*" someone cries. The air becomes discordant, and everyone turns to see Liana finally appear at the cave's entrance. She is old enough to be my actual mother, but she's as fast as any hunter in the Enduar court.

"What's wrong?" I demand, carefully composing myself as I feel my people's attention hot on my neck.

Liana gasps and bends over, trying to catch her breath. When she finally stands upright, the crystals hanging off every inch of her dress jangle, and she points toward the horizon. "It's the giants," she pants, the morning sun glinting off of the piercings in her nose and eyebrow. "I was preparing Sama's necklace when something clouded the magic. The clouds gave way to a vision. They'll be here early."

Tension is thick. "How early?" I ask. As guardian of the Fuegorra crystal, she has the ability to see that which I cannot.

Before she has a chance to respond, a light tremor shakes the ground beneath our feet. Everyone grows impossibly more silent as the mountain stones confirm Liana's words.

Nearly three days early, damn tree rutters. We were direct with our instructions.

My lips curl at the thought of our old enemies, slavers, traders, and greedy bastards. They remind me of my father. I take a deep breath, trying to control the anger that boils in my chest.

"Hunters! Prepare to defend the city," I say, my voice ringing clear through the silence. "Joso, I want all women and children escorted to the lower levels. Now."

My people move quickly, rushing towards the tunnels. The singers' melodies turn into a chant, a song of urgency, and I can feel the power of their crystals strengthening my resolve. I doubt we will fight them, but our long history together has given me reason to be suspicious.

I turn to Liana. "Our agreement was for two carts of supplies. There should be no more than four giants in total. How many did you see?" I demand.

Liana meets my eyes squarely. "The vision was brief, but I counted four, My king," she replies, her voice steady. "There are more slaves this time, and some looked severely deformed. I think maybe sixteen all together."

I nod, shoving down the bitterness. I will have Vann help me take care of the slaves later tonight. If the giants come in peace, I will welcome their herbs.

"Send out a hunter team to scout the area," I order. "And prepare a group to accompany our guests to the viewing room, where I will trade with them personally."

As my people scurry to follow my commands, a sense of calm washes over me. I know I am not my father. I will not allow my anger to cloud my judgment.

I turn to the wise woman beside me and reach out to touch her shoulder. "Mother Liana, you will go with the other women."

She looks up at me and narrowed her eyes. "You think me too old to see the giants? I survived the last war."

I shake my head. "It's not about war—I am determined to ensure that there is no such hostility between us. We have no more Fuegorra readers left. I don't want to lose you."

Liana looks at me for a long moment, her eyes unwavering. "Very well," she says finally, nodding her agreement.

With Liana gone, I turn my attention back to my meeting with the giants while I walk.

"Are you ready?" Vann says as he approaches. The tall Enduar with two missing fingers on his left hand smiles. He's my personal advisor, and we were raised together in our old capital, Iravida.

Right now, he looks as worried as I feel. "Ready enough. Come, help me prepare the viewing room before the enemy enters our home."

PART ONE

CHAPTER 1
IOLITE
ESTELA

My plan is working. The last four days have been spent weakening chain links in secret, loosening a cart wheel, and bribing other slaves with my meals when they catch me working. The price for their allegiance has been onerous. My stomach is a hollowed-out bowl from hunger, and my knobby joints are burning in the wintry air as we walk across dirt and snow and *pull*.

We all wear harnesses that keep us strapped to our cargos filled with dried plants and herbs. Three other slaves are chained with me, including my tall, half-giant brother, Mikal. He can pull a cart like an ox, and I struggle to keep up with his long legs as my feet ache in my boots, and blood soaks into the thick woolen socks they've given us. Unlike Miki, there is no giant blood in my veins to keep me warm.

Most slaves' faces are hidden under fur hoods. My brother, the sixteen-year-old with shaggy brown hair and yellow eyes, catches me watching him and presses his lips together in some semblance of a smile. I quickly look away, aware of our royal master's gaze.

Prince Keksej, also known as the First Prince, has thick hair is red as fire and hangs loosely around his shoulders. In contrast, his beard is wispy and without definition. He's tall, at least eight and a half feet, possibly closer to nine, and his chest is broad enough to almost hide his belly. The deep green of his winter clothes makes the shadows on his face appear darker.

"Eyes on the road, tiny flea," Keksej grumbles sharply. The First Prince knows my name but only uses the nickname publicly for the same reason he walks beside my cart—so everyone remembers the family I belong to.

He'll get his reward soon enough. Today Mikal, Arlet, and I will make our escape. We will go to find the elves in the East, a warm place where slavery is little more than a terrible rumor whispered around cozy hearth fires in warm, wooden homes.

In the distance, I see the tall, black mountain capped with a generous layer of pristine white, and the swirling mists leaking out from the blue ocean and wrapping around the large chunks of rock left over from the great war. The way through *El Paseo de Nubes*[1] is narrow, and we are so close. It's the whole reason I volunteered Mikal and me for this trek.

I count my steps to stop thinking about the pain shooting up my legs. *Uno, dos, tres, cuatro...*[2]

The air smells foul and salty, even with the frigid temperatures, especially since I haven't bathed since Rholker tried to take me to his bed. Despite the grimy furs we'd been given for travel, I shiver while listening to the icy waves crash against the shore. It has been a long journey all the way from the capital, Zlosa, to the small court of vicious Enduares. I'm praying it will be worth it.

Prince Keksej looks up at the sun climbing in the sky and sucks in a sharp, irritated breath. I haven't seen a bottle in his hand yet, and he's making it everyone's problem. "Dammit. *Move faster,*" he growls.

We say nothing, just strive to match the punishing pace. As he moves through the beach shore, his face shows no emotion, only a resolute determination. I sneak a glance at how his hand rests on his hip. A familiar whip is waiting for an excuse to be reacquainted with my back after mere hours apart.

Three other carts are behind us, each full of provisions and weapons for Prince Keksej. I don't know the slaves pulling them outside of our nightly exchanges. However, the tall figures walking alongside them are easily recognizable—warriors tasked with protecting the prince and keeping slaves in line. One of them jogs to catch up with Keksej, and they begin speaking in giantese.

"This is the first time I've seen snow, and I wouldn't be mad if I never see it again," Arlet whispers behind me. She's pretty in a soft, domestic way. Her red hair, round face, and brown eyes remind me of autumn leaves collecting on the ground. We became den-mates after her lover cast her out of their shared dwelling.

The only sound I let escape is a grunt. We're so close, I don't want to anger the prince now.

I hiss when she trips, causing the harness to pull on my raw skin with added weight. "*Maldita sea*[3]."

"Sorry, Estela," she whispers. I take a deep breath. It's a minor slip-up. Not enough to cause any problems, yet I still glance back at the bundled-up redhead to make sure that her chain hasn't come undone. My body protests at the change of position, and I haunch forward to take some of the pressure off my lower back.

"Ho! Form a straight line!" the prince calls, whipping the ground as we shift position.

My nerves are tightly bunched inside of me. Our cart is first, and the giants hang back, watching the others as they move into formation. The first lick of mist against my face burns. The legends of this place say that there is a tunnel about twenty-four paces in.

My counting starts up again. I tap my harness three times, knowing that the small vibrations will go to all of the others through the taut leather. Sergi, the fourth slave with us, grunts with the added weight.

When I'd bribed him, he laughed at us and called us *capullos*—idiots. But promised his silence through mouthfuls of food.

Miki removes himself while the gauzy haze wraps around us completely. He's silent for his size, and he slinks back to wait for the third cart—the one with a wheel I'd been making notches in every night.

The cart is heavier without my brother. Not to mention the lack of visibility and the way my heart pounds. *You're almost there, keep pushing. Mikal is capable. It will be fine.*

At step fifteen, I reach back, working to unhook the metal chain from the cart and take the sharpened rock out of my waistband. Slowly, I cut the leather from my harness. The mists absorb much of the sound, and I can hear the giants behind us, even as I try to be quiet.

I think of the oldest human legends from lands far, far away. Before my people was enslaved by giants, we had our own goddess, our own luck.

"*Por favor,*"[4] I whisper. It's barely more than a breath. *Mamá, help me find the tunnel.*

I hear Arlet work on her chains, too. Each step hurts a little less as we get closer and closer to freedom.

Veintiuno, veintidós, veintitrés...[5]

I stop on the twenty-fourth step and look around in the mist. I can see very little when I hear the crash of the cart. My heart seizes and I jump.

"Stop," one of the giant warriors calls. "Broken cart!"

Thankfully, I haven't heard the whip yet.

The remainder of my harness is off in a matter of seconds, and I am overjoyed with the shaggy-haired boy creeping through the mist. Pride fills my chest. I want to hug him, but we need to find the tunnel out.

Just as we start to move away from the cart, Arlet makes a sound. It's distinct from the prince's shouts at the slaves behind us.

Mierda.[6]

I look back to find her still attached, fighting with her chain. Mikal is already next to her. Our hands fly across the links, trying to loosen the frozen metal. My fingers burn as the craftmanship holds, but determination fuels me onward.

Arlet's face grows ruddy, and a tear freezes on her cheek.

"Go," she whimpers.

My heart hurts. We are so close to freedom. I don't want to leave her behind. I feel the ground shake closer to us.

Prince Keksej is coming, the tunnel's location is still a mystery, and we are standing around without chains or harnesses. *Fuck.*

"Estela, get back into place," Mikal says.

The sound of steps are getting louder, despite the mist. They echo off the walls of ice around us.

Mikal gets back into his place pulling the cart while Sergi starts laughing. My feet refuse to move while I hold out on accepting failure. I always have ideas to get us out of trouble. I plan backup options for my backup options. But now?

"Estela, please," Arlet says, her voice raw.

I take a breath while I try to put back on my harness. My fingers, numb and red from the cold, refuse to work as I fumble with the ropes and leather.

A whip cuts through the mists and cracks against the snow. I flinch hard. My prayers are dead—my mother is not watching over me.

"What's this, tiny flea?" the First Prince demands.

My neck bends forward, and my fingers freeze against my chain. Another giant appears at my side and yanks the chains away. He holds up the two ends to show Prince Keksej.

"Estela," the First Prince snarls. "What are you doing?"

He steps closer, his whole body coming into view. My eyes go to his whip which drags through the snow and mists like a venomous python coming for me.

"You wish to escape?" he asks.

I don't answer. When he gets closer, I smell alcohol and my whole body goes numb.

"My father told me to go easy on you after he heard about what happened with my brother, so I gave you options for punishment. You asked to be brought on this journey. Did you not?"

Silence.

He growls. "Answer."

I squeeze my eyes shut. "I did."

"That's right. You did. It had been my hope that you show me how much you honor being a slave to the royal family. There certainly are worse masters. Do you not fear the trolls?"

Terror wraps around me like a frozen claw and immobilizes my body. This time, he laughs when I don't respond. Hot breath smelling of dried meat and wine lambasts my face. Pain is coming, and I can't move. "Since you have no fear of being stolen by the flesh-eaters, I'll have to find something else to motivate you."

His eyes are cold, like a predator about to pounce on its prey. Sadly, I am no wild animal. The truth is much more pitiful.

"Then come here. Five lashes for disobedience," he demands.

Mikal sucks in a breath, and my whole body tenses up. My

back still hurts from last night, but I know the way my brother sounds when he's about to make a stupid choice. "It was my idea."

The prince looks irritated. "Both of you then," his voice booms. "Five for your sister, and fifty for you."

"No," I breathe, yanking against my leash. The giant holding on to me laughs. I throw myself forward, this time screaming, "No!"

The prince pauses. He is a terrible sight in the mists. "Again?"

I blink back tears as a warrior fixes Mikal's chain and releases both of us from the cart and hands our leashes to the prince.

No.

Mikal is brave—he barely flinches when the prince wraps the leashes around his arms and pulls hard. I can't help but whimper, already feeling the whip's lash on my skin.

When the First Prince meets my gaze, he can see my fear. His yellow eyes twinkle with a mix of rage and amusement. "Stupid, stupid, tiny flea," he murmurs, twisting the leashes and making me cry out in pain as they cut into my skin. "If you had succeeded in escaping, I'm curious where you would've gone—the frozen ocean or the wolf-infested forests?" He chuckles at the idea. "I am a kind master, and I only punish you when absolutely necessary. Since you seem too mindless to remember where we are, allow me to remind you."

He pulls me a little closer. Too close. Mikal strains against his leash and starts to shout, only to be cut off with a rope around his neck.

"Trolls steal slaves; they beat them, rape them, and throw their human skeletons to their cursed volcano after they've been picked clean by their teeth. You humans breed like rabbits, so we endure a loss of disobedient slaves for troll diamonds."

He's told me all of this many times, yet I still wish I could vomit on his bare feet and claw out his eyes.

"Do you want to be lured by their dark spells and seductive songs? Would you like to meet the Butcher and his Cleaver?" The words have time to land their full effect while he continues to study my face. It's the first time I consider I will actually have to face the Enduares. Tears stream down my face as he lifts the whip with the other hand.

"Kneel, human bastard," he directs to Mikal. Then his glowing eyes find me again through the mist. "You alongside him."

I swallow my agony and fear and take my place next to Mikal. He doesn't bow his head, but I do. One of the warriors steps forward and yanks the furs up for both me and Mikal, exposing our backs.

My skin burns, waiting for the bite of his whip, only for another yank to send a stinging ripple across my body. Barely a few paces are separating us when the First Prince's whip comes down on Mikal's back.

My body slackens as renewed tears threaten to choke me with each deafening crack of the whip. Mikal only cries out when the whip slices through another layer of skin. I can do nothing but look on in terror as my brother takes the blows meant for my idiotic plan.

Once.

Twice.

I lose count as my brother's back is shredded. His blood sprays in the air, some of it splattering on my shoulder and the side of my face. Guilt is the familiar song playing under my skin, making my heart wail while he doesn't so much as whimper. He's proud. Too strong for someone so young.

Then, one lash hits my back, cutting into my healing skin and mixing my blood with my brother's before he returns to Mikal. Our hands reach for each other, and I squeeze his long, familiar fingers.

"How touching," the prince says. "The bitch and the bastard holding hands. Not so happy she volunteered you to come now, are you, Mikal?"

Then he wraps the length of the chain around my neck once and yanks on my leash, pulling me back so he can lean down and look me in the eyes while I choke. Mikal grunts in protest as another giant takes his leash, and Prince Keksej's hand shoots out to grab my chin. Our eyes connect while his hot fingers hover inches from my face.

I wonder what would happen if I lowered my head, forcing him to touch me and break his father's rules. But my own personal victories mean more pain for Mikal, who struggles to stand. *Mi pobre hermanito.*[7]

"You make me forget why I wish to be kind," he says. "Both your disobedience and your brother's position put you at risk—I do this so the others do not try to take advantage of you."

The warrior drags Mikal away. Hot tears slide against my cheeks, only to freeze and fall in the snow with soft pats.

"Now, back to your duty," Keksej says and starts to move.

I am so scared; I am so tired. But the punishment is over, so I silently follow, not daring to look back at the prince or the blood coating the ground between us. When I look at the skyline, all I can see is I see the mountain looming before us.

"Estela, physical pain in a reminder of the promises we make," the prince murmurs in a moment of rare clarity while everyone is focusing on pulling Mikal's harness over the slippery blood coating his back.

I hate the way my name sounds on his lips. His giant pronunciation is coarse.

"You have one last chance. Obey me, or I will let the trolls steal you. You'll beg for mercy, calling out my name while they rip you to shreds." He smirks as if he enjoys the thought. "Then who will take care of Mikal?"

My lips curl back as I bite my tongue. The mist snakes between us while he lets his words sit for mere moments before handing me over to the warrior. The back of his shaggy hair hangs down around his shoulders, and I imagine his head being parted from his neck with an enormous broadsword. It's all too easy to imagine how flesh and bone would give way to a sharp edge before landing at my feet. I can picture his unseeing eyes looking up at me, furious over my betrayal. I...

I look at my brother and shuffle over, pretending the prince's threat is carried away by the haze as we continue walking.

"It's not your fault," Mikal whispers in the human tongue.

I loathe myself. My mind starts to spin, and I lose feeling in my fingertips while fear and anger drug my senses. He wouldn't have been hurt if it wasn't for me. So I remain silent, keeping my head high and following the warrior with my chin up until we exit the mists.

Uno, dos, tres, cuatro, cinco, seis... [8]

The air still smells like blood, and it's hard to breath in all the clammy humidity. Arlet hums, and my eyes turn to my brother.

"I'll get you bandaged as soon as we are inside, Mikal," Arlet says.

I know her well enough to hear the guilt in her voice.

"No need, Arlet," I say. Reaching out from the cloud-like air, I take his hand and put in a few chewing leaves I stole last night after my whipping. "I will take care of you, *mi amor.*" Since my angry words cannot leave my lips, I think them while Mikal puts the medicine in his mouth. *Forgive me for not being able to do more. I will curse those damn giants from the afterlife if I die on this trip.*

Sergi chuckles at the exchange. "Damn fools. I told you this would happen, but you were too blinded by dangerous dreams to listen. Hear me now: Pray to whatever god you believe in, and ask them to grant you safe passage out of these mountains. Enduares, trolls, however you call them, they are monsters and they will show you even less mercy than the First Prince. I was the only slave who returned last trip."

All the things Prince Keksej has told me play through my head repeatedly while I pull through the snow. Counting is bitter, but it's all I have to calm my mind.

Diesiseis, diesisiete, diesiocho...[9]

I fight to hold back my fear, but it keeps growing. My mind is in shambles—we were never supposed to go all the way to the mountains. We should be catching our breath in some icy alcove right now.

Instead, the mists thin out. It starts slowly and then clears all at once, revealing the entrance to the Enduar Mountain.

"Halt!" the First Prince calls, and we stop.

The open jaws of the cave are surrounded by red veins of rock swirling like rivulets of blood. I shudder. The crash of the ocean to the left feels at odds with the blanket of white stretching out in the opposite direction. I look at the mountain, eerily peaceful away from all the trees below.

"*Por los dioses*,"[10] Arlet says, cutting off my fears.

Standing in the edges of the mist are pale blue beings, standing like sentinels on the icy beach, arranged in a formidable line of defense. The sight alone fills me with dread as I take in the spears, armor, and swords they wield.

Trolls.

The way they stare at us now, ready to kill without a word, is worse than my imagination. Their muscles are impressive even through the layers of thick clothing and armor. I fear what their strength means for our human bodies.

There are three massive cave bears chained with leashes not much different from my own. They snarl as a giant warrior approaches. A cannon sits in their midst, ready to fire its payload of red-hot, glowing stones. It is watched over by a magic-wielding troll who looks like a dragon guarding its hoard. I hone in on that lava, held into balls by magic, thinking about the volcano used to blow up half the continent during the war. Many giants and humans died on that day, but most of the casualties were of their own race.

"Ho!" the prince's warrior calls out, and one monster steps forward. All kinds of instruments hang off his armor, though his hammers are the most notable. Images of crushed skulls and broken bones intrude on my thoughts.

"What a kind welcome, troll," Prince Keksej spits savagely in giantese.

"We call ourselves Enduares now, prince. And you are early," he calls back, obviously pleased at Keksej's scowl. "By three days. You know our timelines are precise, and we do not take kindly to intruders."

The air is thick with tension when the First Prince steps forward. "Will you turn our supplies away? We've brought more medicinal herbs."

Some of the Enduares shift their weapons, but the one who stepped forward keeps his expression even. My eyes widen when an armored tail with a sharp, pointed tip darts out from behind him.

"We will proceed, but you will instruct your people not to leave their rooms." He bares his teeth at the giants, and I can see the sharpened points all the way from here. "Wanderers will be punished."

The prince's voice booms through the open air. "Lead the way!"

One of the warriors steps forward and scans my cart. He looks at Arlet, Mikal, Sergi, and then his gaze lands on me. My breath catches in my throat. They need someone to take the herbs. Knowing I tried to escape, I've basically painted a target on my back.

He grimaces at my disgusting appearance, points at Sergi and says, "You. Bring the sample box."

My relief is potent, like someone taking the knife from my throat. I don't look at Sergi as he stiffens, then turns to the cart and pulls out a box filled with phials of extracts and small bags of dried products.

We are not allowed inside yet, so we stand, trapped in a period of awful waiting. The best way to occupy my time is to help Miki with his back. I watch the warrior unhook Sergi to pull him into the mountain's mouth and almost miss how Arlet discreetly passes Mikal a few more chewing leaves to relieve his fresh wave of pain. I stumble when he shifts so that I can see the red, crusted mess covering his back and upper thighs.

That kind of mutilation is hard to comprehend. It makes me physically ill, despite having seen worse in the healing hut back home. I swallow the bile and reach out to gently touch his back. But no matter how feather-light my fingers are, he flinches, and fresh crimson liquid coats my skin. "Do you have any extra cloth?" I ask Arlet. "I used most of mine last night."

Before Arlet can answer, the same giant who took Sergi reemerges. He looks furious, and his eyes land on me and my bloody hands. I lean down and grab a handful of snow to scrub as much of the red off as possible.

"You." That is all the explanation I get before the warrior draws near and reaches for my leash.

Oh gods. What happened to Sergi?

Arlet's frozen fingers take my hand. "Do as you're told. The next day will pass quickly, and we will be heading back in no time," she whispers in my ear.

"*Te quiero, Este,*"[11] Mikal says quietly.

"None of that, Miki. I will see you after the viewing," I say, even though I don't know what will happen during the negotiations. "Tell me you love me then, and I might say it back."

He smiles weakly at my promise, and I feel marginally better.

The giant finishes unhooking me and yanks me forward. I find it hard to move my feet as fear grips me. I look back at Mikal and Arlet one last time before we enter the mountain. My fingertips are numb, and the tunnel is scorching my skin as we move deeper. There is a loud pumping sound with lights floating above me and golden designs lining the wall.

It doesn't take long for us to catch up to the rest of the group. The prince is there, sneering at the troll who looks angrily at the ground. That's when I see it.

A blood stain next to the sample box.

---

1. The cloud passage.
2. One, two, three, four...
3. Damn it.
4. Please
5. Twenty-one, twenty-two, twenty-three...
6. Shit.
7. My poor little brother.
8. One, two, three, four, five, six...
9. Sixteen, seventeen, eighteen...
10. By the gods.
11. I love you, Este. (Short for Estela)

CHAPTER 2
WAVELLITE
TEO

Ascending the endless steps my father had once used to separate the rest of the city from his throne is tedious on a good day. Now, it is unbearable. Vann and I hurry through the courtyard filled with poisonous, glowing mushrooms. Giant *lumikaps*, we call them. As we approach my crumbling throne, mage lights float above us, drawing power from the Ardorflame in the center of the city. A fountain spitting bioluminescent water gurgles to my left as we turn into the viewing room.

My advisor and I step inside, and I take a deep breath. This place is filled with mirrors to remind our guests that they are being watched. Soon, the stone bender will join us to further encourage an amicable exchange. I am careful to protect the one commodity the giants desire—dead rocks.

Diamonds, in the common tongue.

Since we have inherited a frozen wasteland and shadowy caves, we can barely grow more than the mushrooms in our garden. It's a simple, but effective arrangement: they take our curses, and we take their plants.

I produce keys from one of the many pockets sewn into my clothes and open the side door where the cut gems are stored, all while the vibrations in the rock beneath my feet draw nearer and rattle my bones. I grit my teeth against the dissonance, and my neck starts to itch.

"Get the new ones. They are the largest," I say, scratching at the spot just above my collarbone.

"The ones from last week?" Vann asks.

I nod, dropping my fists to my sides. They are as good as forged from the blood of Sama's parents.

Vann hisses as he picks up a covered tray with stones the size of his fist. I know he believes the same as everyone else, that diamonds are cursed. "We could give them crystals as large as their fingers, but they ask for these bedeviled chunks of volcano."

I press my lips together. They are also reminders of what my father had done. All stones have energies—some just more than others. Only Enduares sense their songs, and know their potential to heal, unify, grieve, or give the greatest gift of all: a mate. Though, if I am being honest, that gift is something I have long since given up. There are no Enduares left to show up on my doorstep and sing.

I hold up my hand, silencing our casual conversation as the stone bender pauses at the threshold. "My king?" he asks, waiting for permission to enter.

"One moment, Luth." Glaring at Vann, I quickly say, "If this is the only way we can get what we need, then it is better that they are traded far away from our home."

"Yes, my king." Vann's lips turn down, but he continues to take out different stones, and I leave to find the contracts dotted with the insignia of my people: a hammer crossed over a scroll.

"Enter, friend," I call to Luth.

The stone bender steps into the room, a floating orb of lava trailing behind him. He is quiet, focusing all his senses on ensuring he contains the deadly molten rock in a form he projects.

"Any report, stone bender?" I ask.

He nods, lips still pressed into a firm line. "Prince Keksej appears to be in the beginning stages of inebriation. He killed one of their humans while entering the tunnel."

I frown, disgusted. "We will need to sort that out after the feast. Any of the slaves looking particularly in need of respite?"

Luth's frown deepens. "Forgive me, I did not see them all."

I sigh. "How long until they arrive?"

"They are speaking with Lothar. They should be here within the next five minutes."

The temperature in the room skyrockets, and my advisor starts taking out weapons before selecting his sharpest cleaver to display while the giants inspect our selection. "Who are the dead diamonds for now?" he asks.

I sniff. "Prince Keksej's idiotic brother."

Vann growls, waving his three-fingered fist in the air. "Weren't they here two weeks ago?"

I nod, flexing my fingers and swatting a wandering glitter beetle with my tail. "Apparently, there was a problem with the first one. His bride did not like the shape or some nonsense."

"Perhaps she senses the curse they all carry."

The rumbling gets louder, and my ears twitch. Sweat collects under my clothing and slides over the gold circlet resting on my brow. "Unlikely. Giants live in forests. They know nothing of caves and rock."

Ciento uno, ciento dos, ciento tres...[1]

I freeze, my thoughts halting, and turn to my advisor. That was a woman's voice. What the hell are women doing in the upper level? "Did you say something?"

Vann looks up from his cleaver, and his expression twists even further downward. "Not at all."

Lord Lothar, my advisor in charge of the hunters, arrives at the entrance to the viewing room. Dyrn is beside him and wields a large hammer like the other men in his hunting group. They line the distance between the warriors and us.

Ciento catorce, ciento quince...[2]

The words are fuzzy and hard to make out, but the voice is sweet as summer berries. It is a whisper, but somehow it echoes louder than everything else in the room.

If I focus hard enough, it almost sounds like the human tongue. *This is bad.* The giants never bring women on their treks. If the woman has not come with them, then perhaps someone has stayed behind in the palace... *and why do I not recognize such a delicious voice?* The insanity is all-consuming.

My hand reaches for my sword, but before I can draw it, a sharp pain shoots through my head and burns at my neck. I stumble, grasping at the nearby table to steady myself. All the attention in the room is focused on me.

"Your Majesty, are you all right? The giants are ready to enter." The stone bender steps closer, the orb of lava following behind him.

I shake my head, trying to breathe through the pain. There is one answer that could explain such an ache accompanying the voice in my head, but it is impossible. "I—I don't know."

Like a miracle, the small, red and orange Fuegorra crystal embedded at the base of my throat starts to sing. The garnets and citrine crystals decorating the room join the joyful chorus. There is no such beautiful harmony, not even on the Festival of Endu, when our gods sing to each other at night. No one around me reacts to the song, as if they do not hear it.

This can only mean one thing: my mate has entered my home.

A *mate*. For me? After a century alone?

For a moment, everything in the room fades away into a

distant memory as both my eyes and soul are being pulled to the other half of this harmonic call. It is intoxicating, a melody that lifts my soul and tugs at my heartstrings all at once.

I am roused by Vann. "Teo, are you well? They are almost here." The danger in his voice is clear, and I shake my head again, trying to rid my skull of her enchanting presence.

After taking a deep breath to steel myself, I harness my thoughts. The pain is somehow both excruciating and pleasant. Like I am being melted and remade in the forge.

"Leave me. I am well," I assure them, using every ounce of self-control to stand up straight and push Vann away. It takes considerable effort to slip back into my mask of terrifying power.

Vann inspects me for a second longer. "You are sure?"

"Let us in, Troll King," Prince Keksej calls. Luth's report was accurate—he *is* drunk.

I nod once to Vann, gritting my teeth against the sound of the prince and wrapping my braid around the armor on my neck to soothe the burn. The distraction works well enough.

"Let them in," I say.

I am ready to meet my mate. Vann reaches into his pockets and withdraws two silvery sets of pointed teeth. Once they cover my normal canines, I open my mouth to bare the frightening jaws.

"Stay behind me," I order, my voice low and slightly altered by the weaponry.

A young hunter, Tirin, ducks into the entrance and bows deeply. "King Teo, here is First Prince Keksej, Heir to the Giant Throne."

I nod, but my mind is elsewhere. Giants should know a little of the human tongue. Will my mate be a giant? A princess? Or, gods forbid, the queen?

No. Queen Lijasa is dead. I clench my fists and push my soldiers back—If fate has chosen to be cruel and given me a giant mate, I would endure it. Because then I would be able to have a child.

My mind is racing with possibilities of what this could mean for my people, for the relationship between us. A political alliance through mating. But the benefits do not ease the ugly memories flickering in the back of my mind, nor the nausea turning my stomach into the tumultuous sea while I gaze upon the giants.

Their heads are bent to the side in the hallway, still too tall for my palace despite the ample ceilings. My heart clenches when I see no woman in their company—giant or otherwise. Relief is quickly replaced by anger and suspicion.

What if they knew? And they brought her to torture in front of you?

I shove the thoughts aside and step forward. "Prince Keksej, welcome." I try to use honeyed words but do not smile.

The giants stare at me. "The Butcher and his Cleaver. Where are the diamonds?" the prince asks.

"Where are the herbs?" I retort, bristling at the name I was called in the war. If Vann is affected, he doesn't show it.

The prince grunts, his eyes flickering to Vann and then back to me. "We have brought them, as promised."

I look at the hunters who escorted them, and they nod. My gaze travels back to the First Prince, waiting for the samples he usually brings. He glares back at me for a minute before his eyes flick down to my teeth, then at the weapon in Vann's hand and the floating orb of lava in the back.

The tip of a spear as tall as me sticks into the entrance, and I grit my teeth.

The giant concedes as he calls out, "Tiny flea! In here now."

I am confused. *Flea? Why does he call to an insect?*

Chains clink outside the door. Then, the voice starts up once more, and the truth horrifies me. The giants have brought a woman, after all. After a past as broken as mine and an eternity of waiting, she walks into my life from Zlosa—forbidden from me before I can ever touch her. The laws that govern my people are clear: we do not keep humans under the mountain after freeing them.

When Keksej awkwardly turns his head to watch her, I am ready to stab the prince. He reaches out his hand to take the leash binding her to him. I'll tear out his eyes for gazing upon her —for *owning* her. I know better than the other Enduares what the slaves endure at the hands of their masters.

Oh gods. Their teeth?

She is able to see me before I can look upon her. I freeze, enthralled by the sweet feminine voice that is undeniably in my head. Then I remember what I must look like with razor-sharp points in my mouth and glowing eyes. Humans never react well to the way that Enduares dress.

Hola?[3] I will use the meager human words I remember. From what I understand, mates do not hear every passing thought— only what is consciously spoken to their partner—but she is volatile, sending every thought my way, likely without even knowing.

There is no response as a small human woman enters the room. The Fuegorra begins to sing louder, a song that only the two of us can hear. But, instead of joy, her eyes are now focused on the ground. She did not like what she saw—I am a disappointment.

I do not share her feelings, but it does little to ease the heartbreak pulsing in my chest.

Her skin is filthy, and she is dressed in disgusting furs while carrying a box that is too large for her. Dark brown hair frames her light brown skin and hides her eyes. She is small, but her chest and hips flare out in a way that is impossible not to notice.

Hello, beautiful one, I say, this time in the common tongue, keeping my expression stony and cold. Will she gaze upon me again and see past my brutal exterior now?

She takes a deep breath and looks up at me. In an instant, my world is shattered by the force of her piercing brown eyes. They are the color of rich enstatite, with striking lines of tourmaline flaring out from her black pupils. Her gaze is filled with life and passion and reckless bravery. A twinge of pain under the surface makes me realize that she still does not look at me with fascination, but horror.

My attention drops to the spatters of red covering her face. Every muscle in my body tightens, fighting to break through my carefully controlled exterior.

Hostia puta[4], the beautiful voice says. *He wants to eat me.*

Her words wound me, but how can she see anything other than a monster when I bare my teeth like a beast? She has no crystal, and I see no matching mark glowing on the side of her dirty neck. Slowly, so slowly, she walks forward and places the box on one of the viewing tables.

"Open it, girl," the prince spits out. I bristle and cross to my mate impatiently. It comes from a place of care, but I force myself to appear as if she disgusts me.

The woman flinches away when I undo the fastening at the top, causing the box flaps to fall open and reveal the different herbs we need for cures. Niue root for swelling, something they call eucalyptus, and elderberries are just some of the ingredients I find.

"Well? I've produced the samples. Show me the diamonds," the prince says, clearly irritated.

I tear my face from hers and growl at him. A surge of rage builds in the deepest parts of my body. The song is making me irascible.

"Vann, where are the diamonds?"

"Here." My advisor gestures with one hand while he holds

his cleaver in the other. I hear him direct the prince just as another giant tries to enter.

Luth shoots out a small stream of lava from the orb behind me. The incoming warrior gasps when it sizzles his skin, causing the air to smell of burnt flesh.

"Damned cave rat," he gripes, and my mate gasps.

I am acutely aware of the sound, but I refuse to look at her as Prince Keksej whips around with awkward movements. Everything is happening fast, and they'll hurt her if they notice my attention.

"You want to start a fight?"

I spit at his feet. "You know that only one of you is permitted at a time. Insult us again, and we will not hesitate to ensure you never return to our home."

He nods slowly, and I see his skin glisten with sweat from the molten rock heating the room. I tense, looking up to check on the woman once more.

The mirrors above us let me see her from all angles. My mate is starving. Whip marks are strewn across the small strips of bare flesh on her back, in crisscross patterns. It's repulsive.

I nod to Vann, who removes the cloth coverings from the diamonds. The woman gasps at the view of the glittering gems. The effect is instant, and I can hardly stand the pressure in my breeches nor the desire to be near her, to steal her away from these people that she may go to my bed and rest while I have Fira make her new clothes. I inhale deeply and smell the metallic scent of blood on her skin. Some of it is sweet, like her. The other stinks of a giant.

The prince inches forward, his eyes scanning the jewels on the table. Then he leans closer.

Keksej scoffs. "These are smaller than the last ones."

"Not so. Two of them are bigger. You may select one," I say, trying to ignore the singing, making my skin turn to flames with the need to attack and run. To claim. To care for. I have a court to care for, too.

What is your name? I try again, desperate.

Nothing.

I need to get her away from her masters, but there is one in the room and three outside. A considerable amount of raw, brute power, especially since a third of our people are currently sick.

"So, you tried to short-change us before?" Keksej counters, pulling me out of my thoughts. He is angry about the almost-altercation, so now he will make these discussions as difficult as possible.

I loathe the incessant back and forth, filled to the brim with accusations of cheating.

"No, these were mined after your visit." My voice is as cold as ice, trying to warn him not to push me further. The giants do not care about casualties—they return even when we steal their slaves—but Sama's parents died for these gems, and the wound is still fresh.

"This one is acceptable," the prince says, pointing to the largest diamond shaped like a teardrop.

I nod, and Vann places it in a leather pouch. "The herbs are also acceptable. We will sign the contract now."

Vann spreads the scroll on the metal table, and I use the seal on my ring dipped in ash ink. Then, as the prince adds his own name to the paper, I can feel the woman's eyes on me. I try to ignore her, but it's impossible. Her gaze is like fire, making me painfully aware of her presence.

"Is there anything else before the feast?" the prince asks, his tone annoyed.

I shake my head. "No, this concludes our business."

"Enjoy your quarters. We will make sure that the food is prepared on time," I say.

The giant looks between me and the human and then,

without a word, starts to inch out of the room. Crossing the threshold, he calls out, "Come, tiny flea."

My mate hurries out after him. I step forward and then stop when I see the faces of the Enduares under my care. I will need to think of another way to get her alone—one that won't be dangerous. The weight of the realization makes me sag against the table while they fade from sight. We hold our breath, preserving the silence while everyone watches, and listens to them go.

"Tree vermin. I catch their ugly looks and short words. There are not so many. We could—" Vann pauses in the middle of his rant, finally looking back at me. "Shit. You really aren't well. Let me send for the healer."

I look at Vann, and reach under my clothing to touch the crystal whose song is fading with each fragment of distance between me and the woman. My other hand tightens on the table and the metal groans and dents. I can hardly keep from bursting out of my skin, but I am careful not to direct my thoughts toward her in case she can hear me. After pulling the cloth at my neck to the side, his gaze falls on my throat, and his eyes widen. Confusion clouds his wonder.

"You see the problem," I say.

"Holy gods on their stony thrones," he breathes.

I don't know how to do this without starting a war, but she will not leave this mountain.

---

1. One hundred and one, one hundred and two, one hundred and three...
2. One hundred and fourteen, one hundred and fifteen.
3. Hello?
4. Holy fuck.

CHAPTER 3
IDOCRASE
ESTELA

"Did you like it when he touched your hand?" the First Prince asks, hanging back to walk alongside me and hold my leash.

I keep my mouth shut, not wanting to admit how unsettled I feel. Without the box of samples, I am too light, like I might be carried away by the lightest of breezes. Not to mention the music playing softly against my skin. It's like when Arlet hugs me, and her laugh reverberates against my cheek, creating a pleasant sensation that is felt as much as it is heard.

Each step between me and the diamonds should relieve me, but I feel more tangled up. The failed plan from earlier is fading, replaced by the distinct heat in my lower belly and a haunting melody in my ears.

"I saw his eyes, hungry for your flesh and body. If we weren't there, I don't doubt he would've splayed you across the table and torn out your throat."

My skin is already over-tight, but at the mention of him near my throat, I flush from my scalp to my toes. Not with images of death—but his teeth grazing my neck while he holds my hands above my head. I don't cry. I *shiver*.

The image is equal parts intriguing and frightening. Keksej wasn't lying about seductive spells.

"I imagine he will try to steal you tonight," the prince tries again. When I still don't respond, Prince Keksej snorts, passes my chain to one of the warriors, and walks up to the front of the party.

He asks the Enduar something, and the man responds with some clipped grunt. I wish I could block out my ears to all sound. I'll have to warn Arlet and Mikal when I see them again.

My hands are clammy as we walk through the cave's mushroom light and shadowy crags, but I feel better knowing I'll be resting soon. Arlet and I can finish wrapping Miki's back.

The air is musty here and overwhelmingly sulphuric, which pairs well with the ancient carvings on every surface and plane. It's as if I'm transported to another time. We slow, and I'm acutely aware of how close the Enduar is to me. My stomach growls involuntarily when a waft of roasting meat reaches our noses.

I fight the urge to vomit. What if Sergi's remains are being cooked right now? My hands fly to my empty stomach. The skin there is stretched tight, but the thought of food makes me want to fall on my knees and retch.

I make mental notes of each landmark, an old habit from my time as an herb gatherer and amateur healer. A broken temple sits in the middle of the space with glowing orange and red veins pulsing light all around. Lava, I realize as a twinge of fear pricks my chest. The under mountain world captivates me with its horrible beauty for a few seconds. I had assumed staying underground would be dark. However, large glowing orbs now accompany mushrooms, illuminating the way before us and causing my eyes to snag on every detail from the enormous crystals jutting up from the ground to the circular homes.

The swish of an armored tail brings my eyes back to the Enduar. The metal appears flexible enough to accommodate an extensive range of motion. Some utterly deranged piece of myself wishes that he were the king so I could be near him again. I would feel the same rush of blood in my veins, and he would look at me with burning blue eyes, coil his tail around my waist to pull me flush against his large chest and touch my bare skin with his broad hands.

It all comes back to me so clearly. The music, the smell, their unnatural beauty. It was all a trap. I remember the whispered stories told across evening bonfires. Trolls present as appealing, beautiful even, before making it so you could never leave.

Malditos monstruos. [1]

Drawing in a deep breath, I shift under the furs, trying to cool down my body and look back the way we had come. I watch the tunnel leading to the exit until all I can see is carved stone.

"This way, First Prince," the Enduar says, bowing once more before gesturing to a tunnel near the palace framed with intertwining boxy patterns. They look like they're made of pure gold.

Prince Keksej leads the way, and I am stuck between two warriors as we walk down the passage. There is a faint pumping noise, methodical and mechanical, but it's a welcome change from the fading song. Circular doors appear on either side of us, each bearing various elegant geometrical patterns. When we stop, I look at the other giant warrior who has stayed behind to guard the room for the slaves.

"This room is for you, Prince Keksej. This has been prepared for your warriors, and we have another room for your... workers," the Enduar says.

I blink, surprised at his hesitance to use the word "slave." Does he pity us? Can such barbaric people even feel remorse?

Prince Keksej turns around to look directly at me. He raises his chin further in the air. "This slave will stay with me," he orders the Enduar as if he were one of his servants. The warrior hands over my chain.

I freeze, not having time to react, before the door to the prince's room is opened, and my master tugs my leash and calls, "Come."

My legs are used to acting before my brain, so I scurry forward and enter right behind him. Fear makes the back of my neck tingle. I tell myself that he will not touch me.

But...

The princes have always been competitive with each other. Perhaps he will use me and give my body to the monsters. Horror makes the blood in my veins feel like acid.

None of the Enduares would know that he had broken a command made by a king mourning his dead human whore. Undoubtedly, it would satisfy him to hold such a thing over Rholker's head for the rest of eternity. One of them will have finally won in this sick game.

If I could beg for him to leave me be, I would. Instead, I hold my breath while Keksej ducks his head to the side and swats one of the floating lights away. The room isn't compact, but I am suffocated. Especially when he grabs the hem of his shirt and pulls it over his head.

"I see how your eyes dart from side to side, Estela. You are angry with me," he says at last. "Or perhaps you upset about your attempted escape?"

My heart races at his words, and I resist the urge to tremble in front of him. It is not my first time seeing his nude form—he always does this when he wants to dig his claws into me.

"Answer."

I swallow. "I am not angry, my prince." I bow my head, and it hurts my throat to spit out lies. The healing lashes on my lower back burn with the effort.

"I have something for you," he says, dropping my chain, reaching into his pants, and pulling out a key. He tosses it to the ground. "Freedom." He starts laughing when I don't move. "Oh, come now. I'm extending an olive branch. I knew you would try to escape when you volunteered both you and Mikal."

My eyes burn. *Of course.* "Then why let us come?" I say past the lump in my throat.

He shrugs. "I knew you would never make it far. To be honest, I expected it in the forest, not in the ice passage." He laughs again. "Humans really are the least intelligent sentient beings."

My head hangs. I don't dare tell him about *El Paseo de Nubes* —that slave legend is for me alone.

However, he is very conversational today, probably from all the wine. If he keeps talking, it leaves little room for him to attempt something disgusting. "So why not give me to the king?" It would be an apt punishment for everything I've done.

"A prince doesn't answer to a slave," he says as he removes his pants. "Especially his own slave. Shouldn't you sleep better knowing your master is close by?"

Disgusting prick, I think, while keeping my face blank. "Will I be here all night?"

Keksej finishes undressing, ignoring me, and I avert my eyes to anywhere else in the room so he doesn't catch me grimacing at his large, bony body. giants are thicker on top, and they are covered in tattoos. Some are considered sacred, but most are memories of battles won. He is not solid and sturdy like the Enduar king.

I groan inwardly. The Enduar King, who is using his magic to lure me, is the last person I should be thinking about.

Another melodic hum I haven't noticed before permeates the

room. It's softer—much softer than the song that lights my skin on fire. While it plays, flower mantises come to mind. They are forest insects that attract butterflies and bees for pollination, only to trap and eat their prey whole.

Humans are fragile. Most of us are magicless, good for nothing but labor and entertainment. It's a mistake to forget that.

I take a silent breath and inspect the quarters. The room is circular, like the houses we saw, and the interior is warm and lush with several fur-covered surfaces. Golden decorations with precious stone inlays are everywhere. Some gems are opaque, while others are translucent and polished, but they all twinkle under the floating lights bobbing in the air. My master touches one that glows brighter, illuminating the bed modified with a second cushion to make the mattress long enough for a giant's frame.

Then, he produces a wine bottle from one of his satchels. I hold my breath. But he doesn't move closer, so I unclench my hands and look away once more.

There are delicate petals on the walls with golden leaves and stems to create vibrant mosaic flowers. Their gems are as deeply green as the leaves in Zlosa, and as pink as the blush of a newborn babe. My focus lands on the crystals as tall as me that are placed around the round room. I suck in a breath.

The music comes from them.

"Rest before the feast," Prince Keksej grunts. "I've brought you something more comfortable to wear. It's cleaner, too."

Something to wear?

I look back and find the bottle half gone. Sweat blossoms on my forehead. He's pointing sloppily to a bag that I hadn't noticed before. After obediently crossing to the space, I bend over—holding back a small grunt of discomfort—and start rummaging.

It doesn't take long for me to find an emerald green gown, little more than a mere scrap of cloth in the pile. I recognize it immediately, not only from the feel but also from the color. I drop it as if it burned me, and my stomach tightens as horror washes through my veins. It was my mother's. She wore it to see the king when she would service him in his chambers.

"Put it on!" he bellows from his too-big bed. The wet sound of his lips on the bottle's mouth makes me flinch.

Damn all the flowers in the field—hell, curse all the trees and the ugly giants that live between them. How did he get this?

My lungs refuse to work properly. Not when I walk behind one of the dressers, and certainly not when I start changing. When the gown is on, I stay hidden until he speaks again.

"Come out and pester me, tiny flea."

When I step out of hiding, his yellow eyes gleam. The bottle of wine is completely gone now. I cross my arms, uncomfortable as it's not hard to see where he looks. The neck of the gown scoops low between my breasts, showcasing two brands—one from each prince—interlocking on my sternum.

The fabric is too thin, the color is too vibrant, and I've already left smudges on the silk. The only bright side is that he is tired from the journey. I move again, selecting an area as far away from his bed as possible before kneeling down.

"No," Keksej slurs. "You will sleep at the foot of my bed."

I swallow hard as bile begins to come up my throat. Without looking at the naked giant lounging with his back against the wall, I reach my destination and ease down on the ground before his mattress.

"Did you not hear me? On the bed," he hisses.

I stand and sit on the edge of the mattress. His large foot is next to my hip, and I look down at the dirty appendage that has walked across two different terrains over the last four days. His toes are hairy, and the skin is thick and cracked. I close my eyes and curl myself into the tightest ball possible while lying down.

The lights are turned off with the clap of my master's hands. He doesn't say anything else, so I hug my hands to my chest, and he starts to snore. Still no touching.

I let out my first proper breath in a small eternity, only for the pressure in my bladder to alert me. *Por el amor de los dioses.*[2] Moving could wake him, and he hasn't been out long enough to sleep off the alcohol. He'd be furious.

Holding my urges is a learned skill, but even I have my limits. When the sensation only gets more insistent, I know I can't wait until he wakes.

Taking deep breaths, I listen to the snores and wait an adequate amount of time before I slide off the bed and look for a chamber pot. When one isn't immediately visible, panic sets in.

I press my legs together, still crouching, and turn around. There's a door by the entrance.

It has to be there.

I straighten and walk across the room on the balls of my feet. Sweat gathers on my back, armpits, and palms, and the dress carries my distinct smell. It was already getting too warm in this room.

Desperate, I put my hand on the doorknob and turn slowly, trying not to make a sound. It takes forever because I keep pausing, making sure that my master continues to snore through his drunken afternoon nap.

So far, so good.

When the handle is turned all the way, I open the heavy, round door. My mistake becomes apparent the second a slice of gentle, bluish light pours out from the inside, landing right on Prince Keksej's face.

I let go of the handle as if it had burned me. The door slams shut, and I freeze, my heart pounding in my chest. I press my back against the door, hoping the prince won't wake.

But it's too late. I hear stirring from the bed and the sound of footsteps on the fur-covered floor. There's nowhere to hide, so I stand up straight and turn around to face his naked form.

"What are you doing?" he asks, his voice thick and syrupy. "I told you to sleep."

I bite my lips together and clench my legs while ignoring the burning in my bladder.

"Are you trying to escape again?" he demands, still rip-roaring drunk. "I thought you learned your lesson this morning?"

I shrink back, too exposed in this damned gown. "Or, perhaps, you liked the Enduar's face just as much as he liked yours?" His words only serve to enrage him more. "Is that why you slink away while I sleep, little slut?"

I shake. The First Prince reaches over to his things and picks up his whip. My body is already coiling tight, anticipating the agony that will come soon.

"If you think the bite of my whip is rough, you have no idea what the sensation of Enduar teeth tearing your flesh apart is like."

I am trembling so hard, unsure whether he will beat or rape me. I back towards the door, ready to run.

"Dammit. Answer, Estela!"

I flinch so hard that a tear falls down my cheek. "I needed the chamber pot."

My master starts laughing. The sound is rough and grates against me while he prepares the whip in his hand, wrapping part of it firmly around his forearm to give him better control.

"We'll see about that. Turn around," he demands.

I bunch my fists in the dress. My resolve to be obedient was already fracturing before he embarked on his drunk musings.

He's half-mad, and I can't stay here. "I won't run away again—let me relieve myself," I beg.

He picks up his bag off the table and hits me across the face. I fall to the ground in a heap and don't have time to react before he draws back the whip and strikes me.

The pain sears through me, and I can barely make out the sound of the pop through my tears when it hits my skin.

I try to contain my screams, but it's impossible. They are torn from me instantly, filling both my mind and ears. I am powerless against the strength of a giant, and no one will come to help me.

Somewhere in the distance, a voice roars in time with my own. The ground beneath our feet begins to shake, and cracks appear in the walls around us. The floating lights flicker and fade.

Prince Keksej staggers away from me, his eyes wide as he stares at the destruction around us. I don't know if I should stay still or run when the whipping stops. My master is breathing heavily, his face an angry red, and his nose wrinkles while he stares at the room around us. The shaking stops almost as soon as it had begun, and he pushes himself off the wall, wiping his mouth. "The piss makes you smell even worse."

Are you in the servants' room? a voice demands, and I flinch, dread mixing with acute pain. The King. Blue eyes, blue skin, silvery white hair, needle-sharp teeth. *He made the cave shake.*

Thick, hot liquid runs down the back of my mother's dress. My legs are covered in sticky blood and urine, and the carpet below me is damp. Humiliation makes my skin burn, but my defiant spirit flares at the voice's return.

Get out of my head, you monster. I squeeze my eyes shut. This is all a part of what Keksej warned me about. If I can keep the king away, I will walk out of this room alive.

I am coming to you. Every syllable has fierce finality, and I don't understand why he is looking for me. All I can think about is angering Keksej further. My master cleans the blood-drenched whip and looks over at me. His look is familiar—I've stopped crying, and he wants to know why. If he thinks my punishment hasn't been severe enough, then he will call for Mikal. The image of my brother beaten to death fills my head, and my stomach heaves.

Stay the hell away from me, I hiss back, watching the cracks in the walls as if that could prevent more destruction.

You are in pain, I will tear—

Leave me be, you foul creature! You already killed a slave.

I did not. But I will kill that giant.

I don't want you to come. My words should've sounded strong, but they come out pathetic, obscured by the agony from my whipping. Why would he try to come to my room? Why save a woman he wants to eat? It doesn't make sense.

"You see, Estela? You see what they are capable of?" the prince says. For a second, I think I see fear in his eyes, but he looks at me with disgust. I wonder if he worries that they are luring me away to be stolen as we speak.

If I kill them, would you trust me?

My eyes widen. How could more death make up for what happened in the tunnel?

"Remember what happened here while you clean this up. I won't sleep tonight with the smell of human piss in the air," the First Prince orders. Then, as if remembering that we still had the feast, he says, "It's time to wash yourself, too. I'm tired of your stench, and scrubbing your skin will reopen your wounds. All that blood makes you extra appetizing."

I cringe.

"Don't look so sad. If you survive the night, you'll have learned your lesson for good."

His words are taunting, like usual, but I see the worry on his face. These walls are no longer safe for him after the shakes.

Without another word, I duck into the bathroom to get some soap.

I feel the same terror I have the whole day. All the more reason to leave tonight before they try to take me. I haven't been able to speak with anyone else, so I don't know if I'm the only one experiencing these strange sensations. The King of the Enduares is not a man to be taken lightly, and I don't want to be his meal.

He looks me up and down and makes a displeased sound when I bend down and scrub. He doesn't comment on pain, lessons, or even the Enduares. He touches on a subject much more abhorrent.

"I don't understand what my brother sees in you."

I freeze in the middle of working soap into the urine-soaked spot. *Here we go.* I bite my tongue so hard it bleeds.

Members of the Giant Court are allowed one side slave for their personal pleasure. Since King Erdaraj made me into forbidden fruit, Rholker became obsessed with making me his comfort woman.

I doubted the Second Prince's desire had anything to do with my looks, my size, or anything besides that mandate from his father. Keksej is harder to figure out, though my suspicion is sibling rivalry.

The prince starts up again. "But, I didn't understand why my father took your mother either. She gave him a bastard son, and he forbid us from touching you. What magical honey pot do you human women have to make powerful men, great warriors, lose their minds?"

I continue scrubbing, my skin burning. No thoughts. No voices.

"I'm nearly drunk enough to demand a taste."

My whole body locks up, and my gaze stays fixed on the stone floor. His words shock and terrify me so much that I forget how to run. This isn't how I should act. I should fight, make it stop.

Someone knocks on the door, and the tense muscles in my back relax a fraction while I sense Keksej tense. "Milord?" one of the giants says.

The First Prince relaxes at the sound of one of his own men, but I'm on my feet in a second.

"Enter," the prince calls, his voice magically clear again.

"There is someone to see you," the warrior continues and Keksej curses at the realization as the door opens to reveal the Enduar King. Time stops. I suck in a breath.

He still wears armor from neck to toe, and that long, feline tail flicks behind him as he holds up a large jug of mead. The monster doesn't smile. His nose wrinkles as he looks at me with more disdain than the warrior—the giants hate me, but the look of unfiltered rage at my presence here, with the prince, electrifies me. Blood is drying on my skin, and the concentrated smell of piss and soap burns my eyes.

"King Teo," Keksej says, still fully nude. "What do you want?"

"I'm sorry, my Lord. He insisted," the warrior fumbles, looking between me and the prince. "I can see him out if you are indisposed."

"Is it improper for a host to visit his guests?," the king drawls. His voice is dark, and smooth, and it caresses my mind while it slides through my thoughts. Like sweet wine.

"What the hell are you doing trespassing in my room?" the prince demands, grabbing his pants, and clumsily pulling them on. I wonder if he feels how much hotter the room got. My skin suddenly burns as the same song from the viewing room reaches a new crescendo.

"I came as a friend, hoping we could enjoy a few more moments of conversation before the feast," the king breaks off, his eyes flitting between me and the giant before his disgust deepens. He gives a haughty smile that stings more than it should. I grapple to understand my illogical reaction—of course, he doesn't care about me. That voice in my head... it wasn't him. It was someone else.

"Slave troubles?" the Enduar Troll King asks.

"It smells like animal shit in here," the warrior pipes up.

Prince Keksej doesn't blink. "Just a human." Both of them laugh, and my wounds burned more intensely than before. It takes a moment to realize the king doesn't share their mirth.

"Prince Keksej, I came with a bottle of our finest batch to make up for that little quake. We've been experiencing some irregularities in our mines." The sound of this man's voice confuses me, it's too similar to what I heard. But he... he hates me. Why would he threaten to kill the giants?

My master makes a sloppy, pleased sound. "Ah, yes. You had me worried we would have to attack you. I know your people," he clumsily moves his hands before him as if mimicking a spell, "magic the stones or some nonsense."

The king smiles, and the sharp points of his teeth, paired with glowing blue eyes and polished armor, chill me to my bone. He's a demon, come out of some fiery hole.

"I am in no mood for war today. I thought we might have a little game," King Teo says, walking to a small table on the side of the room.

The warrior watches him carefully, and I forget that I'm still cleaning my mess. The pain in my body returns with a vengeance as my back starts to throb. I shiver despite the heat.

"What game?" the prince demands.

The king pulls out a seat and sits down. "A drinking game. I see you're more than fond of a good brew."

I am the one with the least amount of experience in relations between the Enduar and the giants, so I have no reference point for what the interactions should be. But drinking in the presence of an enemy seems... unwise.

Keksej is more drunk than I realize because he smiles. "We've been doing business for years. Nice to see you're loosening up."

The spot on the ground is about as clean as it will get, so I slowly stand up and eyeball the warrior now leaning against the wall. He's scowling at the idea.

"My Prince, maybe you should—"

Keksej's face turns red. "You will not deny me. I never back down to a challenge, so bring the mead!"

No one acknowledges me. A quick look shows that the door is now closed, still unable to reach Mikal. The clink of a glass draws my attention back to the sovereigns once more.

"Tiny flea! Be a good bitch and pour for us," the First Prince calls.

I grit my teeth, trying to swallow down the bile that rises in my throat. These men are monsters. Being near them makes my skin crawl, but I know better than to disobey. I slowly make my way over to the table and pick up the bottle of mead.

It takes everything inside of me to ignore that cursed song piercing through all my defenses. The king draws me in like a moth to a flame, and I want to touch him. Just once. And then—

I stop myself. This is a trap.

"Giant rules, then. Grofiket, you will keep score! The first to pass out or vomit loses." The giant warrior nods, and Keksej looks even more delighted.

"I would be amenable to that," the Enduar King's voice slides through the air, mingling with the song and caressing me in ways it shouldn't.

"If we are drinking, there should be a wager!" the prince says at last.

The Enduar nods. "My thoughts precisely. Tell me, Prince

Keksej," the tall, blue man leans forward, armor rippling as he moves, "Would you like another diamond?"

The First Prince grunts and the warrior standing at attention behind us shifts his weight.

It's an impressive suggestion, but I don't know what more the Enduares could want. We didn't bring enough supplies for more bartering. As I pour, I can't help but think of my hygiene. The alcohol burns the inside of my nose, and I smell little else, but the Enduar likely has heightened senses. What does he think of me?

I balance the jug on my hip and push one drink toward the First Prince. His movements are still jerky. A splash of liquid lands on my dress. *It doesn't matter,* I tell myself. Then I take a breath and start to push the other glass to the king. He catches it before I have a second to react, and our little fingers touch.

A jolt runs through me as our skin meets, and I feel a burning sensation through the shared point of contact. The image of him dragging a damp cloth over my naked skin, washing away dirt, blood, and tears, takes over my mind. His touch is gentle enough to make tears spring to my eyes. Then I blink, and it is gone.

I quickly pull my hand away, but not before I catch a look in his eyes that sends a shiver down my aching spine. They are cold and calculating, and it's clear that he has an ulterior motive for this game.

"Another diamond could be interesting. But what do you want in return?" the prince asks, shirtless and sweaty.

"Make me an offer," the king says, his voice smooth as silk. Prince Keksej waits for the Enduar King to drink first so he knows the mead isn't poisoned.

The Enduar raises the glass to his lips and drinks deeply.

Satisfied, my master downs his drink in one gulp and slams the glass down on the table. "You steal enough of my people. How about I offer you one of the hearty men we brought?"

My stomach drops at the words, and I feel sick with fear. Mikal. The king raises an eyebrow, clearly intrigued by the proposal. For a moment, I'm frozen, unable to move or speak, but then I force myself to look up at the Enduar. There's something about his gaze that takes everything in me to keep my composure.

"A diamond for a slave?" the king says slowly. I hate the way he says it. Like humans aren't worth his jewels. Then, "Very well. If I win, you will let me choose one of your slaves."

---

1. Damned monsters.
2. For the love of the gods.

CHAPTER 4
LAPIS LAZULI
TEO

No less than six of my hunters are stationed outside for when I reveal what I truly want. The tension in the air is thick enough to cut with a knife, but the idiot in front of me continues to drink. A trail of mead trickles down his flaming beard, and there is a damp patch on his hairy chest.

He doesn't know that I have a gemstone pressed on the inside of my cheek to prevent intoxication. He was so surprised when I arrived, he didn't even think to look. Damned fool.

Even still, the burn of the alcohol is a welcome distraction from the anger and grief spiraling through my veins. I steal another glance as my fourth glass is poured.

Right there, between my mate's breasts, is a brand.

Two godsdamned brands, actually.

And she was in here alone, wearing *that* while he was naked. Blood has soaked through the back and trailed down her legs. Her feet leave bloody splotches wherever she walks. I swear on every star in the sky, he will pay for this. Images of slicing his head off, and watching him bleed out at my feet run through my mind while I watch the shirtless giant down another glass.

Frustrated, I grab the jug from the slave, and she skitters away. It's too big for her anyway. Much easier if I pour.

The prince laughs. "She's a small thing—a tiny, little pest."

I eyeball him, and frown. He goes right back to drinking, oblivious to my murderous thoughts. That is for the best since our official trade agreement has kept us alive for many years and war must be avoided at all costs. I see the faces of my people, the mates, the children. Protecting them falls squarely on my shoulders.

The sixth glass comes and goes, and soon, the tall jug is almost empty. He still sits in his seat. The anticipation is making me want to crawl out of my skin.

Soon. It's almost time to reveal my hand.

The Prince sways when he yanks the jug away from me. "I pour now," he slurs.

I oblige and allow him to pick up the jug, he spills some of it into his lap, and I snarl. "Careful," I chide. "That is a very good brew."

He sways again, and he scrunches up his face. He blinks rapidly, throat bobbing. Then, he leans over on his side and vomits on the ground.

It is done. I won. Relief is the sweetest emotion.

I watch the prince wipe his mouth. Then he narrows his eyes and straightens up in his seat. "What trickery is this?" he growls.

I raise a brow. "Trickery?" I echo, feigning innocence. "I offered you a drinking game, and you accepted. You even chose the rules. What did you say? *Giant rules?* This," I gesture to him, "just happens to be a result of your own weakness, First Prince."

He glares at me, his eyes dark with fury. "I will not be mocked," he snarls.

I lean forward, my own anger simmering beneath my calm exterior. "I am not here to mock you," I say, my voice low and dangerous. "Now, I want my slave."

He scoffs and wipes his disgusting mouth with the back of his hand. The acidic smell of his sick is filling my nose.

"I'll take you to their rooms in the morning. You can choose then." He tries to wave me off with his hand.

My muscles are tense. "No, now. I won't have you backing out of the deal."

"They'll be asleep. Who knows what revolting things they do when they're alone," the prince retorts.

I stand. "No need to find out. I already know who I want."

The prince appears completely sober. He waits for my next words with a lethal concentration that shouldn't be possible for someone who just downed enough mead to tranquilize a bear.

"Give me this slave." I jerk my head to my mate, still not daring to look.

The prince is deadly serious. "No. Stop with your games. We will look in the morning."

I lean over the table, grab him by the shoulder, and pull him up to his feet. His weight nearly throws me off balance, but I keep my grip tight.

"I'm not playing games anymore," I growl. "*You* suggested the *male* slave. I agreed that I wanted *a slave*. Her." The laws of the council be damned.

"Unhand the prince, troll!" the warrior yells.

The prince fights against me and spits right in my face. "She belongs to the royal family."

"Not anymore."

Frantic, Keksej looks to the side toward his warrior. "Take her!" he cries.

I press the crystal on my wrist, causing it to light up seconds before the six hunters burst inside the room. They are too late, as my mate is already in the hands of the giant. He holds a knife the size of her head to her throat.

Her petite body moves and contorts in pain as she bucks

against the giant. When she meets my eyes, all I see is terror. A primal instinct roars to life inside of me. Throwing the prince to the ground, I leap across the room. I catch the warrior by his hair, knocking him off balance and causing the woman to fall. She scrambles away as my tail swipes up across his neck, leaving a thick red line. Rage is burning in my eyes.

The warrior chokes as blood starts to leak out of his wound, but I don't let go.

"You will never touch her again," I say, sinking to the ground. The point of my tail plunges into his chest, finishing his death with a metallic gurgle. I stand up and look directly at my mate. She is shaking, eyes wide and horrified.

The prince bellows, *"Help!"* in giantese, and another warrior runs into the room from the hallway. No sooner than he lunges toward me, than one of my hunters swings his hammer, crushing the man's skull.

My mate screams and runs from the room. One of my men follows her. This is all spinning out of control faster than I can blink. I was supposed to win her, and then we would command them to leave. Instead, I have spilled giant blood for the first time since the war.

"Stop," I command, and the whole room freezes.

Two dead giants lay before me, and another stands in the doorway. I whip back around to the first prince. He is telling the man not to attack—that he knows his odds of survival. Luckily, he doesn't know I am fluent in his language. Half of his guard is slain, and with his drunkenness, they would lose their fight before it ever began.

"Accept it. You revealed his hand too quickly," I say in giantese. "There is no reason to rekindle a war, prince."

Now, he is staring at me with disbelief, his face contorted with fear.

"I'll be telling my father about this," the prince spits out, his voice shaking angrily.

I let out a low growl, my claws digging into the stone table. "You started this," I say, my voice low and dangerous. "If you would have given me the slave, all would be well."

The prince backs away, his eyes darting to the two dead bodies on the floor. "I doubt the king will see it that way," he says. "You aren't allowed to own them at all."

"Will the king be so eager to give up the diamonds we trade with him?" The giant prince grimaces. I am not afraid of him. I am not afraid of death. All I care about is protecting my mate and my people. "Leave," I say.

He stands. "I should have known better than to trust a troll." Then he is pushing his way out of the room.

I lunge toward him, but my hunters grab me by the shoulders. Vann. Somehow he got in here while I was dealing with the prince. The other hunters file out, their hammers and spears at the ready.

The hallways are full of heavy footfalls and labored grunts as the remaining giants and their slaves bolt out of our mountain.

"Let him go," he urges.

And I do. I will allow him to flee, with the knowledge that his father will soon hear of what has happened here tonight. I know that there is no going back. War is coming. "Follow them out. Make sure they do no harm."

"Will you come?" he asks.

I nod. "I will tend to my mate."

Those around me freeze. It is still too new for anyone to hear those words lightly.

I wish I felt the hope I see in their faces as they fight for their people. It is unlikely that she will want to be in the same room with me. I can see that accepting our matehood will be a long, painful process–but the most important thing is that she is here.

I will sort out the rest with time. If there is one thing I learned from my father, it's that everything in this life has a price. As king, I am prepared to pay until I have nothing left to give.

It would not be the first time I would have to remake myself in the name of progress. I am strong. It did not break me last time, and it will not break me now.

My thoughts fall to oblivion when a feminine scream pierces the air.

CHAPTER 5
LARIMAR
ESTELA

Hot tears prick the corners of my wide eyes as I stare down at the dead giant at my feet. Panic rises up through me like a tide, and my heart beats faster and faster like a caged bird. My instincts are screaming at me to leave.

The king wants me.

He won me in a bet.

Suddenly, everything the prince warned me of is reality. I'll be brutalized and eaten. A small cut on my throat stings, and I smell blood—blood will be the scent of the rest of my life. Pain. Just like my mother. Agony until the bitter end, and Mikal will be alone.

Everything swims around me as I run, darting past more Enduares and into the hallway. The giant guarding the slaves has found his way into the room in order to save his prince. Fear clouds my mind as I try to remember where the slave room is located. It isn't far from the Prince's.

Terror's vise-like grip closes around my throat and squeezes.

I feel it everywhere—in my spine, my stomach, my hands. Who knows how many of the king's hunters are lurking in the shadows, like the six who tried to take me?

"Stop!" a heavily accented voice calls behind me.

I turn to see one of the Enduares coming after me and scream again. Another ugly bellow from the prince makes me flinch hard enough to trip. The hard stone ground bites into my palms and knees, yet the pain barely registers as I scramble to my feet and latch onto the nearest door.

The Enduar chasing me slows, hanging back as I pull on the door with all my might until it swings open wide enough for me to dart inside. He'll kill me for wandering, like they did to Sergi.

The other fourteen slaves are huddled together on every available surface in the small space, with the contents of our carts overcrowding the space. One man screams, and the sound of a whimper draws my attention to the shadows. They expect me to be an Enduar.

"I'm human," I call, shutting the door behind me after looking back into the hallway and seeing that the Enduar has disappeared.

We only have a few moments before they will come for me.

"Thank the gods," Arlet says, appearing out of nowhere and wiping away tears from her eyes. I feel guilty looking at her.

Mikal grabs me by the shoulders, his fingers unnaturally strong. "Estela, you came back alive." He says my name as if it is a prayer answered by the heavens. I latch onto his hand and pull. Seeing him does little to control the world tilting on its side.

There isn't enough air in this room for me to breathe.

"*Mi amor*[1]," I gasp, then kiss his cheek. He pulls me into a bone-crushing hug, and I yelp in pain.

"What happened?" Arlet demands, eyeing the emerald green dress stained with blood.

I look at her and shake my head. The slices on my lower back will heal while running. "I'm all right. Just more whipping."

I put some space between Mikal and I, staring at the bandages wrapped around his bare torso. Not quite whole, but close enough. I touch his shoulders and run my hands down his arms to make sure he is real.

"We need to leave, Miki," I whisper. Then I am ripping open one of the giant's trunks, grabbing the first furs I see. I toss one to my brother. "You too, Arlet." This cave will be a cruel death. Blood, gore, and burning lava. When we leave this time, no one will catch us.

I tug both of them toward the door. "Now," I plead.

"What about them?" she asks.

I open my mouth and falter. This is taking too much time. We need to get outside. My mind is already scanning through all of the landmarks I took note of before, mentally guiding my way through the tunnels to the outside.

The savage death of the giant invades my thoughts. I close my eyes and draw in a fortifying breath. If they want to brave the cold mountain as well, they should have a chance. "The Enduares have killed two of the giant warriors. I don't know if the First Prince still lives. I suggest all of you run," I call over my shoulder as I grab onto the handle.

"Leave?" one of the slaves says. "Why should we trust your words? Aren't you the prince's tart? Did you suck him off so you could escape?"

Mikal freezes, his angry rage brimming to the surface. After yanking himself out of my grip, I cry his name as he walks over to punch the man squarely over the jaw.

The slave recoils when Mikal hits him again. I race over and grab my brother. "Enough, Miki." I have to take charge of the situation—especially when my brother still lacks the maturity not to make things worse.

"Half-giant bastard!" the slave yells while holding his bloody nose, but I'm pulling Mikal toward the door just as Arlet yanks it open.

We all file into the hallway. There is shouting from the next room, and I see the writhing shadows of Enduares and giants fighting. I grab my brother's hand, and we start running. A sharp sound abruptly draws my attention behind us just as a large hand wraps around Arlet's middle section and picks her up.

I turn around to see the remaining giant warrior holding her, a cruel grin on his face. Mikal snarls and charges at the giant, but I grab at my brother's clothes, knowing full well that he is not a match for the brute while his back is still torn. My heart pounding, I try to think of something, anything, that could save Arlet.

"Let her go!" I shout, my voice echoing down the hallway. I can sense the tension in Mikal's body as he stands protectively in front of me and shoves me back into the shadowy wall. He's too noble. He'll get himself killed.

Four Enduares emerge, charging toward us. "Hurt the humans, and we will not hesitate to kill you."

My brows furrow, not believing what I am hearing. More threats of death from the terrifying creatures. They are... defending us? Nothing about these trolls make sense. It stuns me long enough that I don't notice that the wall is actually an alcove until a large pair of hands slip around my middle section and mouth and drag me into darkness. Away from the fighting.

I am shocked into immobility. The smell of the giant palace, earthy and floral, is what knocks my senses back. *Maldita sea*[2], *the First Prince*. I shove hard and try to ram my head backward into his face. He blocks my blow before he leans down, beard scratching my neck.

"Tiny flea, you think you can escape so quickly?" Keksej whispers in my ear.

His skin is rough against my own. I've never felt it before, and it grates against exposed flesh and gropes at my breast before continuing to my throat. Squeezing. Taunting me with the end of my life.

"So soft. Is this what Rholker felt when he tried to take you to his bed?"

I snap at his wrist and miss. He chuckles and rubs his hand along the column of my throat while I try to shout. The sounds of fighting from the hallway drown out my raw sound. My throat hurts. All of it hurts so damn much. It's impossible to staunch the memories of Rholker showing up at my den, demanding me as a comfort woman and carrying me away.

A human can never win against a giant. I could not keep Rholker off me, and I certainly can't his older, drunker brother from assaulting me in a dark hallway.

Keksej's strength has been manifested in other ways, but now, at the mercy of his scarred arms, he finally breaks his father's command. He will snap my neck before I say goodbye to Miki.

Sixteen years of torture. All to keep taking care of Mikal.

What did it mean?

I stare back into the hallway, my vision of the action limited from the end of this alcove, and glimpse the giant fight against the Enduares. Arlet is nowhere in sight, but half of Mikal's body dances into view. Then he falls back, and I see it all.

A giant swings an ax, and it collides with shiny golden armor. Mikal reenters the scene, ducking out of the way just before an ax catches his flesh. I see him wince in pain and worry about the gashes from his whipping.

"Mi—" my voice is cut off when Keksej clutches my throat again. He pins me in place and forces me to watch.

When an Enduar swirls his hands in front of his body,

pebbles and large stones emerge from the walls and start spinning. Every second, the speed increases as they knock against each other, turning into razor-sharp shards. Slim enough to cut.

My eyes go wide. Prince Keksej must also be enthralled because he stops hurting me. I'd seen the troll controlling a ball of lava, but this is... somehow more terrifying. It's a refined weapon. Not brute force.

One of the shards whips past the giant, catching his cheek. Red blood wells under his eye while he drops his ax, stumbling back and pressing a hand to the cut. Then he holds his arms over his head in surrender.

"Stop! We are leaving!" he calls.

The Enduares cease their attacks, but the one with the shards keeps them floating in the air. It is a clear warning.

"Where is the slave woman? She was in the hallway before this started," the Enduar says.

Mikal pants, notices that I'm not in sight, and scrambles forward. His head darts back and forth, and my heart shatters.

The prince squeezes my throat again, and I choke. Even though there are more than fifteen paces between us, Mikal's eyes meet mine. Recognition of what is happening flairs, and I see a fierce determination that makes me proud and fearful all at once.

"Here!" he shouts and starts towards me. For a moment, I think it will be all right. Mikal will live. Then, the giant hits Mikal over the head and he falls to the ground.

I scream into his hand, and the prince squeezes me hard enough for something to pop. Agony explodes in my body while fresh tears stream down my face. My heart thunders in my chest like a herd of wild horses.

"Mikal," I gasp against the prince's hand, too quiet to be heard. He is picked up and carried by the giant.

Out of sight—away from me.

The Enduares are at the entrance of the hallway in a moment. "My king," one calls back as Keksej growls.

"Stay back! Or I will snap her throat," he taunts, and the Enduares freeze.

One of the Enduar hunters turns and shouts something in a tongue I don't understand.

"Don't worry, my tiny flea," the prince says, quieter this time. "The king wants you alive, but I have my own plans for you, my little tart."

I rally my strength and push against his chest while ducking down, managing to wriggle out of his grip for a moment before he grabs me again, this time harder. I bite his hand hard enough to draw blood, and he yelps back. He towers over me, his yellow eyes gleaming with an intensity that makes my skin crawl. I know there is no way I can defeat him alone, but there is something inside me that defies all logic. Mikal is all I have left in the world.

A new sound comes from the hallway, but my attention is focused on my captor.

"Fuck you. *I am not yours,*" I snarl at Keksej, scrabbling for something to use as a weapon. He's close enough that I can reach for his belt, where he keeps a small array of minor weapons. I cut my finger while grabbing a small knife.

He lunges forward, picking me up and crushing me into him. "Such fire in you," he chuckles, his mouth hot against my ear. "I'm sad I was never able to finish taming you. It will be sweet to remember you this way—to tell Rholker what he was missing."

With a scream loud enough to tear my throat apart, I swing the small knife around, connecting with the side of Keksej's face. He yelps in surprise, his grip on me loosening momentarily again. I take the opportunity to slip out of his grasp and run after Mikal.

I have to make it out. I have to. The Giant Prince comes after me, and I look back to see the dim light show off his furious features and slitted eyes. While turned around, I run into something hard. As solid as stone.

Armored arms wrap around me, and I scream for Mikal once again.

I struggle, but the hold on me is too tight. I look up and see the Enduar King. His braided silver hair hair is slick with sweat. He looks down at me with a hardened expression.

"Stay still," he orders.

A sob wracks my entire body. I try to struggle again, but my body is too weak. The last few days have been too much.

He holds me closer, but it doesn't feel like the way that Keksej held me. He is... mindful of my ruined back.

"*Please,*" I beg. "Please let me go. I need to find my brother."

"You have asked for war. Is that what you want? To ravage the land once more?" Prince Keksej yells.

The Enduar King ignores me as he stares down the giant. "You attacked my people first. You threatened war the second you hurt this woman under my roof."

The First Prince looks incredulous. "All this for that bitch?" He starts laughing. It's an ugly, bloody sound.

The king stands strong. "I will say it only one more time—I won her. You decide how far you want to take this, Keksej."

The ridiculousness of this entire night strikes me hard. Why are the humans important to them? Why am I?

"I have to bring her back," Keksej admits, wiping blood from his leaking wound.

I blink, shocked. *What? Why?*

Don't say anything. He has a tendency to over-speak, the king's voice returns.

I start breathing faster.

"Please. Give her back," the First Prince begs.

What the hell is happening?

"No," the king says. The single syllable leaves no room for negotiation.

The First Prince snarls. "You trolls have always been idiots. I will do us both a favor and end this before it begins." He raises his arms and charges to attack the king.

The armored man throws me over his shoulder, using his tail around me to hold me close as he pulls out his sword and blocks the blow. My body jolts and I whimper, but the prince is sent flying back by the force of the king's strike. I see the blue sparks in the air—enchanted metal.

I tremble so hard that the king sets me down and turns to face Keksej, who is still snarling with rage but has more fear in his eyes than anything else.

The Enduares are bloodthirsty monsters. They should eat me. And yet, they don't move to touch me. In fact, the Enduares didn't attack the humans during the fighting. But... they killed Sergi. I also saw the king slit a giant's throat and stab him in the heart. It's hard to understand what is real.

"You will leave now," the king booms. His voice is commanding and unwavering. "If you ever return here, you will face death."

"I will tell the others that the Butcher still lives. Wait for our messengers, cave rat." Keksej glares at him but backs away slowly before turning around and running off through the tunnel. It is a pitiful sight. The master who had hurt me so deeply, who has stolen my whole world, runs like a newborn babe.

It disgusts me to see his weakness. To know I belong to his family.

Belonged, a voice says in my head.

The king turns back to us, and I see that there is worry in his eyes when he looks at me. The sight shocks me to my very core. It's as if he... feels what I feel. He reaches out a hand as if he wants to touch my face but then stops himself before quickly pulling away.

"You can kill me. Eat me, I don't care," I sob. "But my brother has to live! If he stays in Zlosa, they'll tear him apart. I'll stay here if that's what you want, I promise. Just take him to the elves." My voice has climbed to a screech that even I don't recognize. I've never been so afraid before. My hands claw at the direction the giant had taken Mikal.

A soft, human hand comes over and touches my cheek. I look up to see Arlet, tear-streaked. "I'm sorry, Estela." No other slaves are in the hall with us, but I know they didn't leave. They only took Mikal.

I shove against her. Hard. "Why did you let them take him? You knew," I seethe, "you knew that he is all I have left. What is wrong with you?"

The wail that breaks out of my body is raw, and I fall to my knees, the world spinning around me. My mind races, trying to come up with a plan. Then the Enduar King touches me again.

"You monsters." I claw at his face, and my fist lands on his jaw. "If you won't send your men after him, then at least let me leave."

The king looks down at me, his eyes blazing as he catches my wrists. The song between us becomes so loud that it stuns me. I stop crying, stop fighting, as I am wholly consumed by the man who will tear the flesh from my bones.

His tail comes up to gently caress my cheek, but the metal is cold, and I flinch away. Trembling. The king frowns.

"I know it's difficult for you to trust me. You need to understand that it is unsafe to follow them. We can discuss this later," he says.

I growl and use every ounce of strength to kick at the space between his legs. "No, *now*." My bare foot connects with metal, and I hear the crunch as my foot fractures upon force.

I scream out in pain, collapsing onto the ground. Arlet jumps back as the king kneels down beside me, his armored hand rubbing circles on my back. I grit my teeth and try to hold back tears.

"You are cowards. Does the offer of my life really mean so little?" I sob.

I know you are afraid, his deep voice softly whispers into my mind.

My head snaps up, my teeth still clenching through the pain.

Yes. It is me. I told you I would kill them for you, but tensions are high, and you leaving will only make this worse. His eyes search mine as he speaks, and fresh waves of horror pass over me. A large, armored hand reaches out, grazing my neck.

You do not know what you are offering with your bargain. We can make a deal when you feel better, though there is no need. We belong to each other. You can trust me.

All I hear is him declaring me as *his*. The tone in my head is possessive, borderline obsessive. Like a dragon guarding gold.

I spit at him. "No. Never yours."

He nears me again, and I kick at him with my good foot. Clearly growing frustrated, he shouts something in a tongue I do not understand. When I start full-body thrashing at him, calling Mikal's name through the tears, he uses his large body to cover me on the ground.

The warm, solid length of him blankets me, and my flesh betrays me. Hot warmth pools over my skin despite knowing this position could kill me. I hate the sensation. Crushing someone is an odd way to kill something, but maybe I have been too much trouble for him too soon.

Then his hand disappears, only to return with a crystal. He

holds it against my temple. No sooner than he starts to sing, my vision fades.

Mikal. Mikal. Mikal.

Awareness blinks out slowly and then all at once.

---

1. Means "my love", but it can also be a diminutive term for children from family or friends.
2. Damn it.

CHAPTER 6
AMETHYST
TEO

"Stop pacing," Liana demands.

I halt. The incessant humming that only I can hear is causing my heart to race and my thoughts to accompany my temperament with a dull roar. After taking my small mate to the queen's suite and gently laying her on her bed, she suddenly woke up.

She had been covered in blood. So much blood. From her hair to her ankles. It is impossible to forget her scream because it felt like nails raking across my skin, tearing flesh with her agony. I still see her back bowing and her hands grasping for purchase against something, anything, that could pull her closer to her brother.

Leave, monster, she'd screamed, and Velen the singer put her back to sleep.

Though she rests, I feel her. Brilliant, multi-colored pain from her dreams feeds the flame of my rage. A bruise is blossoming over my jaw, yet my pride is much worse off.

My mate hates me. Despises the sight of me, as if the entire cavern did not sing only for us—easing us into a pair to make the transition from two to one a beautiful, soft period. As easy as breathing.

Perhaps humans do not have mates? What a cruel, familiar twist of fate that would be. All my life hoping for a queen, just to find that she cannot bear to look upon what is hers.

Happiness does not come easily for me. My father had used me as a bloody pawn in his war. I had long since decided that it was my burden alone to carry the weight of my bloodline's sins. So what I have a mate? This has not changed that.

My fists clench. "Tell me what you see."

Liana's hands drop to her sides. "Your mouth is begging to meet my hammer," she says.

"I came to you because you work with this magic. The human woman is volatile. I need to ensure her safety, and you are able to create scrying crystals," I say, my voice low, dangerous. "I cannot be with her. Even in sleep, she fights against me with a strength I've never encountered."

Liana's face softens. "Something is blocking her soul. It's difficult to move around."

My consciousness splits, half in Liana's grotto and the other half hearing that gods-awful scream. I see her, bleeding in his room while she cleans her mess off the floor. I see the brand on her chest. See her held by Keksej in the hallway, as if he was determined to have her one last time before he killed her. It made me insane enough to risk a war.

The call of matehood is too strong. The woman who does not want me is everywhere: the whispered scent in the air, the hum of the stone embedded in my chest, and the blood rushing through my veins. There is not even any name to supply her with besides the awful nickname her old master left.

I look at the crystal in the center of the room, the mother of the stone in my chest. It does many things, from opening our ears to the stones' song, extending our lives, and hastening the healing process when cut.

"What if I performed the ritual to give her a piece of the Fuegorra? Should that clear the block?" I've been here for over a quarter-hour, and I am left without any trace of a solution. My mate sits locked away in some room with the flame-haired woman watching over her. It wouldn't be hard to get a singer to put them both to sleep, and make quick work of the procedure.

The wise woman stops, the crystal piercings on her nose flaring as she breaks from her work once again. "Ma'Teo, son of Teo'Litkh, you will leave that poor woman alone unless you intend for her to hate you. If you approach her with the same raw force you brought to that fight with the giants, we will be going to war in vain."

"War has not been declared. They attacked first." Even still, the thought sobers me, and I slink back. The voice of my father enters my mind.

"One day, you will find yourself understanding my choices. And you will see what I have seen all along—you are too weak to be king."

Looking down at my ungloved hands, I see the ghost of blood. The war returns to me in flashes of brutal pain and ugly deception. I see blood on the dirt, the ghostly white marble walls, my shoes, and my sword.

The breath rushes in and out of my mouth, and my chest pumps to keep up. A hum vibrates, as if trying to soothe me, and the clock measuring time in Enduvida strikes three. My eyelids droop. It's late. We have already climbed to the small hours of the night.

Every surface glitters and sparkles in the soft shroom light, casting shimmering patterns of light and deep shadows that seem to dance in time with the ebb and flow of the stones. It helps the panic and anger retreat once more. I let out a sigh and carefully crouch down in the narrow walkway so that a termination of citrine does not impale me.

When the other sour emotions fade completely, guilt remains. What have I gotten my people into?

Liana makes a frustrated noise and then whispers softly. The walls and ceiling echo and amplify every breath. The Fuegorra crystal lights up like a raging fire, and the wise woman's hands shake, like she's overcome with the spirit of prophecy. Then, as fast as it started, the magic breaks.

"What if I—" I start when an ear-splitting screech fills the space around me as the crystals sing dissonance.

"Out. You are heavy, like a stone. I cannot work with you looking over my shoulder. Go find Ulla. Get her to fix your ugly face. I will bring the crystal to you when I've finished."

I grit my teeth and growl, "I am your king. You don't get to speak to me that way."

She looks up and defiantly meets my gaze. "And you do not get to rush the magic."

I stare at her momentarily, feeling the tension in my body start to build to dangerous levels, then turn and half walk, half climb out of the burrow.

It isn't right for me to take out my anger on her. She did not kill the prince's guards. I did. The faces of the giants, shredded by my sword and strewn across the battlefield, return to my mind. I smell the stench of their bowels. It's a smell that I can never really forget—so different from the pleasant, sulphuric smell of the under mountain.

A lonely old butcher sitting atop a crumbling throne. That is all I am. Once away from the stones, I stop at the royal caves. There are dozens of warm springs inside, and I reach down to scoop up water and splash my face, breathing deeply as I turn to take in the majestic sight of the ancient palace.

The imposing walls of the castle are dimming, and the crystals used to connect to the Ardorflame no longer shine with a clarity akin to glass. Nevertheless, it is beautiful. A reminder of the days of old—back when we were scholars, warriors, and still called ourselves trolls—but it is a shadow of its grandeur. We once thrived in the cities of gold, with kings and queens regarded as exalted gods to watch over their people. Now, we merely survive.

My hands shake, but not for the reasons that they should. I ought to feel bad about senseless death, but I do not regret it. Perhaps that means some piece of my soul is broken.

Two hunters, Dyrn and Tirin, are waiting at the entrance to the back of the palace, spears in hand and dressed in full Enduar armor. "My king," Dyrn says before bowing.

Tirin is young, and when Dyrn bows, he follows, careful to be a good hunter despite coming from a long line of stone benders.

I nod to both of them. "Have the others been brought back up to their homes?"

Tirin glances to the other side of the section, where the giants had stayed, and my eyes follow. An image of my bloody mate flashes before my eyes, causing my fists to tighten. Something beneath my skin stirs, something not entirely my own.

Neither Dyrn nor Tirin had been in the fight, but I'm sure they have already heard the details. Tirin is wide-eyed, but Dyrn seems unbothered.

"No. We were waiting for your word, sire," Dyrn says, keeping his chin low as he speaks, not to making eye contact with me.

I let out a long breath. "How many humans are there?"

"Fifteen in total. The giants only took one when they made their exit," Tirin supplies.

Mikal. My mate's brother. "Are any of them sick?"

"Most of them have injuries, all of them are malnourished.

But, no, they do not appear to be carrying any sicknesses," Dyrn reports.

"Very good. Have they been fed?" I ask. Dyrn shakes his head, and I am irritated. "Why not?"

Dyrn shifts his weight. "The bear killed for the feast was only partially cooked. We needed Ulla's seasonings, and we were unsure if we should risk going to the lower level without reason. Then the screaming..."

I nod slowly and reign in my feelings. "That was wise. Come, friends. We will take the herbs down to the lower cavern so Ulla can give the sick something to help them be moved in peace." There is much more to do. If war is truly coming, I should send the head hunter, Lothar, to the elves, and pray they don't kill him before he has a chance to walk through their gates.

Dyrn nods. "Of course."

Gods only know where Vann is. I will find him later. Now, I must walk, or I will claw my own skin off. Dyrn follows me into the royal enclave and picks up two crates. Tirin trots behind us, still lanky and fresh. He eagerly carries three crates.

After I take two from the pile, we slip into a well-concealed section that houses a steam-powered sidewalk leading deeper into the mountain. Such contraptions once spanned much of the city, but most were destroyed in the quakes after my father's eruption. Sweat slides down my back as the temperature increases.

"King Teo," Tirin starts, and I glance back at him.

"Hmm?" I grunt.

He is what we like to call *ruh'duar*, or "cave-bred." A term used for those completely oblivious to the decorum our old culture called for.

"They say that one of the humans is mated to you."

The words hit me like a slap in the face. The air is thin down here.

"Is that true?" Tirin asks, his voice laced with curiosity.

I swallow thickly, weighing my options. I could deny it, of course, until I am ready to speak publicly with my people about what the humans mean to us. It would be easy to claim it is merely a rumor.

Tirin is young, but he is sharp, and I don't want to lie to my people. Even if it means admitting to something that we still don't understand. "Yes," I say, my voice low. "It's true."

Tirin grins. "I saw the one with ruby-colored hair. Human women look nice. I bet they will look even prettier when they have been bathed." There's a smack, and Tirin groans as I catch Dyrn's tail retreating.

My chest is tight. I know where the humans come from—how their masters regard them as pitiful animals and kill them without a second thought. I do not know how to fix them—especially my mate—but I know that their life here would be better than what they have known.

A fire in the middle of the space lights the cave where my people spend the night. I pass by row after row of makeshift cots and bedding filled with sleeping Enduares, and I cannot help but feel a wave of guilt wash over me. These people are my responsibility, my court. Do they know what I've done?

Dyrn clears his throat, pulling me out of my thoughts.

"King Teo," someone else calls out, and the bustling pauses to greet me. Iryth approaches with her babe tucked against her breast, near the many moonstones hanging off her clothes.

"We bring herbs for the sick," I say, pretending all is well, and several more look up with grateful expressions.

She nods her head, swaying from side to side. "Very wise, Your Majesty. We are well taken care of."

Lies.

"Where shall we put them?" I ask.

Iryth gestures to the other side of the cavern, and I see

Svanna, Ulla, and Eylin adjust long rows of tables for people to serve themselves throughout the night. Their tight expressions shift as they stare at the small crates.

We cross the distance and place the precious medicine on the corner of the table. Ulla comes over with now-shy smiles and gives her thanks while Eylin hangs a pot of water over the fire to prepare a curative tea.

"It is kind of you to bring this yourself. We felt the shakes and feared the worst," Ulla says.

Panic tears at my chest. "Was anyone hurt?"

She shakes her head. "We are made of sturdier stuff. I am pleased to see you well with such monsters under our own roof," she says while my gaze sweeps over a group of children. Then her gaze lands on my jaw and she gasps. "Teo, what happened?"

"The giants have already left," I say. "There was an accident. I was hoping you had bruise paste from the last herbs we bought."

Tirin leans over the table, intruding on our conversation. "Humans can be mated to Enduares!" he calls. Some look up, confused, but Ulla looks like she has seen a ghost.

When she meets my eye, I look away, and she stiffens. "I suppose that is good news about our guest. And yes, let me grab something." Her words are rushed, and I see the way she blinks too fast.

I hum a quick agreement as she tucks into a small basket of her things. An earthy scent wafts in the air around us as the tea is prepared. I do not wish to worry her without reason. The others must be briefed before we let the words spread through the court.

When she rubs the paste over my jaw, her fingers tremble slightly. Her touch lingers a second too long, and a pit forms in my stomach. Ulla should not still care for me. She was there when I returned to the Enduares after the war. As a healer, she not only mended my wounds but listened while I poured out my heart.

"Thank you. Should we take the others up now?" I ask, pulling away.

Ulla shakes her head, hiding the disappointment in her eyes. "Let them rest tonight. We will see you again in the morning."

A small group of younglings laugh from around the fire while they play the pebble game. Their tails stick out and swish back and forth against the rocky ground as the fire lights up their joyful faces despite the somber adults. Tirin goes to play with them, chasing them in circles while Syri and Yret screech bloody murder. The tenderness of the moment slices right through to my heart and takes me by surprise.

If I can make my mate see me for who I am, help her love me, we could inspire others. We could free more slaves. Enduares mating with humans... could mean a full cavern.

My father's kingdom would have abhorred the idea of mixing blood with a non-magical race, but the truth is that my people are dying out. We had been fools not to let more people come into contact with the slaves we'd stolen and freed in the past.

The more I watch, the more possibility blooms before me like luminous fungi. So many feelings are trapped in my chest, and I struggle to free them. Liana is right—I am heavy. The risks have increased, but so have the rewards.

A watery sound fills the air as healing-infused liquid is poured into cups, and singers are already approaching with gems in hand to help minister to the sick. Something about how the water moves strikes up an idea about how I can make the woman stay.

My attention is pulled to Dyrn once again, and I find him already inching toward the exit with the seasoning. I know it is time to return to the surface and help with the food, but I linger for a second more.

"I think that Tirin should stay here for the night. He seems to bring a bit of warmth wherever he goes," I say.

Dyrn nods. "He barely went through the First Cut barely a year ago, but he is fierce. He picked his role well."

"That he did. Let us return," I say.

My people make me strong. The camaraderie with them gives me the hardness to pick up my sword once more—to hurt myself if it means survival.

"Safe night, friends," I call, and then follow Dyrn to the surface.

Upon exiting the tunnel to the palace, there's movement behind me, and I see a hunter following. Faol offers a shallow bow, his hand on his weapon while he joins Dyrn.

"My king, Lord Vann sends word," the hunter with the scarred eye says.

I acknowledge him, "Yes?"

"He has tried to speak with the remaining humans. They are all too terrified to respond," Faol says.

I sigh. "Let them stay together, but get them clothes, blankets, and we'll prepare a hearty meal." Most humans I've met are fearful things. Nothing like the woman who punched me in the face—the one now stored in the queen's suite. "Perhaps stationing a singer in front of their room can also convince them to relax."

Faol nods and leaves, but Dyrn remains at my side. He is not looking at me. The moment is heavy. The weight turns crushing when I remain in one place too long.

Determined to do anything but return to Liana's grotto, Dyrn and I start toward the pavilion. It will be good to see Vann again. He always helps me clear my head.

There is nothing but silence as we walk. Upon arriving, I see a fire lit in the center of the open area.

A mostly raw *ruh'glumdlor* is on a metal spit being hoisted over the flame, and I feel a deep sense of satisfaction that we have such a successful bounty for our new humans. But, as usual, my mind travels back to the dark brown-haired woman, and I wonder if the flame-haired one is taking care of her wounds.

The potent sensation of her fades and twitches. Her sleep is heavy. Vann appears at my side, and the look on his face makes my stomach clench.

"I thought you were with the humans," I say. There is no need for pretense between us, not between the closest of friends.

"I was, but my human language skills are not as proficient as yours, and not all of them understand the common tongue. They huddle together like rats," Vann replies, his voice lowered so the hunters will not hear. "It does not bode well for their time under the mountain."

"We must be patient," I say. "They come from monsters far worse than what the world believes of us. They think we steal their kind out of hunger for their flesh." The bitterness behind my words is palpable.

"Can we prove them wrong?" Vann says, laying a hand on my shoulder. "In the past, none of them wanted to stay. I also recall something about humans needing light to survive. But what the hell do I know? You're the one mated to that creature, and I am too pessimistic."

I nod, still lost in thought about my mate. "Do you have any word on... the woman?" I still don't know her name, she is not officially a queen. What more can I say?

Vann's lips twitch into a smirk, watching my discomfort. "Which one?"

I shove him. It's harder than I intended, but he doesn't seem upset. "You wound me, friend."

He laughs. Then, his smile falls short. "She refuses any help, save from the firelocks. And she smells."

"She's awake?" I blink, my heart soaring far too high for

someone who hates the sight of me. She should have slept longer than two hours. My magic was potent. In an action that is still new to me, I stretch my touch wide, seeking her out. I am met with cold silence. Fear slices through me, so I try again.

Vann nods. "Yes, she is. But she's strong for her size. She continues to throw things at anyone who walks through the door. Did you have to give her a fully stocked suite?" It's then that I realize there is a slightly darker hue to the skin around Vann's eye.

It wounds me that she feels unsafe. We are not the giants. When I seek through the bond in our minds, I still do not find her.

"Peace, friend. She's just been freed. We should sort out the broken bath in her room," I mutter. The panic taking hold of my heart is too much. "And I need to speak with her."

Vann's expression is wary, but he nods. "Very well. I'll come with you."

We hurriedly make our way to the queen's suite. Technically, a tunnel connects the king and queen's suites, but I will not use that until she can look at me without crying. I may force her to stay in Enduvida, but I will force nothing else.

My heart races with every step, and brushes of velvety insect wings send new sensations fluttering across my chest. I know she hates me, but I cannot help but hope that this time she will realize what I am to her.

When we arrive, the redhead is standing outside the door. She looks up at us with narrowed eyes while pressing into the door frame. She fears us. I can see the bruises on her arms from her former masters, yet she is prepared to defend my mate. A flicker of admiration passes through me before I push it away.

"Firelocks," Vann says.

She hisses at him. "What do you want?" Her voice is rough and filled with anger.

"I need to speak with the woman inside," I say, trying to keep my voice calm and steady.

She glares at me, an animalistic rage burning in her eyes. "No. You can't go in there. She's sleeping."

"I can sense she is not. She needs to see me," I insist, my patience wearing thin. "I can help her. Please, let me through."

Vann steps forward, and her head snaps in his direction. "The king has asked you to do something. We are patient but don't expect us to respect insolence. Let us pass."

She steps forward and holds her finger out accusatorially. The absurd bravery these human women possess is enough to bring the greatest hunter to his knees. "You said we were free—that means you can't force her to do anything. She belongs to no one, *demonio*[1]."

Vann grins, and I realize that he has put on his teeth armor again. He's trying to frighten her. He's always been one of the most avid human language learners, but she peppers in insults that even I do not know.

My friend steps forward again until her finger pushes into his chest. Still, she doesn't back down. Her chin lifts higher. "I do not belong to you creatures, either."

"You belong to the court now. As we all do," he says.

The tone makes me wince. I don't think he realizes how he sounds, but I hear it. Of course, our duty has always been to our people. She has never been given such a choice.

"Vann," I start.

"Firelocks—"

"My name is Arlet."

The display between them is heated to molten levels. I don't think he recognizes that her heat is hatred, while his comes from interest. What I wouldn't give to be so blissfully undeterred.

"Lord Vann, leave us," I say with finality.

My friend looks up, the spell broken. He swallows once, bows, and then retreats back into the castle.

The redhead, Arlet, looks back at me. Some of her fire has faded, as if it took something out of her to tell off Vann.

"Arlet," I say gently, stumbling over the words. "I feel I owe you an explanation."

She juts her chin out. "You owe me nothing. Let us go."

I nod once. "I will let you leave any time you want."

This catches her off guard, and she regards me with suspicion. Now is the time to win her confidence through honesty. "What game are you playing?"

"No game," I assure her. "The Enduares do not eat humans. We do not steal you for food—that is a lie the giants tell you. We free slaves every visit."

To say she is shocked would be an understatement. "I—I can leave?"

I nod. She is not mated to anyone. Vann would have told me if he felt something at the sight of her. "I will personally send someone to help you pack a bag. Our storehouses are open to you."

This pushes her off-kilter completely, and she glances behind her at the door to my woman.

I step forward, putting a little more pressure on her. Praying she will cave. "Please, let me see your friend. I need to speak with her."

She purses her lips. "Tell me why you have such an interest in her."

I take a deep breath, unsure of how to answer her. The truth is that I have been drawn to my mate since the moment I laid eyes on her. I feel a connection with her that is beyond my control, and I have been unable to ignore it. I know that it sounds insane, but I can't help how I feel.

"She is my mate," I say.

Arlet looks horrified. Her white skin turns impossibly paler. "Like... your wife?"

I tilt my head to the side. "Yes."

"*Hostia*[2]," she breathes. "That means Estela is a queen? The Queen of the Trolls?"

I blink. "Queen of the Enduares," I correct, but my mind is racing. She surrendered her name. *Estela.* The victory is sweet as I turn it over in my mind, dissecting the syllables from the way that Arlet said it. If my memory is correct, it means something like... star. My star.

"Yes," I confirm.

Arlet looks at me as if I am a two-headed beast. "You... can't speak to her." She twists her filthy furs between her fingers. She's nervous.

My eyes go wide. It all makes sense now, the withdrawal of her presence in my mind. My anxiety. My— "She's not in there," I say.

"How do you know?" the human gasps. This time, when I move toward the door, she doesn't bar my way. I push inside, smelling Estela's bloody, metallic scent everywhere in the room. It drives me insane, riling my being to action.

Stalking over to the bed I had laid her down on, I pull back the covers and find one large bloodstain. I can't stop how my breathes come quicker and quicker.

When I whip around, my braid swings around with me, knocking off a potion sitting on the table near her bed. It shatters on the ground, and Arlet flinches.

"How long has it been?" I demand.

Arlet chews on her lip for a few moments before moving forward. "Less than a half hour? She told me to stay here and distract you if you came."

I know it is irrational, but this feels like a knife in my chest.

Betrayal. My mate has betrayed me by leaving. Does she wish to kill me?

Anger rises within me like a tidal wave. She left without a word. Gone, and I cannot feel her. I have failed to protect her, to be her mate. I feel the weight of my duty as the new King bearing down upon me.

"Where did she go?" I ask Arlet.

The redhead shakes her head. "I don't know. She just said she was going to look for her brother."

Estela could get hurt, or worse, captured by the giants. I need to find her, and fast.

Without another word, I rush back into the palace. There is a tunnel that leads directly out of the mountain. I can ride one of the *glacialmaras*.

---

1. Demon.
2. Shit.

CHAPTER 7
LEPIDOLITE
ESTELA

Mikal is... gone.

My mind swims with a life full of him. Learning to balance him on my hip as I crushed herbs after a long day of scavenging, binding his cuts and breaks, and watching him shoot up like a reed until he appeared tall enough to touch the sky.

His absence is like a deep wound that refuses to heal. I try to push away the memories, but they cling to me stubbornly like a second skin.

My captors didn't realize that I'd stolen a knife from Keksej. The one I'd struck him with was still carefully tucked into my waistband upon awaking. I'll count it as a sweet coincidence. As well as the lack of pain in my lower back and leg.

I feel light-headed. Whether it is from blood loss, healing, or grief, I don't know. All that matters is that I can keep walking. When I left behind Arlet, it was almost too easy to sneak back through hallways until I reached the tunnels leading out of the mountain.

The furs I wore were stolen from the room I'd been given by

the Enduar King. After his cursed songs and crystals didn't succeed in seducing me to death, he tried to pacify me with shiny baubles and clothes. With any luck, I will never see him again.

As I stand before the great doors leading out of the mountain, the flaw in my plan comes to life. The exit is made of that same goldish metal I see everywhere. When I push on a door, it doesn't budge. They are sealed with no visible handle.

"Gods-damnit," I curse. "Mamá, you left me alone in *El Paseo de Nubes*. Why?"

Inspiration sparks. Just a modicum of luck—a small message like what I felt after she died. I could almost see her frowning down at me just before making a comment about my lack of faith.

This is a reminder that she's always there when she can be.

When I look at the door again, everything seems clearer. The Enduares are ingenious—meaning they could hide something in plain sight. I continue feeling my way along the rough ridges of the door until my hand connects with something. I grab it. Nothing.

My breathing picks up. I'm dangerously close to hyperventilating. Every second here is a second I could be caught. But I refuse to give up, so I grasp the object tighter, pulling until my nails break, and I start to bleed all over again.

Something gives way slightly and the relief in my body is palpable. Half-mad with panic, I twist the object and hear a satisfying click. One side of the doors begins to slowly creak open. I can taste my freedom in the air shifting around me.

When I slip out, it's as if I'm leaving behind all my years of chains and shackles. I pause at the edge of the cave, wiping my hands on my clothes and looking back at the swirling red veins coming out of the stone.

Something feels wrong. I can't explain it fully, but there is a pit in my stomach that wasn't there before. I turn away from the tunnel.

The night is dark, the moon barely peaks out from the clouds and the air is cold enough to see my breath, but I have to try. I allow myself one hesitant moment longer before stepping out into the open air. No voice invades my thoughts and the song ceases.

Good, I tell myself, but my head hurts and my heart hollows out, as if I am hurting myself by putting space between me and these trolls. I block out the looming face of the Enduar King, and start to walk briskly. A sharp, fragmented pain tears through my sternum. I raise my hand to touch my chest—as if I could hold my cracking heart together.

This is not your home, so you shouldn't feel this loss in your chest. You, Estela, have no place to call your own.

The extreme cold alerts me to the fact that my feet are still tender, as is my back, but I've braved worse for Mikal. I can finish healing when he is safely away from the giants.

I quicken my pace. The crunching of snow beneath my boots is the only sound in the vast emptiness around me.

My fingers and toes start to tingle, and my nose runs before freezing in trails over my upper lip. I hold the back of my fur to my mouth to help the pain.

I barely make it down the small slope at the base of the mountain before I am so cold I can hardly move. I hadn't realized how much traveling in a group with nightly fires and enormous giants radiating warmth had kept me warm.

Something crunches behind me, and I whip around. My heart races as I stare into the darkness, trying to make out any shapes or movements. There is nothing to see, nothing to hear except for the sound of my own breathing. I chide myself for being so paranoid.

I keep walking—this time, more cautiously. I have the

distinct impression that I am being watched. Has the king come for me? I shut my eyes against the thought, telling myself that all will be well.

Another crunch, and I spin around again. A figure emerges from the darkness, its silhouette illuminated only slightly by the faint moonlight. My heart pounds in my chest with fear and anticipation.

"Who's there?" I call out, casting a puff of white into the air.

The figure doesn't answer right away, instead continuing to approach me.

Maldita sea.[1] *No, no, no.*

"Blood," it hisses in a broken version of the common tongue. "Sweet, human blood."

The hairs on the back of my neck stand up as the figure gets closer, revealing itself. Though not quite as tall as a giant, nor Enduar, its form resembles a man. A jolt of electricity skitters down my spine when I meet its red eyes gleaming in the darkness, reflecting the scant moonlight, while silky dark hair falls over its ice-pale shoulders, and a strip of cloth hangs around its loins.

I take off with a speed I didn't know I possessed, my breath rising in quick gasps. The adrenaline pumping through my veins helps me ignore the growing pain in my feet. I glance behind me and see the creature. Its long limbs are fluid and graceful even as it tears up the pristine snow while chasing after me.

My mind races as I try to come up with a solution to fend off the creature. I know that I won't be able to outrun it for long, but I only have my small knife.

Scanning the area frantically, I search for a weapon or hiding place just as the being pounces. Its sharp claws tear through my flesh like paper. The scream that pours out of me is inhuman. I shove and kick at the lifeform with all my might. Its only response is to pin my shoulders down roughly.

I grab the knife in my waistband and plunge it deep into the creature's side. It howls in fury but doesn't stop lapping at the blood pouring from my wounds. I wrench the knife out of its side and stab it again and again until I falter, weak.

The only sensation I have is the cold ground and frozen lips pressed against my skin. Then, the prodding of something sharp starts at my shoulder. Two pine needles at the point of piercing into my skin.

"Mikal!" I scream. He won't survive without me. My life has always been to make sure that he grows into the man he could become. I am decidedly against dying, so I fight. I fight for him.

"Help!" I cry out as loud as I can when I feel the creature's strong jaw start to contract. It's a futile attempt to save myself, but—

A sound like wind chimes reverberates through the air. The creature abruptly stops feeding and looks around, its eyes narrowing with anger.

I gasp for air, my vision fading in and out. I press my hands to the wounds on my chest, trying to staunch the bleeding. I need to heal, to get out of here.

Then I see a long white stripe, a frozen icicle, glowing and writhing in the air with the grace of a serpent. Atop the beast is a golden armor-clad figure. A long silver braid blows out behind him like a whip made of starlight. The view of him is devastating. A celestial avenger.

I should know who that is. I feel it in the particles that make up my very being, but my vision is fading. It's getting more challenging by the moment to focus on anything but trying to staunch my mortal wounds.

Delirium is setting in. I don't know who I am. Where I am. *Why am I in pain?*

The creature who was just ravaging my body backs away as

something shoots out from the ice beast. My attacker screeches, its body convulsing.

The demon returns to a crouching position. Not dead. An elegant streak of gold darts around in slow motion, latching onto the being who was trying to kill me and tearing him in half. Dark blood sprays and freezes in the air, and the smell of bile fills my nostrils. It is like a corpse rotting from the inside out.

The two halves fall to the ground with a thud just before the ground beneath me rumbles and cracks open. Lassos of red-orange lava snake out, gripping onto the monster and carrying it away.

Scrounging through my mind, I find a name. Mikal.

Is this Mikal? I blink rapidly, not sure if what I see is real. I found him. *He* found *me*. He's safe.

The golden figure's glowing form pulses with a fierce and protective energy. He strides towards me, and I try to speak, to ask how he found me. But my body is too weak, my voice too faint to make a sound.

He kneels beside me and softly takes my hands in his own. He murmurs something that I can't make out through my pain-induced haze, and then I feel warmth radiating from him like an aura. He places his hands on my chest wounds, right above where the creature had pierced them with its teeth, and a bright glow engulfs us. Suddenly, my agony fades away, and I can feel myself healing from within.

Strong arms pick me up, cradling me as we make our way back home.

Everything will be all right.

I nestle further into my savior's arms. Everything feels so much better. Warmth. So warm and I am cold.

The feeling floating through me is so easy to identify. Love. Safety. *Te amo*[2], I think. The only coherent words I can possibly muster.

I'm vaguely aware of being shifted as we nestle on the ice creature once more before I slip away.

~

"I TOLD YOU, TEO. IF YOU DO THIS, SHE WILL NEVER FORGIVE YOU."

The voices disturb me, so I roll over to demand they be quiet. The slave dens are always noisy, but whoever is speaking has come too close to my hut.

"I am not asking. I'm ordering you as your king."

A frustrated grumble. King? The Giant King is in his castle, far from the slaves. He would not bring me to his rooms.

"If we do not do this, we cannot finish healing the damage inside her body. Then she will die."

"Very well."

"Put the gem in."

Something sharp pricks my chest, and I bolt upright, knocking someone back. Music bursts to life. It is louder than anything I've ever heard, demanding... something. They are trying to keep me down. *Mikal.*

"Stay away from me and my brother!" I yell, eyes flying open and adjusting to the soft light.

This isn't the slave den. I am surrounded by a dim, warm room that glitters like gems and gold. Two large, blue beings lean over me.

Dread fills me. I am in the palace of the Enduar King. *No.* Tears spring up, and my memories start to flood back into me so quickly that my mind protests. It's as if something is slicing through my head, waging a war of grief.

"What have you done to me?" I demand, my cheeks wet from desperation and rage.

"I—we have healed you," the king replies.

I look down at my chest to find a glowing red-orange gem

nestled into the skin. The skin is entirely healed, but the sight is grotesque. It is the only thing worse than the brands the princes had placed there years ago. My fingers trace tentatively across the foreign object, but I can't bring myself to tear it out.

"You were near death when I found you."

"Where is Mikal?" I try to move, but the burning in my chest stops me. The singing is loud enough to deafen all other sounds. Acidic dread fills my belly. I had escaped to go find him, and was attacked. I was bleeding to death in the snow when...

The king. I had thought it was Mikal, but the king came to save me. The heat on my chest, and the song surrounding my body takes advantage of the momentary pause in my thoughts. I grab the king's hand and press it to my face, instinctively knowing that his closeness would soothe the pain in my soul.

The King's blue skin is so smooth and warm to the touch. To my surprise, he gently strokes the back of my hand with his thumb, the singing intensifying, wrapping me in warmth and comfort that I haven't felt in so long.

Mine, I say.

The word makes me freeze. I shove away his hand as if it's burned me and scrambled to the corner of my bed. As far away from him as I can.

I look at him and then the woman. She frowns as she gazes at me, as if she's ashamed. Good. I hope she suffered from chagrin over stealing me.

"What have you done to me, *demonios*?" I spit out.

The woman doesn't budge, but the king moves closer.

"I have been speaking with your people, and I know you believe we are flesh-eating trolls. We are not dangerous to you, merely our enemies. We were saving your life."

I spit at him and hiss. He knows my language, somehow. No one speaks human dialects but humans. I'm shaken deep in my soul, trying to fight this crystal. It wants to control me, to subject me to him. I will never let that happen.

"So you keep saying. How do you know my name?" Another piece of me he shouldn't be allowed to have.

"I—"

The stone in my chest warms again as he steps closer. I panic and throw my hands up. "Get out!" I screech.

The king recoils at my outburst, his eyes wide with surprise. The singing grows louder, almost deafening, as if it's trying to compete with my rage.

"I said get out!" I scream again, lunging towards the king. He steps back, but I can see the flicker of something in his eyes. Anger? Disappointment? It's hard to tell.

"We will leave you to rest." The woman speaks softly as if trying to calm me down. But I won't be placated. Not by them.

"Don't come back," I growl. They exchange looks but ultimately decide to withdraw.

As soon as they leave, I curl up in my bed, clutching at the gem in my chest. It's pulsing with a bright light. I will find a way to get rid of it, to free myself from their control.

But as I lay there, exhausted and in pain, I can't help but note this is the second time they've saved me. The song turns sad, and I feel the warmth of the king's surprisingly gentle embrace.

I shove that moment away and return to my brother. This attempt to escape failed, but I learn from my mistakes. I can try again. I cling to hope fiercely and start to count, drowning out the dangerous melody coming from my chest.

Uno, dos, tres, cuatro, cinco...[3]

---

1. Damn it.
2. I love you.
3. One, two, three, four, five...

PART TWO

CHAPTER 8
WULFENITE
TEO

Mother Liana and the six council members that lead Enduvida stand around my throne. Dozens of scrolls have been brought from the royal library, detailing the end of war agreement and the laws we established while settling in Enduvida. Each Enduar wears varying degrees of anger on their faces.

"Section three, article nine states that we would not house humans in the mountains were made nearly thirty years ago. Surely you can understand why we would want to revise them given the situation," I say, my head pounding. I've hardly slept in the last two days.

Estela must be watched and refuses to let me anywhere near her. It is nonsense—she nearly died from the abomination's bites. It was hours of work to ensure that all of the black liquid was out of her system.

It has put me in a foul mood.

Lord Lothar, the one in charge of the hunters, studies the scroll in his hands. "The ceasefire issued at the war's end clearly laid out the terms for our continued peace. Humans were enslaved to the giants long before we ever started fighting, and they were able to retain them to ensure a successful rebuild of their society after a significant population decrease. Both you and the elf king agreed not to join the slave trade to prevent further destruction. We have been walking a fine line by pretending to kill them when they visit our mountain—taking a human to become our queen would be a violation according to our current agreement since it could be interpreted you entered the slave trade by winning her in a drinking game."

Liana lifts her eyebrows. "Come now, that's hardly entering a slave trade. That was a friendly bet the tree vermin lost."

I shift on the broken throne, avoiding the jagged bits of the stone. "I am inclined to agree. She has been freed."

Svanna snorts. "Free? Can she leave the mountain?"

I scowl at her. "In time. When she realizes that we are mates."

The tall woman shifts her braid to display her mating mark. "Do you think that it is what works in a partnership? I heard your father was possessive of his queen, but I thought you wished to rule with a more steady hand."

"Does your mating to Iryth not bind you two together?" I ask, straightening my back.

She shrugs. "Who knows what matehood really is? Is it attraction? Compatibility? All I know is that Iryth has loved and protected my heart from the moment we recognized each other. Does this human woman feel safe and loved, locked in the queen's suite?"

My mouth falls open. "It is only until she heals."

Vann, who usually follows my lead in all, is the angriest of all. "Respectfully, sire, you allow yourself to be ruled by the deadliest of all emotions—hope and guilt. They all need to leave before the giants return."

I shake my head. "The human woman is my mate, and we

did not steal the others. The giants left them behind. Is that not a gray area?"

Lothar nods. "I would say so."

Everyone falls quiet once more until Svanna steps forward. "But how do you expect to care for them? Our skin doesn't require sunlight. We are stronger than they are. Their eyesight isn't suited to our dim caverns long term."

Liana shakes her head. "While we are bigger, one of our greatest advantages is the Fuegorra crystals. We have already successfully implanted one in the small human, and I have seen drastic improvements. We can offer the ceremony to all the others. I think the question that this all comes down to is: are we willing to turn away a potential group of mates for our people when our numbers are dwindling? Ulla, how many births have we had in the twenty years?"

Ulla, in charge of healers, singers, and cooks, purses her lips. "Twenty-three."

Vann shakes his head. "You put too much faith in the stones. If we deplete our bloodline, who's to say that we could survive under the mountain."

"You speak like a troll, not an Enduar," I say.

His eyes narrow, and I see him rub the stubs of his missing fingers.

There's a tightness in my stomach. "Our population is indeed collapsing. We are going quiet into the dark night of death while we grow older, knowing the enormous burden we are placing on our children. This is a chance to fight for our future. Are we really such awful, selfish creatures as to reject that possibility because of bigotry?"

Vann's face turns purple. "Are you accusing me of bigotry because I don't want humans to die under this mountain? Or because I don't want to violate a treaty that has ensured the meager peace we've clung to? This city is already a tomb."

Lady Fira, the oldest of the advisors, speaks up. "The earth is a tomb to our ancestors, Vann. You say the king speaks of guilt, but you are as dead as your betrothed. You wish us all the same fate." There's a noxious silence, but she looks at me. "I stand with you, my king. While some might reject the words of a lowly weaver, I also speak as an Elder in your court. I would rage against the darkness before I let it take me to Vidalena."

"And if we die before we get enough humans to fill our cities?" Vann says.

I growl. "Lord Vann, see reason. Ulla, may I see the census record?"

She nods and passes me the scroll. "The twenty-three births she mentioned are recorded here. After Irsh and Mele died, we are left with eighty-two elders past the age of childbearing, thirty-three women, and one hundred and fifty-two men."

The depressing statistics make everyone's expression dim. Salo, leader of the stone benders, shakes his head. "Of those thirty-three women, fifteen are already mated and married."

Svanna purses her lips. "And not all of us prefer your large blue—"

"Yes, yes," Vann says, more irritated than angry now.

The others see his ire, but I see his pain. At his core, he is concerned with survival. He's just mistaken about the way we achieve that.

Liana crosses her arms, looking brutal in the spell lights. We don't always see eye to eye, but what a force she is when we agree. "Not all of us are destined to be parents, not even mates, but there is one thing we have known across the history of our people. We cannot conceive without matehood. Perhaps it is a survival instinct, but our basest primal selves are recognizing these humans. I say we parade the humans around the Enduares. If there is another recognition, then it is clear we must fight for the humans."

Vann twists around to look at her. "And if there isn't?"

She looks at him. "Then we will give away all of them except for the human mated to Teo. We need a royal heir."

Salo lets out a deep sigh, but I speak up. "Let us vote. Those in favor of keeping the humans to see if there are any more mated pairs?"

Liana, Fira, Svanna, and Lothar raise their hand with me, while Ulla tentatively lifts hers after a few moments. She is carefully avoiding my gaze.

Vann looks at the others like they have betrayed him.

"And those against?" I ask.

Salo and Vann raise their hands immediately.

"Noted. The majority says that we will keep them until we can finish taking them through the caves. If there are more matings, then we will start planning how to take more humans from the giants," I say. "Lothar, would you be willing to start researching that?" Though he is the leader of the hunters, he has an excellent eye for diplomacy.

He nods. "Of course, my king."

I stand, dismissing the rest, and gather the mess of scrolls. Spending time in the royal library calms me, so I will happily take the scrolls back before visiting Estela.

Liana helps me rewind one of them. "Vann needs to watch his tongue if he doesn't want me to cut it out," she grumbles.

I laugh. "Any luck with the scrying crystal? The last thing I need is her escaping now that I have the council on board."

She shakes her head and starts stacking the history of our people. "No. I intend to do some tests when she's healed, but I suspect this human has some drop of magic inside of her."

I think of what Svanna said about protecting Estela while Liana leaves. The miner doesn't know that I am protecting my mate from herself.

As I turn to the exit with an armful of stone scrolls, I catch

Ulla's eye. She's waiting. There is something there, a sadness I cannot name. I hesitate, then approach her.

"Is everything all right?" I ask her softly.

She hesitates. "The woman, Estela, really is your mate." It is not a question.

The muscles in my neck tighten, and I swallow. "Yes."

Her gaze drops. "I wish you both well," she says softly.

My heart cracks. "I am sorry, Ulla. I know that you hoped we would recognize each other."

Her head whips up, almost angry. "You did not?"

My mouth opens and closes. What can I say? I was very broken when I came home after the war; she was a friend. Someone I was comfortable with. It seems unfair to write it off as comfort, as if comfort was not deeply valuable.

After several seconds of searching for the right words in silence, I continue, "Ulla, you are a talented singer and an even better healer. If we were meant to stay together, our stones would have sung. I promise you that we will find you a mate as well. In fact, most of the humans we have are men. You should meet with them first."

Her jaw tightens, the same way it always does before she is about to cry. "Very well." Her courage returns as she looks up at me. "I will hold you to your promise about my mate. Do not forget that I can still beat you in a spear fight."

I laugh. "That was once, and we were children."

She laughs, too. "Did you know that I saw your woman? She doesn't seem like she is made of strong enough stuff to be queen."

I frown, thinking of her kick. "Believe me, she is stronger than she looks."

Together, we walk out of the throne room, and I return to the library and call to Luth the stone bender. He trots over while I lay the scrolls on the long table and lean against one of the chairs.

The air smells dusty from stone paper thousands of years old. "I need your help with the queen's quarters."

"Of course, my liege." He too takes a glance at the rows and rows of our people's knowledge. "Would you like me to come now?"

I push off the table. "Yes. That would be excellent."

He follows me dutifully as we enter through my room and cross the tunnel. I explain what I need quickly, and he listens carefully.

"Light fingers, Luth. I will be displeased if she hears you and wakes," I murmur. I don't tell him I know she's sleeping from how she feels through our connection.

"As you wish, my King," he says with a bow and turns back to the wall to begin tracing along the stone.

I survey the tunnel separating our rooms. It is relatively long, hidden in what looks like a wall from the outside. Traditionally, it was used to give both sovereigns their own spaces to think, study, and rest. They could call on each other when need required their presence.

Members of the crown started visiting every city at the age of twenty to ensure a mate was recognized by fifty. There were great balls held for my parents, and they ruled for nearly a hundred and fifty years.

It is strange to muse what my life would look like if the war had not happened. Such expensive parties are a thing of the past. I was in the middle of a war at the age of fifty. Now I am over a hundred, and I had expected to die with my crown. Estela is a blessing from Grutabela.

The stone bender continues to work on tracing patterns on the wall, and I watch as slabs shift to create a window into Estela's room. At the first glimpse of my mate, relief floods through me.

She is still fast asleep. Her chest is rising and falling with each slow breath as her long brown hair is splayed out on the pillow beneath her. She is wearing a sheer nightgown, which reveals the bandages all over her body. To my dismay, she is still filthy in areas that weren't touched during her healing.

My breath catches when I see the glowing stone displayed on her chest. It glows for me. I am filled with an intense urge to open the door right next to the window and touch her. But I know that I cannot do so until she is ready, until she comes to me of her own accord.

"It is finished," Luth says.

I nod to him. "And you are sure it still looks like normal brick from the other side?"

"Yes, my King. There are many other places throughout the palace that have similar stone enchantments. My father helped make them, as his father did before that," Luth says, his same quiet, unwavering confidence.

I appreciate that about him.

My appreciation evaporates when I look back to find him glancing out the window to look at the new queen. Irritation rises up inside of me, a sensation similar to sitting in one cramped area for much too long, despite knowing that his glances aren't more than curious. I fear the mating bond has made me over-sensitive, but having her means she can be taken away. Luth saw how I was affected over our first meeting.

A voice inside of me says that no Enduar would dare touch her out of reverence, but another voice, the one pushing me since the day I was born, reminds me that I am weak.

I shoot back that a level-headed king does not give in to his demons so easily. "Thank you for your help. You may go now," I say to Luth.

He bows and hurries back down the halls. When he slips through my room, and back to making weaponry, I am left alone with a view of the little human. Sleep makes her vulnerable. The tight lines of worry and pain etched into her face soften, revealing undeniable beauty.

I reach my hand up and touch the stone separating us, needing to be closer somehow.

"What horrors has life shown you, *amor*[1]?" I whisper. The last word is one of her human words. When she had clung to me, bleeding and broken, she'd whispered a simple phrase. One that gave me hope beyond compare, only to be crushed when I realized she wasn't speaking to me.

Te amo[2].

I love you.

A lump forms in my throat, and my eyes burn. I. Cannot. Touch. Her. It is killing me. Death by a thousand pricks of a needle, stabbing me repeatedly as I watch her from the shadows like a coward.

I tighten my fist and decide to make one last adjustment to her room. It does not take the same skill level as this window, and my stone bending will do well enough. Her old bathroom was broken and eventually removed while we rebuilt parts of the palace.

Perhaps giving her a place to wash would help her feel safe.

In the corner of her room, where there is an empty spot, I focus on the stone and memorize its formation. I close my eyes and sense along its surface with my magic. It is good brick, pliable. When I push down, it bows with ease while connecting with one of the warm water pipes. Crystals dot the space, some glowing gently after I pull them up from deposits below the palace. It takes concentration to ensure that none of them are sharp enough to hurt her.

Each beryl crystal will react with her Fuegorra, helping her heal faster.

When the space is filled with warm water, I turn around and

leave. It feels like tearing a stone sliver from my flesh—the pain is far worse than staying and indulging the irritant.

As I exit the tunnel room, I try to push the thought of Estela out of my mind, but the mating bond tugs at me relentlessly. I head towards the throne room, where I have another council in a few hours. Maybe the routine tasks of being a king will distract me.

Soon, the giants will send word about what happened under the mountain. Preparations should be made. The sick should be healed, the humans will require more attention, and weapons and armor should be forged. There is still an entire court to be taken care of.

---

1. Love.
2. I love you.

CHAPTER 9
AQUAMARINE
ESTELA

One second I was at my table working, the next two female lumber slaves are clutching at my arms and holding me down to the ground. They hold a bucket of water over my head and I thrash in their arms.

"You stopped bathing again," Prince Rholker says down at me. He looks side to side, making sure that we are secluded in the trees. "I want you to serve in the palace tonight. We need to get you washed."

I open my mouth to scream when one of the women jams her knee into into my throat while yanking on my coarsely spun pants and shirt. They strip me naked in front of the prince, revealing the scars from his brother's whip and knife. It's cold, and it's nearly nighttime.

I choke on the lack of air, and the Second Prince jumps. "Get off her. You won't fight back now, will you, Estela?"

The woman removes her knee, but my respite is brief when the bucket of ice water is dumped across me. I whimper.

"It would have been warm if you had bathed when I told you to," Rholker says.

I continue to ignore him, closing my eyes so I don't have to see the way his gaze lingers. While their rough hands hurriedly scrape soap over my tender bits, I mentally return to my table.

I refuse to stay in the present, choosing to escape with a world of plants and poultices. Memorizing the potion for the common cold was one of my first tasks as an herb preparer, so I think about making one just in case the chill of tonight is too strong. Endure a little longer, I think, when a jagged fingernail catches my navel.

It works.

When a rough towel is handed to me, I start ringing out my hair and drying off the water. I shiver forcefully, almost missing the hiss of sharp steel exiting a sheath. However, I can't ignore the wet, meaty thud of a head landing on the ground.

I whip around to find the two slaves dead. Their heads lay next to their bodies, unseeing eyes open to the forest brush. The blood leaks from their necks and soils the ground. I step back, covering my mouth and nose as Prince Rholker shakes the blood off his blade.

He looks up at me, remorseful. "If my father found out I was following you around still, he'd be angry. Really, you only have yourself to blame. If you had bathed when I told you earlier, they would still be alive."

My back hits a tree trunk. I'm vulnerable, naked, and terrified.

"I'm not a monster, Estela. I care for you." Prince Rholker reaches his hand out.

A loud, harmonic banging starts up, interrupting my sleep.

I shift in bed, pushing myself up despite every inch of my body protesting. I almost don't notice the ever-present song, singing sweetly, easing me out of my nightmare.

It is strange to dream again. It happens so infrequently, and now I am haunted by my past. The hollow pain in my chest is gone, but it's been replaced by a sad confusion.

A bottle clanks to my left, and it has me bolting upright. I must be in the healing hut. I worked late, I need to get back to my den to see Mikal and Arlet.

No, a voice says. You are under the mountain, and you are safe.

My hands claw at the space around me as I gasp, only to be met with immediate pain. I'm in the Enduar Mountain. That is what the melodic ringing is.

"Stay away," I yell, my eyes adjusting to the darkness. Small glowing lights are all around us, but none of them are bright enough to reveal the details of my room. Something is wrong.

"Hush, child, I will not hurt you," a deep, aged feminine voice says.

My hand presses to my chest. The hardness there is foreign, and I look down to see the scars of bite marks illuminated by a glowing flame-colored gem embedded in my skin. Memories of the monster, the blood, and the agony come back. I start breathing faster, my hand trembling over the spot where I've been deformed.

"Stop that. All is well," the voice says again.

There's more shuffling before several orbs above me flare to life and bathe the world in gentle, yellow light, revealing a beautiful room covered in gold details and crystals. It is bigger than the space I was forced to share with Keksej. There is a spacious dresser, more murals of flowers made with green, blue, and purple gems, and a bath.

My eyes widen. It's been too long since I was clean, and I know that has consequences.

My eyes land on the Enduar woman standing next to my bed. She is tall and lithe and positively covered in crystals. Short, stick-like formations hang off her sleeves, and hundreds of small ones are stitched into her vest. She wears a tunic-like dress that hits her knees with hip-high slits on either side. The fabric is flowy, graceful even. Her leggings appear plain, but jagged, pointed stones are on the tips of her feet.

I look up at her face. There are three piercings on each of her ears, one on her left eyebrow, between her nostrils, and one on her lip. Enduares don't seem to age like humans because their skin, while slightly wrinkled around her eyes and mouth, still appears taut. She isn't smiling.

"You are the one who put the gem in my chest," I say. "You bound me to this place." I think of the hollow heartbreak I felt trying to leave. What happens if I feel that way again? It chills me to my bones.

"You are bound nowhere. My name is Liana," she says sternly while grabbing a small mortar and pestle. "And before you ask, Ma'Teo asked me to stay and care for your wounds. You're almost finished healing, thanks to me."

My stomach drops.

Can you hear my thoughts, too? I think toward her.

No response.

As she grinds something in the bowl, there's a strong bitter scent in the air. I tilt my chin up and sniff. *Willow bark.* I regard her warily for several minutes, trying to decide the severity of our situation.

"There was a sound earlier that woke me. What was that?" I ask.

"A clock of sorts. There's no sunlight under the mountain, so long ago, some of our best astronomers used his magic to sync the tower with the sun's cycles. It will ring every hour, with one note for each hour. Don't worry, the songs change too." She keeps grinding and reaches down to pluck a leaf that I can't quite see. My healing training kicks in, and I look at her ingredients to see what she's making. I see lavender buds, dried marigold leaves, niue root, and willow bark.

I blink. Just a simple healing poultice.

"If you add those leaves, it will taste better," I say to her, pointing at some dried peppermint in the herb box on the table.

She looks over at me again, this time pausing her mixing and raising her eyebrow. "Do you know about healing?"

I press my lips together, easing back. "I was the one who prepared those herbs. I know about healing from caring for slaves, but I am not a doctor." True, but the royal doctor did rely on me more than he should've.

She scoffs. "You humans and titles. One of the men said something similar the other day about mining." Then, she pours the mixture into a metal goblet and stirs. She holds it out to me. "You may ask me whatever you'd like, but your friend should be here soon with breakfast."

Reaching out, I take the glass and look down at it. I should feel threatened, but I don't. It helps that she doesn't have those awful, steel teeth.

It smells right. But what if there is some kind of drug hidden that I didn't see before she started working?

She crosses her arms. Not in a defensive way, the way that a mother might seconds before scolding her child. "Drink. I have glimpsed my future—the only vision I could see with you. We will be close friends, you and I."

I want to laugh at her words, but something in me stills. My mother believed in seers and shamans, and a small piece of that embedded itself into me.

Even still, the idea of befriending one of these Enduares is preposterous. I am here against my will. It takes effort to ignore the pain throbbing in my shoulders and arms from my last escape attempt.

When I look into Liana's eyes, I see kindness. Somehow, it is cold, like stone, but kindness nonetheless. I place the goblet on the table. She all but growls.

"Where am I?" I say, my tone guarded.

She purses her lips. "This is called the queen's suite."

I cringe. "What?"

She gestures around her. "The old queen lived here," she reiterates.

I scowl. "Obviously. Does the king sleep in this room as well?" The giant sovereigns didn't sleep together before the queen's death, but all I know about Enduares comes from battle songs. The Butcher and his Cleaver, killing thousands of humans, giants, and elves. The traitors. The gore-lovers. "Am I destined to be the Butcher's whore?"

Liana whips around, and deadly power leaks off her in waves. "Do not call him that," her voice echoes through the room, causing a sharp sound to pierce my ears. It's more shocking than painful, but the fragile trust beginning to bud shatters around me.

I scramble back into the corner of the bed, holding my hands over my head in a feeble attempt to block her out. The nauseating waves of power subside.

"Drink, human," she says, now more irritated.

There's a knock on the door, but I don't move from my curled up position. I can't see anything but the insides of my eyelids. I feel nothing but the rush of air into my lungs and the rapid flutter of my heart.

"Estela." Arlet's voice is painted with worry, and I unravel to find her and I alone in the room. She's already on the bed, crawling toward me. It hurts to see her and not Mikal. My eyes start burning when she wraps her arms around me. "Are you in pain? Mother Liana said she made you a potion. Here, take this."

She holds out the golden goblet, and I grimace. "Put that down," I say, pressing my hand against my chest to stop the spasms. "I'm... fine..." I pant. The smell of roasted meat draws my attention. *Food. Gods, I'm so hungry.*

"The gem looks pretty on you," Arlet says, her eyes landing on the wide scoop of my gown's neck.

"What?" I croak, my head pounding.

She tilts her head to the side. "The crystal. A few days ago, after you were attacked, they offered homes to anyone who wanted to stay under the mountain. They told us we'd have to perform a ceremony, *dual'moraan*. They say that most Enduares do it when they reach maturity, but it was fun. Did you have a hard time hunting for your Fuegorra crystal? There are only two of us who have done it so far. Well, I suppose you too. How exciting! I know you were—"

"I didn't ask for it to be put in, and I sure as hell didn't go hunting for gems," I snap, rubbing my pounding head as I eyeball the tray on the table. Her face falls.

"No? Well, I heard about what happened when you tried to escape... I haven't been allowed to see you while you were healing. They finally granted permission for me to bring this for your breakfast." She lifts the tray with the delicious-smelling food a little higher, gesturing to what I'm supposed to eat.

My stomach hollows out. "What?" I snap. "That could be poisoned... or better yet, they could have cooked Sergi."

"Honestly Estela, listen to yourself," Arlet groans and grabs one of the glowing lights floating over my head, and I get a full view of her improved appearance. Her hair has been washed, pleated, and twisted above her head in a pretty, swooping bun. Her color has returned, and she no longer wears the clothes of a slave. Her new furs are finely sewn with stones stitched all over them.

"What the hell has happened to you?" I ask, pushing away from her.

Her brows furrow. "What do you mean?"

"You are dressed up like a doll, freely visiting me in the queen's suite. *Look at your hair,*" I shake my head, my eyes burning. "Have you become a comfort woman?"

She looks horrified, her hand flying up to her hair. "What? No. They haven't touched me. This is how unmated Enduar women wear their hair."

I ignore her words, instead thinking of Liana's nauseating

power. Then I remember the king ripping my attacker in half as if it were nothing. I can still feel the splatter of blood on my skin and smell the putrid scent of innards. It's a stench I will never forget.

Arlet takes my hand. "My friend, I know that you fear them. But you've been sleeping for nearly three days, and nothing has happened to anyone but proper meals and baths to scrub away decades of dirt. No one has been killed. This," she gestures to the tray again, "came from something they call a *ruh'glumdlor*, or a cave bear. I helped them prepare it."

She does look healthy. *Clean.* But...

"The Enduares are the enemy," I say.

She shakes her head. "Not our enemy. The giants', maybe."

I press myself into the wall and point to the crystal in my chest. "This is how it starts. How do you know this won't control you to do awful things? What if their hold is so great that you kill someone? Me, even?"

She shakes her head. "That would never happen."

The lightness with which she treats my statement doesn't sit right. "How do you know? They will use their evil songs to lure you into submission, ravage your body, and eat you after becoming their willing pets. How could you forget this?"

She gives me a pitied look, which I hate. "I grew up hearing the tales, too. But I... I don't know if they are real. They told us we could leave, get the crystal, or linger a little while we decide."

My eyes grow wide. "Why haven't you left, then?" I demand. I had been grasping for threads of freedom since the instant Mikal left. She had been offered a way to walk right out the door and ignored that?

"Estela, my sweetest friend, you nearly died. It's not safe to go out of the mountain alone. Besides, I would rather die healthy, with a belly full of this warm food, than return to our old masters and die of a broken back."

I balk at her. "But, you could learn from my mistakes. Don't leave at night, and..." I trail off. The reality of her words is heavy. "We were going to go to the elves, not the giants."

She tilts her head to the side and huffs an ironic laugh as if I am the one acting foolish, not her. "I don't even know how to get to them. You wanted to escape the giants, and we have. Count your blessings."

I purse my lips, ignoring her ugly words and glancing around my room. It is more beautiful than any other sight in the cave, and I have been entranced by many. She follows my gaze to the bath. "Let me help you bathe, friend."

The nightmare is still fresh in my mind. I see women holding me down while I scrubbed. "*No*. I can clean myself."

"All right." She starts fidgeting. "I am glad that you are here too. I know you still want to run, but you offered to stay. That's important to these people."

A memory from the fight with the giants comes back. My eyes widen. I tried to offer my life for Mikal's, but the king turned me down. At least, that's what I think happened—now my memory is fuzzy.

Arlet told me that they said we could leave, but she's also made it crystal clear that she doesn't want to come. That's fine. I can walk out the front door without my friend to save my brother.

Forcing a smile on my face, I look back up at Arlet and come out of my corner. When I'm sitting on the edge of the bed, I take her hand. "I am happy you are feeling better."

The worried look melts off her face, and she squeezes my hand with hers. "Thank you. The last two days... I've never felt better. Estela, they ask nothing of me. No whipping, no pain, just... contentment. Not everyone is as welcoming to the humans, but those that do more than make up for it."

I nod, noting I should be alert when I leave. It's like I can see the rotting nature of these beings peeking up at us through cracks in the attractive facade. It hurts to lose my friend to them.

"I'm feeling weak again," I say gently. It's not true, but it's clear she's too encased in these people with their pretty rooms and clothing. The pain of her letting Mikal go is still fresh. "Can I eat alone?"

Understanding clouds her expression, and I almost feel guilty.

Almost.

Then she leaves, promising to return in a few hours and take me to some light source she says works to keep us healthy. I will be gone before then. They have still left me in this place, with clothes lining the drawers and valuables stacked on the shelves. I could barter for Mikal's freedom. Looking back at the meat on my dresser, my stomach growls with revenge. I am hunger personified.

I quickly grab the tray of food and sit cross-legged on the bed. I close my eyes when I lift the meat to my mouth and bite down gingerly. Arlet was right; no slave I'd ever known would have enough meat on their bones to supply this kind of food.

Juices drip down my chin. It's my first full meal in a week, and I might vomit due to the sheer volume of food I've tried to cram into my taut belly.

When I'm more than satiated, my eyes land back on the small spring. The red and blue crystals there twinkle, as if coaxing me to sink into the waters and keep healing. This wouldn't be a bucket of ice water in the bushes, this would be a quiet reprieve.

I look down at the dirt, smell the distinct odor, touch my grimy hair that is starting to mat, and think. Powerful beings can force those beneath them to do what they want. My filth is a flimsy barrier, and cleanliness brings safety.

But a bath would slow you down. Who would be expecting you to leave right now? The idea comes from somewhere in the corners of my mind. I refuse to think it again in case the king is still listening to my thoughts.

Forcing myself to stand, I act on instinct, looking for a basket or bag. After finding a satchel with a long strap decorated in even more gems, I quickly change out of my sheer nightgown and into furs, mindful of the bandages wrapped around my middle. Then, I begin gathering clothes and stuffing them into the small space. When I find herbs they'd been using on my wounds, I snatch those up, too. I also steal the golden cups with red gems dotting the outside.

As I pack, I try to keep my mind blank. It's more challenging than I thought, so I try to mislead the king's prying magic with memories. When I get to Zlosa, I will go to the common hall, a place Mikal used to drink with the other slaves in the lumber yard. I remember my times scavenging, needing to be careful to avoid the watchers.

My thoughts are carefully guarded as I open the door and run into the under mountain.

CHAPTER 10
YELLOW SAPPHIRE
ESTELA

The air is strangely sweet, though heavy with the smell of burning wood and dust. My heart races as I walk, trying not to draw attention to myself.

My shoes smack against grey stone as I run down the endless stairs, past a garden of mushrooms, and to the bridge. The glowing temple in the middle of the under mountain pulses pleasantly while I cross.

There are voices filtering through the warm air, and I panic. I see a large group laughing in the distance and scan my surroundings for a new path to escape.

Once I see the strange, circular building that marks the cave's exit, I duck into a tunnel. One I hope will be a shortcut. I round the corner, I'm stopped in my tracks by a new group of Enduares.

Though they are still tall and imposing figures with skin like blue stone, they have shed their armor in favor of elaborate clothing, not unlike what Arlet had worn in my room. The crystal in my chest hums as my anxiety mounts, and I can feel its power coursing through my veins as if trying to relax me like a calming drought given to an animal soon slaughtered.

One of the Enduares steps forward, his eyes so blue that they almost seem to glow with an otherworldly light. His gaze pierces through me.

He looks concerned. "You are the king's human?" His common tongue is almost hard to understand. "Can we help you?"

The Butcher's whore, I translate as I shake my head, trying to back away. *I knew it.*

The Enduar steps toward me again. My heart is pounding in my chest, and sweat trickles down my back. I have to get out of here.

"They told me that I could leave if I wanted to," I bluff, sticking my chin out.

One of them shakes his head and murmurs something in the Enduar tongue. My eyes go wide, and I start to breathe faster and faster. The one approaching me nods. "You must speak with the king."

I hold my hands up, telling him to stop, and his nose wrinkles as he inhales my smell. There are so many of them, what if they hold me down too?

"No," I say firmly and dart around their group. I'm fully expecting to be snatched up and dragged, kicking and screaming to the man who made me watch while my brother was taken.

But to my surprise, they don't follow me. I sprint down the passageway, my heart pounding in my chest. As I retrace my steps to the exit of the cave, I pass several more of the monsters. None of them approach as I run under mushroom light and once again across the bridge, showcasing the temple with pulsing veins of lava.

While hurrying up the winding tunnel to the exit, a weight is lifted. They really will let me leave. My plan will work this time. I will—

"It is good to see you are feeling better."

I'm stopped dead in my tracks by a fully armored Enduar leaning against the grand golden doors. His arms are crossed, and he looks down at me, almost bored, as he takes in my filthy appearance, stolen clothes, and satchel. Mere flickers of anger shine through his expression, but I feel them potently. They are sharp bursts from the crystal in my chest.

"Ay, esto es el colmo,"[1] I breathe. That connection between us still isn't dead, and he doesn't seem to notice the state of my body. Power flows off him, but it doesn't compare with his cruel, chiseled perfection. Except his eyes. They are guarded.

He raises a silver eyebrow, and I'm just glad he isn't wearing those awful fangs on his teeth. "More human words? Something about height, I think. Do you enjoy my height?"

I narrow my eyes. I don't know how he knows so many words from the human dialect, but I am getting tired. "It's an expression, *capullo azul*[2]. It means that I'm done playing games. Now let me pass."

His lips quirk up into a smile, the first one I have ever seen. His full lips stretch over only slightly elongated canines, nothing like the steel teeth he wore yesterday. It unsettles me, especially as it is at odds by his battle armor. "Why would I do that, exactly?"

I take a deep breath, trying to calm my racing heart. This is the most he has ever spoken to me out loud. "I don't belong here. I need to find my brother."

"You keep saying that. Will you tell me why you think they'll kill him?" he says after a displeased pause. Still not moving from his spot.

More anger heats my insides. "No. My friend told me that you declared they were free to leave. I'm merely exercising a right you granted me to get the hell out of here."

Desperation leaks into my heart. He raises his hand, and flashbacks from my first escape overtake me. He'd used that same hand to tear my attacker in half as easily as if he were tearing through leaves.

It is impossible to handle the wave of anger and despair crashing over me as I look into his unyielding silver-blue gaze. Somehow, he invades my mind again, sending me an image of me on the ground, laying in a pool of my own blood. Dying, broken. My knees threaten to buckle, and my eyes well with tears at the horror.

"You are afraid of all the wrong things. It is safe here," he says. The sound of metal clinking was the only thing I could hear over my labored breaths.

He reaches out and touches me. A large, warm hand envelops my face, turning my face to gaze at him. He does not merely exist in this world, he does not submit; he *commands*.

"Have you thought about my offer?" I ask.

His eyes gleam. "I had assumed you offered yourself out of desperation. You are calmer now, and you still wish to give yourself to me?"

I blink, struggling to breathe with his hand on my face. "Let me go to save my brother. I will free him, and I will return."

His expression grows harder, more severe, as he watches me speak. "The answer is still no to letting you leave."

I take a step back, feeling the loss of his warmth and the crystal in my chest pulsing. "Send someone with me. I promise I will return. Is that not what you want—For me to stay and be your... concubine?"

More anger. "What I want, Estela," he all but purrs, "is for you to return to your room and heal."

The king leans forward, looming over me, so I must crane my neck as I look up at him. Clearly, he does not care about the state of my hair. The song my crystal sings is unbearable, drawing me in to touch him. To feel his skin on my own.

"Did you know that my cousins, the elves, used to find

spouses for the royal children by stealing commoners," he says, tracing the lines of my body with his eyes. His eyes are full of concern, not lust. "I always thought it was comical that it was safer for them to find a stranger with no money or land over a political union. They even went as far as to make their ceremonies include the husband throwing his wife over his shoulder and running out into the night."

I swallow hard, panicking as the Enduar king speaks. Was that not what he had done in the hallway in front of Keksej?

"Are you saying that we..."

He tilts his head to the side, looking at me with sad, guarded eyes. "We are not married. Enduares call our ceremony the *Grutaliah Bondyr*. It involves quite a bit more singing and blood than a simple kidnapping."

Blood? I think.

The king's gaze flickers over my face, and I can see the gears turning in his mind. My gem hums at his attention.

"I have finished considering your offer. You stay here, and I save your brother." He says the words in a matter-of-fact tone. Hope flutters in my chest. "However, I require one addendum: you will not just stay in this mountain where it is safe, you will also be my bride."

My mouth falls open, and the fluttering stops. "You've been planning this. You put me in the queen's suite."

He raises an eyebrow. "Do you accept?"

"Yes," I breathe almost instantly. My mind catches up soon after, furious. A marriage with the king is a thought as preposterous as a fish falling in love with a bird—a lion coddling a lamb—but it has already been clear that I cannot leave.

The king's eyebrows shoot up. "Are you really so eager to marry the troll king?"

Then, something impossibly soft and furry curls around my ankle. I gasp at the contact. More heat directed to my core pulses through me, and I look down to see an uncovered tail tightening around my leg. It's the first time I've fully witnessed the silver hair at the end or the soft, suede-like skin.

My chest tightens. "I thought you were called the Enduares now," I whisper, and my words vibrate with the foreign object in my chest.

The king's expression remains blank. "And what will you be called when you stand at my side, my queen?" he says, reaching up to touch me and falling short. "Will you count yourself with us monsters?"

I ball my fists. "Queen? A slug can call itself a caterpillar, but that doesn't mean it will turn into a butterfly."

He purses his lips. "Can a new name not encourage a new attitude?"

I shake my head. "I am the daughter of the king's whore. You are a king, and you want me, so I won't call myself a queen—I'll call myself my mother's daughter."

The heat of his anger leaches into my skin. "You, Estela, have agreed to be my wife, therefore a queen, not my whore."

I narrow my eyes. "Does a king not fuck his queen when he desires to produce heirs? How much choice does such a woman have?"

He sneers. "If you invite me into your bed, you will be soft and willing, or I won't have you."

His words inspire a mixture of fear, confusion, and anger in my head. I regret my deal already. I look behind him to the golden doors. I know where the handle is. It's my last chance to try for real freedom. I duck around him. He catches me and hoists me over his shoulder.

The crystal inside of me starts to hum, but I will not give in so easily. "What the hell are you doing?" I screech, pounding on the armor on his back. It makes clanging sounds that echo through the tunnels as he starts walking.

"I've decided the elves were wise to carry away their brides," he grunts. "Are all humans so quick to go back on their agreements? You'll hurt yourself if you keep flailing around, my star."

One more blow and the brittle skin along my knuckles breaks. I can't tell for sure, but I think his breath hitches as he walks faster. The tunnels blur together as we move, my head bouncing against the armor on his back. My blood is pumping through my veins like a wild animal. I try to twist and wriggle free, but his grip on my legs is ironclad.

"Let me go!" I yell again, my voice echoing off the walls.

He ignores me, his pace picking up until we're moving at a near run. Air rushes past my face as we hurtle through the tunnels, and then my head starts to pound from the blood. My midsection is also throbbing from his shoulder, jabbing right into my gut, much less gentle than the last time he carried me.

We only slow when we get back to the palace. I start crying when I see the door to my room. My future. The tears slide down my cheeks, leaving behind hot trails as he puts me down, takes my bag, and opens my door.

"Do you see that door?" He points to the wall at the end of my room. For the first time, I realize that there is a door in the stone. Discreet. "My room is through there. Knock if you need something. Now, go rest," he demands. Then adds a gentler, "Please."

I glare at him, tears still running down my cheeks. "Why would I ever come to you for anything?" I say.

He sighs. "You are free to go wherever you would like within Enduvida. But only after you are finished healing."

I stare at him, his face resolute. A profound sadness sweeps through me, and I try to push it away. I gave my life for Mikal's—it had even been my idea.

Instead of lamenting my choice, I should be rejoicing that Mikal would live and be happy. Love is selfless—that's what my mother had already said. She even proved it by dying to give birth to my brother.

Inside my room, I collapse onto my bed and lay there, staring up at the ceiling. The crystal in my chest continues to pulse and hum, reminding me of everything that's happened to me since I arrived in this ugly mountain.

Tears roll down my cheeks as I realize how alone I truly am. I lay there, grieving when the humming and pulsing of my crystal grows more potent, almost like it's trying to communicate with me. It's as insistent as an ocean current, rolling me forward toward open waters.

I close my eyes and focus on the sensation, trying to tune out everything else. And then, I see it. A vision of Mikal, trapped in some prison, surrounded by giant guards.

My heart lurches in my chest as I watch him sleep. He looks about the same as when I last saw him—not hurt aside from light bruising. Something inside of me relaxes, and the vision fades.

I breathe out and close my eyes. *Bargaining with the king was the right choice*, I tell myself.

As I sink into the soft bed, the grime on my skin becomes itchy. There's also a foreign moisture between my legs, one that makes my thighs slide together uncomfortably. I'm not escaping, so it's time to wash. For my own comfort.

I glance over at the steaming bath in the corner and take a deep breath. It looks warm. So very warm. I push myself off the bed, feeling the ache in my muscles as I stand up.

There are no solutions to be had today. So, I strip off my clothes and sink into the hot water, sighing in relief as the tension in my body starts to ease. The crystal on my chest dims.

I close my eyes and let the warmth of the water surround me, trying to focus on the crystal and the vision it showed me. However, the image is gone, and there is a harmony in this small space. The crystals embedded in the sides of the tub glow to life, singing themselves. Maybe it's just my imagination, but every second spent in this water eases my hurt.

There are bottles neatly lined up around the edge of the basin, next to a towel I hadn't noticed before. Reaching out to touch it, I feel the plush fibers cushion my fingers. It surprises me—I've never seen any fabric quite like it. Then, I start reaching for bottles. Opening each one to smell.

My brows furrow as I cannot identify a single scent. They are all sweet, floral even, but I don't know the flowers. I pour some of the shimmery slime into my palm and rub it in my hair. It lathers, and I start scrubbing until the grittiness on my scalp subsides.

After rinsing, I am spent. I don't know how I expected to run away this time because I am absolutely exhausted. The thought depresses me. Sinking further into the comfort, I fully submerge myself.

I hold myself under for a few seconds. And then a few more. Letting the pulsing rhythm of the water go deep into my soul.

Sometimes, I wish that love left a little bit more for me.

---

1. This is too much.
2. Blue asshole.

CHAPTER 11
SAPPHIRE
TEO

It is foolish to go to the window in the tunnel connecting our rooms, but she *agreed to be my wife*.

Yes, she had breathed.

Almost eager. It was all for her brother, I knew that. It was hard to remember with her in my arms. Right now, my intention is to make sure that she keeps her word and does not escape or injure herself.

How was I supposed to know that she would finally decide to bathe?

I want to look away, but cannot tear my eyes away from her small form. She is so bruised under those clothes. Liana had told me she was covered in injuries, but the wise woman had not prepared me for the purple, black, and yellow on her lower back, accompanied by fresh wounds.

They are just beginning to knit themselves together, but the old scars that had not healed properly are still on full display. Rage and sadness boil inside of me as I watch her slowly lower into the tub.

She is a wounded goddess. One starved and tormented by

mere mortals. I would be more than happy to be a terrible demonstration of divine power.

I lean in closer, trying to get a better look at her injuries. Her head tilts back, and for a moment, our eyes met. I freeze, expecting her to scream. Except, her gaze continues its path across the room undeterred.

Was she looking at the door connecting our rooms?

My heartbeat returns to normal as she starts to wash her body. There's a hot throb below my belt as she rakes her fingers through her hair, breasts barely peeking out of the water.

Her beautiful, curly, deep brown hair is covered in suds. It was unbound before, but seeing it shine in the faint light does something to me. One day... she'll let me braid it.

I turn away from the window, feeling guilty for catching her in such a vulnerable moment. I should never have watched her like that, no matter how concerned for her wellbeing. It's time to go back to my own room.

But despite how much I try to distract myself, her image remains etched in my mind. The bruises on her back, the way her hair lay soaked and heavy across her chest. Something inside of me stirs at the thought of it all.

Yearning.

I try to resist it, to push it down, to tell myself that it's wrong. But the memory of her body in the tub lingers, haunting me. And before I know it, I return to the window.

My heart stops beating. She's under the water. I can barely see her, save for the shadow in the crystal lights. A few seconds pass, and I expect her to come up for air.

A few more seconds pass, and there is no movement. The only thought in my mind is how long I spent, waiting for a mate, and she would rather die than be with me. An onset of temporary insanity has me rushing back through my tunnel, out of my room, and to her door. I grab the handle and push it open, finding myself in the dim, steamy room. Panic grips me; what if she's drowned? What if I'm too late?

But then, just as I'm about to reach into the water, she emerges from the depths of the basin. Water cascades down her body, her hair slicked back against her scalp, and I'm struck by the urge to touch her. To run my hands over her skin, to pull her into my arms, to claim her as mine.

I can finally breathe again.

She is terrified, clutching at the sides of the tub. Her arms and legs scrunch up to cover her body. Then she decides better and launches a shampoo bottle at my head, catching me straight in the eye.

I stagger back in surprise, holding my hand against the injury. I can't help but let out a frustrated growl. The truth is that I don't deserve much less. She doesn't know I was spying on her.

"I didn't call for you" she says, her voice low and strained.

"I just—"

"No. You told me I wouldn't be a comfort woman, so stop reaching for me at every chance you get."

"You are a danger to yourself. I came to ensure you didn't try to escape," I growl, still looking away. The lie is bitter, but sweeter than her anger. Vann hadn't been lying about her strength.

"We just made a deal," she says.

"Yes, and you immediately tried to run out the door."

"Noted. Well, I wasn't trying to escape," she hisses.

"Just bathe?" The words slip from my mouth before I can stop them, bright with accusation.

She looks back at me, defiant and unafraid. She's so much smaller than me. Little compared to the blood-sucking creature that nearly killed her, yet it does not seem to matter for her sense of self-preservation. She would kill me. I do not understand why the Fuegorra chose a mate with so much fire when all I long for is softness, but I am proud of this display.

Suddenly, her expression changes. The fierceness falls away in favor of embarrassment. "Are you asking me if I was trying to..."

I purse my lips. "You were under the water for a while."

"Why would I off myself when my brother's rescue is dependent on our union?"

I can hear the hurt in her voice. So full of surprises. My heart twists in my chest, guilt suffocating me. It's almost as if my question from before is being answered—relentless care for the people we are in charge of. She will be a good queen. When she is ready to rise to power.

"I will leave now," I murmur.

She sneers, disturbing the water around her, and says, "That would be wise."

I do not stay to look at the ripples caressing her brown skin, I leave the room once more. As soon as I am on the other side of the door, I realize that she was not as mad as she should have been. I wonder if someone has invaded her privacy before and think of the First Prince.

My thoughts swirl as I make my way back to my own room. Was I any better than the First Prince? Both of us had been guilty of taking advantage of her vulnerability, of trespassing on her solitude.

I sink onto my bed, still lost in thought. The image of her bruised back flashes before my eyes, and a spike of protectiveness sears my chest. I want to shield her from the world, from all harm, from anyone who might hurt her.

The best way to do that is to finish our marriage contract. Such a thought propels me out of my room and to the library. I reach for the cart full of fresh scrolls from the stone benders. I unroll one, pleased, and place it on my table before going to the royal section and withdrawing my parent's marriage contract.

I sit down, put on my crystal specs, and start to read. There's an uncomfortable stirring in my gut as I study the document. My father's people had been imperious toward my mother—demanding intercourse with the king at frequent intervals as well as dictating the colors she was able to wear. My mother had been an affluent teacher at one of our most respected universities. It hurts my heart to see how she was forced to give all of that up because of something she could not control.

It reminds me of what Estela said in the tunnel. I lean back in my chair, thinking about my mother. Was she just a glorified whore to the king? I had always assumed that my father truly loved his queen—when she died, all the goodness in him died, too.

But maybe that had merely been a romantic idea from a youngling. This contract tells a very cold, controlling story.

Does this human woman feel safe and loved, locked in the queen's suite?

Svanna's words hit me straight in the chest once more. I had broken my people's laws to steal her. We had made a deal to be wed. But would she ever love me? Or would she be obliged to pretend?

When my quill hits the page once more, the words that flow out are intended to include, not control. I make it clear that I will never touch her without her consent, that she will be encouraged to take on the tasks she desires, and be friends with those she likes.

When I'm done, I'm still uneasy. None of these words tell her what she is to me. She knows nothing of our matehood—and I am afraid she will run if I reveal it too soon. Some lies are necessary.

A knock on the door behind me has me hurrying to my feet. When Vann saunters in, he has a sour look on his face.

"What's wrong?" I demand. There are few things that could cause him to look so angry. "Have the giants returned?"

His frown deepens. "No. Mother Liana has sent me to tell you that one of the human men has recognized a mate. Neela."

My eyebrows raise. "Another matehood. What about Ulla?"

He purses his lips and shakes his head. "She hasn't said anything. It seems that the humans will be staying."

I shouldn't feel relief and joy at the revelation. It means a long, taxing future between our people and the giants for their slaves. But...

"Was I so foolish to hope, my friend?" I ask, grinning.

Suddenly, Vann's expression falls. I see the guarded walls he puts up crumble and fall as he lets out a long breath. He blinks his eyes and they look glassy in the spell light.

I cross to him. "What is it?"

He blinks, eyes now red. "Adra and I weren't mated."

My eyebrows furrow. "I don't understand." His betrothed had been a singer, and they had known each other since they were young. They had wanted to be married despite knowing they could never have children.

He looks right at me, his face ravaged with brutal pain. "If you keep bringing humans, then there might be a mate for me. Adra would—I can't—" The tears beading along his waterline drop.

I cross to him and clasp my arms around his back. He remains stiff. "Adra would want you to be happy, Vann."

He returns the hug for a mere moment before pushing away. He looks down at the scroll on the table beside us. The pain in his expression fades as he reads the words. "What is this?"

I swallow. "Estela told me she would marry me if I saved her brother."

"Godsdamn it, Teo. More promises?" he looks irate.

I stand tall. "You have such little faith in my ability to save both her and our people. It's starting to insult me."

He throws his hands in the air. "What the hell do I know?" He opens his mouth to say something else, but instead chooses to wipe his mouth and leave the room.

I'm left alone with the ghosts of hundreds of thousands of words.

CHAPTER 12
CITRINE
ESTELA

"Will I have to say something?" I ask Liana. Today, at the midday feast, we will announce my betrothal to the Enduar King. Six days have passed since the giants brought me to the Enduar Mountains, and my body is fully healed.

She shakes her head. "No. You'll just have to stand there. Of course, we will need to practice your wedding ceremony, but we can do that some other day." She grabs something in the chest she had two Enduares carry in. "This should be your size."

She's holding out a golden dress with bark-colored gems dotting the bodice. There is a silky brocade across the low-dipping neckline. Two lacy sleeves have been sewn to slide off my shoulders, and the skirt will drag across the ground.

"What the hell is that made from?" I ask, holding the thin blanket over my naked body. Giant ladies wore dresses under their gowns, but I was given some sort of undergarment that resembled extremely short pants. The dresses here were far more revealing, not requiring corsets, but leaving little of my chest to be imagined.

Arlet touches the fabric. For some reason, she is desperate to be like them. She wears her hair like the Enduar women, opts for the most elaborately stitched furs available to her, and even makes some earrings to hang off of her lobes. I am doing this out of obligation to save my brother, she seems genuinely content.

"Stone silk," she says. "It's a similar process to how they make paper, but this is mixed with metals that are soaked in something special to create something soft enough to be a fabric. You are going to look stunning. I can't believe how lucky you are."

I roll my eyes.

Liana runs her spindly fingers over my cheeks, forcing me to look at her. "You look so healthy. You know what would make you look even better?"

I draw my eyebrows together. Liana is a strange woman, but it's hard not to feel comfortable around her. "What?"

"A few piercings." She taps my lip and nose. "Here and here. It'll drive the king mad with lust."

I push her away, catching her smile as she returns to the dress. "Right, because that's what I want."

Liana reaches over to pull out a pair of golden slippers. She lays them on the ground before my feet. "Try these."

I step into them, and they slide onto my feet easily. As if they were made for me. I look at myself in the mirror. My hair is shiny, and my cheeks are red.

I look different.

Arlet frowns. "How do you want your hair?"

I glance at her in the mirror. "As it is? I think it looks fine."

Liana raises an eyebrow. "You don't want a bun?"

I furrow my eyebrows. "Should I want one?"

She shrugs. "Human customs are far different to ours. Unmated women wear their hair in buns. For a long time, the man would braid his woman's hair after the mating ceremony, but that changed several hundred years ago when we realized that some preferred their own gender. Our small court holds onto the custom mostly out of nostalgia, adapting it to fit couples like Iryth and Svanna or Morht and Verl."

"I don't know who they are," I say softly as a shiver starts at the base of my spine while thinking of the Enduar King's long fingers sliding across my skin. When he walked into my room yesterday, his eyes had been haunted. Feral for me. I can't stop thinking about it. It's been so long since he's touched me.

I shake my head. *That's a good thing.* "So I should wear my hair in a braid?"

My heart starts to pound at the thought of the king coming to see me again. The last time he visited was to bring me a contract to sign.

The whole affair had been laughable. I've never needed to know how to write my name, so I drew a rude gesture, and he counted it as binding.

He had left with a promise to protect my people. He takes his deals and contracts very seriously, but I have a harder time believing him. There had been slaves, many slaves, who had been stolen. I couldn't forget the slaves who had lived to tell tales of watching their companions gutted while still alive. Sergi's blood stain still accompanied my lonely thoughts, and I couldn't rule out the gem in my chest making me long to see him.

"Estela?" Liana said again.

I blink and look back at her. "Sorry."

She smirks. "Why don't you wear your hair however you'd like? We can make new customs."

I press my lips together and nod. "That sounds good to me."

The old Enduar gestures me forward, and takes the towel I've kept wrapped around myself while Arlet slides the stone silk across my skin. When she steps back, she looks at me and smiles so wide it hurts my chest.

"You are so beautiful," she says, pressing her hands to her mouth as Liana holds up a few jewelry pieces. She wraps gold chains around my unpierced ears, and clasps cuffs on my wrists. She has a ring for each finger, and some of them make strange sounds as they come in contact with my skin. I hold up my hand, inspecting one of the purple stones.

Liana raises an eyebrow. "Do you like it?"

I blink. "Yes. It just feels... strange."

She smiles. "The Fuegorra in your chest is giving you a sensitivity to the stones. It's a good thing."

I don't respond, still flicking my fingers together at the odd, tingly sensation. When both of the women step away from me, I look in the mirror once more.

The person staring back at me is a stranger.

"Are you ready to go?" Arlet asks.

My heart starts to gallop in my chest, and I take a deep breath to steady it. "Yes."

"You skipped going yesterday, so you both need to visit the Ardorflame temple before the feast," Liana says. "You'll feel better after, Estela," she urges.

I groan. "It was a mistake to let you help," I mutter.

Liana smiles as she opens the door. "I will see you soon."

Arlet leads me down the endless steps and past the mushroom garden. We don't speak much. In fact, she is busy smiling at every Enduar we come across, much to my horror. I shrink back, staring at the hammers and knives hanging from their decoratively bejeweled belts. None of them are quite as friendly as she is, but they all seem pleased to see us.

Liana is one thing, but these Enduares are too big, too sharp around the edges to be comfortable.

The palace walls fade away as Arlet and I move to the center section of the under mountain. Pulsing red veins glow across the temple, highlighted by the large blue crystal secured by ropes to the pillars outside the palace gate. Red, orange, and blue crystals of all kinds illuminate the impossibly high ceiling, and small orbs, ranging from the size of melons to flecks of dust, float in the air around me, combining with the gigantic mushrooms with glowing caps to provide soft light.

People are everywhere, carrying dishes and blankets to the same place we are headed. There is one Enduar with a few missing fingers and stern face—the one who had hung onto the king's hip during the viewing—who looks at Arlet and scowls. She doesn't try to say hello either, and I regard him with suspicion. She had mentioned that not everyone was friendly.

He's gone quickly, and all the other passing Enduares smile at my friend. Then, they peer at me with guardedly curious expressions. It's as if they know that I am the only one not allowed to leave. I suppose that in a court as small as theirs, it would be a great source of gossip. The woman separated from her family, forced to stay behind. The one almost killed. The Butcher's whore. The one who ran away.

I think of my vision of Mikal and push away all other thoughts. That is until we reach one of the large bridges crossing over one of the three crevasses separating the different sections of the city.

I peer over the side and see some traces of glowing rock far below, and my fear of heights takes full effect. All air is sucked from my lungs while I freeze. My breaths rush in and out of my body faster than ever, and it burns a familiar path down my esophagus.

"Sorry," I mumble. "It's this damn dress."

Arlet is nothing but understanding as we move.

Was that the lava they used to kill thousands? *Oh gods, what have I agreed to?*

Arlet pats my hand and pulls me along. From the first step on the gilded stone, my heart is in my throat. One slow step at a time, we make it across.

I am presented with dozens of circular homes, all clustered together in a randomized matter. I blink as I look at the gears. Small machines move around each house, doing god knows what, and hammers or weapons are lined up outside, hanging from the walls—no doubt ready to be used for work the following day. There is a quotidian beauty in the architecture, and everything is advanced. Functional. It's both elevated and comfortable.

My hands and feet are still numb, and there's a zinging sensation in my teeth. In no time, we are walking into a large pavilion with a proper feast lining all of the sides. My senses are assaulted by the loud, joyful atmosphere. Children are running around, men and women cooking and sharing meat, others sitting, some holding hands, and others...

Por los dioses.[1]

I look away quickly after spotting the couple kissing in the open. The Enduar has his hand up the Enduar woman's shirt, clearly palming her breast while they tease each other lips.

I make a disgusted sound. Arlet chuckles beside me, clearly amused by my reaction. I shoot her a dirty look, but she smirks and drags me towards a group of women who are laughing and chatting. "Peace, my friend. It's not as if they would make love in front of the fire. Their affections are more... free."

For some reason, that makes my chest hurt. I'm still watching when the couple comes up for air because it forces me to think of the slaves and my contract with the king. The romanticism of whatever that couple feels was once as foreign and inconceivable to me as a body without scars. But there's a magnetism to the king I've agreed to marry. For the first time... I'm starting to wonder about the molten liquid in my lower belly when he is near.

"Ready to keep going?" Arlet asks. "We need to go to the front of the pavilion to wait for the king.

I hum my response. Arlet smiles brightly, and I wonder what goes through her head while watching that. She comes from a relationship where her partner utterly rejected her.

Back in the Zlosa, most women were sent to the breeding pens at the age of twenty. The princes made sure I never went, but Arlet was assigned four times. The last time, they assumed she was pregnant she came back—with Daniel. Families were given their own dens for a period of time, and our whole little quarter celebrated the slave marriage ceremony. Jumping over a broom. After a few months, when it became clear there had never been a child, he cast her out. She begged him to take her back, pleaded. I dragged her to live with us.

I used to think she was sensitive. Soft. Now, I see that she is more resilient than I could ever be. I question if the deep-rooted suspicion I cling to is really so good.

My thoughts stray back to the king. The man who invades my personal space, walks in on me naked, and kills those who threaten me. He inhabits my dreams and waking thoughts alike, despite how furiously I try to shove him to the corners of my conscience.

"Neela! Hello!" Arlet calls to one of the Enduar women engrossed in conversation with two women holding hands. I notice the way one of their hands is obscured, and I wonder if she clutches a hammer like the rest of them.

The woman Arlet knows, Neela, is a stunning creature with deep iron-colored hair and piercing blue eyes. She gives us a kind smile before breaking off from her conversation and coming to say hello. I stand beside Arlet, prepared to attack at any moment.

"Arlet," she attempts, stumbling over all the consonants. "It is good to see you again. This is the other woman? King Teo's human?"

His human? I practically snap my jaws at her—except she's right. The two women holding hands turn to look at me, and I don't miss the strange looks they cast at my hair.

Then I notice the small bundle nestled against one of the women's breasts, and guilt floods through me. She's not holding a weapon. She's a mother.

Neela bares her unarmored teeth. "Control yourself. You are no longer in Zlosa," she warns before leaving.

Arlet yanks me around to face her. "What the hell was that? They were being kind," she says angrily.

I narrow my eyes at my friend. "Leave me be. I didn't know there was a baby right there." I like children, it would never be my intention to hurt one.

My red-headed friend shakes her head. "Neela is nothing but kind, and she's not the exception. They are strange. Tall, gruff, and the tails are unnerving, but they have done nothing to you. It's as clear as day that what you were told is a lie—isn't that why you agreed to marry the king? I know you are upset about Mikal, but the giants did that, not them. He is gone. You've proven that going after him is pointless. You know better than anyone—sometimes it is necessary to cut your losses."

I grit my teeth, anger still simmering beneath my skin. I want to spit on her, remind her that she let him go. Arlet has always been too trusting, too forgiving, and it grates on my nerves. She thinks my betrothal is a change of heart.

"You think too highly of them. I agreed to marry the king *because of Mikal*. Gods, Arlet. I used to spend time wondering how you ever got into that relationship with Daniel, but the way you run into the arms of the predators, I am slowly realizing that you aren't naive. You are simply stupid."

Arlet's eyes widen at my words before tears glisten in her eyes, and part of me wants to take it all back. But the other part, which has been hurt for too long, doesn't want to give in. In the end, I choose repentance. "Arlet, I'm so sorry."

I reach for her, but she pulls away.

"You... don't know anything," she says quietly, her voice shaking. "I'm not stupid. And neither are they. I feel sorry for you and King Teo—being wrapped up in your hatred will make your already miserable life that much sadder."

I open my mouth to respond, but before I can say anything, a loud commotion arises from the other side of the pavilion. I startle and slink back closer to my friend.

She doesn't want me near her. After casting me a disgusted look, Arlet moves away from me, and I am left alone in a sea of Enduares. I slowly turn, shaking to see the Enduar King in all of his cold, blue beauty.

---

1. By the gods.

CHAPTER 13
OPAL
ESTELA

King Teo wears a black tunic studded with silver metal, and a deep vee that exposes the Fuegorra gem on his chest. He wears rings on his fingers, and earrings dangle from his ears. He's beautiful, like a starlit night sky. He's taller than any human man I've ever met, and his body is lean and muscular. His long, silver hair is arranged in a thick braid that falls over his shoulder. While I stare at him, it reminds me how small I am and encourages me to be bigger. Fearless.

His eyes lock onto mine, and a shivers run down my spine. Even from here, I see his nostrils flare, and his eyes grow black. The song in my stone is glad, desperate. My heart races as I try to back away, but he moves toward me, his movements fluid and powerful, before taking my hand and pulling me to the front of the party.

I hurry behind him, enveloped in his warm, clean scent.

"Good evening," he calls to the crowd, and everyone turns their attention to us. He regards the crowds. "It seems that someone has let my secret slip."

Laughter ripples from the Enduares, and several hurry to the large barrels of mead. They raise their glasses to us, but I am frozen. Motionless.

"I am pleased to announce my marriage to Estela, one of the humans who has come to live in our mountain." His large, warm hand presses on the middle of my back, pushing me forward. With all of their attention on me, I struggle to breathe. "I present this gift as a token of our promise to marry on the Festival of Endu. I hope you will all join us."

A gift? Liana didn't say anything about that. The crowd is jovial, but I freeze when his fingers brush my hair to the side. The crystal on my chest starts to glow and everyone is captivated while he places a necklace on my throat. The chain is too short for me to look at the design, but I can tell it is dainty.

He returns to my side and takes in my face and neck. "Behold your future queen," he says. Reverent.

I turn back to the crowd and nod my head to them, but all I can think about is the stories of massacres. I've seen how dangerous they can be, and right now, I feel it.

The joy in the crowd starts to fade the more time that I stand there, unspeaking, so the king steps forward. He smiles at his people, and the world is lit up with white-hot flames.

"To the humans!" he says, raising his hand in the air.

The court raises their glasses in tandem, wishing us well, while his displeasure radiates off him in waves. As soon as they finish drinking, several people flock to him, some holding onto his forearm as they tell him gods know what. They offer him warm, broad smiles, and he addresses them by name. Each person. He knows them all.

It's unheard of to see such familiarity between subjects and their ruler. My back is now fully pressed to a pillar as I watch him smile and *hug* others. He nods at their words, laughs at their jokes.

When they turn to me, they frown and walk away. One

woman wished me a healthy baby, and left. It had me shaken, even though I knew that the king wasn't forcing me to have children. Not that I didn't want them—there was a time when I would have preferred the breeding pens to the giants.

I glance around, looking for Arlet, and see her with some of the other humans. I hadn't seen them come in, but they are already eating and drinking. They, too, are traitors.

I try to keep my breathing steady, but my heart is pounding hard enough to feel in my throat. The moment that the king sets his sights back on me, a prickly sensation sweeps across my skin, and the song grows louder.

With great difficulty, I draw my eyes up to look back at him. His smile is gone, and he walks toward my hiding place.

I want to flee, but my legs refuse to move. He stops a few paces away, his tall frame towering over me, and I have to crane my neck to look up at him. It's a mistake because of the heat that comes from his eyes piercing into mine.

"Well. It is done," he breathes. "Are you well?"

"Your people hate me," I say.

His hand comes up to caress my cheek with a surprisingly gentle touch. "I told you that you should start working with them when you are ready. When they get to know you, I am sure they will soften."

I want to pull away, to resist him, but the song has me paralyzed. "You don't even know me," I retort.

"You are right. But there are some things, deeper things, that I just know." He smiles sadly. "Your color has greatly improved."

His hand is warm against my clammy skin, and my eyes flutter closed. Weak. That's what I am. I'm fighting a losing battle against him, and it's either give in to some of his touches or make eye contact and feel like I'm being burned alive on the spot.

"But your hair..."

His hand slides away from my skin. My traitorous body mourns its loss.

"What do you mean?" I demand, furious again.

He raises an eyebrow. "Loose hair is only to be seen by lovers."

My mouth opens and closes, and my skin heats from embarrassment. I grab my hair and start braiding it at the side of my neck. *Uno, dos, tres, cuatro...*

The numbers don't help. *Just stop looking at him.*

Why? his voice returns almost immediately.

It had been so long since he'd spoken to me in my mind I was beginning to believe that it had been some sort of trick.

He's watching me with a faintly amused expression. It makes me angry. He has all the advantages in this situation because he can think without someone eavesdropping into his thoughts.

I think of the most vulgar expression I could use against someone like him. Something much harsher than *cave rat*.

His eyes narrow.

I smile, pleased with the small victory.

Because, if I keep looking into your eyes, you'll entrance me like you have all the others.

His expression falls open completely. "You think that we have bewitched the others?" he says aloud.

I can't help but smirk. "Well, what else can explain their calm?" I say, my voice dripping with contempt. "I have a lifetime of stories about what you are capable of. Hell, half the continent is gone because of *your kind.*"

The king's eyes flash angrily, and I almost regret my words. Almost. But then again, I'm not one to back down from a fight, even if it means putting myself in danger.

"You speak out of ignorance," he says, his voice low and dangerous. "Your people are now our people. We treat them with respect and honor, and they in turn do the same for us. Do you believe the rumors that we eat humans?

I scoff. "Perhaps not, but you had to steal me to make me your bride. Where did your reputation come from in the first place, *Butcher*?" My cheeks are hot. Every time I'd gotten mad at him before, a softening came shortly after. Something that made him question whether or not it was right to be so harsh with me.

Right now, he doesn't back down. "People and civilizations can change. Look behind you," he demands, holding his arm out toward the party happening around us.

I look behind me, taking in the celebratory atmosphere of the gathered people. They laugh, drink, eat, and everything is light. Then, my eyes follow his arm to look at the children dancing around the fire.

"Our young are the most valuable part of our community. Our future. Do you see many?"

I count less than twenty, but he doesn't wait for me to answer.

"I have helped many humans, and I've never seen any with as many scars as you. It... pains me to think about what you have endured at the hands of the giants. More than you will ever know. But," he speaks passionately, "we are showing you that we trust you because we understand loyalty is earned, not demanded. Why won't you extend us the same courtesy as our future queen?"

"Right, because having the power to crush them like insects has nothing to do with it."

He steps closer into the shadows with me, his breath hot against my cheek. He is everywhere, too close and not close enough. "You think that we use our songs to trick and control you? Would you like to see our power, Estela?" he murmurs, his lips only inches away from mine. "Would you like to feel it?"

I shudder, both in fear and anticipation. It would be insanity to accept. But... the coiling in my stomach and the humming in my chest says yes. Demands it. So I nod, knowing that I'm making a mistake in allowing myself to get so close to him.

He smiles and takes my hand, pulling me from the shadows and into the light of the fire. The flames dance around us, filling the air with warmth and song that chase away my doubts and fears. I feel like I am soaring, free, and unburdened by the world.

"Velen! A new song. One for me to dance to with my bride," the king calls. Then he says something in his language.

A man with a solemn, tight face nods and steps between two of the enormous crystals all around the room. The features of this Enduar are striking, not unlike the way the king's chiseled beauty is remarkable. These men are all sharp, masculine angles and strong jaws. His beauty has me glancing up at the man escorting me by the arm just before I realize that this is exactly what kind of crystal siren could lure me to my death.

When Velen starts his song, everyone goes quiet. His notes reach up and down and outside of the boundaries of what I've known sound to be. It sings of a power greater than we can comprehend, of a longing that cannot be filled.

"You see?" the king murmurs as he pulls me close. He situates my hand on his large bicep and takes my other one with his hand. Then he pulls me close. My breasts brush the space below his chest, but I don't care. Something inside of me urges me closer. "The song comes from the cavern, from the rocks and minerals that make up our world. We simply use it to enhance the feelings of a room, not create them."

Hostia[1]. I suck in a breath. That would mean that my attraction to him is genuine. My eyes are drawn to Teo's face, and there's unbridled marvel in my mind as I allow myself to memorize his blue skin. His eyes pull down at the corners, contributing to the stern expression he seems to wear often, but I can just begin to see kind lines around his mouth—and it intrigues me to see such a blatant example of how his smile never quite reaches his eyes.

Sadness lingers in him. Regret. Torment. It's a mirror into my own soul.

The entire cavern echoes the rhythm and melody back, submerging us all in a sound unlike anything I would ever be able to compare in my lifetime. Pure beauty and vibration while I twirl, helpless in his arms.

My heart breaks with the movements of his mouth. And then, another song joins the singer's melody, and the crystals resonate with the harmonies. My emotions weave through me like threads in a tapestry—there is one who longs for something with a ferocity that refuses to be reciprocated.

To be honest, I have never experienced an emotion so potent. The only love I'd ever felt was toward Mikal. It was the type of enduring love borne out of labor and worry. He is my only family.

This is different. Butterflies come to life in my stomach while I watch Teo, and I long to touch his face to see if this is another dream. The truth is, despite the images of ecstasy invading my thoughts, I didn't know anything about sex past breeding. I'd heard that it could be a good distraction, and some men even made it pleasurable for the women.

If anyone were to touch me, to make love to me—giant prince or otherwise— my value would have been shattered like a glass phial on the rocks. What good is a toy that has already been broken?

But right now, the king doesn't look at me like he'd hurt me. My pulse is almost painful between my legs. I can see giving into the demands between us and kissing him. I'm practically consumed by imagining what his lips would feel like on my throat. If those pointed teeth were as sharp as they looked.

I gasp when the crystal in my chest starts to resonate with

the glorious sound. It's stoking this fire within me. For the first time, I remember to be embarrassed.

Relief comes quickly when I look around and see everyone closing their eyes. Their gems glow brightly to the power of the man's voice. Even Arlet, who lets the tears stream down her face without restriction.

Then, the king lifts my chin, and I glimpse the glowing, otherworldly red and orange of the gem's color embedded in his chest seconds before I look into his silver-blue eyes. I can feel his power pulsating beneath his skin. It is like a current drawing me in on gentle waves.

"Your thoughts are loud."

My cheeks flush, but not from shame. I want to resist, to escape from him, but I can't. I am both captivated and scared of what will happen when I let go and succumb to pure sound. It's like I'm in a dream.

No one is watching us anymore, and he looks at me through half-moon eyes before ducking and drawing my mouth toward his. The whisper of breath on my lips seconds before our mouths meet is intense.

"Still think I am beguiling you?" he whispers and pulls away.

I am left wanting for my first kiss. For some reason, that hurts. My life before feels small outside of caring for Mikal, like I was defined by fear instead of what I could enjoy. It was wrong, and now I am not resisting. I only want.

Want him. His touch.

The crystal in my chest hums so furiously that I jerk back, elbowing him in the arm. He straightens up, blinking rapidly.

The trance is fully broken, and I look at him with enough indignation to melt his circlet right off his forehead. More games.

"What was that supposed to prove? That your songs don't control me?" I spit on him, wiping my mouth. "You are making me want you!" The words are lies, and heat creeps up my neck.

The song stops, and the cavern remains quiet. Watching us all with wary gazes as the king's eyes narrow to slits. One of his warriors steps forward, his hand on his hammer. A zing of fear shoots through me, but I stand my ground.

The king holds out his hand, holding back the warrior. "That is enough," the king grunts, his gaze never leaving mine. For a second, I glimpse that disgust that I saw so frequently in front of my masters.

Does he hate me now? Good. Much better to be hated than to taste his breath on my tongue. If I make him angry enough, surely he'll cast me out. I will be free of giant and Enduar alike.

He grabs my hand, pulling me away from the prying eyes all around the pavilion. Dread drops low in my stomach. This is the moment I've been waiting for. The moment when he becomes frustrated enough with me that he will take his time and have his way. The moment he'll take what others spent my whole life fighting for.

I'm shaking and sweating by the time shadows surround us. He turns to me. I yank my hand away and ball my fists as tight as they will go. His expression is surprisingly gentle despite his obvious frustration.

He's a liar.

"I do not know why you resist so ardently. You must..."

The second he nears me and touches my back, alarm bells are ringing in my ears. Instinct reminds me of the way that Keksej had held me close. I let my right arm fly, hitting him squarely in the jaw.

Pain explodes over my knuckles, and I double over to cradle the injured limb against my chest. The pain is familiar. I remember trying to kick him in the crotch and breaking my foot. My breath starts getting faster and faster.

Malditos Enduares.[2]

The king spits on the ground beside him and steps back, rubbing his jaw. "You hit like a warrior."

Tears are falling down my cheeks as I continue to cradle my arm. "Not well enough to keep you away from me," I say through my hyperventilating. He watches me. What a pitiful creature I must appear to be.

Then he lets out an exasperated sigh and reaches for my hand. I yank it away and wince.

"Stop touching me!" I yell. Grateful, so grateful we are away from everyone else.

The king growls, *actually growls*, and grabs me. After one futile attempt to wiggle away, I release myself to his grasp. He's warm and solid.

"Stubborn human. Why must you make everything so challenging? We treat your people well. Save you, feed you, clothe you. We do not have to be enemies," he rants, his voice thick with emotions I don't understand, while he slips off one of my rings and holds it to my aching knuckles. "We stole the other humans from your masters to free them, not eat them."

I narrow my eyes and look up to study his face. "Then where are they?"

He raises an eyebrow. "We gave them supplies and let them leave. We did not yet have Arlet to tell us the Ardorflame is a good substitute for sunlight."

His words ring true—they are too similar to what Arlet said, but I'm not ready to trust. "Freedom was a dream whispered in the forests. I used to think I would know how to act if I were freed from obligation and assault, but I had no idea until I was left behind in this mountain after bleeding on a trail for four days. Until I was separated from Mikal. When I had a choice, I chose him. The rest of this is a means to the end."

"I have offered to help you with your brother—" the king starts.

"Yes, yes. The contract is signed. From what included in our deal, it never required me to like you."

"Hold still," he murmurs. His mouth is dangerously close to my ear. It would be so easy for him to bite me. My nipples harden under my dress. Being surrounded by him is intoxicating.

The gems on both of our chests start to glow as he whispers a few words that could pass for some sort of song. My Fuegorra grows brighter, and the pain subsides. Without thinking, I lean into him. He stiffens as a deep rumble comes from somewhere near his heart.

I bolt forward and whip around. "Are you purring?"

He narrows his eyes, and his tail flicks out behind him. "Does it matter?"

My mouth opens. "I—"

He steps toward me. "I'll say it again: I am not your enemy."

It's unclear what he wishes to accomplish with this conversation, but I can't let whatever just occurred happen again. "Enemies, maybe not, but I will never be your docile wife. You stole me, you hoped for me to be grateful, and I am not. The lessons learned away from the giants cannot be unlearned by pretty songs and a beautiful view." I shoot another glare at him and smooth the skirt of my dress.

His gaze softens, and he slowly steps away. My body relaxes as he does.

"Our deal didn't require you to enjoy my presence. But it did require you to learn how to lead these people. You seem to be healed. It's time to start acting like a queen," he says quietly before turning away. "You need to be careful."

Then, someone emerges from the shadows. One of the king's advisors. The one who doesn't like Arlet.

He whispers something into the king's ear, and the king nods before turning his gaze back to me.

"I have matters I must attend to," he explains, his tone short and curt. "I meant what I said. Stay out of trouble."

With that, he strides away, disappearing into the darkness. I watch him go.

The throb in my hand is nearly gone, but my throat is raw, and my blood is still rushing through my veins. I am unsure what to do now. I could go back to my room. *Or...* I look back to the pavilion and see the party resumed. My chest aches with how I treated Arlet, I said things out of anger that should have never been spoken. I don't belong there.

I look back at the direction the king went, and a new option flares to life. A queen should also be invited to important meetings, right? He seems so good at finding out my thoughts and secrets. It's time to learn some of his.

---

1. Shit.
2. Damned Enduares.

CHAPTER 14
MORGANITE
TEO

Vann pulls away, and anger is twisting in my gut. *They are here.* The giants have returned with an answer. My tail flicks to the side while I say goodbye to Estela, and leave behind the burning embers of tension between us.

By the time we reach the bridge, Faol appears, carrying my armor. I put it on quickly, using my tail to assist with the straps and ties. When I am finished, I turn to Vann.

"Go for a group of hunters," I tell him. "Make sure that Lothar comes too." He nods and heads down a different tunnel.

In the light of the Ardorflame, I walk alongside Faol through the cavern to the passage leading out of Enduvida. Memories from the year I spent in the Giant Court negotiating a peace treaty swirl before me. Then I think of the First Prince looking upon my mate, whipping her, desiring her.

Weak, my father's voice whispers. I ignore it.

Fate has been cruel to all of us. I have to believe I am strong enough to keep my mate and save my people.

Lothar, Vann, and the other hunters join me at the exit. As we cross into the snowy over world, we are greeted by a tall, brown tent.

The leathered flaps are new, still in pristine shape, and inside there is an oblong wooden table. The skins of the tent smell like humid forest air and expensive oils, the signature scent of Zlosian royalty.

The giants are taking no chances this time. Twelve warriors flank a seated figure. My eyes narrow on the enormous chair, made from a carved tree stump. Intricate flowers and leaves run up and down its sides with gems accenting the handiwork. Those are our gems.

This sweaty mammoth commanded slaves to carry the monstrosity from Zlosa to my mountain so that he could sit and look me in the eye. Though, there are no slaves in this room. I wonder where they've hidden them.

To my surprise, it is not the First Prince seated behind the table. Though we have never met, I believe I am staring at the Second Prince. I think bitterly how the queen called him her favored son. He is smaller than his brother and less scarred—hopefully he will also be easier to manage.

"Giant," I say coolly, not deigning to nod my head. "I do not know you."

His hair, also wiry and red like his brother's, sticks out around his head as he nods, not standing. "Enduar. My name is Prince Rholker, Second Prince to King Erdaraj."

My fists curl. "I have brought Lords Vann and Lothar to discuss your decision." I gesture to the spots on either side of me while they sit. Four more hunters and two stone benders are piling in behind me, clad in armor as well. The space is too full. Sweat trickles down my back under my armor.

The prince leans into his seat. "Even though we anticipated this, I must admit—I'm a little disappointed I can't see Enduvida with my own eyes," he says lazily.

I also lean back into my seat while Lothar laces his fingers together on the table.

"Why have you come to our home?" Lothar asks.

The Second Prince takes a deep breath. "We have come to discuss a truce."

Warning bells go off in my mind. "A truce?" I repeat suspiciously. My hunters shift uneasily behind me.

"Yes." The giant gestures for one of his warriors. "After many meetings with my father, King Erdaraj," the Prince says smoothly, emphasizing his father's name again while clasping his fingers, "he has decided that he's not interested in a genocide of your people. I don't know how many of you rats are crammed in that mountain, but it can't be enough to fight off the entirety of our armies."

Insult after insult. "You assume many things," I say, sitting across from him at the table.

He shrugs. "It is in our best interests."

I look him in the eye and think, *What about peace is good for your interests?* Deciding my words are too bold, I take a deep breath through my nose and say, "Forgive me for not understanding why you would cast off my offense."

The warrior hands the Second Prince a note. Rholker glances over it, and my fingers twitch.

"As I've already said, my father believes in peace between our two peoples, particularly so that we can conserve our trading route. However, we will require a time of penalty as retribution for the two giant citizens that you disposed of during their last visit."

I grit my teeth. My suspicions about the wealth of their kingdom depending on our trades are all but confirmed. It always comes back to diamonds. "Interesting words. Does your father realize that they were the ones to cause the altercation in the first place after I had rightfully won a bet? It was only self-defense on our part."

He sneers. "That is not what the First Prince says... But, my father agrees with you."

"I see," I say, trying to keep my voice level. "What penalty are you proposing?"

"My father has waxed poetic about your people. His terms come in twos. Two diamonds, and," he pauses, placing the note on the table, "the death of two of your own. If you agree, we can negotiate a peace treaty that will go into effect between our peoples for the next five years," Rholker says, his tone bored.

He's not half as idiotic as he looks, but he can't hide the flickers of anger peeking back at me.

I lean forward, the weight of responsibility heavy on my shoulders. It is an impossible position to weigh the lives of two of my people against the future of my people.

"I would like to see the letter you carry," I say.

Prince Rholker scoffs and then pushes the paper lazily across the table. One of my hunters retrieves it and hands it to me.

My eyes scan the words, angry. Hoping for a loophole where there is none. The language is crass, but it confirms what the Second Prince says.

"And if we refuse?" I ask, my voice low.

Rholker's eyes dip to the table. "We hope that won't happen."

"But if it does," I repeat.

"Then war will be declared. And this time, we will make sure you don't have a chance to blow us up first."

I wonder if he knows how far my father was willing to go if his volcano had not worked. One of my hunters shifts behind me, and I take a sharp breath. "I will give you four diamonds, but no deaths."

He raises an eyebrow, clearly interested. However, he still says, "Two diamonds, two deaths."

"Second Prince, you can't be serious," Lothar says.

I grit my teeth. "Two diamonds for the king, one death, and an extra diamond for you."

The Prince leans back in his chair, a sly smile curling at the corner of his lips. "Make it two diamonds for me, and it's a deal. Oh, and I will require the head of the dead cave rat. I'd like it stuffed. It will make a nice gift for my father's wall."

My stomach drops. I take a deep breath. I force myself to think of the faces of all of my people. One of them will die. But not by the giant's hand. There is only one way to preserve the honor of my people, and it is to give them the death they deserve.

I swallow, opening my eyes and fixing them on the Prince's face. "I will agree if you let me handle the death."

"Very well," Rholker says, put out.

I stand up from the table, my jaw clenched in fury.

"We have a deal," I say, my voice cold.

The Second Prince nods dismissively. "Good."

Lothar pulls out a blank scroll. "Finalizing the details of our treaty must come first. We have a few requests to discuss."

Prince Rholker shakes his head. "Prove you are willing to sacrifice for this treaty first, or I will tell my father you declared war." His lips curl up into a smile.

I look back to the giant. "You are young. These things are done with great care. Not in one afternoon." The words I speak are lifeless. "You must give me time to consider."

He smiles. "No. This is the offer. Take it or leave it, old man."

Somehow, I will make him pay for his arrogance and cruelty. It has been thirty years since we last sent hunters to their borders, but it could be possible again. I've been a fool for putting off sending Lothar to the elves.

Maybe the human men living in my city will be amenable to learning to fight. They are hardy.

The prince shakes his head. "Are we not in a tent full of

Enduares? I will not let you pick some weak, dying whip. You'll choose from your warriors, just like you chose from ours."

Rage washes over me. I force myself to turn and look at the men standing in the room behind me. My comrades, my friends. I look at Dyrn, Joso, Lothar, Faol... Vann. My throat tightens as I wish I could send them all away. None of them look afraid, none of them look at me like I am weak. Vann meets my gaze with unflinching respect I don't deserve. I must be quick, or the giant could change his mind.

When Vann starts to move, time slows. I shake my head, a minuscule amount. My mouth opens to silence him—to remind him of his value. He saved me after the war, and I would not have been able to gather my people as effectively if I had not had a personal advisor. Losing his insight and presence would be detrimental to my ability to rule.

Another Enduar saves us both. Tirin.

It is like someone reaches into my chest and tears out my heart. He was the first to come to me after I found Estela, the first to confirm she was my mate. I have been proud of his growth as a hunter.

How will I tell his mother? What will I say in the council meetings with his brother? He meets my eyes and nods, offering himself for this awful obligation. He is too good. Untouched by the war that haunts me day and night. I had looked upon him more than once with hope for the future of the Enduares.

And yet he offers himself nobly, understanding the severity of his actions. He is not a child, and I cannot control a man's right to sacrifice himself.

"Are you sure?" I ask in my people's language.

"No conspiring," the Second Prince barks. "Speak the common tongue, or the deal is off."

Tirin nods, his face resolute as he murmurs, "It is an honor to die for my people. If we can keep the humans, it is worth it."

My throat closes. "This man will fulfill your deal."

The Prince rises to his feet, coming to stand beside me. "Use my sword," he offers.

I take one look at the scuffed, no doubt blunt blade and shake my head. "He will die by my own weapon."

Tirin steps forward, and I gesture for him to kneel.

He does so without hesitation, and I stand behind him, drawing my sword from its place on my hip. It makes a hiss against the tough leather sheath which sears my eardrums.

I have to do this. For my people, for Tirin, for myself.

I take a deep breath and raise my blade high above my head. In one swift motion, I bring it down, severing Tirin's head from his body. Blood sprays everywhere, coating me in a sticky crimson. I hold tightly to my blade, ensuring the prince can't see my trembling hands.

Somewhere behind me, there is a gasp. *Murderer*, the voice says. It catches me off guard, and I turn around to see a streak of gold and brown darting away from the tent flap. Estela. Why is she not in her room? It took me so much to get her away from the giants, why the hell would she try to come close to her old slavers?

I cast her a thought. *It seems you have gotten better at hiding your thoughts.*

No answer. I'll deal with her later.

When I turn back to the display, one of the giants is preparing a basket for the head. One of my hunters is kneeling on the ground, lifting the body to be returned to its home.

If our enemies were not here, I would not hesitate to cradle the body and do it all myself. I would wail and mourn for the loss of a good man in an impossible position. Another casualty.

The Second Prince looks at me with a mixture of disgust and satisfaction and claps his hand on my back. I turn to face him, death leaking out of my pores.

Giants have extremely weak lower back muscles—the perfect spot to stab when they least expect it. I could kill him now.

And ruin Tirin's sacrifice.

As if sensing my thoughts, he snatches his hand back. "If I were you, I would be grateful we do not require you to pay back the hundreds lost in the Battle of Roark, Butcher."

Vann hisses at my side and I push to my feet as my advisor growls, "Do not speak of battles you didn't fight in, boy."

Rholker holds his hands up. "Very well. We will wait for your diamonds," he says, watching his warrior stash the head carelessly.

I push aside the bone-crushing grief—the urge to scream, and wallow in the pain that I alone have caused—and sit down. The air is silent. Stony. Like the essence of a diamond.

I turn to Vann. He looks ready to start murdering anything in sight. That rage is poisonous—he needs to get away from these brutes. "You go for the diamonds and a scroll."

He leaves and I turn back to the prince. *"Then* we will begin the contract. Correct?"

The prince nods, and a silence ensues. The open air seems lifeless without the gems to sing sweetly around us. It is lonely and sad in the snow.

The quiet is interrupted by the prince. "So. Won the tiny bitch in a drinking game, did you?"

His bored expression has turned spiteful, with his legs now hanging over the side of his ridiculous seat. One of the men behind him passes him an apple.

He is immature. Letting him goad me into making even more poor choices would be like losing a game of wits to a toddler." I handle my drink exceptionally well."

A hate-filled laugh tears from his lips before he takes a bite of the fruit. "My brother was very angry about losing." The bit of fruit moves around his teeth as he speaks. I focus on that instead of his vulgarity.

"Yes, I remember."

His lips curl into a smile while he crunches. "I'm sure you do. He brought her here to punish me for taking her to my bed. Can't sleep with the slaves, and all that."

To punish *him*? Estela was scared out of her mind. The effort it takes not to flatten his face hurts my insides. "It's generally a good rule."

More crunching. The sound grates on my nerves, but I keep my composure.

"She's pretty enough. Small tits. Your size will be an adjustment. At least, it was for me. That's the bullshit about humans—they are just too stunted," he says with an infuriatingly casual tone.

He... touched her. I see red. But deny myself an outward reaction. I refuse to let him win. I see the way her body looked after a thorough lashing, the way she cried. I remember the brands on her chest, two interlocking rings. Realization strikes—one for each brother.

When I touched Estela's back, she had punched me. It was a reflex. I know what invisible scars look like. Did he give them to her? Or was it his brother?

Rholker continues, interrupting my thoughts. "You did realize that you were getting used goods, didn't you?" He spits a seed on the ground. "If you want a whore, I would happily bring you a full gaggle of them after we finish up this business. A basket of the freshest apples in the kingdom." Another bite. He's almost to the core when he holds the apple out to me. "Since you like leftovers."

My hand tightens around the hilt of my blade, my grip white-knuckled. He is trying to provoke me. He wants to see me break, to see me lash out so he can have an excuse to kill me. I can't let that happen. I have to stay calm, to stay in control.

"You are interested in allowing humans to live with us?" I ask.

He takes the apple core back and he shrugs his shoulders. "Between us, you'd be surprised how much humans can reproduce in fifty years. We almost have too many. If you give me back the woman, I will find you as many slaves as your stony heart desires."

"Perhaps I need workers to help rebuild my kingdom. There was a young man, practically a boy, that came to our city last time. He was taller than most humans. I would be interested in buying him," I say, watching the prince's face to see if recognition flickers.

The corners of his mouth turn down, a tell for his lies I'm realizing. "I'd have to check with the slavers. After you give me back the woman."

"I can't," I frown.

My eyebrows raise and his smile widens, and I can see the glint of something dangerous in his eyes. "You can't? I think you're like every other man. You want something that will carry your mark, not a rotten fruit. Especially not one tasted by your rival."

"Why has that slave bewitched you?" I ask.

He looks nervous at the mention of witchery and twitches his lips again. "She hasn't."

More lies. Time for some of my own. "Then you won't be upset to know that she is dead, so I *can't* give her back."

He blinks and I can see his fiery gaze grows cold. "Dead."

I nod. "Afraid so. We were a little too rough."

Prince Rholker swallows. I feel no guilt. It is not as if we would need to announce Estela's coronation to the world—aside from trade we aren't connected. That won't change because of our peace agreement.

When we are ready to reemerge into the world, we will be different. Stronger.

"May I see Estela's body?" He asks, almost reverently while his grip tightens on his apple. Revealing too much about his true feelings. *The repugnant bastard loved her. In a sick, twisted way, but he did nonetheless.*

I tighten my jaw and shake my head. I've gotten him right where I want him, but I could still push it further and get the upper hand in negotiations. Consider it the first act in a long, slow revenge against what he did to my bride.

Leaning forward, I meet his eye. He senses the shift and narrows his gaze. "Estela? What an interesting thing to know about a slave. Do you know all their names?"

His nostrils flare.

I smirk. "Your mother always told me that you were immature. She told me that the chances you would turn into a man would be slim—weeping over a dead slave seems like the kind of act Lijasa would have hated."

He sits up in his chair, and the apple core falls to the ground. His mouth is open as he watches, and I see his mind working, piecing together the rumors he's probably heard his entire life. The ones never confirmed about his mother's death and the lover she had before her bloody end.

Just as he's about to respond, Vann returns with the scrolls and diamonds. I am grateful for the interruption, for I don't know how much longer I could have held my tongue. Vann places the items in front of me and I begin to sift through them, grabbing a pen to start writing the contract that will bind our peoples together.

"Now, about the contract. I brought Lothar to assist us in

creating a fair agreement—though I admit I never considered peace. Are you ready to begin?"

Prince Rholker purses his lips, clearly disturbed. "Very well."

"Second Prince, as I've mentioned, we are open to reconsidering our position in the slave market as buyers. Since you have already confirmed that your kingdom is in a position to trade your surplus, I want to visit this point first." I say, my voice even. In time, I will have to explain to my mate that I am not a murderer and this isn't about purchasing her kin—I'm creating the ability for them to stay, therefore setting her up as my queen.

He looks sickly pale when he holds out his hand. One of the warriors quickly produce a goblet of wine. Poor Rholker gulps it down, looking like a simpering fool. He's in no position to negotiate with me, he just doesn't know it. "If it includes more diamonds for my father, he would be amenable to the adjustment."

Lothar nods once and opens his scroll. I watch Rholker squirm, and I am deeply satisfied. Things are turning in our favor, despite the terms I had to strike to reach such an agreement.

"In the interest of clarification. I thought we might review the practices from the war. Long ago, elves, giants, and trolls—Enduares—lived by certain codes between peoples."

I remember the times well. One would act as a mediator between the other two. However, the choice of who to support was left to which side had the strongest bond. Elves and Enduares often worked together before the Great War. In times when there was a peace treaty between the elves and giants, my father favored the elves. He ruined that relationship long ago, I pray we can fix it.

Lothar continues. "While we no longer exist in a cohesive group to ease the inter species conflict, we have several proposed checks and measures we can use. Namely, the Enduar Volcano."

The giants freeze. Prince Rholker's fists go white. "So, it does still exist."

He was young when the war happened, but the echo of lava will ring on for generations to come.

"If you review our trade agreement, you'll see we never denied that it could be used again, only that we wouldn't. Now, let's keep going. I am listing the terms of our peace," I say lightly. Almost casual.

Rholker says nothing.

"Five years? And then we shall reconvene. Is this correct?"

He nods, still strangely silent. Both my lies and invoking his mother left a bad taste in my mouth. But I had spent my youth learning to be a leader, and playing games is just a part of the role—my best self will always be reserved for my people.

Tirin died for the Enduares, and he was glad to do so. His life was worth so much. So many good people were dead.

Their memories lend me strength to cheat, steal, and borrow until we reach that great, illusive tomorrow. When we get there, my people's hands will be clean. If I were asked if I regretted what happened to me, I would say no.

Let history judge me, as long as there are people to look back on this moment.

As my pen finishes, I begin to read aloud. It isn't until the end that Rholker reanimates his body.

Lothar looks over my words, and then passes them to the prince. "Once again, we would like to reiterate that if the peace between our peoples is broken at any time, then King Teo of the Enduares reserves the right to invoke the mountain to do his bidding."

He looks exhausted when he starts to read. "I see that the diamond trade will still continue strong. My father will be pleased."

I wonder if this peace treaty really will have a good reception

—his father must have put great trust in him to send in place of his brother. Unfortunately for King Erdaraj, Prince Rholker had underestimated me, thinking that I was like some giant in his court who would fall for his belligerence.

All this... for diamonds. It makes me wonder if there is something of greater value we are missing. The more that I think about the discussion, it wasn't easy, but it was easier than I had anticipated.

My mind races with the next steps as Rholker signs the document. Vann will need to start sending information teams out to learn more. I'll send Lothar to the elves to tell them of our treaty.

"My father thanks you for his new wall decoration," Rholker says, gesturing to the basket with Tirin's head.

I push back my seat hard enough for it to fall on the icy ground. "Tell the king to send his thanks in a letter. This meeting is over." I need to get out of here before I do something idiotic. There's a funeral to prepare.

CHAPTER 15
EMERALD
ESTELA

I should not have followed Teo. While I creep around the tunnels leading out of Enduvida, I find myself standing in front of the exit in my betrothal dress.

The air has already gone icy, but I've come too far to turn away. My thoughts usually tell him where I am without wanting. However, it seems like he only hears most of my louder thoughts, not general chatter. There has to be a way to stop that.

Before I take another step, I imagine closing the windows in my brain and focusing on keeping them shut while I walk toward the people talking. It hurts my head, but if it works, I am happy to suffer. Not far outside of the entrance, positioned atop the snowy ground is a tent. It is deep brown, the color of forest deer, and I freeze in my tracks. *That belongs to a giant.* I hurry over, kneeling at the side of the thick tent's flap. The breeze pushes the leather open, providing a generous gap for me to peer through.

"Use my sword," the slimy, deep voice of the Second Prince says. I freeze. The king had told me that they would come with a decision. But I hadn't expected them so soon.

My grip on the windows of my mind loosens. The ice beneath

my feet disappears, replaced with flashes of a large, wooden bedroom. Rholker's large bed. I'd known that it was time for him to pick a comfort woman as his wedding gift, but I also had known his father denied his request to choose me.

He couldn't stand being told no. I'd tried to hide in the lumber fields, but he came anyway. We didn't make it far in his room before the Giant King's soldiers came for me.

And now I am here. Wearing a pretty dress and sleeping alone.

As quietly as possible, I move closer to the door and look inside. Several giant warriors are watching the prince and the king who stand near where I sit.

"He will die by my own weapon," Teo says before having his hunter kneel. Enduares don't age the same as humans, but this one looks young.

The king raises his arms. I can't believe he would do something like this as he's been kind to his people. Just an hour ago, he was laughing and hugging them.

Then his glinting golden sword comes down in a smooth arc. I can't see the body anymore, but the sound of the head falling and the smell of blood are confirmation enough.

Murderer. He told me he was gentle, that he cared for his people and protected them. How can I trust a word out of his mouth when he would kill in secret? I turn in the snow and start running back to the cave's entrance. My feet get tangled up in my dress and I stumble into one of the walls.

It seems you have gotten better at hiding your thoughts, King Teo says, and I hold tighter onto my mind while I untangle myself and start running again.

At the base of the tunnel, an Enduar calls out to me. "My lady!"

I don't answer, just keep running. Past the vestiges of the

feast, over the bridge with the eternal flames at the bottom, back up the endless steps to the palace.

As I shut the door to my room, I sink to the ground. He told me he wouldn't come into my room again. But he lied. Will he go back on his word and use me like he used that man?

"Please, please don't let them come for me," I whisper to myself, the words barely audible amidst my sobs. I don't trust myself to think in this moment.

I get up to place heavy furniture against the door—it's a futile attempt at protection against the powerful monsters that reside outside these walls, but I do what I can. My hand hurts less than it did earlier. With any luck, there was no actual break in my knuckles.

The dress bunches around my ankles, and I start tearing it off. The ties are easier to loosen than I thought, and it puddles on the ground around my ankles. Reaching up to grab my engagement gift, I tear the necklace off. When I look down, I see an odd assortment of gems. There isn't much time to dwell before I toss it on a shelf.

While I grab a new tunic and leggings, I think of the feast earlier, and how I longed for him to touch me. Stupid. So, so stupid. He's done nothing but prove to me how dangerous he is—and I gave myself away to be his wife.

Exhausted and defeated, I slump down onto the warm stone floor in the middle of the room, letting my tears flow freely. As I sit there, wallowing in despair, I am drawn to the small collection of herbs scattered on a nearby table.

Liana still hasn't removed them after her long evenings spent healing my wounds from the blood-sucking creature and the giants. Their muted colors and delicate shapes seem so out of place in this dark mountain. In fact, I haven't seen a single plant used outside of the ones we brought. The only thing that grows down here is mushrooms. For a moment, my curiosity takes hold, providing a brief respite from the pain.

As a slave, I collected herbs and prepared them for medicinal use. My fingers tremble as I reach out to touch the soft, dried petals of a crimson flower. As I study the herbs more closely, an idea blossoms in my mind, almost too daring to entertain—but what other choice do I have? The only way out of my contract is death.

If I can combine these plants and their properties, perhaps I can create a poison potent enough to bring down an Enduar. If he is dead, I reason, I can find a way back to Mikal, and I will finally be free.

No ownership, only family. New beginnings.

I grab the various herbs and containers that once held healing salves. I set to work with feverish determination, my hands shaking less and less as I become absorbed in my task.

Speaking aloud protects my thoughts better than anything else I have. "Let's see... this one has a numbing effect," I mutter under my breath, crushing the leaves of a silvery plant between my fingers. The scent it releases is both sweet and sharp, like a blade hidden within a bouquet of flowers.

My heart pounds in my chest as I move on to the next herb, a fragile-looking dried vine. "This one induces drowsiness," I recall from my training. My eyes flicker over the remaining ingredients, my mind racing as I calculate the best combinations to ensure the poison's potency. I can't afford any mistakes, not when the stakes are so high.

The world outside this room fades away, leaving only the carefully measured doses and memorized recipes needed to create something deadly.

As I drop in a little water from my tub, stirring the poison's base with a wooden spoon. The liquid simmers gently, its surface shimmering with an oily sheen. It's beautiful, in a dangerous sort of way—much like the king himself.

Neither he nor Liana knew what I was capable of. They thought me simple.

As the final ingredient dissolves into the mixture, the liquid takes on a murky, greenish hue with the lightest trace of silver. Who knows how much time has passed—and it doesn't matter. I have finished.

"Perfect," I breathe, satisfaction welling up within me. My final chance at freedom and escape is now contained within the small phial clutched in my trembling hand.

My heart hammers in my chest, adrenaline surging through me as I clutch the small phial of poison. The triumph of creating it is quickly overshadowed by the fear of being discovered. I listen intently to the silence around me, praying that no one will knock on the door.

But then, a crash behind me shatters the fragile quiet as the door rams into a chair. My hand tightens around the phial, and I whirl around.

"Who's there?" I demand.

"Estela," Arlet whines. "This is not what friends do, you know. They don't insult the other and then barricade them out of their rooms."

A bead of sweat trickles down my temple as I fumble to hide the phial behind a cluster of dried herbs. My heart races, and I force my face into a blank expression while I hurry to move the chair against the door.

My breath is short by the time it's out of the way. I wipe my hands on my skirts. I can still feel the residue of the poison on my fingers, a reminder of what I've done and what I must do. "Shouldn't I be the one seeking you out to apologize?"

What I had said at dinner was awful. It was a horrid thing to blame her for what happened in her and Daniel's time together.

"Yes, but they sent me to get you," she says, stepping further into the room. "Something deplorable happened." Then her gaze flicks between me, the disarray of botanicals strewn across the table, and my gown on the ground. "Is everything all right?"

Dread twists in my gut.

"Fine," I lie, swallowing hard.

"Indeed," Arlet says, raising an eyebrow. "I suppose this is more productive than running away in the middle of the night."

"Desperate times call for unusual hobbies. I tore open one of my scabs while dancing. Hence the new clothes," gesture to the dress on the ground. I'm eager to get her attention off my work.

She wasn't an herb preparer—her time was spent weaving—but she saw her share of injuries during her time in Zlosa. "I am sorry, Arlet. So very sorry for being such a bitch." I swallow the insults about the Enduares, knowing full and well that she is entrenched in her new life.

Her face softens, and she steps closer to me. "It's okay, Estela. I forgive you." She reaches out to touch my arm, her fingers warm against my skin. I reach over and hug her tight.

She pats my back. "We should go. There was a death in the court. One of the hunters was killed while patrolling the *aradhlumes*. They asked me to bring you to be with Teo during the parting ceremony."

I freeze. "Someone died patrolling what?"

"Oh. Sorry." She tilts her head to the side. "The glow spiders."

My skin burns. Lies. That person did not die killing spiders.

The anger must be twisting my features because Arlet looks uncomfortable. "We really should go," Arlet tries again.

I inch toward the table to grab the phial before looking at her. "You seem to know so much about their customs in such a short time."

Arlet looks guarded. "I like their customs. I like their work, their crystals, and I like the way they treat each other," she stammers. " I think—You don't—"

"I don't what?" I ask, trying to understand where all of this is coming from.

"I want to have a family, Estela. I want to be a mother, and I think that I have a chance here," she says at last.

She doesn't know what I have seen—doesn't understand how deceitful the king is. "You think I don't? I loved caring for Mikal. If I could do that with someone who would support me, maybe I would again. These people aren't that."

She shrugs. "I don't agree. They are honorable."

I narrow. "Wait. I thought the giant doctor told you that you couldn't have children. Have they been making you promises?" Dirty liars.

Her long fingers splay across her carefully stitched skirt. "Have you heard about mates?"

I raise an eyebrow. "Like, animal husbandry?"

She shakes her head. "No. It's an ancient magic for races like the Enduares and elves—humans and giants don't appear to have it. One of the other humans, Luiz, is mated to an Enduar woman. They found out soon after we arrived. After..." she trails off.

My eyes narrow, trying to understand what she is telling me.

"They say that if someone is mated to another, there's a possibility to conceive. Of course, there's also more romanticism to it than that—they say that the gods grace them partners to be happy. I just keep thinking, if I find a mate here, maybe things would be different."

My eyebrows raise. "Are you? Er, mated?" If she is, no wonder she has assimilated so quickly. She's bound here by some cosmic rite.

She gives the strangest look. "I have not heard the song. But I am young. Who knows if one day I could..."

Her words are appalling, but my mind snags on the word song. Is that not what I have been hearing every day since I've arrived?

My mouth goes dry. "What song would you like to hear?"

Her shoulders lift as she shakes her head, and that's when I catch it. There's discomfort in her expression. She's hiding something. "I honestly have no idea."

I purse my lips. "I am hungry. We should leave, but first, I need you to help me with my hair. I was told not to let it hang loose."

"Of course. Let me grab a leather tie." Arlet looks relieved that I have relented, and she smiles. "There is always food after anything the Enduares do. They make sure of it."

I nod, watching her while she maneuvers around my head. I take deep breaths, preparing for what I must do.

CHAPTER 16
FLUORITE
ESTELA

Enduar escorts are waiting for Arlet and I. One of them is the woman, Neela, whom I was rude to earlier. Her eyes carefully avoid mine as we walk. My wariness of her holds me over as I cross the bridge again, pass through the residential section, and into a new tunnel I do not recognize.

The air here is thick with moisture, making it difficult to breathe. I know we have gone deeper into the mountain, away from the freshness I had grown accustomed to. The sound of water echoes through the tunnel, and I imagine a river flowing nearby.

We don't speak. I think back to the conversation with Arlet about mates. As if summoning magic, the gem embedded into my chest hums. Pictures I didn't conjure appear—like painted scenes of him touching my skin had goosebumps rising on my arms. I shake my head, trying to dispel the thoughts, but they persist, unbidden. It is a strange feeling, a mix of revulsion and curiosity, of wanting to know more but also wanting to run far, far away.

Eventually, we arrive at a set of large stone doors which are already wide open, marking the source of the water. A massive waterfall crashes down the stone, misting the entire area. They are adorned with intricate carvings of animals and people, all unfamiliar to me, and purple stones glitter in the wall. It's like staring at walls of stars.

Those same spell lights glow overhead, showing hundreds of Enduares. Crystals are organized around the space for the singers to lift up a song. This one is nothing like the joyful ones I've heard, nor the peaceful ones. It doesn't even compare to the ballad of heartache the king asked the singer to play while we danced.

This is agony. These are the emotions I've locked up tightly for Mikal. For my sweet brother.

The mournful tune fills the air with a weight that settles heavily on my chest. Even without understanding the lyrics, the sorrow emanating from the voices of the Enduar singers is clear. I am led to the king's side where he sits at the front of the gathering. His eyes are closed as he listens to the song, his face carved with pain. He's... vulnerable. So beautiful.

I feel a pang of sympathy for him, that fades quickly when I remember the arc of his sword. Then the song between us starts up. This time, I really pay attention. There are no words, but the melody tells me to touch him and find comfort.

My eyes widen. *No. I must be mistaken.* There's no cosmic force tying us together. Mourning the dead is ugly business. It changes people irrevocably.

In this moment, I'm merely swept up in the fact that the Enduares are not so different from my own people. They too have lost loved ones, have known pain and suffering. Humans can still be evil and monsters can have consciences.

The tears sliding down my face are wet betrayals. I grasp the phial again, feeling the smooth, cold glass in my fingers as I trace the line of the cork. If I am to be with him all night, I will have access to his food.

I need to be patient.

Then a new wail cuts through the air, and my heart jumps with fear. It is a voice that I recognize, one that I never hoped to hear again. It is the sound of my mother, screaming in misery while giving birth to Mikal.

My head whips around, and I see everyone in pain. Do they hear what I hear? An uncovered tail snakes around my back, and I gasp. I look up to see the king looking down at me. His eyes are wide with concern, and the gem in my chest glows in response.

"Estela, what are you feeling?" he asks, his voice full of urgency.

I shake my head, trying to clear the echoes of my mother's screams from my mind. His voice is so familiar, it slices through the grief. His hand slips through mine, and I look down to see my crystal glowing. There is peace between us. I'd swat his hand away, do anything I could to regain myself, but I am on the precipice, and he is the only thing holding me back. Then, all the lights go out.

All that is left is the song, the gems glowing in our chest, and the water.

The king steps forward, dragging me with him. Liana joins us, and together, their voices start to chant. It is a slow, rhythmic story, like a poem. I wish I understood.

When Liana starts to speak by herself, the king leans over. "Far away, there is a place. A heaven of sorts. A place where there is no slavery or death. This is its song. Would you like me to tell you the words?"

I look up at him, just barely making out his features. "Yes," I breath.

He nods sadly.

> *"Far away, in Vidalena's embrace,*
> *Amid mountains warm, a sacred space.*
> *Beneath brilliant sunlight's gentle grace,*
> *In groves of trees, our final resting place.*
>
> *Here, pain and war, they cease to exist,*
> *In this hallowed ground, where spirits persist.*
> *To our family, gone but not lost, we gather to say our last goodbye.*
> *To express our love, and forever cherish them,*
> *In our stones, their memory won't dim."*

Like a sweet vision, my eyes light up. I see it. I can picture it as clearly as if the gentle breeze was before me.

Movement in the crowd makes my sense dull, and we make way for a new being, the only one still lit in its entirety. It is a headless body, carried by more Enduares I do not know.

The man the king beheaded. The wailing increases, and I hear the loss so strongly that I am forced to squeeze my eyes shut. It's dark. Far too dark for a place with glowing crags.

My crystal is hot, and my body temperature increases until... I *see* something else. A blue baby and his Enduar family, I see them fleeing to this cave. I see a life pass in an instant. I feel the pride of the man who died. It all alarms me.

This crystal is changing me. I wish they would have never put it in. I yank my hand out of the king's grip, stepping back from him and the other Enduares. The grief and pain of the headless man's family, the anguish of my mother's screams, and the haunting images of the blue baby's life are too much for me to bear. I can't even fathom how the Enduares deal with the incessant magic of the stones.

The king reaches out for me again, but I dodge his touch. "Estela, please," he says, his voice barely above a whisper. "Your thoughts are yelling at me. Let me in."

I shake my head, tears streaming down my face. "No. I don't want this. I don't want any of this. Take this crystal out of me."

The king's brow furrows, and his gem glows brighter, almost as if in warning. "What is wrong with the Fuegorra?"

I stumble back, fear twisting my insides. The cold, wet stone of the wall presses into my back as I hide from that man.

Stay back, I say, speaking to him on purpose this time. My hand goes back to the phial. In the darkness, he halts. I can see when the glowing gem winks out and he watches the rest of the procession.

As the body is washed away, the singing stops. The screams stop. The only sound is the watery roar in wake of the pain.

A reverence fills the air as, one by one, the Enduares leave. They let the world fade to black as they trail out. We are not the last to exit the hall, and it is I who chooses to leave when the time comes. The king does not try to pressure me.

I walk past him, keeping my eyes down, not wanting to see the pain etched on his face again. But before I can make it to the doors, he grabs my arm, spinning me around to face him. His grip is firm, cluing me in to the tension in his muscles.

"King—" I start.

"Teo," he says firmly. When I don't move to speak again, he continues, "We are betrothed. I am not your king. I am your Teo."

I pull my arm out of his grip, looking at him with hardened eyes. The song nudges me once more, but I refuse to hear. "You are not *my* Teo. I wish you were nothing at all."

The words slip out, and his eyes darken, his jaw clenching as he steps closer to me. "You saw the meeting with the giants. Would you like to talk about it now?"

I clench my teeth. "What is there to talk about? You killed the man we just had a service for," I whisper.

His eyes narrow. "That was the deal for the giants. I was supposed to kill two."

I tear away from him. "Am I supposed to be impressed? Congratulations, you are a murderer."

He laughs, actually laughs. "I am the Butcher, Estela. I have been slaughtering since before you were born—you knew this when you decided to marry me."

I can hardly keep the next words from coming out. "You told me that you believed people could change."

This completely disarms him. He stumbles back, blinking. "People can change. But, there are certain duties I can't deny as a king."

I shake my head. "You lied to me about protecting my people."

He grabs my wrists and pulls me close. I don't fight back. He's warm and this muggy room is cold. "I killed Tirin to protect our people. Don't you see that? You think that peace can't have its moments of bloodiness? If you are grateful that you are still here and not riding back to Zlosa with those bastards, then you'll forgive me my trespasses."

I blink, breathing heavy. He's so close. "Did you ask Prince Rholker about Mikal?"

His face tightens. "You accuse me of not caring for my people, but all you care about is your brother. Do you have any right to judge?"

"Forgive me for expecting more of a king than a lowly, uneducated slave," I spit.

"You will soon be a queen."

I step closer into him. There's something about the way we fight, the way that we strip each other bare with these words. It inspires something more, something greater. It makes me... hope.

"Did you ask?" My voice is unnaturally husky.

That strange, long tail swishes behind him, an action I'm quickly becoming accustomed to.

He releases me. "I did. But there is nothing to report."

The bitterness of our reality crashes into me. He won't change, and neither will I. Which is why I need to go back on our agreement. I let my hands press to my pockets, tracing the outline of the phial.

"Fight me as much as you'd like, but you will eat at my side. Let us join my people. Our people, now," he says.

There is no strength left for me to fight him. It's like that, with my heart in my mouth, that I follow him. We return to the feast hall from before. Tonight, there a few seats laid out around the long table, instead of the usual openness that encompasses the way the Enduares share food together.

King Teo takes one of the chairs and motions for me to sit beside him. I resist the urge to refuse and take the seat reluctantly. The food is laid out in front of us, and my apprehension rises as I watch him bite a skewer full of meat and mushrooms. My plan to poison him seems more daunting now that he's sitting beside me.

As is to be expected, people come and go while we eat. Some to whisper about things I don't understand, others to say something seemingly inconsequential as they sneak glances at me.

It weighs heavily on me as I pick at my food, my stomach twisted into knots. I try to avoid looking at Teo, knowing that his eyes are always on me, but eventually, I can't help but glance in his direction. His gaze is intense, unwavering, and a shiver runs down my spine.

"Are you still angry?" He asks, breaking the silence between us.

I raise an eyebrow, unsure of how to answer. My eyes flicker down to his food, which one of the cooking Enduares has just replenished. When I see a new Enduar hovering behind him, a new idea strikes. The difference between those who merely get by and those who succeed is courage. "What kind of meat is that?" I ask, pointing at his metal plate.

"Cave bear. We call them *ruh'glumdlor*."

I nod. "Arlet has told me."

He returns to his food. "It's the most common food that we eat—*wyrmhlumes* are less than appetizing and *ruc'rades* are too small," he studies me as he speaks. "Sometimes we eat..." he searches for the words, "Glow spiders. *Aradhlumes*."

I nod, cataloging each of the names. "Do you enjoy it?"

His sculpted eyebrows draw together. "Not in the mood to fight anymore?

My skin flushes. "You told me I had to interact with others in our contract. Liana mentioned it again, too. This is me being curious."

He purses his lips, and lets out a long breath. "Yes. And I hope you enjoy it as well, for it is the most common meat you will eat here."

I look up at him through my eyelashes, something I've never tried but have seen plenty of other women do. Attracting male attention hasn't ever been as important as it is right now. "Can I try some?"

He is utterly dumbfounded. "Did you not hear me? We eat it several times a week, if not every day."

The corners of my mouth curl up, and I feel sick. Flirting is foreign to me, and it sounds so disingenuous to my ears after our fight.

"I was hoping," I drawl, "to try yours, Teo."

His eyes widen a fraction of an inch.

"*My* food?" he asks, his voice low. He doesn't understand this change, but he's not rejecting it. "You wish to eat off my plate?"

I nod, trying to keep the tremble out of my hands as I reach for his skewer. "Do the sovereigns not display affection in public?"

He grunts. Teo's eyes never leave mine as I bring the meat to my mouth, and bite down. Teo's pupils dilate, and I see the flicker of desire in his eyes that I was hoping for. It's working.

It's working a little too well if I'm being honest. This is a manipulation for him, but it makes both our crystals hum happily. It makes me want to touch him. There is something about reaching for his plate that is intimate like we really are a pair.

Luckily, the man lurking approaches and steals the king's attention away. Still nibbling on the skewer, I use my other hand to deftly unstopper the poison and pour some on my finger. I bring that hand up, hoping they don't see the greenish hue to my fingertips as I rub them around the hunks of bear.

Then I put the food back in front of the king and sit back. He seemingly ignores me for a long moment, barely doing more than flaring his nostrils as he gives his full attention to this mysterious newcomer.

I refuse to look at my handiwork. As the conversation between Teo and the newcomer drags on, I panic. My palms grow sweaty.

It takes significant willpower not to fidget, so I clutch onto those window doors in my mind to keep him out. It will just take a few moments for him to eat, but the poison will take at least an hour to set in.

At that point, I will have to steal a new fur and leave. It will be all right. *Everything will be all right.*

I allow myself to look. All of my attention is reduced to the king's plate as I try to keep my breathing even. I don't realize that the conversation is over. His large hand picks up the skewer, and I meet his eyes, trembling.

He takes a sniff. "Trying to kill me, Estela?" he murmurs. Then he leans forward, so incredibly close to me that the warmth of his skin leeches into mine. The fear retreats the closer he gets.

A familiar lick of fire lights up my insides. His eyes are unreadable, but somehow, I know he is furious. The first time he's truly been irate *at me*.

"Admirable attempt. You truly are my greatest weakness," he says. "Unfortunately, you must do better than poison if you are really so eager to get rid of me."

I try to move and his tail wraps around my waist, pulling me close. "I made a mistake."

"Agreeing to marry me or trying to kill me?" He bares his teeth.

I take a deep breath. "Both."

He laughs, and the people around us disperse, as if they can sense his ugly emotions mounting. "Yes, the second you walked into this mountain you should've known I couldn't let you go. But you humans don't have gifts from your gods. Do you know what you were about to do?"

Heat fans across my skin. I've never seen him so careless with his words.

He takes my hand. "My star, the reason you are so drawn to me, the reason you war within yourself at my touch is because we are destined to be together." He tilts his long, thick neck to the side and reveals a small glowing mark. "This is a mating mark. You are my mate."

My eyes go wide. Ever since Arlet told me about them, I refused to believe it would be me.

"You just tried to kill your mate. By the laws of our people, that is punishable by death," he says, his voice low enough that no one would hear.

"I don't accept you as my mate," I say.

He shakes his head. "As if that would change any of this. Come."

Sweat beads all over my body. I cower back as he pulls me to my feet, and fixes a fake smile on his face.

We hurry from the feast hall, and he waves away a few who try to approach. I gasp for breath and ask, "Are you going to kill me?"

His eyes are stone cold when they look at me. "I haven't decided yet."

After he brings me back to my suite, the one with a tunnel connecting our rooms, he releases me. I move backwards, looking for something, any solid surface to hold myself up.

He looks down at me with such fury and his hand tightens on his belt. I watch him, shaking.

When he is close enough to reach me with the length of his blade, he stops, and lets his hand fall. "My father would have killed you. He would have hated your human blood, and that you were destined to be mine."

I look up at him, his face bitter and ravaged with such hurt. I tremble under his attention as he looks to the table where I prepared his poison.

Then his eyes land on one of the shelves. He reaches forward and picks up the necklace he put on my neck earlier today.

Slowly, so slowly, his fist closes and he replaces the jewelry.

When our eyes meet, it's scalding. "Despite what you believe, I have changed. Perhaps showing you mercy might convince you of that," he says, and backs away.

"W-will you send someone else to do it for you?" I ask.

He looks at me intently. "No. I will tell no one what you have done. I trust you will afford me the same kindness with Tirin. I have already told those who should know."

My body doesn't know how to react, so I stay there, pressed against the wall, frozen as I watch him leave me alone.

I stay there for a long time. Only breaking the spell when I look at the doors that connect our rooms. Something inside of me comes to life. I walk toward them, holding my hand up to touch the space.

Everything that I had thought about the Enduares told me that they would kill me as soon as I arrived. It wasn't hard to see that the Enduares were gentler toward us than we could have hoped for. Everything I had ever known was wrong. And now... the king had his chance to get rid of me for good, and he let me live.

I don't know what to make of all the information. It's too much to understand, but there is something shifting in the depths of my soul.

I am starting to trust him. Ironically, now that he may never trust me again.

Are you on the other side? I say to him through my mind, and wait far too long for an answer that doesn't come.

CHAPTER 17
ONYX
TEO

It was impossible to sleep last night, so I went to visit Liana.

Your mate is still learning our ways. Give her time, she had said. As if I hadn't been spending every waking hour since she'd arrived trying to ensure her people were well cared for.

I stare at my mate through the window in the hallway between our rooms. I stand frozen as I watch her cry on her bed. It makes me nauseous to see her tears.

The betrayal stings. It's like I can feel the pull of our destiny and the anger warring within me. It is a mess in the queen's suite.

I should have known better than to leave her without supervision.

Endu curse me for thinking that she was resting after what she saw in that meeting room. Why wouldn't she want to kill me? I beheaded one of my own men and she had no idea why.

The evidence of her poison crafting is everywhere, on the table, the ground, the wall. She was trying to kill me so that she could be free. Some part of me is impressed at her strength and ruthlessness—both good qualities for a queen.

If my nose couldn't detect the sour smell in the air, as potent as her anxiousness, I would be dead right now. And yet, all I can think is that it must be a gaping wound for her to be forced to be here with me.

It seems that the only solution to her pain is retrieving her brother as soon as possible, a complicated task because it is tied up in the tentative peace I have with the giants.

It is time to reach out to the elves. I turn on my heel and leave her to her tears.

Walking to my study, I think of what she said in the Parting Cave. *Take this stone out of me.* I glimpsed her pain through our bond—and it was awful. She is a wounded animal acting out of instinct.

As I cross the threshold, I find Vann studying a scroll. He looks up at me. "You left the feast quickly with the human. Everything all right?"

"The human's name is Estela," I say gruffly. "And she will be your queen in a week."

Vann nods, understanding in his eyes. "Estela," he repeats. "I heard the word mate on your lips as you left. Does she know?"

"Know what?" I ask, just to be petulant.

"That your destinies are tied together from now until eternity," he clarifies, not without a heavy dose of sarcasm. I know his wounds run deep after his betrothed died with the rest of our people, but it is hard to speak to him about my heart when he's like this.

I take a deep breath. "It's complicated."

"Complicated?" he echoes.

"If I tell you the truth, you must swear to never tell another and accept my choice," I say.

His eyebrows shoot up. "Now you must tell me."

I shake my head. "Swear it."

He holds up his left hand. "I swear on my parents' watery graves."

"She tried to poison me," I say, my tone clipped.

Vann's mouth falls open in surprise. "What?" he exclaims. "Why would she do such a thing?"

"She saw me behead Tirin," I explain.

"Hmm," he huffs. "What choice did you have? These humans are infuriating. Irresponsible, ungrateful."

I narrow my eyes at him, studying his neck which is covered by his tunic. "You promised to accept my choice. I told Liana about it, and she helped me see clearly. If you had recognized a mate, you would feel differently."

His energy changes.

"Wait, have you found someone?" For a second, he doesn't respond and I think he will tell me yes.

Then he shakes his head. "No."

I purse my lips. "The humans will warm to us in time. We will offer them a good life." It is my job as king to let others see all sides, even if my heart is breaking.

Vann raises an eyebrow, but doesn't respond. He's been with me long enough to know when I'm in a foul mood. "So, what next, My Lord?" he asks instead.

"The elves have been silent since the negotiations after the war. However, since we have signed a contract with the giants for peace, we should establish a line of communication. Let them know that we would like to rekindle our allyship."

"Do you think they've forgiven us for lying to them?" Vann asks.

I frown. "My father lied to them. I did not." In fact, I could not have lied to them, I was on a very different mission.

"Yes, but the elves see you as an extension of your father. He was the one who trained you for this role, so you will harbor some of his... philosophies." Vann leans forward and picks up the copy of the peace agreement. "I have been poring over these words. Trying to find any clues as to why the giants are so obsessed with the diamonds. For a long time, I didn't question it. But since you have brought it up, it has plagued me. What if the elves already have a secret relationship with the giants?"

I shake my head and my jaw clenches at the idea. "Unlikely. Elves are notoriously isolationist. It took twenty-five years to broker the peace treaty with them the first time." I move to the window and stare out at the cavern in front of us. It is not what it once was, but it is beautiful. Surely Estela should be able to see that with time.

Vann nods. "Very well. I will send someone to retrieve your message soon."

I take a seat in front of him. "Make it Turalyon. He has a good head on his shoulders, I think he would be well suited to diplomacy with Lothar."

My oldest friend nods, glancing back at the scrolls he's left scattered on the desk.

"Thank you, Vann." My eyes burn as he stands. Tirin is one death of many. I think of Estela's cowering form and visit the darkness in my soul. When my father sent me to seduce and murder the queen, there were slaves in Zlosa that Lijasa ordered slaughtered to prove my devotion.

Estela's words about change plague me. And I allow myself the time it takes to dwell on my pain. She was right—it doesn't matter if I save most of my people and free dozens of slaves, stains like Tirin, like those nameless faces, are never washed away.

It takes me a moment to realize that Vann is still in the doorway, waiting for me as he often does when observing me lost in thought. "Are you sure you are all right?"

"We don't speak of the war often," I say, staring at the gilded swirl on the end of a stone paper scroll.

"Would you like to?" he breathes.

I hear the discomfort in his voice. His wounds are as deep as mine. "Do you have regrets?"

"Are you referring to Tirin? He honored us all by his action." Vann crosses his arms and puts his missing fingers on display.

I shake my head. He is silent for a moment, and then says, "Yes."

"Do you believe in second chances?" I ask, still staring at that scroll.

He smirks. "Perhaps life is one big chance."

I nod. "Yes."

"Everyone has regrets, brother."

"I think I have more than others. They are starting to catch up with me. Staining my soul, weighing me down. I-I am tired." How can I tell him that I think what happened with Estela is well deserved?

He shakes his head. "One of the hardest consequences of our actions is having to live with the choices we thought were right at the moment." He comes over and puts his hand on my shoulder.

Silence stretches between us. "I need to do something for Estela," I say at last.

Vann raises an eyebrow. "After her trying to kill you?"

"Yes. When we made our marriage agreement, her terms included a brother who she wants saved. He was one of the slaves that came with the last caravan—the only one taken back to Zlosa. She is... protective of him. If we can retrieve her brother, she might cease to be a liability and a danger to herself and to me."

"Understood," Vann says with a nod. "I will find out everything I can. Did she give his name?"

I cross one leg over the other. "Mikal." The room around us is stuffy, and I'm tired.

"Before I go, should we speak about the Festival of Endu next week?" Vann is hesitant after so many heavy words hanging between us. "Or, should I say your wedding?"

I shake my head. "Not now, Vann. I need to think."

Vann nods, then takes a deep breath. "Teo, you're not a bad person. Even now, you are thinking of your mate—what she needs, what she wants—while balancing all of our people. I haven't forgotten what you did on the day of the eruption. You saved my life."

"You saved mine, too." I blink back the moisture in my eyes, but he's not done.

"You believe that one good act does not strike out an evil one, and you might be right. But I believe that our gods will weigh the purity of our hearts and our loyalty to our family. When it is your turn to be put on judgment by Endu, I believe your heart will be the purest of us all. You have carried the hardest burden from the beginning. It is an honor to follow you." He presses his fist over his heart and bows. Then he leaves the room, shutting the door behind him.

I'm left alone with my thoughts, haunted. I think of Estela crying on her bed. Every time I have lowered my guard, I find myself betrayed. I might deserve it, but I don't know how to be her mate.

The demands of destiny are impossible to deny. Like hoping the sun will not rise on the over land or thinking that the earth below us will not quake.

I sit down at my desk and reach for the quill. It is time to begin drafting a letter to the elves, hoping against hope that this will be the first step in rekindling an alliance that will help us all.

As I dip the metal pen into the shimmery inkwell, my mind begins to wander, and my thoughts return to Estela. She dances through my veins to the song of our matehood, infecting my mind with her sweet features and fiery voice. I can feel glimmers of her emotions, flickering in my own body. I feel the sadness, the anger, the helplessness.

With a heavy sigh, I begin to write my message to the elves, taking care to choose each phrase. Diplomacy was my favorite part of learning from my father—though I have no great talent for stone working like others, words are my tools. Finding the right ones is like finding that perfect pocket of ore or that precise temperature to temper a sword or spear.

As my hand moves across the parchment, my anger settles. After three drafts, I have finally drafted the perfect words. Just in time, because Turalyon arrives.

He bows as he enters the room, his eyes darting between me and the scroll I've been working on. "My Lord," he greets me, "I am honored to be sent on this mission with Lord Lothar."

I nod in acknowledgment, handing him the scroll and giving him detailed instructions on what to do next. "Make sure you are cautious. Elves are not to be trifled with, and they may see our attempt as a sign of weakness. We need their support, but we must also be prepared for any eventuality."

Turalyon nods, his brow furrowing in concentration. "Of course, my Lord. I will be careful."

As he turns to leave, I speak up again. "Turalyon, stay alert, and return as soon as possible."

"I will, my Lord," he assures me, bowing once more before exiting the room.

I am left alone with my thoughts once again, still staring out the window. I stand up from my desk, and start restlessly pacing. Perhaps a walk through the caverns will clear my mind. As I make my way through the winding tunnels, I hear shouting.

My pace quickens as I move into the residential section, only to come across four of the human men. They are saying something to a small group of my people.

Svanna is there, still wearing her mining equipment. With dust coating her face, it emphasizes her silver eyes and pointed white teeth.

"What's the matter?" I ask them.

One of the humans looks up at me, anger etched into the lines of his face. "King—" he stutters. His fierce bravado is completely erased at his fear.

Am I really so terrifying to these people?

"Yes?" I try to move him along.

Svanna speaks up. "Of course the humans are welcomed here. But they are more mouths to feed, we only ask that some of their men help us hunt."

Another one of the human men steps forward. "King, I am called Mauricio by my people. We understand that we must help if we live here, but there is something in the tunnels they sent us to hunt in."

My thoughts race, trying to figure out what could be frightening the humans.

"Take me to where you saw it," I say, knowing that I cannot let anything that could endanger my people reside in our caverns.

Svanna follows as they lead me to the tunnel entrance, and I can feel the energy shift as we descend into the darkness. It's cold, the kind of cold that seeps into your bones and stays there. My breath mists in front of me as I move forward.

I'm reminded of the being that attacked Estela—she was so cold when I saw her. I had assumed it was because of the snow, but now I realize that even I had felt a chill.

As we move deeper into the tunnel, a strange, eerie mist swirls and dances around us like it's alive. The humans are right to be afraid.

We stay there for over an hour, searching. Waiting for the worst. When nothing happens, I turn back to them. "This is unusual, stay out of this section. Svanna, will you tell the others we need a council meeting? We cannot risk any accidents before we know what is happening."

Svanna nods. "Of course, King Teo."

Unease continues to mount within me. Something is not right. And with so many to care for, including Estela, I cannot rest easy.

As we make our way back to the residential section, waves of panic wash through me. First, it was the threat of the giants, then we had the humans, which was promising until my mate tried to kill me. I was supposed to be worrying about the elves, but this is something much more immediate.

CHAPTER 18
RUBY
ESTELA

T all trees surround me. A bright orange sun is just sinking into the skyline, and the forest smells the same as it always has: sweet, wooden, and fresh. Since the slaves were sent back to our dens, it is as peaceful as can be expected on the night of the autumn feast.

The Giant Court is loud enough to filter all the way out here, but another year has passed, and the king's declaration for me not to be touched and for my brother to remain alive is still strong. They don't ask for me to join them at these parties as a server anymore.

My bare feet grip at the tree trunk while I climb higher, and higher, to reach a ball-like plant we slaves call 'hoja de bola'. Though it is poisonous to giants, it's Mikal's favorite breakfast, and my stash is running low.

I spot the bunch of yellow-orange leaves on one of the boughs and quickly snap it off before beginning my descent back down the tree.

Sweat trickles down my back as I hurry, my eyes scanning the ground below for anyone who could have seen me. After ensuring that the area is clear, I run through the trees and around the fields, weary and sore.

Soon, it won't matter and I will be able to sleep.

As I exit the field, I am surrounded by familiar dens—fenced-off areas where we sleep and store our meager belongings. I hurry to the hollowed out tree I carved out a few years back to stash my food.

That's when a scream pierces the silence.

I see the head with blood-red hair peeking over the houses and freeze. Prince Keksej is there.

Not again. I had waited more than a month to go scavenging for the hojas de bola so that they wouldn't come looking for me.

Then the First Prince draws his hand back. A short whip with three tentacles flicks back in the air before coming down. This time, when the scream breaks out, I recognize Arlet's voice and start running.

"I will ask you again, where is she?" his voice echoes over the space.

"I don't know," she yells.

There's a pause, and his head disappears. "You have such dirty nails. Let me help you clean them," his voice rumbles.

Another scream pierces the air as I reach their location. Most slaves are huddled inside of their dens while she is tied to the whipping post in the center of the town. I push myself hard until I reach the clearing and see Arlet's torn clothing and the bruises already forming on her skin.

The prince holds up her bloody hand that now has one missing finger. She wails from pain, opening and closing her hand as if it could stop his blade.

"Stop!" I scream. "I am here! Let her go!"

I rush forward, quickly scanning the scene for Mikal, before my eyes glimpse Daniel trying to watch Arlet from his pitiful window.

Hatred flows for that man, watching a woman he claimed to love hurt over and over again. I rush forward so that they will see me.

It's then that I realize Prince Rholker is here, because he stands, and I see the gashes on his arm. Brawling during the feast again, likely.

"Tiny flea," Prince Keksej says, forcing me to look back at him. He lets Arlet go as if she'd burned him and steps forward. I fall to my knees next to her.

"Get inside with Miki," I tell her, grabbing her finger off the ground. "I'll fix this. I promise."

Prince Keksej nudges me with his bare foot. I get a whiff of spirits. "The healer said that you knew where the extra simka leaves are."

I straighten and nod, acutely aware of Arlet stumbling away. Just as I start to turn toward the herb hut where I prepare the plants used for the royal apothecary.

"Wait," Prince Rholker calls. "Where were you?" His elder bright lets out an exasperated breath but doesn't stop him. Like always.

"Foraging," I say.

"Where are your plants?" Prince Keksej demands.

I hesitate, not wanting to give up my hiding spot with all the slaves listening.

"I don't believe you," Rholker says. His voice has that same calm quality I've come to hate.

I turn back around and find his hand in the fire, holding something. "You were with someone else. Admit it."

My hands go up. "No, Second Prince. I was looking for food."

He shakes his head. "That doesn't make sense. You get fed every day. I think you went to fuck a farm hand. Do yourself a favor and admit it!" he roars.

I stumble backward. "I promise I didn't."

"Swear it on your mother's grave," he demands. He withdraws a long, metal rod with a circle on the end. A brand.

My eyes widen as I take a step back, realizing what he intends to do. "Please," I beg.

"Swear," he insists.

"I swear on my mother's grave," I say as fast as I can.

"Humans are easy liars. I told you last time," Prince Rholker continues, holding the brand up to my face. *"If I came for you and you were not here, I'd brand your skin. Whatever man you were rutting will know you belong to the royal family."* Then he points to Daniel, who is still watching Arlet, and runs out to hold me down. I fight against them, struggling with all my might to get away and not allow them to brand me. But their strength is too much, and I am overpowered.

"I wasn't with a man!" I scream as the brand comes closer to my skin. A searing pain that is unlike anything I have ever experienced.

"Good. Then this will remind you to behave."

I don't even know who says it because the hot metal sears my flesh, and I scream out in agony.

I awake in my room, completely alone. My throat hurts, and my skin is coated in sweat. I roll out of bed and rush to the tub in the corner before plunging in fully clothed. The warm water soothes my aching body, but I can't shake the memory of the dream. It had felt so real. I run my fingers along the area where the brand was, but it's occupied by the new gem that the Enduares gave me.

I take deep breaths, sinking further into the water as I wait for my roiling stomach to calm.

You aren't there anymore. You are all right, I say in my language while I relax. *You are to marry the king, and the giants will never touch you again. The king always comes for you.*

The words are so sure, so potent. It's true. He comes when I need him.

Then, like the sun breaking forth over the horizon, I remember what I did.

Someone knocks on my door, and I am out of the bath and into fresh clothes in mere moments. I sit on the bed, expecting it to be the king's Cleaver, come to finish up what the king could not bring himself to do. Guilt has been pressing down on me like the weight of this entire mountain.

When the door swings open, it's Liana. Her eyes are extra vibrant in her worn, wrinkled face.

"Has your nightmare passed?" she asks while looking at the dripping waves around my face.

I stare at her, unsure what to say. How does she know? Did she hear me scream? "Yes."

"Good, we can get right to business. I am tired of your narrow mind. You tried to kill him," she says flatly. "Do you know what he is to you?"

I remember his admission and get off my bed—I don't like sitting with her standing over me like that. As I walk around the room, I straighten the mess I've been living in for the last day.

"He hates me. It matters not what we are to each other," I mutter, pulling open a drawer and rifling through it for dry socks for my bare feet.

The woman snorts. "Is that what you think? I know that you aren't delighted with being mated, but you are to him what he is to you. You think that he cannot forgive attempted murder by his mate? Ma'Teo could forgive much worse if you gave him a reason to."

I roll my eyes, but the truth is, her words give me pause. I do not hate him as I should. As I have tried to. It seems that he is also my weakness.

"Ma'Teo?" I ask. "Is that his full name?"

She purses her lips. "It is an old way we trolls used to refer to each other."

Interesting, but she doesn't expand so I turn to her and meet her gaze. "What is it you want from me?"

"For you to see reason and forgive Ma'Teo for the things he cannot control. You act as if he did this to you," she replies, without missing a beat. "Do you know that his father trained him from the time he was old enough to walk to kill one person—the Giant Queen Lijasa. He became the Butcher, as you so awfully call him, after that."

I stare at her for a moment, trying to comprehend her words. "What do you mean?"

"He won't tell you. He would prefer to forget that entire part of his life. Ma'Teo made a mistake during a battle. His father was angry, and your mate was sent to deal with Lijasa. She had taken an interest in the Enduares, and she bedded him for a year before he could kill her."

I stumble back, shocked. I had told him that he could never change, that he was stuck as the evil sovereign I believed him to but... but Teo has as much reason to hate the giant royals as me.

Liana steps forward and grabs my shoulder. "Queen Lijasa was only his first punishment. The Giant King killed Teo's mother in battle soon after. Now he is given something real? And you can't even stand to look at him?" Her words are firm, if not a little unkind.

The woman's eyes are soft when I look up at her. "You are still new to this world, so I will speak plainly. Some might say that the king deserves nothing from you, but I understand the complexities of life much better. You were also taken from your family. This change is not something I expect from you this exact moment—nor do I think it will be easy to attain. But I believe if you take the time to understand and heal what is between you and the king, it will be... rewarding. For both of our peoples."

I am still stunned, working through everything I know about the man. Every interaction is stretched out before me for me to examine with this new lens. He was afraid. Hoping for family.

Frustrated, I pick up a tunic and start to fold.

"In my culture, I am something of a—" she takes a moment to find the right words, "prophetess. I see things with my magic. We need a queen, and your people need liberation."

She smirks when I stop folding a fur tunic and turn to look at her.

"Yes, you haven't thought of that, have you? Gods, *that man tells you too little*. Peace is why Ma' Teo had to kill Tirin. With a peace treaty, we can allow your people to live under our mountain. Think of the ballads which will be written about you. Once slaves, until a human became queen of a well-feared race? We would have half-human heirs."

Anger raises up inside of me. I don't want more children right now, not when Mikal is still lost. "A human queen of a pitiful, hated race?"

Her silver eyes flash toward me, full of irritation. "I have seen the future, Estela, and I have seen glimpses of the present. You can't tell me you still believe those lies."

I place the tunic on the table and step toward her, still feeling queasy. "Your people devastated the elves, giants, humans, and Enduares in the last war."

She crosses her arms again, effectively making dozens of crystals hanging off of her body create a musical tinkle. "King Teo's father did."

I keep going. "He nearly wiped out his own people. Look at how many of you there are!"

It's almost possible to hear her grind her teeth. "You believe you are making a profound point, but you do not know us. Would you judge an entire people for the actions of one very dead madman? This is why Teo changed our court's name."

I freeze. My mouth hangs open with a rebuttal on my tongue.

Satisfied with her effect on me, she continues. "Do you understand that the bond between a mated pair is not something to be taken lightly? It is rare and precious, and when it's between a human and an otherworldly being like the king, it is even more significant. If the king can be mated to you, others can be mated as well. In fact, they are finding mates. Our people will be saved."

I raise an eyebrow, skeptical. "This only seems beneficial for you." Humans are little more than chattel. We are worthless. Our masters don't even care if we live or die.

"You are a short-sighted thing. With that crystal in your chest, you will live longer. It will heal you when you are sick, and with time, you will grow strong," she says.

I look down at my arms, my feet. All of my wounds are healed. Sure, there are scars, but physically speaking, I have never felt better.

Before I have a chance to respond, she continues, "I will teach you how to be a queen, and you can lead our people to fighting for a better world." She's clearly spent a lot of time thinking about what she wanted to say, because she removes a scroll from her robes and hands it to me.

"What is this?" I ask tentatively as I reach out and take it.

She quirks an eyebrow. "I have written down my thoughts on the matter. A gift, if you will. Don't worry, it is written in the common tongue."

I blink. "I can't read."

Realization dawns on her face. "Right, well. In that case, I shall interpret it for you."

She begins to read out loud, the words flowing like a song.

"A human queen will bring the light of hope
To those in the shadows, forgotten and alone
The strength and courage of a noble soul
Will be the catalyst for a new tomorrow

A union between your two species
Will bring forth a new meaning of peace

Your actions now as the queen
Will build a path of freedom unseen

The world will be a place of grace
Where all will run, filled with peace and grace
A world of harmony and prosperity
Will be yours, with the human queen's decree."

I draw my eyebrows together. Entranced by the way that the stones reverberate to Liana's song, including the one in my chest. For the first time, I don't despise the sensation. It is impossible to explain, but this conversation with her has left me *feeling* things more clearly.

It's easy to recognize what she says is truth.

"You keep mentioning this stone in my chest. The one that you all have. Tell me this—should it give me... visions?"

Her eyebrows shoot up. "The Fuegorra?"

"Fuegorra," I drag the word out for the first time since having it put in, letting the R sounds roll on my tongue. It almost sounds like a human word. "Yes."

For the first time since she's barged into my room, she looks deeply unsettled. "It is making you see visions," she repeats.

I nod.

Her full lips purse, causing the beautiful lines of her face to deepen. Something different has bloomed between us in this conversation, and I can't help but think of all the people I've known who have never grown old enough to have such wrinkles.

Then, unexpectedly, she holds out her hand. "Come with me."

I stare at her for a few seconds, tentatively placing my hand in hers. As I do, something else—another sensation—rushes through me. It's like a jolt of static electricity, but it warns me of something else—a presence waiting for me.

She takes me out of my room and down a long hallway. We eventually make our way down into a small chamber filled with crystals. A large, glowing one protrudes from the center, and I know immediately it's the Fuegorra.

The woman leads me before the stone and my skin starts to buzz. It's different from the intensity that comes when the king touches me. Instinctively, I reach my hand up, and the crystal starts to hum.

"Impossible," Liana whispers.

I'm not sure what she means by that, but my attention is quickly pulled towards the crystal. It starts to glow and send warm pulses against my skin.

The humming turns into a melody, a sweet and soft tune that slowly spreads across the room. The crystals around us start to glow as well, matching the rhythm of the Fuegorra in the center.

As we stand there, the pulsing crystal slowing down, I see something. A vision.

I'm in a dark room filled with shadows. I can hear whispers all around me, but I can't make out what they're saying. Suddenly, a light pierces through the darkness, and I can see a figure standing in front of me. It's the king, Teo.

"Estela," he says, his voice echoing through the room as he raises his arms, as if to embrace me. That same impulse to reject him flares, but I have no control over my actions. I step into his arms, and the beauty of the song between us is almost unbearable.

There is a distinct heat between my legs and a dampness that makes my skin tight and my breath hitch.

"*Te amo[1],*" he whispers in my human tongue. Telling me he loves me as his large, calloused hands stroke over my arms.

I don't know why we are in a court before others. This

moment should be between us. But then, the crystal on his chest starts to grow, and mine follows. It as if I am sucked into his magic, lost to both my vision and him.

The mountain comes alive around me and rumbles as if it were a living being. Fire erupts from the ground and tears through the sky, lighting up the world in shades of red and orange. I am bathed in the warm glow, and I feel as if I am part of the earth itself.

Suddenly, the vision ends, and I am back in the chamber with Liana. I am breathing heavily, my hands shaking as they grip onto the fabric of her robe.

"What was that?" I ask her, unable to take my eyes off the crystal.

She frowns, studying me intently. "It is a sign that you are meant to be our queen. The Fuegorra has chosen you to be one of its wise women, like me." Her face brightens, like the moment a match is struck. "We must tell the king." I am still reeling over how it felt to be held by Teo. It was much more intense than the faint inklings we've had up to this point.

For the first time, I realize that, in my carelessness, I had forgotten about Mikal. Guilt returns, and I freeze up.

Liana notices, "What is wrong?"

My eyes start to burn. "The first vision I had was of my brother. He was sleeping, but alive, back in Zlosa."

She pauses. "You still wish to be with him. Don't you see? This crystal will help."

That does it. Tears stream down my face. After endless days in this space under the mountain, I finally have a plan. Something I can do to help me get back to my brother.

I look up at her, unsure how to ask for help. I have spent my whole life doing things mostly alone. "Will you..." I trail off.

Her expression is soft as she lays a hand on my shoulder. "I will teach you how to use the Fuegorra." Then she smiles, a wild, pointy-teeth grin. "But only with a few conditions."

My stomach drops into my ass. "What do you mean?"

Without warning, she draws me into her, effectively hugging me. "We all have duties under the mountain. The contract said you would find one as soon as you healed. You look lovely and healthy to me, so if you wish to learn to use this with me, then you will find one." She must feel me tense because she continues, "This is not about slavery, young one. You were right, our people are few in number, which means we must all pull our weight. If someone does not go hunting, we all starve. I promise you that there will be no pain. I just want you to get to know the people, to let their actions speak for who we are."

After pulling back to look up at her, I wipe my eyes. She smiles down at me, gentle and beautiful.

"I will do it," I say.

"Good. Let's go now," she says and grabs my hand.

I step back from her. "No! I don't wish to be near him yet."

She raises an eyebrow. "Do you go back on your word so quickly?"

Heat creeps up my neck. "No." It is a painful, shameful moment for me.

She holds out her hand. "I am an old woman. Who knows how much time I have left in this rocky world? If you want me to pass down my knowledge, I get to be demanding."

I chew on my lip. "Fine. We will go." It does not matter.

Liana takes my hand and leads me back down the hallway towards the throne room. The vision of Teo and the powerful feelings it evoked are still fresh in my mind, making my heart race and my body ache. I wonder if he felt the same intensity that I did.

As we enter the council room, I find the king sitting atop a deep grey-stone throne. Rigid power leaks off him, accented by the crumbling bits of rock on either side of the otherwise pristine room.

Teo sits proudly—stoically, even—surrounded by his advisors. One of them, a woman I've seen watching him during meals stares at him with unbridled emotion. Her forlorn gaze causes acid to pool in my stomach. He breaks away from her as we approach, his eyes locking onto mine. The intensity of his gaze is almost overwhelming, forcing me to avert my eyes. It's like he can see right through me, like he knows my every thought and feeling.

He does not look gentle or happy. He looks like he wishes he would never look upon me again. I don't know how I can recognize it, but he looks far colder than I have ever seen him.

"Your Highness," Liana says, bowing before him. "We have news for you."

"What news?" he asks, his eyes still fixed on me.

Liana clears her throat. "The Fuegorra has chosen *Lady Estela* to be one of its wise women. Our future queen is a seer."

He raises an eyebrow. "This is good news. Thank you for telling me. If you would excuse us, we are in a meeting."

I blink. He is as frigid as the snow I had to walk through to get here. It shouldn't hurt, but I'll be damned if it doesn't burn as I walk out of the room.

---

1. I love you.

CHAPTER 19
YELLOW SAPPHIRE
TEO

A Half Hour Earlier

Estela is locked away in my thoughts. I am determined to give my full, undivided attention in my meeting about the tunnel and this mysterious mist that is preventing my people from hunting. Five of my six advisors are here, as Lothar went with Turalyon to speak with the elves.

I swear the room is colder than normal. Just a degree or two, but I can still hear the hydraulic pumps in the background, working extra hard to heat the city and bring in fresh air from the outside. Something in my gut tells me that it is connected to the mists, but another part of me doesn't wish to alarm my people before it is necessary.

Svanna looks bored. She's the only one sitting back in the chair, picking at her nails with one of her mining tools. I know she's listening. She's just very different in these meetings as opposed to the decisive leader she is in the tunnels.

"Tunnel seven is still open. The *ruh'glumdlor* population

won't be affected if we continue to rotate through the other tunnels, but only for a short time," Vann says.

Ulla still refuses to look at me after our exchange directly following the last meeting. Her gaze is carefully fixed on Vann as she says, "The *aradhlumes* also lived in tunnel seven. They are the *ruh'glumdlor* bears' main food source, which is extra pertinent since bear mating season has just begun—we need to make sure that enough cubs are produced to continue feeding our people."

Vann nods and grins, clutching his cleaver. "We'll have to go hunting for spiders."

Lord Salo, Tirin's brother, looks displeased. This is his first meeting since the funeral, and I have heard he's been distant with the stone benders. "It may need to be time to start hunting outside of the mountain. There are deer in the forest below. Would those not serve us better than the fatty *ruh'glumdlor* meat?"

Ulla shakes her head. "Changing a core part of our diet isn't advisable unless we absolutely need to."

I carefully listen to their thoughts. "How long do we think it will take to clear the tunnel?" I ask.

Svanna scoffs. "Yes, Lothar, how long will it take to inspect the tunnels? Oh wait, he got to go on a trip by himself."

"With Turalyon," I correct, and she resumes preening. "It will take time to scout the elves. I would suspect it could take anywhere within a month for them to return. There is little risk that the giants will return before then to test the boundaries of our treaty, so this is our priority now."

Salo purses his lips at the mention of the meeting with the giants. He knows what happened, his mother even told me she was proud of the sacrifice her son gave. The price seems hard to justify at this moment.

You are a weak, coddled bastard, my father's voice hisses.

Vann answers next. "Since Lothar oversees the hunters, no

one has sent an inspection group to examine the mists. We decided it was best to wait for Liana to confirm we weren't dealing with *wyrmhlumes*. The humans," the slight distaste in his voice is clear, "are the only ones who have reported seeing a being. What if the mists happened because of a temperature change in the underground waters?"

Fira, the only member of my counsel who also worked with my father, holds up her hand. "I was born in Vidalena, and lived there till the day King Teo'Likh destroyed it. However, I've been coming to this city since before the war. That's nearly one hundred and thirty-seven years of information, and I have never seen anything like this."

Salo shakes his head. "I agree. Tunnel seven is not connected to any water sources. If that were the case, we should see the same problem in tunnels two and five."

"Exactly. We haven't had any problem in the mining section, either," Svanna agrees.

The conversation has strayed, so I reenter the debate. "Members of the royal council. One moment, we are talking about providing enough food for our court, the next, we have moved on to bear population control, only to switch yet again to the threat posed by the mists." Everyone before me remains silent. "My thoughts are these: hunting is not a great concern yet. If the problem persists for more than a week, then we can reconvene, but first, I want to speak with Liana. Then I will commission a thorough inspection of tunnel four."

Vann, Fira, and Salo look back at me while Ulla and Svanna busy themselves with notes.

"Yes, My King," Vann says. The others murmur it as well.

There is an awkward moment that passes as they wait for me to adjourn the meeting. Too damn bad. It's been a restless night and an unsettling morning.

"I would like an update on the humans," I say. "As per our

last report, we have thirteen in our city. Each has accepted the Fuegorra crystal. Are there any new mates?"

Ulla shifts uncomfortably, practically hiding behind Salo. I hone in on her.

"Ulla?" I prod gently.

She bites her lip. "Aside from Neela and a man named Luiz, Ismael and Drinya have started the matehood song."

I blink away the melancholy. "This is good!" My voice is a little too loud. "Have both of them accepted?"

She nods. "And the other pair is doing well. They've moved into Neela's home. He has been training in cooking with me."

A smile tugs at my mouth. Another mated pair. "This is wonderful. Any others?"

The news is so good that it doesn't disappoint me when no one else answers. "How are the rest adjusting to the cave?" I've been so consumed with Estela, I've been a little negligent with my reports.

Fira speaks up first. "Arlet, the redhead, was a weaver as a slave. Not only did she figure out that the Ardorflame is a good source of light for humans, she has proved to be one of the best in my crew. I think she might even have a talent for gem setting. None of the others have shown much interest in the crafts."

I glance at Vann and find him trying not to look interested. Whatever he is doing with that woman is starting to annoy me. I shall speak with him later.

After thanking her, I turn to Salo. "I take it that none of them have started to exhibit magical abilities. Have any approached you as a stone bender?"

He shakes his head, so I turn to Svanna. She straightens. "Seven of the men are working in the mines. They worked in the lumber yards, so they are exceptionally strong. I believe the other four went to be with the hunters."

I nod. "Very well. Keep an eye on them, all of them. We want to make sure they are adjusting well," I say, addressing the whole council. "If there are any issues, I want them brought to my attention immediately."

Then, the door to the throne room is opened. Liana comes striding in with my mate trailing behind.

"Your Highness," Liana says, bowing deeply. "We have news for you."

The air grows thick. The timing feels serendipitous, and I wonder if she knows something about the mists. My eyes wander to Estela. The blood starts to heat in my veins when she meets my stare. "What news?"

Liana steps closer, into the throng of advisors. "The Fuegorra has chosen *Lady Estela* to be one of its wise women. Our future queen is a seer."

My eyebrow shoots up. I am shocked. Possibilities start to flow through my mind, more glimmers of good news in a sea of bad.

Except... she tried to kill me last night. My hope hardens as I look into her eyes. Fear is the only emotion present. Fear of whipping. As if she has any reason to be. Sadness lurks behind my anger.

The back of my throat is dry, my tongue is thick. "Thank you for telling me. If you would excuse us, we are in a council meeting."

Vann stiffens next to me. The meeting is just about to end, but Estela doesn't know that.

I watch Liana bite her tongue, clearly wanting to speak. "Of course, King Teo."

I watch them leave, still stuck in this impossible feeling.

"Forgive me, friends. You are all free to leave," I say and Svanna snorts.

"Was there something you required of me personally, Your Highness?" Salo grits out, staying behind.

"Lord Salo, allow me to ex—" I start.

He holds up his hand. "Please. My brother believed in the possibility of mates to be the best discoveries for our people. He chattered about it nonstop. Do not dishonor him by feeling guilt over his death—he has given you all a gift. Let him rest in peace."

My eyes burn and I think of Tirin's First Cut ceremony, when he mined his own stone and had it placed in his chest. So eager. So bright. "Of course. May your brother rest in the stone."

He nods his head once with a harsh, jerky movement. "Again I ask, anything else?"

I shake my head. "No. Thank you."

He leaves, and my insides are swirling vortex. Vann turns to me. "I will oversee the hunter group and tell you what I find later."

"Thank you, friend." I place my hand on his shoulder.

"Strength, like the stone beneath our feet, King Teo. Congratulations on your queen," he says and slips out.

CHAPTER 20

OPAL
ESTELA

When faced with the option between spending the rest of the day in my room and going out to start working, I chose the latter. Enough time has passed wallowing in fear.

Liana leads me down the hallway, glancing back at me. "Do you want to go weave with your redheaded friend?" she asks.

I shake my head. "Do you garden down here? It doesn't seem like you have many fresh crops, but I have worked with plants and herbs."

The crystal-laden woman looks over her shoulder and bites the piercing in her mouth. "I'll send you with Ulla."

My eyebrows draw together. "Who's that?"

She smiles. "She's the head healer, but she also oversees the singers and the meals. You'll like her."

I glance up at the woman. "Why?"

Liana laughs. "She might be the other person who tires as quickly of Ma'Teo as you."

"Lead the way then," I say, following Liana down a flight of stairs and into what seems like a greenhouse. Rows of various mushrooms, all of which I can't identify, are growing on the shelves. A woman with silver hair pulled back in a tight bun is tending to one of the rows, humming softly to herself. She turns when she hears us approach and smiles warmly at Liana.

I freeze. It's the woman who keeps looking at Teo like he broke her heart.

"Liana, what brings you down here?" Ulla asks, placing a few mushrooms in her basket and wiping dirt from her hands onto her apron.

"I have someone who would like to help with your cooking," Liana replies.

Ulla's gaze falls on me, and her smile dims. "The king's bride." She yanks her gaze back to Liana. "Surely she should be working with something other than food. Perhaps the crystal caverns?"

Liana shrugs. "I should speak with the king before taking her there."

Ulla raises her eyebrow. "You? Ask permission? Weren't you the one who just barged into our meeting, telling anyone who would listen that she was chosen by the Fuegorra."

Liana nods. "Yes, I was." Then she turns on her heel and leaves.

I stand there, unsure of what to do. Then, one of the other slaves comes in. He's wearing a bright expression, which softens his pockmarked face. My eyes study how he now wears a braid in his short hair.

"Hello!" he calls cheerfully. "Estela, right?"

I nod. "Yes." Then I grow uncomfortable. "I'm sorry, what is your name?

His smile grows impossibly wider. "Luiz. I've been hearing all about you. Glad to see you are well."

My throat runs dry. "What do you mean?"

He smiles. "You were the first human mate. Because of you, they lined us all up and made us meet every Enduar. That's how I met Neela, my mate." His look is wistful, and I can see the love in his eyes.

I smile back at him, surprised by his kindness, especially since I had been rude to Neela during a dinner. Guilt festers in my chest. I've been shortsighted with these Enduares. "It's nice to meet you, Luiz."

Ulla watches us, confused. "Don't you two already know each other?"

We both shake our head, but it's Luiz who says, "Slaves were friendly with each other to a point in the slave dens, but nothing like how we act here in Enduvida."

Ulla nods slowly. "Interesting. Well, if you're going to stand around talking, you might as well make yourself useful. Here, take this basket and start harvesting those amethyst caps. And don't break their stems or they'll excrete a bitter flavor." She points at a beautiful mushroom with a pale purple top and dots of turquoise.

I nod and take the basket, grateful for something to do as my unease increases.

The hairs on the back of my neck stand up, almost like a prickling awareness I'm being watched. I turn around, only to find the darkness of the caves, so I return to the mushrooms and Ulla starts humming again. It's a beautiful melody, one that I don't recognize. I ask her about it.

She seems startled that I would notice. Not quite upset, just uncomfortable. "It's a song about our main goddess, Grutabela," she says, her lips tight. "I wrote it a long time ago, when I was more hopeful about finding love."

"It's beautiful," I reply. "Do you still write songs?"

Ulla nods. "Usually for the festival. It will happen soon, I suppose you... You will be there."

I look up at her. "You mean the Festival of Endu?" That's my wedding date.

Luiz, somewhat oblivious to our strained interactions, announces that he will head to the cooking pot with his bounty, so I turn to look at the Enduar.

She nods. "Yes. That's the one."

"I won't just be there, I will be getting married. Is that a problem?" I start to prod. The jealousy in my chest is unreasonable. I've never had to fight for another man, and I don't know how to handle the ugly emotion. It takes mere moments to check and make sure Teo can't hear my thoughts.

She shakes her head. "No."

"Are you Teo's lover?" I blurt out. The urge to cover my mouth is strong, but I don't want to back down. The suspicion has been creeping since the first time I saw them together. It has wormed its way into my mind, and I can't let it go.

She looks at me, horrified. "You humans have mouths full of dirt. He is yours now, isn't that enough?"

I tighten my grip on my basket. "But you had a relationship?" She rutted him. It shouldn't make me disappointed.

She faces me full on. I realize I've picked a fight with someone too tall for me, yet again. My knees start to shake.

"How old are you, little human?"

I look up at her, refusing to back down. "Twenty five."

She laughs. "Twenty five years?" she cuts off the ugly sound. "Teo is one hundred and four years old. I am ninety-four."

My mouth hangs open in shock. I knew there was a difference in lifespan between humans and Enduares, but the number still catches me off guard. Ulla, despite her stern exterior, suddenly seems fragile and old.

"I didn't mean to..." I trail off, my voice softening.

Ulla cuts me off with a wave of her hand. "It's fine. We Enduares live longer, but it does not make us immune to feelings," she says, her voice low. "Teo and I, we were once lovers long ago. After—It matters not. We have not been together in a very long time."

I nod, unsure of what to say. The revelation brings me little comfort, yet it explains some of the tension between the two of them.

Ulla turns away from me to continue collecting, and I follow suit. The task of harvesting the mushrooms is surprisingly soothing, and I let my hands move almost automatically.

The tension in my soul eases the longer we work. The silence is nice, and when she takes me to a table to cut, she watches me for several moments. I keep my head down and let unspoken words hang in the air.

CHAPTER 21

UNAKITE

TEO

My sword slices through exoskeleton and the *aradhlum* screeches just before I cleave off its head. Its fangs glint in the spell light and its thick, viscous innards drain onto the ground. I don't have time to watch the eight long legs twitch before I jab at another spider.

"A little further up next time, Teo," Vann says, laughing. "You're spilling out all the good parts."

I chuckle and wipe the sweat from my brow. "How about I slice one right down the middle for you?" I reply.

We have been hunting these *aradhlumes* for hours. It's an excellent distraction from the humans.

As I charge forward, my blade glinting in the dimly lit cave, I can't help but feel a thrill rush through me. This was what I was born to do: fight to protect those I love.

Suddenly, there is a high-pitched squeal from behind me. I spin around to see a particularly vicious *aradhlum* wrap its long, hairy legs around Vann.

Without hesitation, I rush to Vann, my sword drawn. The *aradhlum's* grip is strong, but I can see its vulnerability. I quickly slice through its legs one by one, freeing Vann from its grasp. The spider writhes in agony, only to grow still when Vann smashes it's head with his cleaver.

"Any bites?" I ask.

Aradhlum venom can burn if not wiped away fast.

Vann shakes his head, panting with exertion. "No, I'm well."

I nod and sheath my sword before I start to gather the bodies. "Let's take these to Ulla so that she can prepare them for the *ruh'glumdlores*."

He grins and piles the gory spiders on his back. When I bend down to inspect the one that I beheaded, I look into its dead eyes and tighten my jaw.

"Come now, back to real life," Vann says over his shoulder. I finish stacking my three spiders on my back and move ahead.

As we make our way through the winding cave system, I wonder if I will see Estela. She's been working with Ulla, but I haven't spoken to her since the funeral.

When we reach the top of the tunnel, it spits us out into the city, and I catch sight of her standing next to Ulla. A part of me wants to drop the bounty before we arrive, but that's cowardly. I didn't spend all that time killing spiders to turn back now.

Estela hasn't spotted me yet. She looks beautiful as ever with her dark brown hair tied back and her dark eyes shining as she works with the food. The first time I saw her after she started eating regularly, it was a transformation. Seeing her stand with our people makes my heart swell.

"My King, Lord Vann," Ulla greets us. "Did you have luck with the *aradhlumes*?"

I nod and drop the spiders off at Ulla's feet. "We got a good haul," I reply.

Estela looks up at me and freezes. "Are you all right? You look exhausted."

I frown. "I'm fine," I say, trying to sound convincing. "Just a long hunt."

Estela approaches me, and her eyes scan my face. A burst of anger erupts. I thought I had forgiven her for the poison, but seeing her now, not having heard the apology from her lips, I pull away.

"I'm going to rest," I announce and leave before my mate can utter a word.

I walk through Enduvida, heading towards my chambers. The streets are almost empty, as most of our people are either working or resting at this time of day. I don't care for the emptiness. The silence only amplifies the thoughts in my head.

When I reach my chambers, I lock the door behind me and collapse onto my bed. I need to clear my thoughts through meditation, but they keep swirling, like a never-ending vortex. With a groan, I sit up and grab a bottle of mead from my bedside table. It's not the best coping mechanism, but it's all I've got right now.

As I chug the mead, I try to push away the thoughts of Estela, but they keep creeping back in. I wonder what she's doing now, whether she's thinking about me.

It stays like that until I drift into sleep.

∽

WHEN MY EYES OPEN, THERE'S RED AS FAR AS THE EYE CAN SEE. IT COATS *my armor, my hands, even streams in my eyes. The stench of bodies overpowers my nose.*

My mother is in the middle of the field, hanging from a tall post. The Giant King is positioned near her body, watching as a pack of wolves tear apart her legs.

I am filled with an intense rage, a desire to destroy the giants in my path. Another spear swipes toward my head. My sword is already in my hand, and I'm slicing through enemy soldiers as if they were made of paper.

"Troll Prince!" the king calls. "You thought you could kill my wife to end the war?"

I don't respond to him. Instead, I focus all of my energy into defeating him and his army. My sword cuts through their armor, and I move forward with ruthless determination.

Vann appears at my side, hacking away at the mid-section of another giant warrior. The ugly, squelching sound of blood pouring out accompanies the grunts and shouts of the giants.

Five lay at our feet, then ten. Then I lose count as my sword lobs off another head. It won't change my mother's death, but it will teach the giants a lesson.

A horn breaks through the battle. My father. I look up, trying to see him amidst the piles of bodies, only to look back to my dead mother. The rage reignites and I lift my sword about my head and charge.

Something smacks me. My instincts take over, grabbing the person standing above me and pinning them onto my bed.

I'm drenched in sweat, my heart pounding in my chest. I try to catch my breath and remind myself that it was just a dream. But the images are still so vivid. I can't even see beneath me.

"Teo, wake up!" Estela says, panicked, her hands on my cheeks. It's disorienting. "You were having a nightmare."

I take a deep breath and sit back, wiping the sweat from my forehead. The room is dimly lit, the only light coming from the flickering candles on the bedside table.

My eyes drop to the woman pinned to the bed beneath me. The nightmares fade as I take in her flushed cheeks and furious expression. My gut stirs. *What plans I have for that pretty mouth*, I say to her mind.

She startles and pushes herself up. "You hurt me," she accuses, pointing to the beginnings of a bite mark on her throat.

My cock presses against my breaches. Bite marks aren't intended to hurt. I push off the bed, trying to escape the heat.

"Well, you tried to kill me," I pant. "What are you doing here?"

She scowls at me. "You looked sick. They made me bring you food."

"And how did you get in?" I demand, clearly remembering locking the door behind me.

She shifts her weight, and I look at the hallway between our rooms. *It's open.*

I groan and rub my temples. Has she seen the window? This is exactly what I needed, Estela being here, after the dream. "I don't need food," I said. "I need space. You can go now."

Her face turns red with hurt and anger. "Forgive me," she says, her voice cracking. "If I haven't said it yet, I am sorry."

I close my eyes, and the images of my mother, and the giant king cloud my mind once more. The dream was a reminder that I can't trust anyone, not even Estela. "Nothing's changed, Estela. You still tried to kill me. I don't need empty apologies." *Isn't that exactly what you wanted?* I think. But no, she has to mean it.

Her lips purse, and she stands up. I panic.

"Don't use the passage between our rooms again."

"Fine." Then she leaves.

CHAPTER 22
NEPHRITE
ESTELA

Two days have passed since Teo bit me and the world feels different. Liana still hasn't let me have my first lesson with the Fuegorra, Teo avoids me, and I hardly see Arlet while I work with Ulla. Each day that I walk over the bridge to my workstation is a day I feel stronger. The healthier I am, the better I will be when I finally get to free Mikal.

I keep coming back in the mushroom house, finding solace with the fungi. I like learning about their shapes, their flavors, and the way they grow. They inspired me so much that I brought the few herbs left in my box.

"These flowers have seeds in the center. Do you see?" I say, rubbing silky pink petals between my fingers.

Ulla nods. "But how do we use those to grow under the mountain? Plants need light, yes?"

I nod. "Exactly. But I have been thinking, if the Ardorflame works for humans, why not plants? Liana told me the spell lights are powered by the Ardorflame, too. If we put the plants under them, and you sing to them once per day, perhaps we could encourage growth."

Ulla smiles as she kneels next to me. Her large, feminine fingers splay out over her knees while she watches me pop out another seed. When her humming starts up again, I pause.

"I wonder if there is a song for plants," I muse.

She pauses. "There may be yet. We have songs for everything else. I will have to look through the remaining ancestral library."

I start digging a hole in front of me, but my eyebrows draw together. "I never learned to read the common tongue. We humans... well, the written words we once had are meaningless."

Ulla picks up a few of my seeds. "Would you like me to teach you to read in my language?"

I look up at Ulla, surprised. This newfound willingness to help catches me off guard, considering how hostile she was initially.

"I would appreciate that," I reply, handing her the seeds. "The more I can do to help, the better. Maybe I'll stumble upon something useful."

Ulla nods in agreement, fingering the seeds as she studies me. There is something unreadable in her expression, then she uses her finger to draw a symbol in the dust on the ground.

"These are our letters," she starts listing them and each of their sounds.

In the middle of repetition, a new Enduar woman appears at the mouth of the greenhouse. She seems familiar, and her hair is worn in a braid down her back. Her armor and grit-stained face showcase her as a miner.

"Time for defensive training," the new woman says. I finally recognize her as one of the council members—the one mated to the woman with a baby.

Ulla smiles. "Svanna! We are learning to read Enduar."

Svanna quirks an eyebrow. "Our reluctant queen? Learning the Enduar tongue?" She laughs and asks me directly, "Finally see us as real people after Tirin's death?"

Pangs of guilt and shame for my past thoughts and actions hit me in the chest. I find myself nodding fervently at Svanna's question.

"I was wrong," I admit.

Svanna regards me for a moment before nodding curtly. "Yes, you were. For that, you will be my fighting partner today."

She turns on her heel and marches out of the mushroom house, leaving Ulla and me in silence.

My new friend grimaces. "It's not a wise idea to keep her waiting," Ulla says, breaking the silence. "Shall we?"

I nod and rise to my feet, brushing the dirt off my pants. As we deposit the seeds in a small bag and make our way out, I am surprised by how many Enduar warriors are gathered to train. They are all dressed in armor, carrying weapons and shields.

For a moment, I forget that I no longer fear the Enduares. They are a vision of their terrible reputation. Stories of trolls ravaging the battlefield are much easier to understand with singers bolstering the group with a dark, guttural song. I think of waking Teo from his nightmare and the way his silver hair scrambled around his face while agony painted the planes of his face deep purple.

Svanna stands at the front of the group, her armor and face scrunched up into a fierce expression. She gestures for me to join her.

"Lady Estela finally joins us!" she says, turning to her troops. "Tell the group, small human. Have you ever held a weapon?"

Memories of when I stabbed Keksej cloud my mind. I swallow hard, trying to push past the fear rising in my chest. "I stabbed my old master," I choke out when Svanna rests her hand on my shoulder.

Her eyebrows shoot up. "Interesting. Well, today, we'll teach you how to properly defend yourself. Let's get started."

Svanna grabs a stone sword and hands it to me. I take it with shaking hands, feeling ill-equipped to hande such a long blade. But I push away the fear and remind myself that I'm here to learn—to be better.

We start slow, with basic defensive moves, but soon, we're sparring back and forth, and the sound of our swords clashing fills the air. Svanna has been using her body as a weapon against stone and giants for longer than I've been alive, but I'm determined to keep up with her.

As we continue, my fear fades. The reverberation of our swords and the sweat on my brow make me feel exhilarated.

I think of Teo above me, looking down at me with dark eyes. Wanting me. I had been foolish not to lean into his touch then. When I spin and lunge, I think of him. Proving to him that I can live down in this mountain. Making him want me again.

For once, I'm not just surviving. It hurts that Mikal isn't here to share it with me, but he will come soon. And when he does... this cave will be our home.

Who would have known that I'd find my home with the monsters?

CHAPTER 23
OBSIDIAN
TEO

Liana sits on the table next to me, surrounded by the scrolls I've spent days picking off the shelves.

There's a letter in Liana's hands.

"We are overjoyed at your decision to invite us to your wedding, King Ma'Teo. We will arrive with your emissaries in four days' time. Sincerely, King Arion," she reads and looks at me. "This is good news."

I groan and put my head on the table. "Is it? The elves haven't said anything to us in three decades, and suddenly they are coming to our caves at the same time as we are dealing with a monster infestation." Pushing back, I sit in my chair.

"What exactly are you hoping to accomplish with this visit? You want the promise of allies?" She lifts her eyebrows and tilts her head to the side. "Or, are you going to test if the elves can mate with humans, too?

I pause. "Believe it or not, I hadn't thought of that." When I look at the wise woman, she smiles down at me. Pushing to my feet, I take her hand and kiss it. "You are a genius. I've been trying to find answers without much luck."

She laughs. "This enthusiasm is contagious."

I look at her sideways. "Arlet hasn't been mated yet, right?"

A strange look crosses her face as she shakes her head. "No."

I nod. "Good. Get her a dress made. We'll introduce her to Arion on the first night. And then..." My mind races. "Then we'll tell them that we need to go against the giants and free the humans."

The wise woman smiles. "Then you will be able to bring Estela's brother back?"

I purse my lips. "I think I may need to do that first. The Second Prince seems amenable to selling us slaves for the right price, but I am not eager to deal with him yet. The ugly sop was spewing disgusting rhetoric for most of our meeting. I may have lied and told him that Estela was dead."

"I can imagine." Liana nods her head. "From where I'm sitting, all we can do right now is solve the mystery of the monsters in the mists before the elves arrive."

I look back at her. "Any ideas?"

She tilts her head to the side, her expression falling. "I believe the monsters in the caves are the same species that attacked Estela on the mountain. They are magical, but something we haven't seen before. I've watched enough of them feeding on animals to know they are some sort of succubus, but little else. If you send a couple of hunters, I believe they'll be able to clear everything out quickly."

I put a cork in the ink pot that I've been draining for the last day and sit back in my chair. "That is good. I'll send Vann in the morning. He'll fill in while Lothar is gone."

Liana hesitates. "I have considered having Estela touch the Fuegorra to see if she can get a clearer image of the monsters, since she's already had an experience with them."

Her name brings a wave of bitterness and excitement. "How has her training been going?"

She shakes her head. "Not well. A part of me fears what will happen once we start—I've never trained anyone before, and much of our mysticism has been lost. There are things, hidden truths, that I have let fall through the cracks. It's also hard to know how a human will react to Enduar magic. For example, I don't know how to train her without draining her health." Tapping her fingers to her mouth, she looks back at me.

I shrug. "She's a hardy woman. Every drop you add to her knowledge is still a drop added. It would benefit us all. I say you should push her harder."

Liana's smile spread into a wicked grin. "Is that so? Well then. Perhaps there is something else I could show her. You were the last to take a *glacialmara* for a ride, yes?"

My nostrils flair. "You're not taking her to see the crystal wraiths."

She smiles. "What if I took her to meet *drathorinna*?"

I sit up. "Absolutely not. *Drathorinna* is off-limits to all except you."

Her head tilts back, and she lets out a deep laugh. "I thought you wanted me to push her since you are so displeased with her actions of late? Peace, you stubborn man. Did you forget that your bride is also a Fuegorra reader? She'll be fine." The wise woman casts me a sidelong glance. "You, however, are not guaranteed safety if you try to follow us."

My grip tightens on one of the scrolls. "You just told me you were afraid to finish training her because she's weak."

Liana shoots me an unimpressed look. "And here I thought that you would be in a good mood because of the elves."

"I am glad about the elves. I just..." There are many things weighing down the corners of my mouth. The bruising bite on Estela's neck, death, monsters under my own roof, and, as always, the giants wanting more diamonds. If they are selling them to amass wealth, who is buying from them?

"You have just convinced me to let her finally have her first lesson," the woman says, biting her mouth piercing.

I growl. "Be careful."

Liana smirks, and absentmindedly picks up one of the scrolls. "Did you know that her brother is half-giant?"

My specs are crooked on my nose, and I take them off to rub my eyes. "Estela's brother?"

She nods. I think back to the smell of giant blood on her, it could have been his. "Vann sent a scout to get information. Many thought he was her actual child, but he is only nine years her junior."

Liana slides off of the table. "Was she raped by one of the princes?"

I take a sharp breath. "I don't know. The princes were commanded to never touch her, but Rholker said he had."

She replaces the scroll and returns to the table. "I have not seen much of her life, as she will continue to be clouded until she learns. One thing I must say," she looks directly at me, "when you finally break past her walls, it will be glorious."

I let out a mirthless laugh. "It is strange. On the one hand, I want to forgive her. To trust her completely, but on the other hand, she tried to poison me."

Liana pulls out a bottle and places it on the table between us. "Have you talked to her about it?"

I roll my eyes. "I've been busy."

When I don't take the bottle, she picks it up and takes a swig. "Well, I'm off to torture your mate."

The growl that rips past my lips is a warning.

She smirks. "Drink up—I brought this for you since the bags under your eyes tell me you haven't slept in a week."

When she holds out the bottle again, I accept it tentatively. "Yes, yes. Now leave me be."

Liana pushes off the table and walks out of the room.

"*And be careful,*" I call to the wise woman.

No response. I take a deep breath and ease back. It is better to be surrounded by scrolls than a woman who would try to kill me.

Checking to ensure I am alone, I reach for a romantics scroll and continue reading. The words are starting to blur together, I have taken on too many topics at once—from mating across the centuries, to elves, and trying to decipher more about the mists in our cavern.

After rolling up one of the romantics tightly, I plop it into the metal container and return it to the wall of texts. When Lo'Niht wrote that a mate was the greatest gift, clearly he had never tried a strong shot of mead.

When I return to my seat, I pick up my bottle instead of another scroll and let my senses swim away.

CHAPTER 24
MOONSTONE
ESTELA

Another nightmare scalds my sleep. Taunting me with memories of the Second Prince touching me, trying to pin me down once again, this time with the intent to ravage.

I wake up with a start, gasping for air and shaking with fear. Sometimes, I vomit after night terrors; others, I just stare at the walls of my suite while I sink back into the depths of the tub, thinking of all the people who avoid me.

Arlet and our distanced friendship. Teo. A few hours soaking does good for my body, but little for my mood.

When Liana comes for me, it is a sweet respite.

"Enough moping," she says. "There is a visitor coming who will help us with the giants and the slaves. That means I have time for you to learn about our sacred stones."

We hurry out of the room, and my heart jolts. Did Teo send someone to get Mikal? "Who left Enduvida?"

"Ask Teo," she says and I frown. I'm too weary from sleepless nights to fight.

She takes me behind the castle, and down a tunnel I don't

recognize. Everything in Enduvida takes forever to walk to, but this is deep. Far deeper than the Parting Cave we visited.

The air is hot and steamy. We stop in a small construction that looks like a stable. A twinkling sound starts seconds before something bucks against one of the stalls.

I jump back, terrified, and look at Liana. "What the hell was that?"

She smiles. "These are *glacialmaras*. Crystal wraiths, we ride them when we must travel far." She crosses to one of the stalls and opens the doors, revealing something that looks like a long floating icicle. Its body bends back and forth like a serpent.

I gasp. "Teo brought one of those to save me."

She nods as what I assume to be the wraith's head nuzzles into her hand. She grins at the eyeless creature. Then she gestures for me to join her.

Tentatively, I approach the open stall. The *glacialmara* turns its head to look at me, and I shiver. It's beautiful and terrifying all at once, and I'm not sure I want to ride it.

Liana notices my hesitation and chuckles. "Don't worry, they're quite gentle. But hold on tight, they are fast."

I take a deep breath and climb onto the *glacialmara's* back. Its icy body is smooth and cold to the touch, but it begins to warm up as Liana climbs onto the back of the creature in the stall next to me. Suddenly, the *glacialmaras* take off at an incredible speed. Wind whips through my hair and I scream in exhilaration and terror.

As we speed through the tunnels, I can't help but feel a strange sense of freedom. For a brief moment, I forget about my nightmares and the weight of my duties.

When we near a fork in the tunnel, I turn to the wise woman. "Where now?" I call out.

She winks. "Take the right side." Then she speeds up, leaving behind her laughter.

I follow along, also laughing as the creature speeds on. The Fuegorra on my chest lights up as we move, and I am shocked by the ease with which I can navigate, as if the creature reads my thoughts.

The cave twists and turns a few more times, and then we are spit out into an enormous cavern filled with icy white light. In the middle, there is a wraith easily a hundred times the size of the one under me.

I rear back, and the *glacialmara* responds, slowing to a stop. We dismount, and I gawk at the massive monster in front of us.

"What the hell is that?" I ask.

Liana approaches the entity fearlessly and begins to speak in a language I don't understand. The wraith responds with a tinkle, and suddenly Liana presents me with a small crystal. "This is *drathorinna*. Mother of all our little wraiths."

I blink, taking one step forward and guiding my wraith with my hand. "Are you telling me the one I'm riding will grow to be that size?" This world is far more magnificent and wonderful than I could have previously known.

She shakes her head.

"No, it won't. Drathorinna is the mother, a queen among the crystal wraiths if you will, but she is unique. Only one is born every thousand years. She's a rare and powerful being, and we consider her sacred." She pauses, looking at me with a serious expression. "Much like you. I know we have not spoken more of your talent, but you must understand what it is to be a Fuegorra reader."

Liana reaches out and touches the enormous beast. The hand around her spot starts to grow. "Each wraith has a special connection to its rider, but the connection can easily be changed from one day to the next. *Drathorinna* only accepts women like you and I."

My heart pounds in my chest as I listen to her words. The

depth of the responsibility she has bestowed upon me is not lost. "What do you mean by accepting only women like us?" I ask, already knowing the answer before she speaks.

Liana smiles, her eyes alight with a fierce determination. "*Drathorinna* is a creature that only chooses certain women to ride her. Women with power, strength, and the ability to read the Fuegorra. Like you and me. When the last reader taught me how to work with the crystals, she brought me here first. Now, I bring you."

I swallow. "You expect me to ride her?"

Liana shakes her head and grabs onto one of the crystal scales lining the *drathorinna's* back. "Not today, no. But, to be considered a wise woman, you will ride her one day."

Though Liana is old, she climbs up onto the wraith with ease. I watch in awe as she moves with grace, her movements fluid and practiced.

Liana beckons me to come closer. "Stand there, by her side," she says. "Feel the power emanating from her body."

Slowly, I step forward, afraid that if I move too quickly, I'll spook the wraith queen. Waves of power crash into me, emanating from every scale and crystal.

"All right down there?" she calls.

I look up and nod. My hand reaches out toward the icy crystals, and a jolt of electricity runs through my fingers as I touch them. A deep buzzing sound reverberates through my body, and I close my eyes, savoring the feeling of the wraith's power washing over me.

Liana chuckles, and her boots land right in front of me. "Don't let it go to your head, child. You still don't know the names of the crystals. We have much to do."

I open my eyes and turn to face her. "What do you mean?"

She's already walking away. "Come on. We'll ride back to the surface."

I grab my *glacialmara* again and follow after her.

As we ride back through the tunnels, Liana falls silent. I take my time, feeling the muggy air whip across my face while speeding past glinting crystals of every size. When it's time to put the creature back in its stall, I feel sad.

"Don't worry. We'll return," Liana says. "You'll just have to wait until after your wedding."

I look at her and grin. "Thank you."

She chuckles and continues walking.

"You humans have no sense of what you might call crystallography in the common tongue. Enduares feel the stones like you feel the wind, the air." As she speaks, Liana leads me to the small grotto tucked away at the back of the palace. She's laid out three red stones on the ground, but my eyes are caught on the Fuegorra in the center of the room. I think of the visions it's shown me. That image of Teo and I, where we were happy. Mated.

"Eyes down here," she says as she squats. "Here is your first lesson—tell me which is the Fuegorra."

I kneel beside Liana and study the three stones carefully. They all look the same shade of red, and each radiates a faint glow, but one is definitely brighter than the other two. When my hand hovers over the stone, I can feel a faint warmth emanating from it.

"That one," I point to the Fuegorra, and Liana nods in approval.

"Hmm. Yes," she says. "Now, what are the others called?"

I blink. "I don't know."

She harrumphs. "Just as I thought. This is red beryl—we use those for healing. This other one is red topaz. We sing to this one as a message of respect and loyalty during mating ceremonies. It symbolizes faithfulness, Estela."

Heat spreads across my cheeks like a rash. "I am hardly a part of you people. How can you demand my loyalty to a man I barely know?"

Liana gives me a long, hard look but doesn't say anything for a moment. "I cannot answer that for you. Let me show you something else."

She reaches into her deep pockets and pulls out something that seems to make the other crystals dim. Her long blue fingers unfold to reveal a diamond, much like the one I was dazzled by on my first day here.

Though it still catches the light streaming in from the mushrooms outside, it seems dull and ugly in comparison to any of the other stones we've looked at.

Liana's expression tells a grim story. "This is a blood diamond. It was formed from the lava that ravaged the continent. It carries the blood of giants, elves, humans... Enduares. It's cursed and brings misfortune to any Enduar that possesses it."

Liana holds the diamond out toward me, and I tentatively take it. As soon as it touches my skin, a cold shiver runs down my spine. This stone feels wrong. It's not just that it doesn't glow like the others, but it is heavier somehow—like it's tugging downward on my hand.

I remember the nightmares, the betrayal, and the fear that have been my constant companions lately. It all screeches in my head, making my temples pulse. I yank my hand back and let the stone fall to the ground.

She nods. "The magic is strong inside of you. Stronger than most Enduares. Most can sense the wrongness of this stone, but few would be hurt by it."

I rub my hand. "Do you sell these to the giants to curse them?" I think back to how much wealth these pretty gems have amassed for my old masters.

She shakes her head. "If only it were that simple. It is cursed for us, and us alone. But it is the only way we can have contact with the outside world. Only certain miners can work with the diamond deposits, and they are stored in a room in King Teo's wing of the palace."

I pause, slightly upset by her words. "How does it curse you?"

She looks grim. "Irsh and Mele were one of our mated pairs. They had a son, Sama, and they were killed in an unusual collapse while mining the diamond for the giants. The stone cutter, Flova, who was shaping the diamonds, fell ill."

I suck in a breath. "Is he all right?"

She nods, bending to pick up the stone. "Yes, the herbs you brought us healed him in a few days."

As she tucks the diamond into her pocket, she continues, "But the diamond latches onto the psyche of those who possess it. It drives them mad with greed and desperation, just like Teo's father. Many say they are dead stones, but I believe each one carries a bit of Teo'Likh. We keep them locked away, but sometimes I fear it's an unnecessary evil."

I wince as I consider the implications of the cursed stone. They seem like they don't truly understand why the giants were so enamored with the gems. "Do you not know why the giants ask for so many?"

Her eyebrows draw together in a frown. "No. They seem to value them for their beauty and rarity, but beyond that, we do not ask questions if they bring the herbs."

I weigh her words in my mind while I think of all the information I gleaned while a slave. The giants trade with other lands. I do not know how the people are called, but they have been amassing allies and wealth for quite some time.

The words to tell her are on the tip of my tongue, but Liana's smile returns, and she pulls out a small leather pouch from her pocket. "Let me give you something you will enjoy much more. It's called hematite. It's known for its grounding properties and is often used in meditation and connecting with the earth. Here, hold this one and close your eyes."

It takes me a few moments, but I keep the words inside and do as she says, feeling the cool weight of the stone in my palm. Immediately, a sense of calm washes over me, like a weight has been lifted from my shoulders. It's a welcome rest after the diamond.

We continue like that, with her handing me different stones and chirping notes to make them sing. When the mid-day tones of the clock sound, I leave the tunnel to help Ulla prepare a meal.

I'm heavy with thoughts of the giants and what they were doing with the diamonds.

As I enter the kitchen, my mind is still whirring with ideas. Ulla greets me warmly, and I smile back at her, trying to shake off the heavy thoughts.

"Is there anything I can help with?" I ask, looking around the warm, cozy kitchen that smells of mushrooms and meat.

She nods. "Yes, thank you. You can start chopping these for the soup." Then, she hands me a basket filled with black fungi.

As I start slicing the fragrant mushroom stems, Luiz rejoins us, bringing water for the soup pot. Neela helps him in, before leaning down to kiss him and wander off. She still ignores me, but I do not mind.

"Luiz, did you and Neela already have a mating ceremony?" I ask, my conversation with Liana still on my mind.

He pauses, brings a leg of some animal to his own cutting table and nods. "It was quick, private. We didn't invite anyone other than Liana and Ulla."

My brows furrow just as a child comes in, running up to Ulla. The child has long, straight silver hair and bright blue eyes, and she holds a small wicker basket filled with crystal shards. She asks something in the Enduar tongue, smiling with small, pointed teeth.

Ulla smiles, and grabs a bit of mushroom off of my board to hand to the girl. There's familiarity between the two, but it is different from what I felt taking care of Mikal.

I am used to children, but slaves with children didn't live where I lived. My reading lessons with Ulla have been going well, but I can hardly understand the girl. Ulla says something else, I think it's about speaking the common tongue, and the girl smiles.

"Look, Flova gave me, Ulla!" she exclaims in the common tongue with a thick accent. It is good to see so many children speaking two languages, just as the slaves once did.

Ulla smiles and takes the basket from her. "These are beautiful, Rila. You should give them to your father for his singing."

Rila bounces on her feet, her eyes darting between Luiz and me. "Help?" she asks, looking up at Ulla hopefully.

Ulla shakes her head. "Not right now, dear. Why don't you go play outside with the other younglings?"

Rila nods eagerly and runs back outside.

"*Mierda[1],*" Luiz mumbles while grabbing his basket. "Forgot the other meat." He walks back out of the pavilion and I continue chopping in silence for a few more minutes before I speak up again.

"She is sweet. Slaves were taught the common tongue young, too," I say conversationally. It is uncomfortable to put myself out there, but Ulla is kind.

Ulla pauses, looking up at me while she passes her elegant hands over her apron. "Yes. We have something like a school for the younglings. It is small. We have less than thirty children in our halls. Her father is a singer, and her mother is a miner. Siya."

I nod. "That is nice." I think of these people, their culture hidden from the world while they slowly die. It is wrong.

"How many Enduares are there?" I ask.

"Around three hundred, with the arrival of you all."

The silence that follows is uncomfortable. We always had enough children in Zlosa, we never worried about our future, just working. I meant what I said to Arlet—I would enjoy having a child. Especially a child in a place where children were so completely and utterly treasured.

I finish chopping the mushrooms, and Ulla adds them to the pot, stirring the soup and humming to herself. Eventually, Luiz comes as well, and we work quietly while my mind swims with thoughts.

They continue to call me an Enduar, tell me I have something to offer. That I am needed.

Ulla gives me something else to cut, and I start working on the root quickly.

A shout breaks the silence. It reminds me of times when a slave wasn't properly put down after a rage-induced whipping.

Mine and Ulla's heads snap up, and my careless knife stroke cuts through my finger. I yelp, and Ulla's attention is between me and the Enduares being brought into the hall.

I stick my finger into my mouth to stop the bleeding and slink back as as a group of Enduares carry one of their men over.

Another scream pierces the air, and the hair on my arms stands up as I watch them. The injured Enduar is covered in blood and thrashes against the two hunters holding him. Though he is tall, like all the Enduares, the men carry him as if he were nothing.

Ulla starts barking instructions as she points to the station I had been working on.

After helping them clear off the mushrooms, knife, and any other utensils that I had been using to prepare the food, they put the Enduar with the mangled chest in front of me. His bloody form is something of nightmares. His braid is falling out, and strands are stuck to the hot, red blood, while his powerful limbs hang limply around him.

"Oh gods, Dyrn," Ulla breathes. "He looks like something chewed him up and spit him out," she says in the Enduar language. I'm straining to listen to her words and understand them.

Neither the name nor the man's face spark recognition for me. There is so much blood leaking from his chest and upper arms, coating his entire body. When he breathes, his spine bows like a fish gasping for breath. The Fuegorra on his chest flashes.

"What the fuck happened?" Ulla demands in her native tongue, her hands already darting across his body. When she yanks them away, both her apron and her skin are stained with the deep-colored liquid.

I'd seen the other Enduar killed by Teo's hand, but this is different. It's a tragedy to feel his life slip through my fingers. The blood is red, just like human blood.

Another hunter who had helped carry him, a man with a scar running along his face, takes out a roll of thin woven cloth from his pack and starts to tear it into strips. As he binds one of Dyrn's shoulders, the injured Enduar gives a shout in his language. Ulla shouts back something I don't understand.

The hunter grimaces, then gapes at the wounds on the table. Horrified at the pain.

"Faol," Ulla says, addressing the man.

He backs away a step, then another, then turns around and vomits on the stone.

No one bats an eye. I wish that I could vomit as well, from the roiling in my stomach, but then Arlet comes. She's hurrying along with another one of the Enduares.

"Oh, gods. *Vann*," she practically screeches as she sees Lord Vann's form. My eyebrows draw together. From what I had seen of the two, they had always been cold to each other.

"There was an attack in the tunnel. *Tranquila*[2], Arlet. Everything is all right." I say quickly.

Her hands are skirting around his face, across the blood leaking from his shoulder. She murmurs something I don't understand, but Vann's wounds aren't as severe as Dyrn's, so I turn my attention back to the other table.

With so many humans here, the Enduares continue in the common tongue. "We were exploring the mists. He started walking ahead of us, and he was attacked. Then Lord Vann started screaming as well. The creature was gone by the time we got there."

For a moment, I stand there, shocked while Ulla comes alive. "Did you seal off the tunnel?"

The hunter nods. "Lord Salo is helping the stone benders right now."

Another scream fills the air, ugly and slightly wet sounding. Dyrn's breath is more labored by the second.

Ulla nods but doesn't ask any more questions. Everyone here knows their place—Luiz is tending to the pot over the fire, other Enduares are preparing meat, and I am just standing there. Watching. Horrified at the Enduar's gasping wet breathes.

It isn't until Ulla grabs a few crystals out of her clothing that I realize her hands are shaking. She places the gems around his body. Then, she starts to sing.

Her humming had been soothing, but this is different—like the difference between the taste of stagnant water in a barrel and the bright freshness from a running river. Her melodic tune is precise, intending to serve one function: mend.

I was not awake for most of the healing that had been performed on me, but now I am witnessing the potent breadth of this magic. It seems as though there is nothing it couldn't cure. Except... even the minor lacerations are dripping blood.

"Where are the herbs we brought?" I ask. "He isn't clotting. There is a leaf in the sample box we brought that will help."

Everyone around me looks shocked, but it's Luiz who

answers. His face is tight with fear as he stirs. "Don't you remember? They were all used to heal you and those afflicted with the coughing sickness."

My hands go numb, and I think of the ones in my room. Not all of my herbs had been used on my injuries, I used some to make that poison.

Ulla continues to sing, but the bleeding still doesn't stop, even as red covers the table and drips onto the ground.

Another scream rips from the hunter's throat. The Fuegorra in my chest slowly blinks awake after many hours dormant from the experience in the crystal cave. Its familiar warmth encases me. It feels... kind. Kind in a way I had never known kindness.

Another Enduar comes around, placing steaming water and rags next to the injured hunter. The man isn't getting better, despite the singing. His crystal flashes erratically, and he is still writhing in pain.

I can't stand here and watch this. "Shh, keep still," I command, "Or you'll bleed out faster." I place my hand on his armored leg, and a burst of heat washes through me. The brilliant light of my Fuegorra is reflected in the glow of Dyrn's crystal. I reach up and take his hand.

Ulla gasps and jumps back. She mutters something I assume is a curse, but Dyrn's breath changes. He eases. A lightness takes place in my chest—I am doing something. Healing him, perhaps? Tears slip down my cheeks as I smile. It is a way for me to give back after they wasted their herbs on me.

"No, wait," Ulla's eyes go wide. She looks at me. I replace her at the top of his body. It's sticky with blood.

"That's better, isn't it?" I say gently.

He coughs. "It hurts."

I hold his hand tighter, and the glow brightens.

Suddenly, his eyes find mine. The silver of them sears my vision in a moment of soul-to-soul connection. He silently begs me to continue whatever it is I'm doing. The crystal on my chest glows brighter. Dyrn's breaths get slower. "Teeth," he murmurs. "Watch for the teeth."

I nod. Cold? Teeth? It sounds like what attacked me outside of the mountain. Fear strikes me hard.

"The teeth hurt you. Let me help," I urge.

He nods. "It hurts. I can't feel my feet."

My tears come harder. He's still bleeding. Why isn't the magic working? I thought I was healing him.

"I can't feel my feet," he says again, this time louder.

"You'll feel them soon," I promise. It's all happening too fast. He's lost too much blood.

"My legs," he groans. Then, his breath stills. There's something about his face that is youthful as it relaxes from all of the pain he'd been feeling seconds before. He looks boyish.

"No," I gasp. Desperation claws at my chest, and I press my hands to his bloody wounds, trying to feel for a pulse. Nothing. "NO! I was healing him!" I scream.

I'm surrounded by people, but none of them attempt to approach me. Ulla has already moved over to the other injured Enduar, apparently having more success, judging by the lack of screams. None of them look at me, except Arlet.

Her eyes are fearful as she looks between me and Vann. I look down at my bloody hands.

"I was healing him," I say. No one responds, wrapped up in Vann. I wrap my hands around my rib cage and back away.

I need someone. Anyone.

I keep backing up until I hit something hard and inhuman. I don't need to look up to see an Enduar. My erratic thoughts have betrayed me once again.

"My star, what have you done now?" he asks, snaking a hand around my midsection and pulling me further from the scene.

The tears continue to spill down my cheeks. "You came."

He smiles sadly. "You called."

I start to sob and collapse in his arms. He picks me up with comforting ease and carries me as I cry.

---

1. Shit.
2. Calm down.

CHAPTER 25
AQUAMARINE
TEO

E very bone in my body hums in relief. I'm exhausted, but with Estela close, I feel stronger. Whole. It's ridiculous, honestly. So many days spent apart—all for what?

I do not know if the recognition of a mate could be considered love at first sight, but when Estela walked into the viewing room, I knew we belonged to each other and quickly prepared to put everything aside so that she would stay in the mountain and rise to the destiny fate had chosen for her. Unfortunately, she didn't want me or any of this. The scheming human tried to kill me, even with the stone in her chest nudging her toward matehood.

Perhaps I had used those words too lightly—had expected too much too soon—because, after more than a day of hating her, of wanting to punish her for the crime she'd tried to commit, she is in my arms. Simply because she called for me. Perhaps it is not love, but it is something much stronger than recognition or mere attraction.

It was good that I had come. With the tunnel search having

gone wrong, and my studies of the elves interrupted, I could be there for my people. They need someone to be strong, even if my stomach is churning. Two dead in a matter of days.

As I returned to the queen's suite, Estela holds onto my neck and cries. The right side of my leather tunic is thoroughly soaked with her tears, and it is as instinctual as breathing to stroke her back. The crystals in our chests hum insistently, but the sensation is not demanding. The magic knows best. It simply soothes Estela as her millions of tears dry up.

Her small hand slides down from my neck, only to rest on my chest. It is minuscule compared to my arm. For the first time, I realize how little we know about each other—there has been little time to talk—my decisions have been the ones of a king trying to secure a battle, not a man trying to court a woman.

It is time to stop chasing and let her come to me. I open the door to her room, and she looks up. Her face is red and swollen from her sorrow. After placing her on the bed, I step back.

"Why did you call for me?"

She gapes up at me. "What?"

"I was working on a meeting with the elves," I say plainly. Then I shake my head, agonizing about what she feels. "You call us monsters. But you call for me when you are hurt, especially after the night you escaped."

She stands up. "I don't know what you are talking about. I was hurting, I was—" she swallows. "He just died so fast."

"Why did you beg for someone to come?" I demand.

She blinks faster now. "Because it hurts too much. I can't—I need someone to take it away." She starts to wring her hands. I've never seen her like this, helpless. Worried.

My instincts are stirring, demanding I help her. "You want me to take away the pain."

Her eyes go wide. "What? No." Then her expression shifts, like she isn't sure if she believes what she just said.

I look around her room, scanning her cleaned shelves and neatly arranged clothes before my gaze lands back on her. I would be lying if I said I didn't crave her touch. "Would you feel better if I held you?"

She blinks. Something in her face is desperate, and I realize she's straining. Protecting her thoughts. Something inside of me almost feels angry—we are right here. Alone. We both could find comfort in this moment. "You have me wound around your finger, refusing to take what is yours. Why don't you touch me?"

She watches me, her eyes still wide. "Why would I touch you? Why would you want me to after the poison?" There isn't malice behind her words, she dares me to tell the truth.

The magic between us is troublesome. It asks me to forgive her too easily after days apart. I take a deep breath.

To hell with everything. "You know that there is a tunnel connecting our rooms, but you have never tried to use it." I gesture to the wall where the door is, alongside my secret window. "You do not know that I can see through it."

She swallows. "You... watch me?" There's an unspoken question that hangs in the air. She wants to know why I did not come to see her.

I take a deep breath. "Occasionally, yes. I made sure you never left." Honesty is liberating, especially after so many days dragged on in the pursuit of ignoring her. The constant nausea in my stomach eases and I can relax, despite admitting my secrets.

The softness in her face has been replaced with anger. "Show me?"

I nod and move toward the wall, unlocking the door and twisting the nob open. She stops breathing as I reveal the simple hallway between our rooms, then brushes past me to walk into the short space. Electricity skitters across my skin from where she touches me, and I hear her footsteps against the uncovered stones. The scrape of her leather shoes as she turns and looks at my window grate against my ears.

"It makes sense," she breathes.

I swallow. My fear claws up my throat, threatening to choke me while I search for the words to tell her how afraid I was she would die. "You'll have to forgive me. I have learned to protect what is mine after the giants killed my mother. I can't lose you too."

She faces me. There is still no anger there. "You watched me bathe. That time, you barged into my room to ensure I wasn't drowning."

Shame is hot as it pours over my head and back. She makes me insane. "Yes."

She bites her lip and takes a deep breath. She should be angry enough to cut my head off. The woman I stole from her masters would be.

Instead, she says, "I know about what you did with the giant queen."

I blink. Of all the things I expected her to say, those words were not remotely in my mind. Shame heats my cheeks as she uncovers the part of my past I wish I could forget. "You don't know what you're talking about." Those wounds are buried deep. I try to never think of what that woman did. Does she know what my father did while I was tangled up in Lijasa's sheets?

"I think I do. I've hit a nerve," Estela says, glancing at the window briefly before returning to me.

I ignore her question. "No one had the right to say anything to you. Who was it?" But even as I say the words, I think of Liana.

She raises an eyebrow. "So, you are able to be upset about me knowing something you did not share, but I am not?"

I clench my fists. "Be as angry as you wish, but I didn't want to lie to you anymore."

She steps closer, but I can't handle the closeness now. I move back. "You were comfortable lying about the rest of your life." She gestures to the window. "Slinking in the shadows like the demon I thought you were."

Anger flares within me at her words. "I did not lie. I have chosen to reveal the truth at strategic intervals while making decisions for the survival of our people."

"By keeping me here against my will," she retorts. "And omitting the entirety of your history. You consider the window an act of dishonesty because you saw me naked—watched me sink into the depths of the water and didn't like how you felt. I have seen many men in my life, most of them wanting me for what the king did. You are as easy to identify as a leaf, *Teo*. So sure that you will have me, that you will be the first to touch me—yet you want me willing." She steps forward, taunting me again.

Her words stir something in my gut. They confirm that the Second Prince had lied—that she was left alone. It strikes up a primal need to claim. "What man would not want you willing?" I realize just how close we are. How easy it would be to touch her. To taste her, finally.

Then, something flashes behind her eyes and her haughtiness drains out of her. "The Giant Princes. Hell, even other slaves. I am the daughter of the Giant King's famous whore."

I grit my teeth. "Fated to the Butcher of Giants. Do you not understand that I killed humans for her? My mission was to be close. I killed her comfort slave to get her attention, and then I—"

Her honeyed amber eyes flash up toward me—intense, as if she's seeing me for the first time.

"I've seen your scars, Estela, and they don't scare me. I think, however, that I still scare you. It is wise to fear the monsters in the dark." She doesn't react when my words leave my mouth, so I continue. "My father raised me to be someone very different than I am, but do not ever think I did not intend to kill every last giant who touched you."

"You are an Enduar. You are strong enough to make those choices," she snaps back.

"You are an Enduar now, too. The Queen of the Enduares."

She glares at me, but it lacks the venom I've come to know from her. "You wish for that. How does a slave become a queen?"

I lean forward, unable to resist. The honesty flowing between us is sweet. "How did the whoring son of a king become a leader? He learned."

Her gaze peers into my soul. "You dream too much."

My tail stirs. "You should see what we do in my dreams." My tail slides up, the furry end tracing her delicate face. She gasps and then shivers. I feel a sense of victory as she responds to my touch. I have dreamt of this moment for so long, and now that it is here, I can't help but crave more. The crystals in my chest hum with anticipation as I step closer to her.

I lean in, my lips hovering above hers, close enough to taste her sweet breath. "I can make them a reality, Estela."

She closes her eyes, her breaths shallow and fast. Afraid of what she feels. "You shouldn't."

"But I want to," I whisper, my hand cupping her cheek. "I want you splayed on *my* bed, calling *my* name while I pleasure you senseless, Estela. It's as easy as breathing, and not just because you are my mate. I did not expect to find you, especially not at my age. Do you know that the first time I heard your voice, saw you, I felt hope. Like light shining in a dark cave. Then you came to dinner, with your hair long—Enduar women only wear their hair down with their lovers. I wanted to take you away then, and braid your hair so no one could see how enticing you looked with it brushing your waist." Just thinking about it, about having someone to perform that ceremony with, made my insides hurt. My skin is tight, over sensitive. "Please, Estela. Taste what you are missing."

Her eyes flutter open to half-moons, depicting a mixture of desire and fear. "I—I've never..."

I breathe deep. "I can smell that you want me too," I reply, my thumb brushing over her bottom lip. "They hurt you. Let me show you what it means to be whole."

A moan escapes her lips, and she leans into my touch. "What if I say that is just the crystal making me feel this way?"

"Then I'll leave you be," I say firmly. "Or we can speak about the thoughts that weigh you down. About Dyrn. Anything you wish. Just, be with me."

For a few seconds, it is just the two of us suspended in time. Mouths hovering close. None of this conversation went how I was expecting—I was sure she would try to hit me again and shove me away—but the scene in the dining hall changed her.

"Teo." The sound of my own name brushes my lips. "This is only happening because I'm hurting. Everything is changing too fast."

Her words cut through my haze of desire, and I step back, giving her space. "I understand," I say softly and back away.

She nods. "I—" she stops. "We are both quite thoroughly ruined, aren't we?"

"Yes." I murmur, keeping a distance between us. It hurts to step away from her, but it could be worse. I've given her the knife to cut my heart out, and she's left it on the table.

"I miss my brother like I would miss breathing, but I'm tired of pretending that it doesn't hurt me when one of you dies." She looks up at me, then reaches her hand up before realizing her mistake and letting it fall back down to her side. "I must prepare for the ceremony with Dyrn."

I pause. "What about the window?"

She looks at me long and hard, "Cover it. I won't run again. Time under this mountain has addled my mind, and there's something comforting about knowing I have you to come for me when I need help." Then she turns and walks back to her room, and closes the door, effectively leaving me alone in the hallway. I lean against the wall, closing my eyes and taking a deep breath.

It is like the ground beneath my feet has shifted, and I walk on new ground. Everything is disorienting. So close to breaking through, but there is still a chasm of space between us. Frustrated, I storm back out of my room and face my duty as a king. One week, two deaths. I need to make sure that my people are protected—we simply can't lose any more Enduares.

I also leave to prepare for the ceremony.

ESTELA CAME. SHE HELD HER HANDS UP WITH THE SINGERS AND WEPT with the rest of us. Like a true queen mourning her fallen soldier. It would have been a sight to behold, except numbness has sunk into my bones after watching the water take Dyrn away to the ocean, and now, all that is left is the unnaturally cold air in Enduvida. It causes fear to tighten my chest. The pumps should keep the temperature steady from day to day. Whatever those mists bring, it isn't good.

After quickly crossing the bridge and making my way to the residential section, I find myself on Vann's doorstep.

Svanna and her mate live next door, but I am still surprised when the sound of a crying Sama precedes Iryth walking up to me. She looks tired, and I instinctively reach for the babe. It takes less than a second for Sama to be passed into my arms so that I can rock him.

I hear a shout inside the hut. Definitely Vann.

"I would say to ignore him, but he's the whole reason this

one woke up from his nap," she says. Her braid is almost completely fallen out, and she yawns while I sway back and forth.

Little Sama's fists curl up in my tunic. I look down at him, "Your king tells you to sleep so that your mother may rest too."

He stares at me, perfectly contented to be held in the arms of a man many considered dangerous. Children are the best part of life.

"You look like a father. May the stones bless you and your mate to have children soon," she says.

I look back up at Iryth and think of the conversation Estela and I just had. She is so broken. Would she even want a child when Mikal is gone? My brokenness made me long for a family, but what if hers has left her without sufficient space in her heart?

I do not know the answers. I only know that we had our first moments of her not pushing me away. It is enough.

Sama smacks his lips sleepily and his eyelids start to droop. "Iryth, I will take care of Lord Vann. Let me hold Sama while you sleep."

She smiles, thanks me, and turns on her heel without thinking twice.

When I knock gently, I'm surprised to find a human open the door with a shock of red hair.

"Arlet," I say, shocked. She looks furious. "What are you—"

"If he calls me firelocks one more time, I will personally shove a hammer up his ass." Then she looks at the drowsy child in my arms, her lips pinch together. She points back into the house. When she speaks again, it is a whisper shout, "I helped bring that ungrateful bastard here, and he repays me by biting me. Why do I try?" Then she marches past me, muttering something furiously under her breath.

Vann calls from his sitting room, "Ignore Firelocks. She's just mad."

Arlet reverses course and storms back into the house. "My name is Arlet, asshole. And stop yelling, there is a baby." Then she storms away once more.

When I walk in, I find him stretched out, covered in bandages. His face is pale, but he lives.

"*You bit her.* Are you mated? Because biting a woman is rarely platonic," I say, absentmindedly stroking Sama's hair. "If there is something between you, tell me now. We are planning to use Arlet to help make our case with the elves."

He attempts to swallow the bitter taste in his mouth. "A bite doesn't mean a matehood. Both our crystals are silent."

I take a seat in front of him, looking at the healing materials which are scattered on the ground. "Do you wish to mate her? It would be unwise to court her just to get into her bed. These humans are not like us."

He growls. "I know that, Teo. Not everyone is delighted at being mated to a weak race."

"That is a very old idea," I say, narrowing my eyes. "I've just returned from being with Estela, I am in no mood to dance around words."

He purses his lips, then grabs the blanket covering his bandaged top to display his neck. "Does this look like a mated man?"

I blink, debating whether or not I should point out that my mating mark has not yet started to glow either. The stone will always sing first. I decide against it, as he is not in a place to see reason. "I am glad to see you are well," I say.

He shrugs, and it's then that I see his red eyes. "I am as well as to be expected."

I nod. "Dyrn's death weighs heavily on my soul."

He nods, then gestures to some scrolls on the side of his sofa. "I have been reviewing your research on these cold ones. Their fangs are sharp, and their magic is like ice."

I nod. "While I was speaking with Estela, I had a thought. I believe they are the same creatures that attacked Estela in the woods."

Vann leans forward. "The one that nearly killed her?"

I nod. That night was unpleasant. It had been a long time since I needed to use my magic in such a way. "They can be killed, but it is not an easy feat. We will need to adjust the hunter training Svanna has been overseeing."

Vann nods. "What do you have in mind?"

"We need to attack soon, tomorrow, perhaps," I say.

He nods slowly. "Has Estela been training with the other slaves?"

"I am not sure. She is starting to fit in—to warm to the idea of this life. If I push too hard, I think she will start fighting again. Dyrn's death hurt her." Sama stirs in my arms, and I reach down to stick my finger in his mouth. My digit is a poor substitute for a breast, but he doesn't seem to mind in his sleep.

Vann leans back, his eyes scanning my face. "I watched her use the crystal. She thought she was healing him, but the crystal was easing him into his death."

My mouth goes dry and I piece together her words about the death. "Godsdamn it all. When we spoke, she was subdued because of guilt."

Vann clucks his tongue. "It is convenient that you can correct such thoughts. Perhaps next week at the Festival?"

I groan. "Vann, celebrating when everything is still so uncertain is not one of your better ideas. Getting drunk surrounded by bloodthirsty creatures is not prudent. It is downright idiotic. Just think of my little game with the giants."

Vann adjusts a bandage, his gaze intense. "Teo, hear me out. The Festival is a time of celebration for love. We have two new mated pairs—is that not reason to be grateful to Grutabela and Endu? In the last month, we have lost Mele, Irsh, Tirin, and Dyrn.

We are mourning and terrified. Even with the treaty, no one feels safe. It can help raise our spirits after such a difficult time and remind people to hope for a brighter future. It's not just about inebriation."

I rub a hand over my face as the weariness sets in. Having a sleeping babe in my arms reminds me that I haven't slept well in days. "Fine. But we need to have the tunnel sorted before then."

Vann nods, a hint of a smile on his face. "It is good we still have an entire week. Just think of your pretty mate wearing something appealing for you. You will have an apt reward."

I scowl at him. "Do not assume I can't kill you with a babe in my hands."

He raises an eyebrow. "See what I mean? The humans are trouble."

I bristle at his words, and lean forward to inspect his dressings. "You look well taken care of. I am going to take a walk around the *lumikap* garden."

He smiles. "Yes, let me sleep while you babysit."

My tail whips out and grazes his arm. He laughs as I leave his home.

CHAPTER 26
TOPAZ
ESTELA

Dyrn's ceremony hurt like falling from a tree. I couldn't breathe, couldn't move. When they placed me next to Teo, I barely looked at him.

I'd hardly known Dyrn, but I still wept when they read the story of Vidalena. These people are surrounded by a world far more magical than the forests where I grew up—and they have twice the ability to tear out my heart.

As I sit in my room, my mind wanders. My life had been one-note for so long, and now I am trapped in a symphony of sound, magic, and whatever I feel for the king.

Wrong. I was so very wrong about everything. It was the grace of the sweetest gods that I had been brought to the Enduares from the giants, and I had ruined it all by trying to escape.

When my eyes land on the table that held my herbs, I stand up. Guilt for what I had done, using those plants to hurt, and then paying the price in shame and a man's life eats away at me, leaving me hollow and numb. Like I am made of wood.

I thought I could heal him with magic I didn't understand.

And then I watched the life fade from his eyes. Foolish and selfish. That was what I was.

When Teo had told me he'd killed slaves... I should have felt something. But all I could think about was how I'd turned a blind eye to so many hurting to protect myself and Mikal. I'd cared for Arlet the best I could, but now she pulls away from me in a testament to my subpar friendship.

While sinking to the ground, I press the heels of my hands to my eyes. There's an ache just behind my eyes that refuses to relent. It pounds and pounds.

And while my mind races, I think of Teo again. First, I turn off all of the lights, trying to find a refuge. When that doesn't work, I start to pace.

Cautiously, I open the door to my chamber, the weight of anticipation and uncertainty heavy upon my chest. The room's darkness spills forth into the corridor, melding with the dim, flickering spell lights above my head.

Stepping out, I allow my senses to sharpen and hone in on my surroundings. Every sound, every whisper of air, every movement—all are magnified as I enter the world I have spent the last month trapped in.

My eyes, accustomed to the darkness, slowly pick apart the gloom before me. I scan the palace for the Enduares, my breathing slow and measured.

But there is only silence. So I continue down the hallway, out of the palace, and to the bridge that I'd once feared. I walk to the mushroom house to check on my plants when I catch a glimpse of the last person I'd expected walking around. My heart leaps into my throat, a wave of adrenaline coursing through me as I prepare myself for whatever may come.

The response comes not in words, but in the appearance of a figure emerging from between the circular homes. My breath catches as I recognize the tall, blue-skinned form of Teo. He cradles a baby in his arms, his expression soft and tender – a stark contrast to the oppressive atmosphere that has enveloped me for so long.

A mix of curiosity and something unfamiliar stirs within me, causing my feet to carry me a hesitant step forward while closing the windows on my thoughts. Why am I drawn to him, when I have fought so hard to remain detached, to keep my heart guarded and closed off?

As I watch from the shadows, Teo gently bounces the baby in his arms, cooing softly in a language foreign to my ears. His tender gaze remains fixed on the infant's cherubic face, each smile and gurgle eliciting an affectionate response from the imposing figure before me.

"Sama," he murmurs, as though he fears breaking the spell of serenity that has settled over them. "You are so precious, little one."

It is then that a surge of warmth floods through my chest, a sensation so unfamiliar it nearly steals my breath away. It seems as though a fire has been lit within me, its flames licking at the icy walls I have built around my heart. For the first time in what feels like an eternity, the cold that has defined my existence begins to thaw, giving way to something new and terrifyingly powerful.

The babe cries out. "Shhh," Teo whispers, his large hands cradling its tiny form while he rocks. It's a sight so disarmingly gentle that it sends a shiver down my spine, further stoking the fire burning within me.

My fingers twitch, longing rising up like a tide, threatening to sweep me away. To reach out and touch the soft tufts of hair on the baby's head, to experience the tenderness I have never known, seems both terrifying and tantalizing. A cold sweat breaks out across my brow, and my breath hitches in my throat.

My heart pounds unnervingly against my ribcage, my breath

coming in shallow gasps as I struggle to contain the conflicting emotions that threaten to tear me apart. My fingers clench into fists, every muscle in my body tensing as I fight against the overwhelming urge to run away from these unfamiliar feelings, to retreat back into the safety of my solitude.

And then it comes—a sound that pierces the darkness and seizes my attention with a vise-like grip. Teo's laughter, rich and deep as the midnight sky, reverberates through the corridor, filling my senses with its resonant melody. It is a sound that tugs at something buried deep within me, an irresistible force that draws me closer to him—as inexorable as the pull of the moon upon the tides.

I turn away from him and hurry back to my room, not wanting to risk getting caught.

CHAPTER 27
TIGER'S EYE
TEO

Once sweet dreams have turned to nightmares. When I close my eyes, I see Lijasa's face. Then I see the bodies of those she killed, and the ones I killed to get close to her. Rotting corpses lined up for her like a garden of putrid flowers.

I sit up in bed, both covered in sweat and nauseous. There is much to do that will distract me from these hellish memories. Much that can save me from myself and the darkness that lingers in my soul. The one that damns me from deserving a mate in the first place.

After peeling off the damp covers, my eyes wander to the door in the wall leading to Estela's room. The window has been fixed.

TUNNEL FOUR HAS BEEN CLOSED OFF WITH SOLID ROCK AT BOTH THE front and the back section to prevent the further spread of the invasive species. However, while there haven't been any attacks in the last few days, mist is seeping out from unseen cracks. It's lowering the temperature of the entire city.

Svanna stands at my side, and a group of stone benders is watching the entrance. "Everyone is doing well with defensive techniques. The warriors seem ready, as well. The strategy you suggested—crowding, and then slicing at the creatures with the intent to sever—seems like it will work well."

My fingers brush against the hard rock, which is frozen like the outdoor snow. "Is there a breach?" I ask Luth.

The stone bender scans the rock. "No. It is holding strong. I have tried to find a crack several times, My King."

I nod. "Whatever magic these beasts have, it is strong. Run the attack sequence one last time with all of the hunters and stone benders, we will attack later today."

This will not be an easy fight, even if we are prepared. Dyrn's parting ceremony is still fresh in my mind and I am not eager for anyone else to die.

Svanna and Luth voice their agreements, though Luth stays while Svanna follows me back into the common area. The overall light in the cavern has decreased, and it's not hard to see that the *lumikaps* are dimming. My head hurts and my back aches while I try to balance and solve a dozen problems day after day. "I need to speak with Ulla about the light," I grumble as she follows.

"You intend to follow us into the fight," she observes. "Training yesterday was arduous. It would be wise for you to sleep first. You could collect Estela and take her to your room. Time with Iryth always strengthens my weary body."

I lean away from her as I walk, trying not to look at the glowing mating mark on her neck that peeks back at me. The last time I spoke to Estela, she rejected me. It was hard to be furious with her for protecting herself after having a better understanding of her life. "She would not come."

Svanna is silent as we near the dining hall. The bustle of

breakfast is everywhere, but Ulla is not. I sigh and we continue to the place where the meat is prepared and the mushrooms are harvested. As we walk behind the pavilion, There is a large group of Enduares—dotted with humans—moving through a sequence of defensive positions. While the humans lack the natural grace that comes to my people, their movements are strong.

My eyes land on one form, smaller than all the rest. She moves with an unexpected fluidity, ducking and weaving with a grace that seems almost unnatural.

Svanna huffs a laugh. "She is a little warrior. It's a shame that Firelocks was called away to help Fira. They are good fighting partners."

I glance up at my life-long friend. "She doesn't like to be called that. Arlet is her name."

She scoffs. "Oh really? Many have started to call her that. She only seems angry when one person uses the word."

I shake my head. Arlet and Vann grow more aggravating by the day. "Vann should be healed by now, but he's still having a problem with bleeding. I need him to help me organize the people tonight."

When my gaze goes back to Estela, I am impressed. Her movements are sharp and precise. Pride is warm in my chest. It only sours when I think about Zlosa.

I continue toward Ulla's normal spot and push my mate from my mind. The inside of the area is covered with the dank smell of fungi, but Ulla is at the back end, tinkering with a spell light.

"Ulla?" I call.

Her head snaps up. "King Teo! Svanna, I have been up to my elbows in dirt for an entire day. Come, see what we have been working on."

We hurry over to find a small patch of dirt cut into rows with mushrooms and spell lights shining through crystals.

There are small green buds just beginning to peak out of the dirt.

My eyes widen. "Are those plants?"

Ulla nods, a small smile playing on her lips. "Yes, they are. After studying the light requirements, Estela had an idea to use the Ardorflame and the spell lights to mimic the sun's light on a smaller scale. These plants will grow faster, and we can still harvest the mushrooms around them without affecting their growth."

Svanna reaches her hand down to the touch the streaming light and gasps. "It is very warm." Ulla smiles brighter as Svanna sticks both of her hands into the rays and rubs her hands together.

The little garden looks out of place in this cave. The small green leaves are vibrant like viridescent crystals. In the face of more life, my soul expands to meet its call. To try harder to fight against that which would steal life. It reminds me that life is not dark and desolate.

The time of the Enduares will come again.

"I came to speak with you about the shroom lights around the city. Everything is seeming just a bit dimmer—Hopefully we will have the chill banished by nighttime. What can be done?"

She sits back on her heels and thinks for a few moments. "It must be the temperature. I will look at them and see if there is a warming song that can help speed up their recovery."

"Excellent," I say, just as my eyes drift off to the place where the Enduares are working on fighting. "You are doing good work."

She notices my gaze and shoos me away. "Come back if you need anything else. Svanna, tell Iryth that I will come by later to keep her company while you are fighting."

The lightness between us dissipates at the mention of the gravity of our infestation. Svanna nods, somber once more, and I cast one last stream of grateful words before we leave. My stomach is still unsettled, and I stop at the corner of the path to watch training now turned into sparring matching.

Estela stands at the corner of the ring, her features glowing in the low illumination while she waits for her turn. I turn to Svanna. "I will come soon."

Her gaze travels between me and the ring, but she nods. "Take her to rest after. I will get you when it is time."

I nod and make my way towards Estela, my heart beating fast. She must feel my presence because her eyes flicker in my direction. Her lips turn up in a small smile when she sees me, and the sight of it sends a jolt of electricity through my body.

We stand there for a moment, just looking at each other. Her eyes are a deep brown, flecked with gold in the glowing light, and they seem to search something in mine. The song between us is intuitive and devastating.

"Sire," the hunter leading the training calls over. "Have you come to share news?" He looks as nervous as we all feel.

I look up. "Nothing quite like that, my friends. I would like to be my mate's sparring partner."

Estela is irate. I feel it through our bond. There's a hush that falls over the crowd as they watch us step into the ring. Estela gives me a quick nod before taking a stance and we begin. The first few moments are tentative. I am playing the monster, and she is trying to defend herself. Though she starts slightly off balance, she soon falls into a rhythm that feels almost natural. Our movements are quick and fluid, and I feel my blood pumping through my veins with each lunge and parry.

It's almost as if we're dancing, and I can't help but feel a sense of exhilaration coursing through me. I can tell that she's feeling it too, the way her eyes sparkle and the flush that spreads across her cheeks.

Then, she turns into the aggressor and flames light up inside of me, practically in the region just below my stomach.

My movements become more fluid, and a rush of excitement propels me on as we spar back and forth. Estela is quick and agile, her body moving like a weapon as she dodges my strikes and lands her own. It's like nothing I've ever experienced before, and I am completely consumed by the moment.

The heat between us is palpable, and I can see it in the way she moves. Her skin is slick with sweat, and I can smell the rich, heady scent of her arousal. It drives me wild, and I become more aggressive, pushing her harder and harder until we're both panting and sweating. Her fingernails scratch at me, and I luxuriate in the feeling.

If I am hurt today, would she mourn for me? Would she come to my room as Arlet does for Vann and yell at me for being careless? If I died... would she feel the loss? Desperation seeps into our movements. If only I could know that we would both be tearing at each other's throats tomorrow.

Finally, I make a move that catches her off guard, and I land a hard blow that sends her reeling backward. She lands on her back with a thud, and for a moment, I am worried that I have hurt her.

But then she starts to laugh, and relief washes over me. I reach for her, sweeping her up before anyone has a chance to comment. Finally, the gem inside of me sings. Finally, I can steal her away.

I'm breaking our rules. Again. But I can't seem to stop the moment.

For a moment, she fights against me. "Wait, I was practicing."

I shake my head. "No longer. We must speak."

CHAPTER 28
ENSTATITE
ESTELA

My palms are sweating as Teo takes me into his private chambers. Once inside, he locks the door and turns to face me. The king's chamber is bathed in an otherworldly luminescence as flickering spell lights cast eerie shadows upon the cold stone walls. I look up at him, heart racing.

Once inside, he looks over at me. "Liana has seen nine of the cold creatures that attacked you. We have been training for them, but the risk is significant."

My eyebrows draw together. "But you killed the one that attacked me easily." The memory is so vivid that it makes my breath come out faster than before.

He shakes his head. "That was one. There are nine now. The other one was also caught off guard, and these ones have had time to plan—if that's something they are capable of." He pauses and walks over to a shelf in his room, picking up something and turning it over in his hands. "When I was younger, being king was as sure as the sun rising in the morning. There was some foreordained logic that coincided with the cosmic path of the heavens. Until there wasn't. When my father sent me to work on the peace treaty, my goal was to seduce and kill the queen. She forced me to her bed for months before I stabbed her through the heart and went to the final battle. There, I found my mother dead. The war wasn't over, so my father used the volcano. I—I saved who I could."

I hold my breath, studying the planes of his face that are illuminated by the gentle light. He looks much older than I've noticed before, his face ravaged by time, loss, and pain. So much pain.

"You are strong. It is hard to picture anything taking you down."

He turns to look at me. "Yet you tried. You, the one who is meant to love and care for me, cannot stand the sight of your mate. You tried to kill me." Those lines of pain are so much deeper now, and I am defenseless.

"I—" I close my mouth. "None of your people doubt you are a good king."

"Estela," Teo's voice resonates through the chamber, echoing off the walls and reverberating through my very being as he closes the space between us. "This isn't about anyone else. We are to marry in a handful of days. I am not strong enough to bind myself to you if you hate me. If you want to leave now, I'll let you go."

"Teo," my reply came out as barely more than a whisper. "I won't leave." The music between us is slowly changing into something beautiful. Our gazes are locked, and it is as if our souls were reaching out for one another, entwining like desperate lovers. The space between us crackled with an electric energy, tension taut as the strings of a harp.

"I doubt that I will die. But Dyrn was so quick and unexpected. I fear..."

I stop breathing. Then, my hand comes up and reaches for

him. Both my hands cup his face, fingers brushing across his cheekbones. My heart thuds loudly.

"Estela, in you, I found a new life. I can't lose that. Please, tell me not to die," he says all at once.

My chest sags and my lips part. "Teo," the words that come out of my mouth are gone because I have a chance to overthink them. "Do not die."

I lean forward and press my lips to his. I can hardly believe I am the one to kiss him. At first, my mouth is soft against his. Then his mouth opens beneath mine, and the kiss deepens. His tongue is like velvet.

I explore his mouth with my tongue, tasting him for the first time as sparks of desire fly through my body. Our mouths move together in a syncopated rhythm, struggling to mesh closer still. This was the kind of kiss that would leave us both wanting more.

I'd crossed a line and it couldn't be uncrossed.

The crystal near his bed starts to flash and he pulls away. "That is a message from the others. I must go."

A sudden urgency chills the air, a bitter reminder of our reality. He steps back, his voice steady despite the turmoil brewing beneath the surface. "I must go."

"Yes," I reply, struggling to keep my own voice from breaking. "You should go."

"Nothing will keep me from returning to you," he vows as he reaches for the armor on a stand near his bed. It's so much more intricate than I've ever realized, each metallic scale imbued the artistic power of Enduar forges.

As he dons the heavy breastplate, I watch his muscles ripple and appreciate the beauty of his masculine form.

Perhaps he is putting on a show for me, but this seems like more than a mere physical transformation; it is a rite of passage. Just like everything he did, it was a testament to his unwavering devotion to his people.

"Estela," he murmurs, shocking me out of my reverie. "Will you help me put on my helmet?"

For a moment, I'm frozen. It's clear he doesn't need any help from me. This is a deepening of the vulnerability between us. "Of course," I answer, but my hands tremble slightly as I lift the ornate headpiece.

When I slide it onto his head, I feel a primal force that seemed to emanate from the very depths of the earth concentrate in the stone on my chest. It was a sensation both exhilarating and terrifying, a dark reminder of the sacrifices that had been made and those that still lay before us.

"Thank you, Estela," he whispers, my breath catching as I fasten the final strap.

"Good luck," I say, feeling like we have reached a space past words. "Be careful."

"I will be," he assures me.

With one final, lingering look, he turns and strides out of his chamber. My mind is filled with the haunting image on the base of the mountain when I tried to escape. I thought I would die that night.

As I watch Teo's retreating form, his armored figure glinting in the light, a hollow ache starts in my chest. But there was no time for me to dwell on the pain; I am a part of these people. They might need me, too. With a deep breath, I force myself out of his room, with the other Enduares. It's time to join my people.

When I reach the pavilion, the first person I see is Ulla.

"Estela," she calls out. "Good that you have arrived. We need your help." I already see the beginnings of a meal around her.

I nod, fighting back the tears that threatened to spill over. "Of course. I'm here for you."

Together, we work side by side as we start to prepare the hall for the meal. This will be the food that Teo eats when he is finished.

"Here, Estela," Ulla says, handing me a large pot filled with steaming broth. "Make sure everyone gets their share."

"Understood," I reply, my voice hoarse from suppressed emotion. As I ladle the nourishing liquid into the waiting bowls, I can't help but think of all the hunters entering the tunnel, wondering if they will make it out.

"Thank you, Estela," murmurs one of the young Enduares, her eyes dull with exhaustion as she accepts the food. I marvel that they welcomed us when I gave them very little reason to. I am lucky to have them in my life.

When I see Arlet on the other side of the room, I pause and go sit by her. She is talking with some of the other women, specifically Neela.

When I draw near, they all look up at me. I'm surprised when it is Neela who speaks up. "How was King Teo before you left him?"

Heat creeps up my neck for them to know that we were just together, but it makes sense. We left in a very public way. "He is confident all will be well."

She nods.

I catch Arlet's eye and she gives me a small smile. "I worry for them too. Come, sit with us. Everyone can finish their meals in peace. Let me teach you how to play the pebble game."

I pause for a moment, grateful for Arlet's kind gesture. It felt good to have friends in this new place, to feel part of something again.

CHAPTER 29
ROSE QUARTZ
TEO

The world away from Estela is cold. Her words run through my mind.

Do not die, she says in her tongue through our bond.

I hold my breath, wondering if she even knows she is doing it. The cavern around us is cold, but the Ardorflame has already started to glow more brilliantly in the center of the space. Once we finish this mission, we could prepare for the festival. All would be well.

"Remove the wall," I command Luth and Salo. As their hands twist in front of them, stones start to rearrange and the wall breaks apart, revealing the dank, misty tunnel beyond.

The stone benders had tethered spell lights to follow each of the five hunters. We move cautiously. There are ten of us in the group, outnumbering the cold creatures by one. Salo and I lead the line, while Vann and Luth trail close behind. Faol, Joso, Keio, Svanna, Niht, and Vorin follow after in rows of two.

I pause at the beginning of the mists, looking back at my advisor. His injuries hadn't killed him, but they had been slow to heal. Some sort of darkness lived within, as Liana said. "Are you sure you want to go?"

"Yes. This is personal now," he responds.

And that is all it takes to have me fully submerging myself into the curling, gray air. Tunnel four is as long as the walk through the residential section and spits out into an abandoned section of the mine. It's full of twists and turns. Lots of hiding places.

The mists thicken quickly, and the ground is slick with moisture. I tread carefully as my men follow in silence. The air swallows all the sound from our boots as we walk. I clutch the sword on my hip, my instincts taut and ready to withdraw it at a moment's notice.

The tunnel begins its first curve, and I still haven't seen a thing. My estimation would be that these monsters inhabit similar spaces, but move in a solitary fashion.

A sound overhead alerts me to a shifting in the rocks. I gesture for everyone to stop and hold their breath, withdrawing my sword and using it to motion for them to fan out. Vann is trembling by my side, but his grip on his own weapon is steady.

We wait in silence, and I can feel the tension radiating off of my men. And then, a snarl reverberates through the tunnel, and Vann growls back, ready to attack. I catch his arm and steady him. That seems to snap him back into the moment.

We hear the skittering first. It's coming from the direction of the snarl, and it's getting louder. I stand my ground.

And that's when I see it. Red eyes on the ceiling before the first creature drops to the ground. The beast that had attacked Estela looked like a man with black hair, red eyes, and moonlight-pale skin. This one is the same, but injured. As the spell light cuts through the mist to see him, his right arm is a twisted amalgamation of flesh and bone that shouldn't exist.

I raise my sword in defense as the creature lunges towards

me. It's quick, but not quick enough. I swing my blade, and it lands on its arm, severing it from its body. The creature howls in pain, but doesn't give up. It keeps coming at me with its other arm, but I'm ready for it. I dodge its attack and thrust my sword straight through its chest, killing it instantly.

As the creature falls to the ground, part of the mist clears, and we see the rest of them in the distance. They're closing in on us fast.

My heart pounds in my chest as I ready myself for the fight ahead. My men follow my lead, their weapons at the ready. The mist around us is thick, but I can see the shapes of the creatures as they stand up. Eight pairs of glowing eyes.

Luth and Salo start stone bending, causing chunks of rock to fall from the top of the cavern and onto their heads. One falls, and I use my stone magic to move a slab of stone atop the beast.

A crunch resounds as Luth and Salo continue their assault on the remaining creatures. They focus on the ground beneath the beasts, causing sections of the tunnel to crumble and trap them in place. My men and I take advantage of their immobility and strike them down one by one.

Blood decorates the walls of the tunnel, and the scent of death lingers in the air. I wipe the sweat from my forehead and take a deep breath while the rush of adrenaline courses through me.

I turn to the hunters and stone benders, looking at each of them in turn. They're all injured to some extent, but their eyes gleam with determination. They know what we're up against, and they're not afraid to face it head-on.

The crash of metal against stone echoes through the tunnel. I whip around to find Vann facing off an exceptionally tall beast, one slightly taller than either of us. The creature stands there for a moment, its glowing eyes assessing us and our battle skills.

I take a deep breath before joining him in the fray—the two

of us working together to take on the creature. The Butcher and his Cleaver. Our blades clash, and sparks fly against the stone as we fight against it with all our might. Every strike is met with a defensive counter and every parry is met with a powerful attack.

Finally, we manage to wear it down enough that it is vulnerable. I grab onto its hair and pull. Taking this opportunity, Vann thrusts his sword forward straight into its chest and crudely cuts out the part of chest where its heart once was. We wipe the sweat from our brows and admire our handiwork—the monster now lays dead at our feet.

The creatures are scattered across the ground. We take a moment to catch our breath before beginning to make our way back up towards the surface of the mountain range.

"Well done, men!" I cry, embracing each hunter in turn.

The stone benders bow their heads reverently in response, and then I turn to my advisors. I pant with the adrenaline of death.

"We have won a victory through courage and struggle," I declare to Vann, Salo, and Svanna.

Vann and Svanna smile proudly at me in agreement, but Salo's face is cold and unreadable. Something about his expression causes my gut to lurch. Liana had said only nine were in the tunnels. Without warning, something comes up behind me.

I spin around, brandishing my sword like lightning. But it is too late. One last creature has found us.

An intense blaze of pain ruptures my neck as the teeth penetrate deep into the flesh. My vision swims as the writhing darkness begins to cloud my senses, yet still, I grasp at the vast wound as blood gushes between my fingers. I am unable to look at the damage inflicted upon me. Agonizing heat scorches down my back, and then all fades away into blackness.

CHAPTER 30
TURQUOISE
ESTELA

The rules of the pebble game are simple enough. Everyone is given three small stones, which they toss into a ring at once. After the count of three, we all dart for the scattered rocks. The one with the most wins.

The women up the stakes by betting chores, or even crystals. I point out the tourmaline and feldspar. They were my favorites to touch, and I am proud of my progress with Liana. I have not gone to the mines yet, so my own collection is lacking.

"I'll win this one," I boast to the group, grinning.

Neela shakes her head. "Not so fast, you have to offer something up as well."

I smile. "I'll give you one of the plants Ulla and I have been growing."

Plants in this dark, albeit beautiful, under mountain were impossible before I came. There's something about the triumph of nurturing life in such a harsh environment that excites and motivates me. And Neela seems pleased by my offer, so I know it's a fair bet.

Then Liana wanders into the space. She doesn't move like

normal, she saunters with her familiar confidence. Her grace has been earned by her long years spent on this earth.

"This looks like a game best played drunk," she laughs.

I chuckle at her joke and point to the pile. "Play with us? Winner takes all."

It's then that I realize the others have been quiet and respectful of the wise woman. I look back, remembering that they all view her with respect. Like she's a royal as well.

Liana, catching my gaze, nods in agreement. "I could use a little fun," she says. She removes her shawl, revealing her toned arms. "But I wouldn't enter a friendly bet without something to back me up." Then she reaches into her pocket and withdraws a small phial that glitters in the dim light of the cavern. Its contents are a red powder of sorts.

One of the women behind me snorts. I turn to see Iryth, Svanna's mate. "A whole phial? Are you trying to kill us? Not everyone is mated in this group."

"Some of us like to have fun," Lyria says, raising her hand to smooth back her tightly coiled bun. "There are so many new men to meet with the humans."

"What's that?" I ask, trying to stop thinking of the kiss and the way my lips continue to burn.

Liana holds up the phial and twists the cap off. Inside, a fine dust sparkles in the light. "We haven't covered this in our classes. Carnelian powder. It's used as an aphrodisiac."

My cheeks heat up as Liana explains the powder's purpose. I exchange a glance with Neela, who is still laughing. But the excitement in the air is palpable, and I can't help but feel a tingle of curiosity run through me.

"Shall we begin?" I say.

Neela laughs. "Yes. Our king will need to be occupied somehow when he returns from his fight."

There's an unexpected hurt from their words. They don't

understand how complex my life has been before now, but a part of me is grateful for the moments of levity. I don't know what to say, but no one pays attention to me as we take our positions around the ring, and the count begins.

"One, two, three!" Liana shouts, and we all lunge forward, our hands grasping for the pebbles on the floor.

The game starts with a frenzy as we all run for the pebbles, trying to grab as many as possible. There's laughter all around me, but I am determined to win. I feel my feet slipping on the smooth stone as I lunge forward.

The room starts to whoop while we run. I hadn't realized they'd started watching us. Some cheer for their friends and family. No one cheers for me.

But I don't let that cloud my focus. I reach down and grab three pebbles in one go, feeling their weight in my hand as I stand up and grin triumphantly. But my victory is short-lived, as I see Neela has grabbed six pebbles and is already heading out of the ring. I groan inwardly.

Just as I reach for a pebble by her feet, a sharp pain wracks through me and I stumble, dropping my pebbles. A pain in my neck so acute black edges my vision, and I scream.

Arlet is at my side in a second and that's when the screaming in my head starts. Deep, utterly masculine agony.

"Teo," I breath.

Liana rushes over to me and helps me up. "What's wrong?" she asks worriedly, and I grip her arm for support.

"The King...he's hurt," I gasp while the pain in my head intensifies. "We have to go to him."

The women around us exchange concerned glances, and Liana steps forward. "I'll go with you," she offers, her expression serious.

I nod, grateful for the help, and we start to make our way

towards the source of the pain. As we move through the tunnels, the pain grows stronger and more unbearable with every step.

We finally reach the entrance to the tunnel, Vann and another Enduar is dragging him from the tunnel. His silver hair is coated with blood, and there is a wad of cloth on his neck, also soaked through with red.

My mind can't comprehend the image. As my breath picks up, I think of what he told me. He wasn't afraid of dying. He told me he would come back.

I start to panic. His beautiful, large body is limp. I rush forward, falling to my knees to check his pulse. He's still alive.

My hands skim over his slick armor as I try to figure out what to do. Liana is next to me, pulling out a crystal from one of her many pockets.

"I don't have any damned leaves. Liana, what do I do?"

She presses one of the crystals to his wound. "Hush human, your herbs work well for sicknesses, but his Fuegorra can work with a crystal to help with wounds. That's how we healed your wounds and your hand, remember?"

"Yes," I say, watching as she places the quartz on Teo's wound. The crystal glows bright green, slowly healing the wound. I am relieved at the sight of Teo's wound healing. He'll survive this.

Lord Vann kneels next to us. "Dyrn tried to kill him."

The blood drains from my face. His death was painful. Disorienting. "Dyrn is dead. We gave him back to the water a few days ago."

Vann shakes his head. "He was still dead. But he had turned into one of those awful creatures."

Liana whispers something severe under her breath. "They have venom?"

I nod, feeling a sense of dread wash over me.

Vann nods. "I believe it's a venom that can turn someone into one of those creatures if not treated immediately."

Vann grimaces. "We didn't know. We were finished with the group Liana had seen in the Fuegorra. And Teo..." He trails off, looking at the unconscious Enduar king with concern.

I turn to Liana. "We need to get him back to the palace. He needs proper attention, and it would help him to lie down."

They nod, lifting Teo's limp body and carrying him towards his quarters. I follow beside him, my hand gripping Teo's larger hand tightly.

When he is on the bed, he starts twitching. I pour water over a wash rag and try to wipe away the blood so we can touch his skin. He feels like Dyrn did—cold.

That poor hunter had to die twice. I'll do everything I can to keep Teo alive.

CHAPTER 31
HEMATITE
TEO

"Teo," my own name is whispered against the silence of the room, but it reaches my ears and anchors me to reality for a fleeting moment.

"*I think he's waking up.*"

My eyes flicker open once more, finding Estela hovering above me. Her features are a mix of concern and urgency, her brow furrows over wide, frightened eyes that mirror the tumultuous emotions surging through me.

"Estela," I rasp, hearing the weakness in my voice and wincing at the sound.

"Shh," she hushes me gently, her fingers tenderly brushing against my jawline as if to still the words that refused to form. "Don't speak, Teo. You need your strength."

The pain intensifies, a burning fire coursing through my veins and consuming all coherent thought. I don't understand how such a simple act—the mere movement of air across my wound—can cause such agony. It is as if my very soul is being cleaved in two, leaving me in pieces, broken and vulnerable.

"Stay still," Estela orders softly, her voice strained and tinged with fear. Her hands tremble as she works, her heart pounding in time with my own. "You'll be all right, Teo."

"Easy...for you...to say," I manage to choke out. My chest feels like it has been cleaved open, leaving nothing behind but raw, exposed nerves and the persistent throb of blood pulsing through my veins.

Liana's form comes into view. "Damn it. If we don't get the poison out, he'll end up like Dyrn. This is bad. Place it over his wound."

The elderly woman's hands land on my chest, hovering over the wound with jewel-laden fingers and beginning to glow with a soft white light. I can feel the magic coursing through me, purging the poison and slowly easing the pain. The magic connects with the Fuegorra in my chest, burning like I am being cooked alive. My back bows under the intensity of the heat. My throat hurts when I scream.

"Estela, come help me," Liana says. Estela nods and moves to assist Liana, their hands working in unison to heal me. The pain slowly ebbs away, replaced by a sense of exhaustion and weariness. Something is being pulled out of my body. It hurts. I choke when I finally try to breathe again, and I cough.

"That's it," Liana murmurs, the light growing brighter as my sickness dissipates. "Teo, you need to breathe and stay still."

"He's looking better," Estela says. Through it all, my mate's voice pierces the darkness, an anchor in the storm. Her human skin slides over my bare flesh, and I shiver. It feels cold, so much colder than it did before. I know I should fear the cold and protect her from it, but I don't remember why. "Come on. You promised me not to die."

Her lithe figure blurs into focus, and I can see the desperation etched upon her face, her eyes wide with fear. As she reaches my side, her body tenses like a coiled spring. She's holding large black stones, and I wonder where she found the obsidian.

The pain returns, and my world tilts on its axis, my vision swimming with stars, but I hold on. I will not allow this pain to consume me, not when there is so much at stake.

"I need to get more crystals. Stay with him," Liana commands my mate. I can't stay awake long enough to know if Estela does.

PART THREE

CHAPTER 32
EPIDOTE
ESTELA

Darkness clings to my eyelids, reluctant to release me from its grasp as I stir into consciousness. There were no nightmares while I slept last night.

For a moment, I can't place where I am, but the feel of silken sheets against my skin and the unfamiliar scent gradually roused me from the depths of sleep. The haze within my mind begins to clear, revealing that I am lying in Teo's bed.

Yesterday comes back to me. His neck wound. He lost so much blood. He asked for me to stay, so I did. Just to check on his wounds. It seems that after I changed the first dressing, I fell alseep.

The last fragments of dreams slip away as I become fully aware of my surroundings, my eyes adjusting to the dim lighting. While I slept, I splayed out, and I got tangled up in bare blue skin, with my leg slung over his hips and my head on his chest. A hard mass touches my thigh, and a hand grips my knee.

The song between us is more insistent than ever, as evidenced by the slickness between my legs.

I shift slightly, trying to disengage myself from Teo without waking him up. I'm glad to see hardly any blood soaking through the bandage on his neck, and his breathing is even and deep.

Thankfully, he doesn't stir as I extricate myself from his embrace. I get up from the bed, self-conscious about my body's reaction to his closeness. I make my way to the bathroom, closing the door behind me.

In the bathroom, there is a bath which is much larger than my own. I look at myself in the mirror. My face is flushed, and my eyes are bright. I'm a stranger to my old self. My face has filled out, and there's a glow to my cheeks despite weeks in the under mountain.

Weeks running from my feelings. Weeks falling further and further into... something with the Enduar king. I think of his kiss, his touches, and how afraid I felt when I thought he would die.

Then I think of the throb between my legs while we were holding each other close. My skin is on fire. I need to do something to extinguish it—something that doesn't include waking him.

My hand brushes my heavy breast. Then I push lower, allowing my hand to stray between my thighs and explore the warmth.

I've never been in love. My first kiss was a shock to my senses. I have never given myself pleasure and, to be honest, I don't even know how. But if my destiny is the beautiful man lying in his bed, I want my first experience to be something I can control.

My skin is tight and sensitive as I pull off my clothes. The heat of the bath is heavenly as I sink into the water, my body relaxing in the luxurious warmth. I close my eyes and breathe in deeply, my mind wandering to thoughts of Teo.

As I submerge myself into the water, I let my hand wander back down, across the curve of my belly, towards the growing heat between my thighs. I gasp as my fingers touch the slickness there. It's different from the water and my body arches upwards as I explore the new sensations.

I close my eyes as I imagine Teo joining me in the bathroom, his hands on my body, his mouth on mine, his hard length filling me up. The image is so vivid that I can almost feel him there with me.

My fingers move faster, and I moan in pleasure as I reach my peak. I lean back in the water, breathing deeply as the pleasure subsides, my body still humming with the after-effects of my first release.

For a few moments, I can't move. I'm relaxed, yet a little sore. Satisfied, and yet hungrier than ever.

I panic, this was supposed to fix my problems—not make them worse. I need to get back to my own room.

Reaching for the cloth, I bathe, washing myself clean of any trace of what I've done. As I pull myself out of the bath, I hear movement from the other room. Quickly, I wrap a bathrobe around myself, grab my clothes, and step back into his room. My plan is to sneak through the passageway and come back when I have calmed down.

"You stayed?" Teo's voice is soft and gentle from the bed.

I freeze, looking over at his eyes, which glow in the dim light. "Yes. I wanted to make sure you didn't lose too much blood."

He sits up, and the blanket falls away from his bare chest. I know he is wearing pants because I was just with him, but my fantasy is still fresh in my mind. I can't contain the song in my chest, and... I don't want to.

I don't realize I'm being careless with my thoughts until he growls. "Estela."

He's crawling forward, then he's in front of me, and his tail wraps around me, bringing me into his lap and cradling me in his arms. His hands trail my back, my neck—his touch igniting fires all over my body.

The song hums louder, but all I can do is look into his eyes and feel my heart racing. Then he pulls back as if anticipating me pushing him away.

"Thank you for staying," he murmurs, pushing the hair from my face. The words mean more as I think of all the times I've tried to run from him.

"You came for me when I was crying. It felt right to be there for you when you needed me," I say, breathless. The way he's holding me is causing the robe I'm wearing to send delicious friction all over my skin.

My eyes drop on the glowing mark on his neck, like a small glowing pebble. His mating mark. I have the sudden urge to bite it.

His arms stiffen around me and his hard length presses against the side of my upper thigh. My pulse spikes.

"What are you thinking?" he asks.

I can feel my cheeks flaming, embarrassed at my thoughts. I shake my head, but I don't move away from him.

"Nothing," I say.

He gently takes my chin in his hand and tilts my face up, so I can't hide from him.

"That's a lie," he murmurs. "I want you to tell me about those intriguing ideas. Tell me how much you want me with those pretty lips."

My gaze lifts and meets his.

"Not everything can be said," I whisper. "I am still learning what it is I feel."

A slow smile spreads across his face. "Will you ever let things between us be easy?"

My mouth opens. "Fine, then. Kiss me." The dare doesn't have time to hang in the air between us. He's all too willing for the next step.

He leans in and captures my lips with his, sending a surge of pleasure through me. His lips move against mine, and the song builds up inside of me, like a crescendo of music. Not as soft as before, this song is demanding and passionate.

A second later, he releases me and traces his thumb along my lower lip.

What else do you want, my queen? he asks in my mind.

He's used that term before, but at this moment, it doesn't feel like a hollow phrase. He genuinely wants me.

"More," I murmur.

More kisses? He asks in my own language.

Just teach me, I beg.

He lets out a stream of words that shock me.

You're getting better at the human tongue, I say.

And that's not even all I can do with my mouth. He's the picture of restraint despite the desperation I sense under his skin.

I take a deep breath but still struggle to say the words. I think of what I felt in the tub, and let my mind open to him. I've never quite felt anything like it before, to have someone with me for a moment.

I feel him react to the picture beneath me by parting my robe and revealing my legs. My skin is damp from the water, but I'm not cold. He moves his hand further down my body, grazing my skin as he moves lower. I'm trembling, my breaths coming out in short gasps. As his hand moves around my hips, his other hand lifts my chin, pressing his lips against mine.

Once we do this, I can't take it back. Are you sure?

We've never spoken so long through the bond. It's disorienting, but not in an unpleasant way.

I meet his eyes, letting one leg fall open to give him access. His nostrils flare, and his pupils dilate. *I am ready.*

Slowly, his hand moves up my body, brushing against curves and planes of my skin. I close my eyes and focus on the sensations, savoring each touch. Then he presses a finger against my slick entrance, and I gasp in pleasure.

He stops.

"Look at me," he urges. "I want to see your face when you realize what you've been missing."

I look up at him, needing for his hand to return to its previous spot. This is better than what I felt before. Much better. When he slides a finger inside of me, I choke. Then he begins rubbing my apex with his thumb, coaxing out sensations I didn't know I could feel. I'm full, just from his large finger. That ache that's been building is tightly bunched up inside of me when he puts in another finger.

He groans, whispering something in Enduar that sounds like the word for "*delicious.*" I don't have time to dwell because his touch is like lightning, and my heart beats faster and faster as I give in. I whip my head back and cry out as I reach my climax, the pleasure rolling through me in wave after wave.

After everything fades, Teo holds me close to his chest, his heartbeat echoing through his chest and mine in perfect unison. His lips brush my hair as he speaks. "You can try to run away, Estela, but I'll always bring you back to me. You belong here, in my bed. And I belong between your legs."

The words linger in the air like a promise, and I lay my head against his chest, my heart swelling. I'd finally experienced something I'd never felt before and I wanted more. Not just from Teo, but from life in general.

I'm glad I stayed, and I'm glad he is healed. I looked up at him, my eyes full of questions. He pressed a gentle kiss to my forehead and smiled.

"When you are ready, let me be your first lover," he murmurs. "Let me show you what pure pleasure feels like. There's no pain in this room, my star."

I exhale and lean forward, only for the crystal on the side of his bed to light up. I know that means someone is calling him away.

The moment is shattered. When his gaze returns to me, I look away. I straighten the robe, and he doesn't stop me when I stand up. The urge to touch him is too strong. My fingers meet his neck and his eyes flutter closed. "I just need to check your bite wounds," I say.

He doesn't respond as I peel back the bandage. The wound has already started to turn pink, and there is nothing but crusted flecks of blood. I think of the crystals filled with black that Liana and I took out while he was healing, and I am grateful whatever darkness was in him is out.

"You are fine," I say, stepping back.

"Would you like to eat together later?" he asks, brushing his large fingers over my hand. I can't help but think where those fingers were moments ago. "We have much to discuss."

I nod slowly, and he gently removes his hand. I take a few steps towards the door, my heart aching for more.

"Be safe, Teo," I say, looking back at him one last time.

He smiles at me, and my heart soars as I open the door between our rooms and leave.

CHAPTER 33
DIOPTASE
TEO

My room smells of Estela. Not just her arousal, but her soft, sweet human aroma. She is in my nose, wedged into my mind, and running through my veins.

I need more, but she is not ready. So the torture continues. And yet, it would be a lie to say that we are stuck where we started. She has changed towards me. It is a blessing.

For that, I can be nothing but grateful as I pull on fresh clothes and move to the bathroom to wash off the sweat and grime from before. When I open the door, I'm hit with another wave of her and I can't breathe.

All my youth, I was told that having a mate was the ultimate gift in life. That it would bring a sense of completeness, of fulfillment. But in reality, it only leads to a never-ending yearning for more. Here I am, hooked on Estela, addicted to her smell, her taste, her touch.

While I stand over the metal basin filled with spring art, I look in the mirror. I've seen better days. My eyes go to the wound on my neck, which has already started to heal over. Estela had done well healing it—the scar will be smooth. But then I look at the glowing mating mark on my neck and remember that Estela had looked on it with possessiveness—her thoughts had been cast freely toward me—and pictured biting it. I groan.

I dampen a cloth, and I revel in the hot water as the towel slides over my skin, trying to wash away the thoughts of her.

Once finished, I step out of my suite, facing the real world and the weight of what happened yesterday, and hurry toward the throne room. When I walk inside, I'm greeted by Vann, Liana, Svanna, and Salo. Their faces are somber, and both Vann and Salo look as though they didn't sleep.

The wise woman takes one look at me, and her frown deepens. "Where is Estela?"

I blink. "I believe she is in her room?"

Liana purses her lips. "She was supposed to stay the night with you and ensure your wounds were properly healed."

Vann's eyebrows shoot up, a bright emotion cutting through the gloom, and Svanna crosses her arms, smirking. Salo is silent, but he watches.

"Mother Liana, the matchmaker," Svanna murmurs.

Liana preens, raising her jewel-studded fingers, and crosses toward me. "We need to talk about what happened with the fight yesterday. She was the other person healing with me. Thus, we need her in this meeting," Liana insists.

I nod slowly. "Lord Vann, will you retrieve Estela?"

"Lady Estela," Liana corrects.

No one balks at the title and I look at the wise woman. I smile. "Yes, *Lady* Estela."

Vann nods and walks out of the room.

When he is gone, the room returns to its former melancholy. No one looks at me as I ease onto the broken throne.

"Was anyone else injured by the tenth creature?" I ask.

Liana looks up at me. "No."

"And do you know why you weren't able to see all of them?" I prod further.

She pauses. "I would like Lady Estela to be here when I tell you."

I furrow my brows and look at the other two advisors. Svanna is playing with the tail of her braid, and Salo stands at attention. Neither of them do anything but contribute to the dread in my stomach.

When Estela walks into the room alongside Vann, a bolt of electricity skitters down my spine. Her eyes find mine first, and the song starts up—this time playing a new tune. There's an added layer of melody as sweet and heady as berry wine.

I stand in her presence and see Liana nod her head. Svanna looks to the human and offers a halfway bow. Salo follows along, just barely.

She looks confused as to why she is here, but then she smiles a little and nods her head back. "The gems sing for a good morning," she says in my tongue.

I blink, shocked at her Enduar accent while the others return her greeting. Liana leads her over to my side at the top of the throne. I guide her to sit, and then take my place on the one good arm.

The room is tense, but I can't stop glancing at my mate. How she's changed.

Liana begins her concerns immediately after, notably speaking in the common tongue. "King Ma'Teo, Lady Estela, we bring bad news. Earlier you asked me why I did not see the tenth monster. It is because, at the time of the vision, the creature did not exist. I—" she blinks furiously, "Dyrn. It was Dyrn, changed into one of those horrible beasts."

Estela sucks in a breath, but nods. "When we were healing yesterday, you told me that there was something in King Teo's blood. We worked with crystal after crystal to extract some black substance."

My mind starts to race. I did not know about any of that.

Liana nods and reaches into the pouch at her hip to withdraw a piece of quartz. Normally, the stone is a clear white, but now it is a deep, purply black.

Estela recoils, Salo steps back, and Svanna hisses. Vann stares at the stone. The energy emanating from that is ugly, *wrong*.

"What is that?" I demand.

Liana looks to Estela and my mate speaks up. "It's the venom, I believe." Her face pales. "If we had left it, do you think that Teo would have turned as well?"

She purses her lips. "I am not sure." Then she turns to Vann. "This morning I extracted a crystal's worth from Lord Vann. It would be right to say that is why his wounds were not healing."

"I keep wondering why it didn't poison me. Was it because of my Fuegorra? My ability?" Estela shifts in her seat. "When I thought I was healing Dyrn the day he died, was my Fuegorra just trying to ease the effects of the infection?"

She nods. "That is what I think as well."

I shift my weight so that I am more standing than sitting on the arm of the throne. "We killed them all, yes?"

It is Salo who speaks up this time. "Yes, your Majesty. However, we brought the remains to be burned in the forges during the night. We kept Dyrn's body separate, and I scattered his ashes in the Parting Cave."

Svanna speaks up. "The hot flames there worked well for our purposes. The rest of the monsters were tossed into the lava."

I take a deep breath and try to process the information. Dyrn, one of our own, had been turned into a monster. And the venom was in both Vann and myself's blood. I turn to Estela. "When you tended to my wound this morning, did you find any lingering magic?"

She looks at me with a soft gaze, and her mind opens to me, showing me a brief glimpse of how she felt. "No. You are healed." She turns to Vann. "I do not sense any darkness in you either."

Vann looks relieved, and he bows his head.

"All of the men who fought should be checked for this... taint," I say.

Liana nods in agreement. "I have the necessary ingredients in my quarters. I will retrieve them while Lady Estela will help me." Then she pauses. "I am not in these counsel meetings often, but I am what we might consider the old matriarch of this court. We just eliminated a serious threat to our defenses, and our people are afraid. The mists are gone, the caves are warmer, but they need the festival. My suggestion would be to start planning today."

I nod. "Yes, we can begin planning sometime—"

"Today. Svanna has already told me that Eryx the stone cutter can help you pick the crystals. Which is your job as sovereign."

I narrow my eyes, irritated at her interruption, but willing to get the crystals we will use to help focus the Ardorflame's song. It is not easy to find four identical gems to work with, but it will be a welcome distraction.

"Very well. Lady Svanna, Lord Salo? Anything else you'd like to report?" I ask.

Lord Salo nods his head but Svanna says, "No."

I clear my throat. "I wanted to finish dealing with these cave monsters, but I am happy to report that Lothar, Turalyon, and the Elven King Arion will be coming for our wedding and the Festival of Endu."

Estela's eyes go wide. "But it's only in a few days."

Liana steps in. "Do not worry, my king, since I already knew, we have begun planning. The rooms are prepared for the royal arrival."

"Very good. Let us go make preparations to receive our cousins." I smile at my mate, and adjourn the meeting after saying, "By the grace of the Ardorflame, we will have an excellent festival. The humans will never wish to leave the under mountain."

Liana smiles, and the others filter out. When my mate follows behind Liana, I feel the trepidation that started this morning.

Just before she leaves the room, she pauses and looks back at me.

Are you well? she asks.

I smile sadly. *Weary, but I believe that everything will be all right.*

She nods. *Thank you for earlier. That... It was not easy.*

My blood rushes through my veins as I think of her face during release. Of the sweet parting of her lips and the sounds she made.

I cast the thoughts to her and she freezes. Embarrassment sours the mood before I have a chance to speak. "We should do that again," she says hurriedly and rushes out of the room.

Dragging my hand over my face, I scent the ghost of her heady arousal as I leave the throne room.

Out of the doors, I find Eryx. He is shorter than me, but also uses spectacles. He has an attachment resting around his head that houses a retractable set of magnifying glasses. Good for inspecting crystals.

"King Teo," he says with a bow. "Lady Svanna and Mother Liana have directed me to take you to the mines to select the complementary focusing crystals."

I nod and we cross the space between here and the mines in a relatively short time.

Enduvida does indeed feel warmer, and I savor that sensation as we move near the forges. I think about the monsters and Dyrn. It is a sorrowful thing that he had to suffer the way he did.

While we pass through the forges, I see the beginning of the ceremony preparations already begun. There are long bars of metal, which will be used to support the gems, and I see a few adjustments made to sitting chairs to place all around the temple.

As I watched them labor, their bodies coated with sweat and stone dust, I could not help but feel a deep sense of gratitude and pride.

When we reach tunnel eleven, the one that leads down to the Cave of Spears, I stop. It is protected throughout the year because of flooding and the water wyrms as large as me. Luckily, it is hibernation season during the Festival of Endu, and the water drains away for a few weeks so we are free to find the gypsum formations.

"Open the gates," I command the two miners who have come to help us. The massive iron doors to the tunnels creak and groan as they swing open, revealing the labyrinthine network that stretches deep into the heart of the Enduar Mountains. The scent of damp earth and rock fills my nostrils, mingling with the subtle energy of the precious crystals hidden within.

"Your Majesty," says Eryx, his voice hushed and reverent as we enter the yawning maw of darkness. "It is a great honor to assist you with this but it is my duty to remind you to walk softly around the crystals."

"Of course, Eryx," I say with a smile. It is just like a stone cutter to be more concerned with rocks than his king. We begin walking, my eyes adjusting to the dim light that filtered in from the entrance. With each step I take, the air smells different.

After a half hour of walking, I see the first long, sharp rod of opaque white crystal that savagely juts across the tunnel.

It almost looks like a spear, hence the name of the cave. The crystal's edges are jagged and rough, the result of centuries of growth and friction against the surrounding rock. I reach out to touch it, feeling the cool smoothness of the surface. Gypsum is used to help provide calm to those in distress, which is close to how I feel today.

One hundred and sixty-three men, both Enduar and human, are living in our halls, most unmated. Two have been stolen this week without finding a mate. There are still eleven women without mates. Seeing Estela sit on my throne did something to my insides. I want her to be strong, to unite and grow our people more. Luiz and Neela are happy—we will be happy as well.

As we continue on, I feel like I am walking through a forest of crystalline trees. The formations jut out from the walls and floors, forming intricate patterns and shapes that cross over each other like a battlefield. Eryx moves ahead of me, testing each crystal formation with his tools to see if it has the necessary properties to be used for the Endu and Grutabela's song.

"Look here," Eryx gestures toward a narrow fissure in the tunnel wall. "The formation of these crystals is truly remarkable."

I join the stone cutter and peer into the darkness, my keen eyes scanning every nook and cranny for signs of instability or danger. The jagged edges of the crystals glisten like fangs in the shadows.

"Indeed," I reply, my voice tinged with awe. "Our ancestors were wise to recognize the power contained within these stones and leave this mine mostly untouched."

"Of course, Your Majesty," Eryx agrees. He's quiet, but I enjoy his presence.

As we continue our descent into the depths of the mountain,

the air grows more humid, and stale, wet sound assaults my nose.

We pass into a section where the crystals are broken and scattered. It looks like something that could have happened in the quake I caused during the giants' visit. I quicken my pace as we approach a tunnel section that appears to have collapsed.

"Is this recent?" I ask.

Eryx joins me at my side. "I cannot be certain, Your Majesty," he admits. "But it is not unusual to have some breaks in a mine with water wyrms. Perhaps you have not noticed them in the past. I have heard other stone cutters speak about them in the past."

I am quiet as he guides me around the mine. When I find two crystals that appear to match closely in shape and size, I reach out to touch them. The power of the stones thrums beneath my fingertips, and I know that they will work perfectly for our purposes.

"Very well. These will suffice," I say.

Eryx nods in agreement. "I will bring my tools with Flova later today to help cut these out."

"How do you see Flova? Is he fully healed?" I ask.

He nods. "I believe so. He still has a cough, but I suspect it is more a cause of the years spent inhaling dust, not sickness. Ulla tells us that the humans have found a way to grow some of the leaves they use to heal him. I am not worried."

I smile, and we make our way out of the cave, heading toward the upper level of Enduvida.

"That is good to hear."

And it was—another pocket of light in the darkness. For the first time in days, I don't worry about giants or monsters. I think about how we will use these to reflect the sound of the night—Estela has never felt the power of Grutabela's song. I want the three stages of the ceremony to be beautiful. There are a few caves behind the palace, near the scrying grotto that have been untouched.

I could spend time cleaning one out. The waters there are warm, and it is private. She would be comfortable there.

CHAPTER 34
IOLITE
ESTELA

I can't seem to escape the relentless pull of my thoughts, every single one of them returning to this morning. It's as if a fire has been ignited within me, raging and uncontrollable, fueled by the intensity of my desire for Teo. I oscillate between regret for not going further and gratitude that I let him be.

The eight hunters who fought the monsters are lined up in front of the station Liana and I have set up in front of the palace. Each of us has a small pile of crystals and a table with cushions for the men to lay on while we work.

It's my first time working closely with these men, but my song is so loud it's distracting. I can't stop my heart from racing at every echo of footsteps, hoping it's Teo approaching. The shadows cast eerie patterns upon the walls, teasing my imagination with visions of twisted limbs entwined in a passionate embrace. I drop my hands to my side and let out a long, frustrated breath. Perhaps, if we finally made love I would be able to clear my head.

"Lady Estela!" Liana's voice jolts me from my reverie. "Are

you even listening?"

"Of course," I lie. In truth, her words have become nothing more than a dull murmur, lost beneath the deafening roar of my thoughts. I have to actively force myself to focus on the men.

"Then repeat what I just said," Liana challenges, her violet eyes narrowing suspiciously. I rack my brain for any semblance of recollection. But it's no use; my thoughts are too far gone.

"I'm sorry. I'm ready for the first hunter," I say quickly.

She puts her hands on her hips. "Do you remember what I told you—these are your people, too. If you are daydreaming about the king, you aren't accepting the responsibility that comes with him. You weren't just chosen by this stone to find love. Call it the divine, call it destiny, but *someone* has great things in mind for you. You deserve to find out what it is."

Her words hit me hard, and the spell is broken. I straighten my back and walk to the table where the crystals we'll use for extraction have been left out. I pick up one piece of quartz and turn it over in my hands.

"Lady Estela," a deep voice says. I turn around to see Lord Vann, the one who seems to dislike Arlet, yet is close with Teo. I don't know how to feel about him.

"Lord Vann," I say slowly. "Liana told me that you had met with her this morning. Are you feeling unwell?" My tone is tight and he notices.

"I was told to come here like all the rest. Better safe than sorry, don't you agree?" he says as he lies down on the table.

I hear the annoyance in his tone, but I pick up a crystal and walk over to his side. I think carefully about Liana's movements from yesterday—I am to move slowly and wait for my Fuegorra to sour at the touch of the venom. I'm making my way over his chest when that tingly, ugly prickling in my palms starts up.

"My apologies, Lord Vann. It seems like it was a good thing you came, there is still a little stuck in your chest," I say while finding the right spot to press the tip of the crystal into his shirt. "I'll need you to remove your shirt."

He obeys without another word. Like the other Enduares he is strong, but this touch elicits nothing from me. This is nothing more than medicinal work.

Replacing the crystal to the injured spot, I begin to extract the venom. Lord Vann's eyes are on me, watching my every move. Not suspicious, but wary.

"Are you in pain?" I ask, adjusting my shoulders which have begun to creep up toward my ears under his scrutiny.

He shakes his head. That movement, the carelessness of it, rubs me wrong. For the first time, I wonder if he just doesn't like humans. "Do you have a problem with my people?" I ask.

That catches him off guard. "If you mean the Enduares, who are your people now, then no," he murmurs.

I press the crystal harder and he sucks in a breath. "I mean the humans."

He narrows his eyes and looks at me. "You are King Teo's mate. I will accept you because the gods know better than I."

I remove the crystal from his chest and find a small, purplish mark on his skin from my stone. "What of the others? You seem particularly displeased with my friend Arlet."

He snorts and sits up, reaching for his shirt. "Are you friends? I don't see you two together often."

I bite my lip. Our relationship had suffered since I'd been angry with her for being so happy to be here. It was foolish, especially since I have started to enjoy living here—but he doesn't need to know any of that. "You are avoiding my question. Why do you dislike the humans?"

His further lack of denial angers me. While he buttons his shirt, he looks at me. "You are ungrateful. The Enduares are strong, resourceful people. We have saved dozens of you, and let them all go because they could not survive in the darkness.

When we learned we could mate with your kind, we risked a conflict with the giants. You reject us, but we have not rejected you."

His words hit me like a slap in the face. I feel ashamed of my past behavior. I open my mouth to apologize, but he interrupts me before I can form a coherent sentence.

"Save your apologies, Lady Estela. You are not the only one who has been misinformed about our people. There are many misconceptions about us Enduares, and it would do well for all of us to learn to be better." With that, he slides off the table and starts to leave. "Just so we are clear, I won't have you telling Teo I was cruel. I like you well enough. I'm just waiting for you to prove yourself to all of us—gods know we have proved ourselves to you."

I stop him as he lingers by the door. "So you tolerate us? What of the men working in the mines? I know that Arlet has spent time weaving. The only person who has been ungrateful is me, and I am trying to remedy that."

His fists tighten when I say Arlet's name again and my eyes widen. "Arlet," I say the name again and he flexes his jaw. "You like Arlet." I fold my arms, pleased with his response. "You know, in the human tongue, we have a phrase—there is a thin line between love and hate. Perhaps you should reexamine your feelings toward her."

Lord Vann's eyes narrow again and he takes on a monstrous look that makes me pause for a second. It reminds me of how powerful this race is.

"I like no one," he says in a low voice. "And certainly not a human." He turns and stalks out of the room, leaving me alone with my thoughts for mere moments before another man walks in.

"Lady Estela," he says brightly. This Enduar seems older than Vann, and decidedly kinder. "My name is Niht."

"Night?" I repeat.

He laughs and shakes his head. "Close enough!"

His voice is so boisterous that it makes me smile. "If you could lay down first, I will do the inspection quickly."

Ever obedient, he is on the bed in a matter of moments. "They say you've got a talent with the Fuegorra. Do all human women have magical powers?" he asks curiously as I begin to pass the crystal over him. "It would be something to have a mate with that kind of power."

My brows furrow. "No—I have heard there are some humans with magic. *Brujas*[1], we call them. But I know little about humans who didn't live in the slave pens." My thoughts split between his excitement for someone. I doubt any Enduar could be lonely with a court as close as theirs, but I suppose there is something about having a person dedicated to being your partner that makes life... easier. I'm learning it slowly.

He purses his lips. "Nasty trade those giants got into."

I don't respond as my crystal finds a small pocket of darkness and extracts it. When he is whole, he gets off the table and leaves quickly.

I meet with three more: Joso, Keio, and Svanna. They are all polite, and continue to use the title that Liana is insisting on. I find myself tired and hungry as I gaze at the twelve crystals all filled with venom. They'll have to be fed to the lava and there is something, almost sad about it to me.

Teo had told me he would enjoy eating with me later, so I begin to clean up just as Liana comes over. "Well done," she says, surveying my crystals. "You could've been a bit smoother with your extraction, but no one is complaining."

I laugh. "I told you I listen to what you say."

"Most of what I say," she chides.

While we stand there, I remember the bet she made while we were playing the pebble game. My cheeks go red, but my curiosity is stronger than anything else. "What happened to the phial of carnelian powder that you brought earlier."

She wipes her hands on a rag and laughs. "I was wondering if you would ask me about that. Technically, Iryth won. I suspect she needs it, with all the hard work she has in caring for the newborn."

I nod, a little disappointed. It seemed like it would make this new part of myself a little more exciting.

Then she comes over and wraps an arm around me. "You know, there are few people I talk to as directly as I do with you. Perhaps you have noticed, but I am happy to be your friend. I'll make you a new phial, consider it a festival gift."

I smile and look up at her. "Do you normally give gifts during the festival?"

She nods her head. "Yes. Hasn't Teo told you?"

I blink and shake my head. "He doesn't tell me much. I—I don't know what an appropriate gift would be."

A feminine snort comes from behind us. "Mother Liana, I didn't know you were so invested in a royal baby."

I whip around to see Lady Svanna. I like her, she's a good teacher, but I'm not ready for this conversation with someone else. "We were discussing gifts for the festival the day after tomorrow."

She smiles. "Yes. Iryth is quite good at such things. Which brings me to why I'm here—unfortunately, we needed extra help setting up the temple for the festival, and the king is quite tall. He won't be able to make it for your date."

My heart sinks at the news. I had been looking forward to spending time with Teo. "It's all right," I say with a small smile. "I understand how important the festival is."

Lady Svanna smiles in return. "I'm glad to hear that, seeing as how it's your wedding day, but I was thinking you could eat with me and my mate. I know you usually eat by yourself after helping Ulla cook, but Arlet sits with us as well. You might enjoy it."

I consider it for a moment, then nod my head. "Thank you, Lady Svanna. I would love to join you and your mate for lunch."

She nods, pleased. "Lunch—I like that word. Excellent. We can head over now if you'd like, I'm sure you are hungry."

I nod happily and quickly follow Lady Svanna through the corridors of the castle. I can hear the sounds of preparation for the festival all around us, and excitement builds inside of me.

When we cross the bridge over the crevasse, I see Teo with seven other men setting up large scaffolds with crystals atop. I suck in a breath. He is shirtless, and I can behold ever carefully sculpted muscle on his glistening back and chest.

My heart hammers in my chest as I try to avert my gaze, but it's like his magnetic pull draws me in. I can't help but admire the way his muscles bulge while we walk into the residential section.

As we enter the dining hall, I see Svanna's mate, Iryth. She's holding the baby on her knee, bouncing as she feeds him spoonfuls of something mushy from a bowl.

"Iryth, I brought a friend," Svanna says.

Iryth beams up at me. "Wonderful. What a joy to have the Lady Estela eat with us."

As I start to say my hello, Arlet appears. Things between us are not unpleasant, but I still feel uncomfortable.

She reaches over and pulls me close. "Estela, I'm so glad to see you," she says. She's a forgiving woman, and I appreciate that.

As we sit down, I look at the two Enduar women. They are quite a bit different from human bodies with their long torsos and stunning fingers. Iryth passes Svanna their baby, and the miner kisses her child tenderly.

It's a sweet scene, but a part of me feels pain at the view. This is the kind of childhood that Mikal should have had.

Iryth misinterprets my stares for something else. "We have been caring for him since his parents died a month ago. He is a healthy baby. Do you wish for one?"

Arlet stiffens next to me and I suck in my own breath. Reaching for my glass, I take a long drink. "I do like children. I raised my brother after he was born."

Svanna pauses as she eats, and I see a look pass between the two women. Telepathic thoughts, no doubt.

"What happened to your mother?" Iryth asks gently.

I take a deep breath and look at Arlet. She hadn't known me then—so she understood the basic stories, but I had never gone into detail. Details are almost always painful.

"My mother was placed in the breeding pens with my father. She gave birth to me nine months later, and was given a small den with my father," I say softly. "Unfortunately, the Giant King had been picking out slaves to pass to his favorite councilmen and saw her. He took her as his comfort woman soon after I was born. She was a fertile human—she was pregnant more than once. But the king always ensured it was taken care of.

"Until I was nine, and she fell pregnant for the last time. He was traveling a lot that year, and she bribed the herb workers to let her keep the child. She died in childbirth. I was all Mikal had left."

The room falls quiet as the weight of my words settles over us. I take another sip of my drink, grateful for the warmth it brings to my chest.

"I'm sorry," Iryth says softly, her eyes full of compassion. Arlet puts her hand on mine, and I smile up at her. "I completely understand why you would want to take your time to think about children."

"It is the past," I say, forcing a smile. "I've learned to cope."

For so long, I had kept my secrets close to me. There is no family among those considered not much better than animals, but there is power in speaking about my story. I am surrounded by friends, like a warm blanket.

"That's why you have been so insistent on bringing your brother back," Svanna says.

I nod, feeling a sense of comfort that she understands.

Iryth holds her child closer, and Svanna holds them both, tucking their little family in the crook of her arm.

"I know the king is waiting until after the Elven King leaves, but if you bring the issue up in the council meetings, I will gladly support you. We could send a few scouts to the giant border," Svanna says.

I am touched by Svanna's offer. "Thank you, Lady Svanna. Your support means a lot to me."

Iryth smiles at us. "Would you like to hold Sama?"

I pause, knowing what a great act it is to trust another with a child. I nod, reaching forward as she passes the baby over the table.

As I hold Sama, I'm reminded of the time I spent caring for my brother. Sama looks up at me with big, bright eyes, and I can't help but smile.

---

1. Witches.

CHAPTER 35
SELENITE
TEO

The arrival of the Elven King Arion is a quiet affair. Estela is at my side, standing a few paces away and fidgeting with her gown. Mother Liana, Lord Vann, and the rest of the council are also present.

As King Arion approaches, I notice that his step is light and his face is serene. He is the son of the last king, and I do not know him. Despite the weight of his crown and the responsibility that comes with it, he carries himself with ease. There are twelve elves traveling with him, all sporting the same long, blond hair and pointed ears. Their skin is pale gold, unlike our blue. They also lack our useful tails.

I settle further when I see Turalyon and Lord Lothar. They smile and nod. Their faces are tight, but they appear unharmed.

"King Ma'Teo," he says, bowing his head as he addresses me. "It has been a long time since our peoples have spoken. Thank you for an invitation to your wedding."

I nod. "King Arion, it is our pleasure to have you here. This is my council." I gesture to one side, and then turn to my mate. "And this is my human bride, Lady Estela."

King Arion's eyes flicker over Estela for a moment, his lips curving into a small smile. "A pleasure to meet you, Lady Estela." His attention flicks back up to me. "I have heard much about her... unorthodox arrival in Enduvida," he says, his voice smooth and cultured.

Estela dips into a shallow curtsy, a pink flush staining her cheeks. "Thank you, Your Majesty. It is an honor to meet you as well."

He ignores her, and turns to Lord Salo, who bows in turn. "I am Lord Salo, leader of Stone Benders and cutters."

He continues down the line to Vann. "Lord Vann, personal advisor to the king."

More nods until he reaches Svanna. She opens her mouth just as he turns to me and says, "Who is this?"

I groan inwardly. Fifty years and things don't change. "Lady Svanna, leader of the mines. Then Lady Fira, one of our elders and leader of the weavers and crafters, Lady Ulla of the singers, healers, and cooks, and Mother Liana. Our Fuegorra reader."

He takes in each woman as I speak, and then twirls around to face me again. "Tomorrow you will be married. Is it true that you are mates?"

I take a deep breath. "Yes." I turn my head to the side and point to the mating mark.

His eyes harden as he inspects my throat.

"Does she have one?" King Arion ask, his gaze shifting to Estela.

"No. But she is unique," I reply, my voice tinged with pride. "And strong. She has proven herself to be a worthy queen."

"Indeed," he says, his attention returning to me. "Do you have any other human women I could meet in this mountain?"

I nod my head. "There is one named Arlet. She has agreed to join your group during the festival tomorrow. She is not mated to anyone in our city, so your men are free to see if she had a spark with any of them."

King Arion nods, his eyes sparkling with a hint of amusement. "Excellent. I look forward to meeting her."

As King Arion and his entourage make their way to the guest quarters, I feel Estela's hand slip into my arm.

Is it normal for him to ignore women? she asks, a frown creasing her forehead.

I look down at her. *The elves don't have women in positions of power. Anyone mated to him would be a consort.*

She raises an eyebrow. *Is he mated?*

I shake my head. *I don't know. I suppose we will find out more tomorrow night at the party.*

She shakes her head. *I don't like him. Someone should watch over Arlet during the wedding.*

I cast a pointed look at Vann, who looks like he could crush stone with his bare fists. *I think that is already taken care of.*

"Would you like to eat dinner with the rest of my court?" I ask the elven king as we stand in front of his room. I sense Estela tense as she nears the place where she was whipped.

Don't worry. This is not the same room. You will never have to go back there, I say through the bond.

The king looks at me and offers a tight smile. "I believe we will get our cultural fill tomorrow. We are happy to eat in our rooms this evening," he practically sings. "Good night," he says and closes the door.

The elves he brought with him also shut their door and we are left alone in the hallway.

"That was... unique," Vann says, and Svanna glares at him.

Lothar lets out a long breath, one that it seems like he has been holding for weeks. "You have no idea."

I look at my advisor. "Do you think he'll agree to help us?"

He nods. "They are strange, but I wouldn't have brought them if they didn't seem interested. Their populations are suffering the same as ours."

We all turn and leave the hall. I'm left wondering if it was a mistake to bring them here.

CHAPTER 36
TOURMALINE
ESTELA

I'm sitting on my bed, staring at the door connecting my room to Teo's room. Tomorrow is the festival—my wedding. I would be lying if I said there weren't butterflies in my stomach.

Liana had left a small phial of the powder she promised me. I look at it, nervous about what will happen after Teo and I are wed. So far, he's been gentle and receptive. A part of me worries that will change.

I fall back on my bed and sigh. This started as an agreement to get Mikal back but has revealed itself as one of the most intricate plans of my life.

Teo has barely touched me since that morning in his room. Tomorrow night... it will be time.

I swallow just as someone knocks on my door. Vaulting off my bed, I rush to open. Every part of me knows it won't be Teo, but it still hurts a little when I don't see his tall, blue frame.

"Arlet," I say, smiling wide. She is an excellent surprise, and she's carrying two gowns. I push the door open wider. "Come in."

As Arlet steps inside, I close the door behind her. She walks across the room with the dresses, one blue and one pale pink, and hangs them on the back of my chair. "What brings you here?" I ask, sitting back on my bed and motioning for her to do the same.

"I just wanted to make sure you are all right," Arlet says, smiling warmly. "I know tomorrow is monumental."

I nod, a lump forming in my throat. "You could say that."

Arlet nods. "I realized earlier today that I never apologized for becoming so distant when we arrived. I just was so happy, and you were determined to hate this mountain."

I frown and shake my head. "For good reason."

She looks up at me. "Do you still hate it here?"

"No. For better or worse, this will be my home."

She brightens. "I helped make your gown. Would you like to see?"

I smile in return. "Of course, I would love to."

Arlet stands up and unfolds the blue gown. It is breathtaking. The color reminds me of the clear sky on a perfect day, and the lace details around the neckline and sleeves amplify the elegant design. "Arlet, it's beautiful," I utter, running the soft fabric between my fingers.

"I'm glad you like it," she replies, beaming with pride. "It was one of the most challenging dresses I've ever made. I wanted it to be perfect for you."

"It is more than perfect," I reply, gazing at the gown with wide eyes. "Thank you. Is the other for meeting the elven king?"

She nods, then flushes. "When King Teo told me he needed my help, I decided to make this with... uh, seduction in mind," Arlet says, her face turning redder by the minute.

I raise an eyebrow, reeling back. "Teo asked you to seduce the elven king?" All I can think about is how he completely ignored all the women.

Arlet shakes her head. "No. I thought it might be useful to have a distraction if things got tense."

I nod slowly, my mind racing. "And did Teo approve of this plan?"

She shook her head. "I didn't tell anyone. Only you."

I take her hands. "You need to be careful with the king. I met him tonight when he arrived. He's very handsome, but he refuses to speak to the women. He doesn't seem... caring. Not like the Enduares."

Arlet's face closes. "He would change if he met his mate. Everyone says that our king changed when he met you."

I reel back. "Arlet, no. You don't want him as a mate."

She doesn't say anything for a few moments, her gaze distant. "You are mated to a king. Why not me?" she asks, biting her lip.

"What about Lord Vann," I ask. I know it's the wrong thing to say when she glares at me. "I saw the way you acted when he was hurt. He can't seem to stop staring at you."

She flares her nostrils. "He's a prick. I don't care for him at all."

I take a deep breath. "Very well. But Arlet, Promise me you won't try anything with the elven king. I don't want you getting hurt."

She narrows her eyes but nods reluctantly. "I promise."

"Good." I stand up, still holding the gown. "I should probably try this on. How does it even work with all those laces?"

Arlet grins, standing up as well. "I'll show you tomorrow. It's quite elaborate, but the effect is stunning."

CHAPTER 37
ARAGONITE
TEO

The morning of the festival has been hectic and boisterous. Now everyone is crowding out of their houses and standing in front of the Ardorflame temple. I must admit, it's beautiful. The light of the lava veins is bright and the spell lights reflect off the crystals embedded in the massive pillars that hold the temple up. The people are dressed in their finest clothes and jewelry, their faces bright and eager, as if they are all in a trance. They talk excitedly, waiting for Mother Liana to appear and begin the festival.

I wait on the steps of the palace, observing my people from afar. Even from here, I can see the elven king and his posse. Arlet is also visible, with her bright red hair and pink dress. She is talking with her hands while the king merely watches her.

I don't have to agree with him to get his help, I remind myself just as a familiar voice enters my mind.

Teo?

I suck in a breath. *Yes?*

Will you come?

Just like that, I'm spinning on my heel and practically flying to her room. When I arrive, she opens the door, and I behold her in her festival gown.

It's a sight to behold. The fabric of her dress is as blue as the ocean, and it falls in gentle cascades around her feet. The bodice is studded with sapphires, and her hair hangs loosely around her shoulders. I want to run my fingers through it. The neckline dips down to her ribs, revealing that beautiful stone on her sternum and showcasing the betrothal gift I gave her—forty gems laced together. She looks like a goddess, and for a moment, I'm left breathless.

"Happy Festival," she says, stepping forward and placing a leaf in my hands. I look down at the small green thing and then return my gaze to her.

She smiles. "It's from the plants I've been growing. It's a niue root leaf."

I grin, so proud of my mate. I draw her into my arms. "Thank you. This is a really beautiful gesture." I think of how much we need plants, how dead this mountain was before she arrived.

She pulls back and looks up at me. "Will you help me braid my hair," she says softly, beckoning me to come closer.

I suck in a breath, knowing what that means for mated pairs—a sign of our attachment for one to braid the other's hair.

I take a step closer, my fingers twitching as I reach for the comb on the vanity. There are several metal cuffs with gems waiting to be scattered throughout her hair. My fingers grip the carved bone, and I want to be anything but gentle, but my mate is soft. So much softer than I could have imagined.

She sits on her bed, and I sit beside her, separating her hair into sections and combing each strand carefully. It's a delicate process, and I'm grateful for the silence that surrounds us.

As I braid her hair, my fingers weave strands together until it forms a perfect plait. With every pull and twist, I can feel her breathing become deeper. I realize that this is more than just a mere task, but an intimate ritual between mated pairs. It brings us closer, and I can feel the energy between us surge.

When I'm finished, I stand up and step back, surveying my handiwork. Her hair has been unbound for too long, I can hardly stop myself from tracing the shell of her very round ear. I turn back to the vanity, grab one of the jewels, and secure it above her ear when she turns to face me.

She presses her hands to the waist of the gown. It's been so long since I've seen clothes like those used.

"Do you like it?" she asks. "Arlet made it."

I nod, admiring the intricate beading and embroidery on the bodice. "It's beautiful," I say. "And you look stunning in it."

A small smile tugs at the corners of her lips, and I can't help but lean in to kiss her. Her lips are like velvet against mine, and desire shoots through my body. I deepen the kiss, my hands cupping her face as I explore her mouth with my tongue. She moans softly, and I feel a sense of pride at eliciting such a response from her.

We pull away reluctantly, and I press my forehead against hers, taking deep breaths to calm myself. I can't lose control now, not when the festival is about to begin, and my people need me.

"Shall we?" I ask, offering her my arm.

She takes it, and we make our way out of the palace together.

The walk to the Ardorflame temple is so much shorter than I remember.

As we approach the temple, the sound of singing and chanting grows louder. The crowd parts for us, and we walk down the middle of a wide aisle lined with people on either side. Everyone is dressed in their finest attire, but all eyes are on us. I can feel their stares, some curious, some envious, and some filled with admiration.

We reach the front of the temple, where a marble altar has been placed with a crystal dagger on top.

"It's okay," I whisper, squeezing her hand reassuringly. "All the hard work is finished. All that is left for us is to enjoy."

She smiles weakly, but I can tell she's still nervous. I turn my attention back to the ceremony.

"Where's Liana?" she asks.

I draw near, smelling the sweet vanilla scent of her skin. "She'll come out soon. First, we shout. Then she will sing the Song of Life while we are wed, and then we will spend the rest of the night basking in the harmony of our gods."

My mate nods, and we stand there in silence, watching the priests light the Ardorflame. The flickering orange light illuminates the temple, casting shadows on the walls. Soon, the singers begin to chant, and the crowd joins in. I feel the energy pulsing through my body, the shared connection between all of my people like another limb.

Then all goes silent, and the lights in the cavern go dark, even the crystals in our chest. They do not cease to work; they simply recognize the power. Estela gasps, clutching my arm as I pull her close. My eyes are better than hers, so I can still see vague outlines.

"Are you ready to let go?" I murmur. She doesn't answer.

The same gong we use for telling time sounds three times before the cries begin. The sound makes my chest cave in. Our pain, our cries, our failures reverberate in the air. I keep my mouth shut for fear of startling my mate, but she relaxes at my side. She steps forward and opens her mouth.

The sound that rips out of her throat is like nothing I've ever heard before. It's a mixture of pain, longing, and a deep yearning for something more. It chills me to the very bone.

I watch her body shake with the force of her shout, and I can feel the energy pouring out of her. From the tilt of her head to the way she squeezes her hands in front of her, her pain is palpable.

Finally, I join in. Letting the sound pour from me, too. It is cathartic, a release of emotion that I have been holding in for so long.

The gong sounds once again, and the shouting stops. The ground beneath us trembles, and the lava veins in the temple light up like they've never done before. The gems surrounding it sparkle, particularly the focus crystals up above. The small slit in the top of the cavern that lines up perfectly once a year bleeds through the air.

Still faint. Then, atop the tunnel, Mother Liana appears. She stands with a white hooded cloak hiding part of her face. Gems glitter all over her, creating their own sound. Her sleeves are embroidered with silvered stars, and her time-graveled voice echoes throughout the space.

"Welcome, my children, to the Festival of Endu! We are pleased that both our humans and our elven guests have joined us this evening. Tonight, we embrace the power of the divine," she cries out. The two large crystals we spent all yesterday placing shatter into the finest dust, glittering in the light. The enchanted stone moves to the sound of the song, forming the moon's shape just above the focusing crystal.

"Come forward, Lady Estela and King Ma'Teo," Liana says.

We move forward through the shimmering air, hand in hand, and both kneel before the stone altar. The wise woman raises her hands in the air, all of the gems and crystals across her body shimmering. "Do you accept your matehood?"

I look at Estela. She takes a deep breath and squeezes my hand while she picks up the knife. "Yes," her voice is strong. She takes my hand, and creates a shallow cut in my palm.

I follow after, barely slicing her own hand before I press our hands together, mixing our blood and adding, "I will protect you with my power, influence, and, if necessary, my own body. If we are blessed with a family, I will also protect them. My old self is dead—from this moment onward, I will live for you only."

"Grutabela and Endu," Liana calls out. "One trapped in the sky, the other in the ground, but forever bound together in love. Bless our sovereigns."

Estela's eyes shine. The crowd erupts into cheers and applause, but the sound from above is louder. The air begins to glitter with light as Liana starts her song. The melody is hauntingly beautiful, etching its way into my soul. As she sings, my mate takes my hand, her fingers interlacing with mine. The pure, crystalline tones of Ulla's voice blend with the deeper, richer tones of Velen, and then we all join in, our voices creating harmony.

Tears burn in my eyes when I realize Estela is singing along. The gems in our chests glow as the air around us glitters, and the temple pulses with life.

I wish I could trap the joy and bottle it up into my soul, but the song ends. The harmony does not.

One by one, couples start to pull each other up towards the temple, sharing a kiss to the cheers of the people. When Svanna and Iryth head up, Svanna turns back to me and yells.

"To Teo and Estela!"

When our mouths meet, it is to seal a promise. I am shocked when her voice enters my mind.

You are mine.

I pull back and grin, helping her stand.

"Your people seem... intrigued by me," she remarks, her voice tinged with something that might have been amusement.

"Can you blame them?" I reply, a smile tugging at the corners of my mouth. "You have been a rare sight until the last week."

"Perhaps," she agrees, her lips curving into a grin. "But I think they find our entwined hands even more fascinating."

"Let them stare," I say, squeezing her hand gently. "For tonight, we are simply two souls lost in the enchantment of the festival."

Her laughter rings out like a bell, bright and clear, cutting through the gloom that has hung over me since I first saw her. "Lost, indeed," she murmurs, her brown eyes dancing with mirth.

King Arion approaches slowly, bowing in front of us. "My congratulations to the new sovereigns. All of this is very enlightening," he says.

I nod. "How are you finding your conversation with Arlet?" I ask.

He glances back at Arlet, and his expression shifts. "I understand the appeal of the humans."

He doesn't seem antagonistic, just genuinely curious. "Enjoy yourself this evening. Please don't hesitate to send someone to notify me if you need something."

He nods as I move Estela forward. As the cacophony of vibrant laughter and lively music surrounded us, I became acutely aware of Estela's proximity. Her warmth is a beacon in the stifling darkness of my world. Leading her through the labyrinthine paths, I revel in the opportunity to showcase our kingdom's rich culture.

"What is he doing?" Estela asks, stopping in front one of the miners who is contorting his limbs into unnatural positions.

"Ah, that's Eshar," I explain. "He's a stone-bender, with a talent for dancing."

"Unique indeed," she replies, her eyes wide with a mixture of fascination and horror. We continue on, our path illuminated by the glow of countless lanterns, each one casting its own shadow.

"Over here," I beckon, guiding her toward a smoky stall where a woman prepared skewers of spiced meat. As the aroma wafts through the air, it speaks of life's transient pleasures, enjoyed only fleetingly before the inexorable march of time claimed them.

"Try one," I urge, handing her a skewer. "They're a festival favorite."

"Thank you," she murmurs, taking a cautious bite. A smile spreads across her face as the flavors meld together on her tongue.

"Delicious, isn't it?" I ask, my heart swelling at the sight of her enjoyment.

"Absolutely," she agrees, her eyes sparkling with appreciation. "And almost the same as every other night."

We laugh, and I lead her further still, back to the palace, until we reach the entrance to the water cavern. The air is thick with the scent of damp stone.

She looks up at me, surprised. "What is this?"

"These were private caves for the royal family. I grew up swimming here—the water is warm, like the ones in our bathing tubs." I say.

She steps forward. "Why have you brought me?"

"Because," I reply, taking her hand in mine and leading her down the steps into the shimmering water, "I want to share every part of my kingdom with you."

As we cross the threshold, the caverns unveil their hidden beauty. Estela's eyes widen, her breath catching in her throat as she takes in the ethereal glow of the bioluminescent plants that clung to the walls and ceiling. Their soft light reflects off the shimmering pools, painting the cavern with an otherworldly radiance. It is a sight I had beheld many times before, but seeing it anew through her eyes fills me with a renewed sense of wonder.

"I thought there weren't any plants under the mountain," she breathes, voice barely above a whisper.

She steps further in, entranced by the shifting hues of the

bioluminescent plants and the haunting echo of the water's song.

"They are called *luminiflor*," I explain, tracing the delicate veins of a nearby leaf with my free hand. "They feed on the minerals in the cavern walls and emit this gentle glow as they grow. They are good for little other than light—we consider them poisonous."

Her eyes flash up at me, and her mind opens. I see her preparing the poison and feel her regret. "I am sorry for what I tried to do," she says.

"It's forgotten," I reply, pulling her close to me. "Fear can cause us to do things we regret later. We have both made mistakes, but we continue onward." I can't resist reaching out and touching the gem embedded in the shell of her round ear.

Her attention is back on the plants. She reaches up and brushes one, pulling back her hand to inspect the glow. "It's somewhat shocking to see how something so beautiful can flourish in such darkness," she muses.

I look at the gilded halo of her body."Perhaps it is the darkness that allows them to truly shine."

"Maybe," she conceded, her gaze wandering over the pools that dotted our path. "And what of the water? It seems almost...alive."

"Ah, yes," I nodded, understanding her fascination. "The caverns are fed by an underground river that carries with it ancient minerals, imbuing the water with its shimmering quality. It is said those who drink from these pools are granted a wish—but be warned, they taste awful."

She laughs. "Perhaps I'll try it anyway."

We continue our journey through the dimly lit water caverns, the soft moss beneath our feet muffling our footsteps. The quiet song left over from the festival is punctuated only by the occasional water drip echoing throughout the chamber. The glow of light is comforting in its intimacy; it was as if we were traversing a world meant solely for us.

We reach the place I had prepared with blankets, food, and towels, she pauses.

I follow her gaze to the secluded alcove, hidden away from the main path. A small waterfall cascades into a crystal-clear pool, surrounded by delicate mushrooms with tails that shimmer with an ethereal luminescence—*luminiflor*—all framed by glowing amethyst and tourmaline. It looks more opulent than common quartz.

"This is the most beautiful thing I've ever seen," she breathes.

"Come," I urged, leading her towards the alcove. As we approached, the warm steam from the waterfall mists my face. "I've brought you something to eat."

We sit on a moss-covered rock, our fingers intertwining as naturally as roots seeking sustenance in the earth. Together, we watch the water dance and sparkle, and I find myself drawn not only to the hypnotic movement of the water but also to Estela's rapt expression.

While I pass her a few more skewers, she gingerly picks at the meat. Her warmth against my shoulder anchored me as the eerie glow intensified, casting an ever-changing dance of crimson and indigo across her delicate features.

She looks up at me, and I can't breathe when I see the trust in her face. "No one has ever treated me the way you do."

My heart swells with an emotion that I cannot describe. I brush a loose curl from her face, and for a moment, the only thing between us is the specks of glitter that drift in the air.

"I vow to always treat you with the respect and dignity that you deserve," I say, my voice barely above a whisper.

Her eyes meet mine, and I can see the longing in them. "You mentioned that you used to swim in these caves."

"I did," I reply, a smile spreading across my lips. "Would you like to join me?"

I stand up, peel off my ceremonial shirt, and pull my mother's ring from my trousers before kicking them off, too. I stand before her in the nude. She hesitates for only a moment before she stands up and steps out of her shoes.

"I can't take off the dress myself," she breathes.

Without a second thought, I reach for the laces on the back of her gown, tugging them loose one by one until the fabric drops to the mossy ground. She quickly turns around, and I suck in a breath. Her body is a canvas of soft curves and delicate lines, and I find myself staring in wonder at the sight of her before me.

"You can't look at my back," she says quickly, trying to hide her breasts.

I step forward and take her hands. "You are the most beautiful woman I have ever laid eyes on. I know what the giants did, and I vow to avenge your honor. But you need to know that your scars do not define you—it is your heart and your strength that do. Let me see, and one day, let me bring you the head of the man who gave them to you."

The words are harsh for such an intimate moment, but she doesn't seem to mind, and she stands there, letting her arms fall down. I let myself gaze upon the curve of her shoulders, her breasts, rosebud nipples, and down to the curving vee between her legs where a thick patch of hair blossoms.

She hesitates for another moment, but then she steps forward and takes my hand. I spin her around and suck in a breath. Crisscross patterns are splayed all across her back. They even dip down past her tailbone and onto her upper thighs. Such ugly, harsh marks for a soft goddess.

When I see the First Prince again, I will kill him. I'll take my time inflicting every single one of her scars on him before I hang him on a post and let the *aradhlums* finish the job. He will pay for every second of agony she's ever felt at his family's hand.

I reach out and touch one of the mangled lines, tracing its cruel pattern from her spine to her left buttock.

I hear her gasp. The sound reminds me to keep a tight rein on my anger. The giants won't steal this moment from us. I squeeze her hand and turn her back around before leading her into the water.

Together, we wade into the warm pool, our bodies sinking beneath the glowing water. Our movements are slow and languid, as if we are in our own private world. My fingers trace lazy circles along the skin of her shoulder before she pushes away.

The water caresses every inch of our skin, wrapping us in a cocoon of warmth. As we swim, her laughter echoes in the cavern, drowned out only by the rush of water over the rocks. I watch as she gracefully twists and turns in the water, her body illuminated by the light of the *luminiflor*.

As we emerge from the pool, we are covered in a fine sheen of water that catches the light in a thousand different ways. She wades to one of the shallower parts of the pool, and her body glistens as she steps out of the water, her braid clinging to her skin as she approaches me. My eyes trace the curve of her breasts, the dip of her waist, the fullness of her hips—everything about her is enchanting.

My blood is rushing within me as she presses up against me, her hands wandering up my chest to my shoulders. I lean down for a kiss, and I can feel the heat of her breath on my lips. Our mouths meet, and for a moment, we lose ourselves in the warmth and softness of each other.

As we pull apart, we gaze into each other's eyes, and my desire for her grows with every passing second. "Estela," I murmur, "I want you."

CHAPTER 38
NEPTUNITE
ESTELA

The song in my ears is lulling me into a state of what feels like permanent arousal. My heart races as I grapple with the combination of desire and nerves tangling together into a knot that tightens in my chest.

Liana gave me a drink to stop pregnancy yesterday. But I am not worried about a child, I'm worried about how I will feel after this.

I've seen it in the way Teo looks at me—a hunger that mirrors my own. I can't deny the magnetic pull between us, but can I truly give myself to him?

The answer is yes. It's my choice.

As our bodies meet, the air between us seems to crackle with energy—a potent mix of passion and power. Our lips find each other again in a searing kiss that sends shivers down my spine, igniting a fire within me that burns with ferocious intensity.

"If we do this," he murmurs against my head, taking out the clasps he'd worked into my hair and pulling my wet locks free, "you will be mine. I know what they said earlier, but this is the true acceptance of a mate. I will be yours—it will be as if you've crawled under my skin. We can't ever go back."

Teo's hands roam over me with a sense of ownership, firmly gripping my waist and pulling me closer. My body responds instinctively, molding itself to his powerful form as if seeking refuge in the storm of emotions raging within me.

"I know." I gasp when he puts his hands between my legs once more. "Please... teach me what you like."

And then, with an almost predatory grace, he leans me back onto one of the mossy stones. I gasp when his fingers brush over a scar on my back, but then I feel the proof of his arousal prodding my thigh, stealing all memories of pain.

All I can think about is his cock. It's long and thick. The thought of it filling me up seems borderline painful.

"Estela," he murmurs, his voice commanding yet tender. "When will you learn that what I like is you?" he asks, his hand reaching up to stroke my cheek gently. His soft tail curls around my thigh and squeezes. The pressure is welcome. "Are you ready?"

I nod. His lips descend on my throat, and I reach up to touch the glowing mark that claims him as mine.

"I wish I had one of these," I murmur.

He growls, and his teeth tease the sensitive skin on my neck. Paired with the rhythm of his hand, I nearly come out of my skin. I recognize my wetness slick my inner thighs.

"Did you enjoy that, my star?" he asks.

I moan in response when one of his pointed canines returns to the same spot. "Yes," I whisper.

"Good," he says. "Let me give you my own mating mark. I'm going to bite you."

Wait until you are inside me, I think.

He goes feral at the suggestion. And then he moves lower, to my chest, devouring me with his tongue and his fingers. His hands soon find my breasts and tease my nipples until I moan with pleasure.

My body moves instinctively in response to his touch as if it was made for him. The soft, damp end of his tail continues to brush over my skin like a feather, light and torturous, as he inserts a finger. I gasp with delight. It feels as if my muscles are quivering and shaking with every gentle caress of his.

My head begins to spin, and my whole body lights on fire. All thoughts have disappeared, and I'm lost in the pleasure. I'm helplessly drawn to it—unable to resist, unable to control myself. All I can do is feel. His touch is pure bliss as it penetrates me.

When he removes his fingers and lines up to my entrance, I whimper.

"I think you're too large," I say, looking into his lap.

He pauses. "Do you want me to stop?"

I cling to his back. "*Gods no*. But you have to go slow."

He leans forward and kisses my forehead. "Of course." Then he pushes in. He moves one bit at a time, kissing my neck while he moves inside. The song humming between us is frantic, and my body has to stretch to accommodate him. At first, the pain is sharp, and then it is pleasurable.

Bite me, I think. He groans and leaves my breast to return to my neck, biting down hard enough to pierce my skin as he seats himself completely. I cry out, seeing stars. I am completely filled with him. I feel him in every inch of my body.

He releases my neck and licks the blood off my neck. "Estela, you're perfect," he breathes while pulling back out.

The tight discomfort gives way to the dull ache—*need*—inside of me. And in that moment, I know our promises have been made true. I'm inexorably his—body and soul.

The experience is overwhelming. I revel in the bliss of being embraced by him as he moves inside of me. He goes slow, claiming me with each powerful stroke of his hips.

"I am yours," I repeat, arching off the mossy rock. His pace picks up, carrying me closer to that sweet edge. "You are mine," I grind out seconds before something explodes inside me as I reach my climax.

At that moment, I find my freedom. I've finally stepped out of the bounds of my past and into his arms.

The intensity of the moment gradually fades, and when I open my eyes, I realize that I had never felt so safe. We lay together in each other's arms, our bodies entwined and connected in ways that transcended any words we could ever say or write.

The water laps against my skin, and I am so sensitive it's almost painful. I turn around, look at him, and pause. The moment is perfect. Too perfect.

When he looks down at me, he holds up his hand and pulls something off one of his fingers.

It's a golden ring with a line of four gems set inside of the leafy designs. "Happy festival," he murmurs as he slides it onto my finger. "This was my mother's, but I have changed the stones. Amethyst, melanterite, obsidian, and ruby."

My whole body trembles at the intensity of his words as my eyes fill with tears of joy. "It matches my necklace."

He hums, and we steal a few more moments, wrapped in each other's arms. Then I take a deep breath.

"Teo, I need to speak with you about something," I say.

He tightens his grip on me. "What is wrong?"

"I am so happy tonight. It has been the most beautiful night of my life. But there is always something in the back of my mind, something I can't let go of. When will you bring Mikal?"

I feel him exhale against me, and I wait.

"Men are scouting the area, but I was waiting until after our meeting with the elves," he says. "I want to tear Zlosa apart for what they did to you all, but we are few. If we do it before we have support, things could end poorly."

I pull away. "Please."

Teo exhales. "Do we have to talk about this now?"

I meet his gaze. "Yes, we do."

He purses his lips. "Very well. We will call a council meeting and send someone in the morning. Is that acceptable, my queen?"

I nod, and he kisses me. Already, my stomach is stirring with his nearness. All thoughts fall out of my head again. I can't help but reach down and grab his silky length. I can't even wrap my fingers his base.

He groans and pushes me back onto the rock. "Don't start games you don't want to play."

I look up at him. "You'll find I can be quite competitive." I angle my neck, showing off his mark on my neck.

He growls and flips me around. I barely have time to gasp before he thrusts into me again, filling me with that delicious heat. I cry out, feeling my insides stretch and pulse around him. His breathing is ragged, and I've never heard a better sound.

This time is not slow, nor gentle, but it touches my heart just the same. Being joined to him makes me feel safe.

He moves in and out, and I can feel the tension coiling tighter and tighter inside me. I pant, wanting to touch, wanting more. He slides a hand between us and finds the spot he touched before to make me come. Then he starts teasing me mercilessly.

I arch away from him, driving his thrusting to a new angle. "Teo," I gasp.

"Say my name again," he demands.

I do, and he groans before driving into me harder, sending me over the edge. I call his name, lost in the sensation coursing through me.

When he's finished, he gathers me in his arms. We stare at each other. Lost. Wrecked, and remade.

"What have you done to me, my star?" he asks, stroking my face with his warm fingers.

I smile up at him.

"I'm going to take you back to our room so you can sleep," he murmurs.

I look up at him, boneless while he drapes my clothes over me. "That sounds nice."

CHAPTER 39
CARNELIAN
TEO

I'm in the middle of laying Estela's sleeping form on my bed when I sense the wrongness in the air. The crystal on the side of my bed lights up, and every muscle in my body tenses. I kiss her forehead, pull on fresh clothes, and leave our room. When I bound down the steps of the palace, I hear shouts.

My adrenaline starts pumping, and I sprint towards the source of the commotion. I swallow hard the second I see the giant's head peeking above our crowd. Hurrying across the bridge to their rooms are the small group of elves. I rush over to stop them.

"What is happening?" I demand of King Arion.

He looks up at me and smiles. "I didn't think it was right you only invited me to your wedding. I took it upon myself to also invite the Giant Court to such a joyous occasion. It seems they have arrived."

"You bastards," I hiss. "We invited you in good faith."

King Arion looks at me with a long, hard gaze. "Perhaps your memory is short because your people are all dead. We elves do not forget how you lied about the powers of your volcano. Keep your humans, we will be staying out of this war for the time being." The elven king tries to push past me when I grab his long silky robe.

He whips around and looks me dead in the eye. "I am not your enemy yet, Enduar. Be very careful about what you do next."

I drop the king's robe and snarl. "An eye for an eye, *ardalínor.*"

He laughs and continues walking with his archers. Fires are starting in the residential section, and I race over with dozens of Enduares now wielding hammers. There's no time to get everyone underground, we'll have to get everyone out now. "Vann!" I roar, searching for my leader.

Lothar comes sprinting up, panting. "There are ten. They've come to demand Estela," he pants.

I look at him. "Gather as many hunters and stone benders as you can. Then go back to my rooms in the palace and protect Estela," I order before dashing toward the Ardorflame, armorless and without weapons.

"Troll!" booms a voice like thunder. "We have come because you stand accused of lying to our high king."

I freeze and spin around to face a warrior with more scars than Keksej. He stands with a spear in one hand and a shield in the other. "You have intruded on my people," I bark back, my voice steady despite the quivering anger that threatens to consume me. "We have done no such thing! Where is your proof?"

The lead giant sneers down at me, his lip curling in a cruel mockery of a smile. "Didn't you tell High King Rholker that the slave Estela was dead?"

I feel a cold sweat break out across my forehead. "High King Rholker? What the fuck are you talking about?"

"Answer the question," the giant bellows.

Before I can speak, the lead giant answers my question with a mocking laugh. "Your face betrays you, troll. Your lies have been exposed. You'll surrender the human slave woman to us, or we have orders to kill as many trolls as we can reach."

I stand tall, meeting his gaze with steely resolve. "Estela is my wife, and she is under my protection. I won't hand her over to you or anyone else. You giants have no right to make demands of us."

The giant's eyes narrow as he nods to one of his comrades. The hulking warrior steps forward, producing a blackened sack. With a sickening flourish, he upends it, and the severed hands of the missing Enduar fall onto the cobblestone courtyard like the petals of some grotesque flower. "We've also caught your people lurking along our borders. These aren't the actions of countries at peace. You have chosen blood!"

When a scream lights the air, something primal winks to life inside of me. A power I haven't dared to touch since the Great War. The lava pools beneath me respond to my call, the molten rock bubbling and boiling as I draw on its intensity. With a roar, I unleash a stream of liquid fire toward the giant before me, the intense heat sizzling through the air like an inferno. I back away to the bridge, standing over the eternal flames of the lava below. I raise my hands up on either side, summoning the strength of the mountain. I'm even stronger and faster since the mating ceremony, and it's reflected in my magic. I tug at the earth with invisible chains, and the ground beneath us shudders.

"Leave my mountain," I roar. The Ardorflame pulses with energy. Lava bursts from the ground, whirling in the air before me and forming a sword, cool to the touch when I grip its hilt. "Enduares, to arms!" I shout out, lifting my sword high into the heavens. "We fight for our home!"

The courtyard explodes in a deafening chorus of sound as my people yank out their weapons and surge forward to be by my side. I can view the shock on the other giants' faces as our army thunders toward them, swords glinting in their hands. The clang of steel on steel reverberates through the cavernous space, cut through by the screams of the wounded and dying. I feel exhaustion creep into my limbs, sweat pouring down my face as I block blow after blow. But still, I press onward.

I spy Mother Liana across the way, muttering with her crystals. Her voice rises higher than the clamor of battle, her eyes shut tight in concentration. The gems attached to her neck and ears sparkle as they shift about in the flickering light of raging fires.

I lunge and strike as I move forward, cutting off an arm before plunging through a chest. I catch sight of Vann with his hammer, and Svanna with her pickax. They clash against two giants simultaneously as they move closer to the houses.

A sound comes from my left, and I use the weight of my blade to gain enough momentum to swing through the air, aiming for the giant's back. The blow connects with a sickening thud, and I feel the satisfying weight of the molten rock as it slices through the giant's flesh. He roars in pain and staggers back before tumbling to the cavern below. I dodge to the side, narrowly avoiding his massive sword as it falls through the air. Without hesitation, I strike towards another giant, my sword finding its mark in the newcomer by plunging through the giant's armor and into his chest.

I pull my sword free, watching as yet another giant falls to the lower level. They brought ten, and I have killed four. The fiery power within me continues to surge, the molten rock at my feet responding to my every command. There are only two left.

This time, when I shoot a stream of lava out, it crashes into the giant's body, and the heat of the liquid fire melts through their armor and incinerates his flesh. I watch as he screams and writhes in agony. Finally, the last giant dies, and I gaze at the bodies strewn about our festival decorations like broken dolls.

The cavern is filled with the sounds of our victory, the cheers of my people ringing through the air. I release the power within me, my focus shifting back to the reality of the moment. The haze clears from my eyes, and I sink to my knees. My breaths rush through my nose, scalding me from the inside out.

My arms are wreathed in fire, the heat of the glowing magma stinging the tips of my fingers. The flesh between my toes still tingles from the residual power of the lava, and my eyes burn from the acrid smoke that fills the air.

I can hear Mother Liana's footsteps as she approaches me, the sound of the heels of her boots clicking against the solid rock of the cavern floor. I do not need to look at her to know that her eyes are dancing with the heat and flames of the battle, her gaze hot enough to set the air alight. She leans over me, her fingers lightly raking against my skin. Soft sounds escape her lips as she traces the outline of my wounds, a small smile curling the sides of her mouth.

"It seems as if you are being well handled by the magic, Ma'Teo."

A groan escapes my lips as her fingers press into my flesh, her power mingling with the magma that courses through me. Slowly, the power ebbs away, and I feel a cooling sensation from my insides coat my skin. Behind the magic, I reach out across my mating bond to feel the comforting presence of my mate. I am met with silence.

"Do you see Estela?" I ask.

No one answers.

I push to my knees, dizzy and ready to faint, and stand. I look around the crowd and find my people are already starting to clean up. Liana reaches for me again, but I push her away, half running, half crawling across the bridge to the palace. I still can't breathe properly after using the magic.

"Ma'Teo!" Liana calls. But I don't stop. My heart is pounding in my ears, and my stomach churns with a mix of fear and anger. Estela was nowhere to be seen, and the thought of her being taken by the giants sends a fresh wave of fury coursing through my veins. As we run past the mushroom garden, I find a bloody scene on the steps.

Then I see Lord Lothar lying in a pool of his own blood, his body twisted and broken. Liana curses and leans down to help him, but I continue to my room.

Estela is nowhere to be seen. My heart feels like it drops into my stomach as I look around frantically. There is no trace of her in my chamber, and the rage I felt moments ago has given way to a growing sense of dread. My mind races, trying to piece together what might have happened.

I run back out to the palace steps and find Liana healing Lothar. "He lives," she says.

I stumble to his side, and grab his blood-soaked shirt. "Where is she?" I roar. *"Where is my mate?"*

His eyes blink open, and he lets out one gasping breath. "The... elves."

CHAPTER 40
EUDIALYTE
ESTELA

"**M**amá is dead," I say down to the wailing baby in my arms. "You can't cry in front of the king, or he'll be angry. Make a good impression."

A giant warrior leads me up the white marble steps to the palace to meet with King Erdaraj. He looks down at me and Mikal with palpable disgust.

"Make that kit shut up."

"Yes, sir," I say and hold Miki closer to my chest while I pat his back. Once nuzzled against my clothes, he eases a fraction. The fractured pieces of my soul settle while I walk. Though not alone, I feel that way.

"We're going to meet your father, mi amor. You should feel lucky —to know your father is a rare thing," I murmur against his thick black curls. Mamá had hidden the baby in her belly, and I don't really understand why. He should be happy to have another son. I feel him gurgle against my ear as we cross to the throne room.

More white. Too much white. The ceilings are tall and the cool breeze drifting through threatens to knock me over. Mikal is already too heavy.

"My King," the giant warrior says. "I present Aitana's son and daughter."

I look up at the king sitting on his throne. His hair is white, and his skin is wrinkled, but his eyes are as yellow as sunflower petals—just like Mikal's. On either side of him are his sons, the giant princes. They stand near the wall, glowering down at me and the too-big baby in my arms.

The king extends his arm toward me just as Mikal starts to cry again. King Erdaraj blinks and sucks in a sharp breath. "Come here, slave."

The First Prince laughs at me and leans behind his father's throne to whisper something to his brother. Prince Keksej does not laugh; he watches me intently.

Slowly, I step forward. Terrified. I don't belong here, but he does. A member of the Giant Court steps towards me when I reach the top of the carpet, and he plucks Mikal from my arms.

My baby brother immediately starts to scream. I clench my fists at my side. He will be fine with his father. I tell myself that fathers care for their children.

One of the warriors draws his sword. I feel a chill down my spine at the sight of the blade. The warrior approaches me, and I tense up as he wraps his hand around my waist and presses his sharp weapon to my throat.

I squeak. The other giant warrior holds out his hands toward the king, offering him his son.

The king snarls and spits on Mikal's face.

"Kill the bastard, father," the First Prince says, withdrawing a dagger from his waist and passing it to the king.

I feel my heart stop beating, and a cold sweat breaks out on my skin. This can't be happening. Not to my baby brother. "No," I scream. My voice is too small.

My body tenses as I brace myself for the inevitable. But then, a white light invades the throne room, blinding me. I struggle against the warrior holding me captive and fall to the ground. A voice cuts through the tension like a hot knife through butter.

"Stop."

The voice is soft yet commanding. It echoes through the palace, and for a moment, all eyes are on its source. A woman stands on the steps of the throne room, her long white dress swishing around her ankles as she move forward. Her curly black hair is painfully familiar, as are her brown eyes. However, the crown on her head is new, as is her braid with gold bands.

The king is on his feet, and Mikal is still in the arms of the giant lord.

"Aitana," the king breathes. His face has gone sickly pale, and he stumbles back as I hear someone whisper, "The king's whore."

The First Prince is incensed. He pushes forward and grabs the knife out of his father's hand, blade first. He doesn't even wince as he cuts himself, and blood drips from his palm.

"I'll do it myself," he growls, and moves to stab my brother.

But my mother is faster. Her hand darts out, and the First Prince's wrist is caught in a solid grip. He cries out in pain as she twists his arm behind his back, and the dagger starts to fall to the ground. She catches it.

"I said stop, you filthy pig," she says, and her voice is like steel. She thrusts the handle into his thigh, and he collapses to the ground, writhing in pain. Blood leaks to the ground and he shouts obscenities at her. Two giants advance towards her and she throws them back with the wave of her hand.

Everyone looks at my mother, terrified. I am proud. She is so beautiful.

"Aitana, what did you want?" the king asks.

I don't understand why he sounds so afraid. I thought he cared for my mother. Shouldn't he be happy to see her again?

Her chin tilts upward. "I will kill you all if you or your sons ever *try to kill Mikal again. And you will leave Estela alone. She is not to be a comfort woman."*

He looks at his son, writhing on the ground. *"I swear it will be done. My sons will never touch your daughter or kill your son."*

The dream was a memory—but the details are all wrong. The king never tried to kill Mikal. I blink my eyes open, the world around me a blur of dark shadows and flickering light. My head throbs with each pulse of my heartbeat, and I groan softly. It takes time for my senses to return, like sand slipping through an hourglass, slow and stubborn.

As my vision clears, I can make out the faint outlines of the room, but there are bars around me. I'm still wearing my stone silk dress, but it's so much colder now.

"Where am I?" I call out, my voice hoarse and weak. Panic claws at my chest, making it difficult to breathe. "Teo?"

The cage encasing me was cold and unforgiving, its metallic bars stretching upwards towards the ceiling like skeletal fingers, their chill seeping into my flesh, turning my bones to ice. My breath emerges in short, shallow gasps, the frigid air burning my lungs as it scrapes past my throat.

My ears pick up the distant echoes of footsteps, chains rattling, and muffled screams. The cold, hard surface beneath me sends shivers through my body, and I struggle to remember what had happened.

I try to sit up, but my limbs feel heavy and unresponsive. I scan the room I've been placed in, seeking any weaknesses in the bars that enclosed me or any tools that might help me escape.

Suddenly, the door to the room creaks open, and the Second Prince Rholker enters. Fear coils in my stomach as I realize that I am trapped in Zlosa, my worst nightmare come true. In the same room as my torturer.

"Ah, you're awake," Rholker sneers, his voice dripping with

malice. "I was beginning to wonder if you'd ever regain consciousness."

"Your concern is touching," I reply, my voice trembling despite my best efforts to control it. "But I assure you, I'm quite fine."

"Of course you are," Rholker mocks, prowling closer like a predator stalking its prey. "You always did have a knack for surviving, didn't you, Estela?"

"Survival is a skill that's served me well," I retort, trying to match his confidence. "Especially in this wretched place."

"You have changed. Where did all of this confidence come from?" he boasts, his eyes gleaming. "You're nothing more than a mouse trapped in a cage."

"Perhaps," I admit, swallowing hard. "But even mice can sometimes escape their traps."

"Is that a threat?" Rholker asks, his lips curling into a cruel smile.

"More of a promise," I shoot back, my heart pounding in my chest. "You'll find that I'm not as easily broken as you might think."

"Interesting," he purrs, circling the cage like a vulture. "I do enjoy a challenge."

"Then I suggest you brace yourself," I warn him, hoping he couldn't hear the fear lacing my words.

"Such fire in your words, Estela," he taunts. "But we both know that you're powerless here. For example, I know you have been looking for your brother. If you want to know whether or not he lives, you'll have to please me."

I snarl and spit at him. "I will find a way to tell your father about this!"

As I say the words, the day before comes flooding back in, and my heart stops in my chest while the cruel giant smiles.

"Didn't they tell you? King Erdaraj is dead. My brother, too. I am king, and you will be my comfort woman."

"Never," I whisper, gritting my teeth and clenching my fists. "I'll never be yours, Rholker." All I can think about is Teo. The way his skin felt on mine and the way I promised myself to him.

I try to suppress the shiver that runs down my spine at his words, but it is difficult to keep my fear at bay. My heart thuds wildly in my chest, and I can feel the heat of my own panic threatening to consume me.

"Let me out of this cage," I demand, trying again.

He shakes his head and laughs. "All right."

"Rot in hell," I spit back. My hands tremble as I grip the cold, metallic bars of the cage, and I fought to steady my breathing, counting each inhale and exhale to regain control.

Then he pulls out a key and starts to work on the lock to my cage.

I desperately try to think of something, anything that could keep me from falling into his arms. I rub the back of my hand, and find the ring that Teo gave me. My fingers splay across my throat and also find the necklace.

The nightmare from before returns. I think of the king and the princes, all superstitious fools. When Rholker manages to finish unlocking the cage, I shrink back.

"I'm telling you. Don't touch me," I warn, the words tasting like venom on my tongue. "This stone," I gesture to the gem embedded in my chest, "will curse you if you do."

"You lie," he murmurs, but his gaze never leaves the stone. He is trying hard not to appear afraid. I've underestimated him before, but he is not an idiot.

I will do whatever I can to keep him from touching me. "If you wish to bring me to your bed, I suggest you remove this stone, or you'll die before you ever have a chance to enjoy being king."

His eyes widen, and a series of curses in giantese slip past his lips. "They've turned you into a witch."

Emboldened by the lack of bars, I take a step forward. And then another. "I'm going to make your life a living hell, giant."

The look on his face, as deepening terror replaces his anger, is priceless. Truly, it's one of the few rewards I'll get for all of this. But there's still one more thing to do. With a nudge from my mind, the Fuegorra in my chest starts to glow.

He stumbles back, tripping over the wooden floor and scrambling away from me, a look of unadulterated terror on his face.

"If only your subjects could see you now. If you kill me, I will haunt you for the rest of your days. If Mikal is alive, and you lay a finger on him, you will wish you had never been alive."

Rholker's once arrogant and confident demeanor shatters completely before my eyes. For all his brutality, I have never seen him so vulnerable. Pity should have filled me, but I feel nothing but satisfaction. He deserves everything that was coming to him.

"You wouldn't dare. You bitch!" he yells, slamming the door on my cage. "I will find a way to get that stone out of you."

With that, he turns on his heel and runs out of the room, the echo of his footsteps a bitter reminder of the change from stone to wood. I was wrong in the mountain; *this* is what it was to be trapped with monsters.

Teo? I say through our mating bond.

Silence.

Such ugly silence.

I unclasp the necklace around my neck and look down at the ring, remembering what he had told me when he handed me my ring.

Amethyst, melanterite, obsidian, and ruby.

He had said the words like he was trying to tell me something.

Amethyst.

A.

My eyes widen, and I trace the letters on the ground. *A M O R.*

Amor. One of my words, written with Enduar letters.

I gasp and look back at the necklace. There are forty gems on that one, most of which I don't recognize.

"Teo," I murmur. "What message have you left me?"

THE END... FOR NOW.

If you enjoyed To Steal a Bride, *please take a moment to leave a rating or review—it really makes a difference! Book two,* To Ignite a Flame, *will be releasing in 2024!*

ACKNOWLEDGMENTS

This book came out of left field. One second, I was finishing a trilogy, and the next, I was writing thousands of words per day, racing to finish this story.

Thank you to the novel gods, for helping me write this book. Thank you to my writing group, Sydney Hunt and Elayna R. Gallea for handing my manic story ideas.

Thank you to my writing friends who have talked me through every major obstacle in this novel. To the beta readers, to my editor, Pauline, but most of all, thank you to my husband.

I'm kinda crazy. Thank you for always being with me.

About the Author

Daniela A. Mera was born into a royal Fae family in Scotland. She was a free spirit who loved traveling and cloud watching while laying velvet-soft grass. When she came of age, her mother forced her to travel to Las Vegas in order to kill a dragon and conquer a neighboring kingdom.

The dragon turned out to be a man, whom she fell wildly in love with. The couple ran away to the gentle hills of Mexico where Daniela ate lots of tacos and fruits the size of her head.

Something along those lines, anyway.

She writes whimsical tales full of lore all around the world, full of emotionally available men and women who run the world.

She can be found listening to sappy romance ballads while writing scenes meant to emotionally damage her readers.

When not writing, Daniela can be found doing yoga and playing video games. Join her newsletter for freebies!

Visit: http://danielaamera.com/

- facebook.com/AuthorDaniela.A.Mera
- instagram.com/authordaniela.a.mera
- amazon.com/~/e/B09JDDZQX7
- goodreads.com/authordanieaamera

Made in the USA
Las Vegas, NV
23 February 2024

86194796R00213